A native of Seattle, Glen Erik Hamilton was raised aboard a sailboat and grew up around the marinas and commercial docks and islands of the Pacific North-west. His debut novel, the first Van Shaw novel *Past Crimes*, won the Anthony, Macavity, and Strand Critics awards and was also nominated for the Edgar, Barry, and Nero awards. The second Van Shaw novel, *Hard Cold Winter*, followed in 2016. He now lives in California with his family, and frequently returns to his home town to soak up the rain.

@GlenErikH
www.glenerikhamilton.com

Further praise:

'Outstanding . . . The suspenseful, fast-moving plot is a good match for the empathetic, nuanced lead.' *Publisher's Weekly*

'A home run off the first pitch – this guy has got what it takes.' Lee Child on *Past Crimes*

'Make no mistake, Van Shaw is a remarkable fictional creation.' *Thriller Books Journal*

'Brimming with action, conflict, and realistic and compelling characters . . . Aficionados of the genre will eat this one up.' *Library Journal*, on *Hard Cold Winter*

EVERY DAY ABOVE GROUND

ALSO BY GLEN ERIK HAMILTON

Hard Cold Winter

Past Crimes

EVERY DAY ABOVE GROUND

A VAN SHAW NOVEL

GLEN ERIK HAMILTON

FABER & FABER

First published in 2017
by Faber & Faber Limited
Bloomsbury House, 74–77 Great Russell Street
London WCIB 3DA
This paperback edition first published in 2018

First published in the USA in 2017
by Willam Morrow, an imprint of HarperCollins
195 Broadway, New York, NY 10007

Printed and bound by CPI Group (UK) Ltd, Croydon, CR0 4YY

A CIP record for this book is available from the British Library

ISBN 978–0–571–33236—6

FSC
www.fsc.org
MIX
Paper from
responsible sources
FSC® C020471

10 9 8 7 6 5 4 3 2 1

For our Mia
A penny to share
your thoughts, we add another
to make art from dreams,
and a third placed between those
for all the rest of your days

EVERY DAY ABOVE GROUND

ONE

MY HOUSE WAS NOTHING but bones. A rigid lumber frame of two stories and an attic, the windows defined by perfect squares and the doorways tall rectangles. Sky and only sky between every line, like the drawing of a small and painstaking child.

I was balanced at the peak. The carpenters and I had completed the trusses earlier in the day, and I wanted to check the joists against the house plan before the sun finished its dive below the horizon. The house was set on a rise at the top of the block. It was the tallest thing for a quarter mile, if you ignored the evergreen trees. So when the black Nissan Altima paused in its slow drift in front of the property, I was looking almost straight down on the car from sixty feet off street level.

The Nissan pulled in to the curb and the driver stepped out. He looked up the stone steps that followed the rise, up the framework of the house, up to me. He raised a hand in tentative greeting.

"This the Shaw place?" he called.

"More or less," I said.

The man was a little older and a lot smaller than the national average. He wore a black watch cap and a jean jacket still stiff from the factory, and gray Carhartt dungarees over bright white sneakers. His smile flashed a full allotment of teeth. A white barcode sticker was visible through the Nissan's spotless windshield.

"You're looking for Dono," I said.

"Yeah."

"Come on up."

The small man walked quickly around the car to the stone steps. I unclipped the safety tether and clambered down to hang by my fingers, and dropped with a boom onto the plywood sheeting that formed the rudiments of a second floor. The whole structure smelled of cut pine and sap, pleasantly heavy in the July heat.

I hadn't built subflooring on the first story yet. When I climbed down I was standing on a bare concrete foundation. My visitor came to the top of the stone steps and halted. He had nowhere to go. The steps used to meet the porch of the old house, and would again someday. But for now they ended in midair, like one side of a small Aztec pyramid. We looked across the six-foot gap at each other.

"Dono died," I said. "Early last year."

His broad smile vanished in a wink. "Christ."

"You knew him?"

"I did." His gaze shifted quickly past the scars on my face—everybody's first stop—to my black hair and black eyes, which were a match for Dono's. "I know you, too, though we ain't met. Dono's grandson, yeah? I'm Mickey O'Hasson. Maybe he mentioned me?"

"Sorry. I don't recall."

"A long time back." Up close, O'Hasson's blue eyes were lively and clear, belying about six decades of hard living on his face. He stood barely over five feet tall and the cap and sneakers made up a full inch of that. The good-humored smile crept softly back onto his wide freckled face, like beaming was his natural expression.

He inspected the edges of the steps, where scorch marks stood out fresh and bold against the pitted stone.

"What happened here?" he said.

"This year hasn't been much better."

"And so you're rebuilding. Good. It was a real nice place."

Nice might have been pushing it. But it had been home, once. "When did you last see Dono?"

"Thirteen, fourteen years."

"You just get out?" I said.

O'Hasson stared at me. Then the intricate lines around his eyes crackled in squinty amusement. "How'd you figure?"

"Your jacket's brand-new. Pants and shoes, too. The car's a rental, and it's fresh washed. Straight from the airport, maybe."

"Near enough." He shook his head. "I remember Dono saying you were a real terror. He meant it good."

I hadn't needed the clothes or the car to make O'Hasson as one of Dono's crowd. My grandfather had been a thief, a robber, and in his younger days the kind of terror that nobody would call good. If this little guy was an acquaintance, then he had probably been an accomplice, too.

"You come to Seattle just to find Dono?" I said.

"Not just that. But he was high on my list." He glanced around at the empty yard. "No roof material yet? I guess you have to get the drying-in done pretty quick."

"You know construction."

"I know it rains a lot in Seattle. You can't leave framing out in the weather like this forever."

"I'm gambling on a dry summer."

"While you come up with the dough?" Those bright blueberry eyes narrowed in calculation, before he shrugged and nodded at the lapsing sun. "Quitting time. It's Van, right? Same name as your granddad, Donovan, but people call you that?"

"Good memory."

"Well, if you'll let me bend your ear a little, I'll buy the suds. 'Less you got somewhere else to be."

I didn't. Hadn't for a few months, not since Luce Boylan and I had broken up. I spent half of each day in one of the part-time jobs I'd managed to scrounge up, and the other half working on the house. Which was no longer an option, until I could afford the rest of the construction. The bones would stay bare.

And I had to admit, O'Hasson had me curious why a man would seek out my grandfather, first thing after tasting the air outside.

"Might as well," I said.

I locked up the tools in the big backyard shed, which had somehow survived the blaze, and changed into a t-shirt that was a couple of stains cleaner than the one I'd been wearing to monkey around the sap-covered lumber. O'Hasson followed my clattering Dodge pickup down to Madison and farther east, to a tavern called Lloyd's Own. It wasn't a dive—the neighborhood was too upscale for that—but it was away from the foot traffic and I could sit and think in peace.

O'Hasson and I settled into a booth at the back, away from the handful of patrons staining their lips with buffalo wings. He kept his cap on. Pem, the skinny hipster kid who worked the two-to-eight shift, drifted over and asked if I wanted a Guinness, like usual. I did. O'Hasson ordered the same. He glanced around at the walls, which were laden with County Cork landscapes, and then at Pem.

"A black boy pulling the taps in a mick bar," he said.

I looked at him.

He waved a hand hastily. "Just a long time since I been anyplace where people didn't stick to their own. Since I been anyplace at all. It's an okay thing, is what I mean." His left hand kneaded at the bicep muscle of his right arm. Across the room, Pem set the half-full pints of stout on the bar to settle.

O'Hasson nodded. "They pour it right in this place. 'S why you like it, yeah?"

"And no one gives a rip if I'm covered in sawdust."

"You do that work professional? Making houses?"

"Real contractors do the heavy lifting. I just pitch in with what Dono taught me."

"Right, he was a builder. I'd forgotten that." He rubbed the bridge of his nose sheepishly. "He taught you other stuff, too."

A statement instead of a question. I waited.

O'Hasson gave his arm one last squeeze. A tiny scab crested one of the veins on the back of his bony hand. I'd had a few scabs like that myself, left by IV needles.

"I'm not prying," he said. "Dono mentioned some things, while we were in Nogales, last time I saw him. You remember him making that trip?"

I did, now that O'Hasson mentioned it. Most of the thieving I'd done as a kid had been with Dono. But not all of his jobs had included me. Occasionally he'd cut out for another area of the country, leave me with cash for food, and come back in a week or two. Open-ended. I sometimes knew where he was, and rarely knew exactly when he'd be back.

It had always pissed me off, being left behind. The Nogales job had been one of those. I'd been about sixteen years old. Dono had come back with fifty grand.

"You set that job up?" I said.

"Yeah. He tell you about it?"

"Not so you'd notice."

"Well, it was solid. Very solid."

Pem brought our pints, placing them dead center on cardboard coasters. A cell phone burred from somewhere in O'Hasson's stiff jacket. He fished it out—an Ericsson four or five gens old—and looked at the screen. He hesitated a beat before muting its ring and setting it on the table.

"Dono did the box work in Arizona," he said once Pem had left. "Faster than anybody I ever saw."

I'd once watched as Dono opened a Sentry combination dial just by feel, and that was near impossible for any boxes built in the last three decades. The days of stethoscopes and dexterity were long past.

"He was good," I said.

"*Damn* good. Always figured I'd set up another job with him someday. But time passed, I had other work, somebody dropped on me for a different thing, and that's when I started my seven-year vacation. That doesn't matter."

O'Hasson leaned in so suddenly he was in danger of knocking over his pint glass.

"What matters is why I'm here. It's very big. I thought Dono might want a piece."

"Moot now."

"And I'm damn sorry for that. Here's to him, and those we've lost." We took a pull on our glasses. I always liked the first sip, when I got some of the foam with the beer. O'Hasson grasped his arm and gazed mournfully into space for a respectfully slow count of three before hitting me with the question I knew was coming.

"You keep up with it?" he said.

"No."

"Not regular?"

"Not at all."

Which wasn't the whole truth. Recent events had given me reason to knock some rust off, greasing alarm systems and finding myself in places people didn't want other people to go. I still had the touch. Just not the same motives as when I'd been my grandfather's apprentice.

"This is serious work," said O'Hasson. "A small fortune for each of us. Even better, it's practically clean."

"Practically."

"I mean the ownership of what we're talking about is—well, nobody's laid eyes on it in something like twenty years. It's forgotten."

I drank my beer.

"So tell me what you think," he said.

"I think nobody forgets a fortune. Small or not."

O'Hasson smiled and drummed his hands lightly on the tabletop. "Not if they're in their right mind. But our guy isn't." He glanced around to make sure no one had moved within earshot during the last ten seconds.

"I spent the last three years of my time in Lancaster. You know it?" he said.

"Near L.A. Maximum sec."

"Yeah. Shithole. They're all shitholes, I figure. Anyway, I got myself a job as an infirmary attendant. It's an easy pull. Lotsa downtime. You get to talking. One of the other attendants, he tells me about this patient he looked after before I came along. Alzheimer's got its hooks into the unlucky prick."

"Why didn't they let him out?"

"Who the fuck knows. Maybe that was in the plan before he croaked. Or maybe being senile made him more dangerous than ever. Point is that the geezer was off his nut. Especially at night, when he got tired. He thought my buddy was his cellmate from half a lifetime ago. He mumbled about everything. Jobs he'd pulled, scores that other people pulled, and he started talking to my attendant friend about a safe."

"Your friend have a name?"

O'Hasson tilted his head. "Let's keep that—what is it?—need-to-know. Just like I didn't tell him I'd be talking to Dono. Safer for everybody, yeah?"

The little man's grin stretched wide enough to make his eyes squeeze tight. "This nutjob used to be the prime West Coast runner, when heroin was making its latest comeback. Supermodels looking like junkies. Whole new generation."

"Runner for who?" I was getting caught up in the story, despite myself.

"The big man in Los Angeles. Karl Ekby. You know who he was?"

"I do not."

"Doesn't matter, he checked out a long time ago. But he was the heaviest. Any horse that flew into Seattle from the Golden Triangle, the nutjob would be right there with Ekby's cash. Back and forth, twice a month, regular as Amtrak. He had a cover business here and everything. And every trip, he'd skim a little. Expected, really. Hazard pay."

"Let me guess. The runner saved all that cash in his safe."

"Naw. He was even smarter than that. He bought gold. Kilobars, you know, the thin ones? A fucking investment. *Those* he put in the safe."

"So he had a pot of gold," I said. "And his cover business was named Rainbow Incorporated."

"You're joking."

"And you're not, which is the craziest part of this whole fairy tale."

"Hey, I figured it was bullshit myself. But my buddy had enough real facts that we could check it out. Taking our time so nobody notices, right? The building where the runner had his office is still here in Seattle. I'll bet anything that his safe is still hidden under the floor, right where he said. Shit, if the building owners ever came across a pile of fucking *gold*, it'd have been big news, right?"

"If there was ever any pile of gold to be found."

"Well, it's worth a look, isn't it?"

I finished my glass. Pem saw it from across the room and tilted his head in a question. I waved him off. Story time was about over.

O'Hasson's phone rang again. His hand reached for it automatically before pausing.

"Go ahead," I said. "I'm gonna hit the latrine."

When I came out, O'Hasson was still talking on the phone, leaning against the wall of the booth with his shoulders relaxed from the hunched urgency of our conversation. His wolfish grin had softened. He nodded along with whatever the speaker was saying. A wife, or a girlfriend, I guessed.

He hung up and pocketed the phone as I approached.

"I've never cracked a safe," he said. "I need a sure bet, somebody I know."

"You don't know me."

"I know you enough if you're Dono Shaw's family. Come on." He licked his lips. "We go in, we tear up the floor. If the safe's there, we open it."

"And then?"

"Whatever's there, we split three ways."

"Your buddy is a generous guy," I said.

"The clock's ticking. That building's due to be torn down. And a third of a score is a shitload better than having all of nothing." O'Hasson shrugged like it was obvious. "I'll hang on to his share until he gets out in a few weeks."

"Damn trusting, too."

"I'm not crossing him."

He meant it. Whoever O'Hasson's unnamed buddy was, he'd put some fear into the bargain.

I shook my head. "It's not for me."

"You'll get your end. Right there on the spot," he said.

"No."

O'Hasson's face twitched, struggling to shore up his habitual grin. The effort failed.

"Where'd you get that?" He thrust a finger at the left side of my face. "During a job? That why you're so gunshy?"

"In Iraq," I said.

"So you served. All the more reason life owes you a little something."

I pointed at his black cap, mimicking his jab. "Your turn. Unless you want to stick with that bullshit about working in the infirmary."

He glared at me a moment before reaching up to remove the cap. What steel-wool hair he had was high and tight, not much different than the standard Ranger cut. He turned to show me his right side. A surgical scar made a smooth curve from the top of his ear to the base of his skull. It was fresh enough that I could see pockmarks where stitches had been.

"Gli-o-ma," he said, stretching out the syllables. "A tumor."

"That why they let you out? To get treatment?"

O'Hasson grunted. "No treatment. Not this time. They opened me up, took one look, and that was enough. Shit's all around the blood vessels."

"You seem to get around all right."

"Not much to it, not yet. My arm gets numb." He pressed a hand into his bicep. "Face and neck, too, lately."

He was right. The clock was ticking fast.

"So if you were the one in the infirmary, who was your generous friend?" I said.

"An attendant, like I said. I told you, I checked it out. Everything jibes with what the senile old fuck told him. Look." He reached out and grabbed my wrist. "I didn't want you to think I couldn't hack it, okay?

It's no problem. There's a fucking fortune, believe me, I can do whatever it takes."

"To spend your last months like a maharajah," I said. "Live rich, die broke."

He withdrew his hand. "Not the sympathetic type, are ya?"

"At least you get a warning bell. I've known a lot of guys who didn't."

The grin was back. I could feel the aggression that fueled it now. "'Scuse me if I don't feel fucking fortunate."

He threw back the last of his stout and fished a crumpled fast-food receipt out of his chest pocket. He scribbled on it. "Here's my number. Just think about it, right? I'll be around."

O'Hasson stood, all five feet of him, and marched out of the bar. I'd be damned if his step didn't have a spring in it.

TWO

GIRIDHARI MATTU, PH.D., HAD an office on the ground floor of the small professional building that his firm shared with two dentists and a chiropractor. A junior partner like Mattu rated just enough square footage for a rosewood desk and two Eames knockoff chairs. The single blank wall was given over to a framed Rothko print and Mattu's diplomas. U of O undergrad, U-Dub doctorate. They were positioned behind the desk where a seated patient would always have them in view. I could have drawn them with my eyes closed after the first few visits.

"How much have you been drinking, Van?" he said.

"Not much."

"Coffee, other stimulants?" He pointed to the travel mug I'd brought with me. In a previous session Mattu had noted that I brought it every time, and we'd gone on a tangent about whether I was a creature of habit, edging into more pointed questions to see if I was showing obsessive tendencies.

"A lot of coffee," I said. "No meth this week."

Jokes never got a reaction out of Mattu. I made the jokes anyway. Maybe it was obsessive.

"Do you feel the coffee might be adding to your sleep troubles?" he said.

"No."

"But you're still waking in the middle of the night."

"Less than before. The new dosage is right."

"Spell out 'right' for me." Mattu had thick bristles of brown hair and a boyish plumpness to his face and body. A casual observer might guess he was still in his twenties. He liked wearing corduroys and high-end hiking boots and sweaters, until the Seattle summer finally warmed up enough to force him to switch to denim shirts. On our first meeting, he had shaken my hand and drawn me in for a hug.

"I wake up once every two or three nights," I said. "Usually after a dream."

"A nightmare."

When I woke I was inevitably drenched, my heart hammering, but strangely calm despite that. I considered that a win.

"I don't recall the dreams much," I said. "It's not the same one on repeat. Not anymore."

"That's good. Social engagements? Have you spent time with company?"

"Nothing lately."

"What about your friend Leo Pak?" He didn't have to glance at his notes to remember the name.

"He's at home in Utah. Reconnecting with family."

"After his inpatient program. Do you feel that program was beneficial for him?"

"Yes."

"I haven't recommended similar treatment for you." Leaving the question hanging.

"I don't need it. Leo's issues are more severe."

Mattu nodded and tugged with satisfaction at his denim cuff. Leo was setting a fine example.

"Have you been dating?" he said.

"No."

"And the rebuilding of your house?"

"It might have to go on hold."

"Because of your finances. Are you still working security?" What Mattu called bouncing.

"I'm still pulling a couple nights a week. And . . . there might be other work coming. More profitable work."

My hesitation hadn't gone unnoticed. "Is that good?"

"I'm not sure I want it."

"Why is that?"

"It's not the kind of job I want to do," I said.

"You realize that's a circular argument."

"But accurate."

He ran through the few remaining questions from his greatest hits list, making careful notes as he proceeded. The official form would be turned in to the VA, as confirmation that Mattu's firm was donating pro bono time toward PTSD treatment. The VA would get their biweekly paperwork, and I'd get my prescriptions refilled.

He glanced over at the brass clock on his desk. Neither of us needed to look at its spidery hands to know we had two minutes left. But it was Mattu's unconscious way of signaling that time was getting short and he was about to launch into his summation.

"I'm not terribly concerned with the decision you have to make about this job," he said. "Whether you choose a steady income over your preference of work, either way could be the right path. I *am* concerned about the large block of time that will be available when you can't work on your house. That has been a focus for you, Van. Maybe overmuch."

"You're saying I need structure."

"In the military your time was extremely regimented." Mattu had made a pun, but I wasn't sure he knew it. "You've adjusted to civilian life very well, after so many years and many intense cycles of activity. Your family house has been at the center of your thoughts. Be careful when that center cannot hold."

We stood up. He shook my one hand in both of his, three pumps. Habit.

THREE

HOLLIS BRANT WHACKED THE throttle with the heel of his broad hand. The *Francesca*, his fifty-foot Carver cruiser, responded with a mounting rumble and Hollis and I leaned forward to counterbalance as the bow rose from the water. He turned the wheel a few easy degrees, pointing us in a direct heading away from his marina at Shilshole.

"Not so long ago, you'd have pissed all over the idea of cracking a safe," Hollis said over the noise. "And maybe all over Mickey O'Hasson for suggesting it."

We stood on the flybridge at the top of the boat. The waters ahead were clear and about as flat as Puget Sound ever got. To our stern, a couple hundred vessels ranging from speedboats to schooners crowded the shoreline. Pleasure craft, hell-bent on enjoying the long Independence Day weekend. If half of their owners touched a helm more than twice a year, it would be a shock. Sailing close to land was like navigating a freeway crowded with student drivers. And no lanes. Hollis liked a little distance from the chaos.

"Tell me about O'Hasson," I said.

Hollis's bowed legs, about the same length as his apelike arms, meant that he had to jump a little to reach the tall pilot's seat. The wind pushed his tight orange-white curls to and fro. "Dono was never much for running his mouth. Look who I'm talking to. You know that. But he hadn't worked with O'Hasson before. And Nogales was a long way from home."

"So who put them together?"

"Jimmy. It's why I invited him along this morning." Jimmy Corcoran was down below, using the head. Probably as a receptacle for whatever he'd eaten for breakfast. Corcoran's face had been paler than usual, even before I'd cast off the *Francesca*'s lines at the dock.

"The job in Arizona, that I remember something about," said Hollis. "Dono had to drive back to Seattle with a few paintings in his car, and he picked my brain about ways to hide them."

Hollis was a smuggler. Anything that seemed low-risk for moderate reward, which left out the kind of contraband that law enforcement declared wars against. To my knowledge, Hollis had never been arrested.

He spun the seat around to reach for his coffee cup. "Dono told me afterwards that the job was so fast, he never bothered to stay overnight in Nogales. They drove in. The house was where and how O'Hasson said it would be. They took the paintings. That was that."

"So O'Hasson did all the casing? He was reliable?"

"Dono was happy with the results, I can say that much."

The thump of the cabin door sliding open on the lower deck interrupted us. Under the thrum of the engine came an equally steady stream of curses.

"Y'all right there, Jimmy?" said Hollis with a wink to me.

"—can't believe you talked me into—Yes, you shithead, I'm just great." Corcoran came up the ladder to the flybridge, carefully taking each rung in turn. His hairless head and light eyes gave him the look of an especially pallid eel. An angry one, a moray ready to bite some careless skin diver's hand off. Jimmy C. was brilliant with electronics. A virtuoso. Maybe all that talent had stolen bits from the rest of him, with charm and courtesy being the first to go.

Corcoran pointed to the bottle of Baron Otard cognac that Hollis had used to strengthen his coffee. "Give me that."

I didn't question his choice of remedy. Corcoran snatched the bottle from me and downed a gulp large enough to distend his throat. He gasped.

"Fucking ocean," he said.

"Talk quick and maybe Hollis will turn us around."

"It's a good day," Hollis protested. He spun the wheel and knocked the engines to idle. The *Francesca* settled into an easy drift. "Look, calm as a sleeping babe."

"Spare me," said Corcoran. "What's this shit with Mickey O'Hasson?"

"He wants me in on a job," I said.

Corcoran's eyebrows furrowed, and his characteristic sneer edged up to try to meet them. "Ha. Suddenly you're not the white knight. What's wrong, you burn through your pension from Uncle Sam?"

The Army wouldn't have handed me a pension unless I'd served a full twenty, and I guessed that Corcoran knew that. But he wouldn't pass up a chance to needle me about my career choices. To Corcoran, any straight job was a sucker's job.

"Hollis says you vouched for O'Hasson with Dono, twelve or thirteen years ago," I said.

"Cutting right to it." Corcoran eased himself down onto the all-weather vinyl cushions. He took another small swig. "I didn't know O'Hasson, but I knew guys who'd worked with him. He was a house burglar, mostly. No tough-guy shit. You seen the man in person, yeah? Can't blame anybody the size of a damn peanut for sticking with the soft approach."

"Was he any good?"

"He had chops. You think I'd have spoken for him if I wasn't sure of that much?"

"Nobody's calling you a liar, Jimmy," said Hollis.

I held up a hand against the glare off the water. We were a couple of miles out, closer to Bainbridge than Seattle. A freighter trundled past, two hundred yards off our starboard, pushing with deceptive speed south toward the piers. Business in progress, over long, long distances.

"How did the connection start?" I said. "Who called who?"

Corcoran shrugged like it was obvious. "O'Hasson had reached out to some people in Seattle. Asking if they knew a safecracker. They knew me and I knew Dono."

Hollis frowned. "Why would O'Hasson want a box man from all the way up here?"

"Maybe every professional he knew in L.A. was connected," I said. "Their bosses would want a big cut. Or just take it all."

"An outsider." Corcoran nodded. "That's the word I remember being kicked around."

Hollis took the bottle of cognac from Corcoran and poured half a shot into his mug. "So O'Hasson was an independent. Like Dono."

"I didn't watch a fricking biography on the runt. He steals shit. I dunno who he steals it for, or why."

I had been wondering that myself. Why a dying man would spend his last days chasing dreams of gold.

"Thanks for the background," I said to Corcoran. "I owe you."

He snorted. It was apparently the wrong thing to do, because his face went the color of a hard-boiled egg left out in the sun. He lunged for the ladder, shouldering me aside in his haste.

When the cabin door had slammed again, Hollis sighed. He stuck a finger in his coffee and stirred it absentmindedly.

"You need money this bad?" he said.

I had been granted a deferral on property taxes the previous year, after Dono's death. Those were now due, and this year's on top. On Friday, the assessor's office had turned down my application for a second deferral. Plus there was the looming cost of rebuilding the house. A bank loan was out of the question. After ten years in the Army, most of it overseas with no real property to my name, my credit rating was low comedy.

During the afternoon hours yesterday on my newest part-time gig, dull seasonal work packing boxes in the warehouse of an outdoor supply company, I'd run the numbers in my head. The taxes amounted to four months of earnings, assuming the work stayed steady. And if I didn't need to pay rent. Or eat.

My silence was enough answer for Hollis. "I could scratch up a few dollars, if it'll keep the wolves away," he said.

"Thanks. But no."

"I supposed not. You've made up your mind about O'Hasson, then?"

"Six times in the last hour," I said. "I didn't think the house meant so much, until I saw the land without it. It looked like—it *felt* like—a tooth had been torn out at the root. That place was the last thing left of him. Of Dono."

"Except yourself."

"Not what I mean. He's dead and gone. His bar belongs to somebody else. But our house—he left that to me. I lived in it for less than a month before it burned down, and all of his things with it." I exhaled. "Dono didn't give a shit about what he owned, I know. Every dollar he earned from a score, he'd sink fifty cents into setting up the next one."

"Your man cared more about having his own rules," said Hollis.

"And to hell with everyone else. Jesus, I heard that philosophy enough times." I put the coffee mug down harder than I'd intended. It banged off the metal catch-rail and a chip broke from the base.

"It's nothing," Hollis said before I could apologize.

I turned my back to the sun and gazed at the city in the distance. Only the very tops of the tallest buildings were visible over the hills. As the *Francesca* bobbed on the water, rays of morning light would bounce off the glass and steel, giving the skyscrapers glittering crowns.

"Screw it," I said. "If I had the money, I'd rebuild. But I don't, and I won't steal to get it."

"You don't need to convince me."

"I'm convincing myself, Hollis. I've broken a lot of laws since coming back home. Maybe this thing with O'Hasson is a kick in the ass to remind me where to draw the line."

Hollis picked up the shard of broken coffee mug from the dash and examined it. "I might not be the most impartial judge, but Lord knows you've had good reason to bend the rules."

"Better reasons than just paying my bills. Or wanting some last hurrah, which is what I suspect is driving O'Hasson."

"Could be that."

He began to clean under a fingernail with the sliver of ceramic. I looked at him. He remained intent on his inexpert manicure.

"You want to show whatever card you're hiding up your sleeve?" I said.

"Sorry." He coughed. "Just making some decisions of my own."

He opened the chart locker and took out a slim manila folder. "I've a fellow who works for a private dick in Los Angeles. He's not a bad sort, for a citizen. When you said you were looking for background on O'Hasson, I took the liberty and had my friend pull whatever public records he could on short notice."

I smiled as Hollis handed me the folder. "Have you got a friend in every town?"

"And a lady in every port. Keeps me young."

I opened the file. Tightly spaced columns of text on the first two pages covered the long criminal history of Michael John O'Hasson, age fifty-eight. I'd taken him for older than that. Mileage outpacing the years. He'd been busted a lot for petty crap as a youth, less often as he gained experience and also spent a few idle seasons behind bars. O'Hasson's latest stretch of seven years had been the result of a larceny conviction and an eight-to-twelve sentence. His third fall.

Printed on the third page was a screen capture of a County of Los Angeles birth certificate. Cyndra Ann O'Hasson, born at Kaiser Bellflower. On the line for *Full Name of Mother* it read *Lorelei Michelle Eaton*. Michael O'Hasson was listed as the father.

Cyn. Twelve years old, on her last birthday. She must have been about five when O'Hasson was put away.

The next document I recognized instantly, before I'd read a word of it. It was the summary cover page from a foster child's record of temporary guardianship. Cyndra Ann had gone into the system at age six. The following pages showed that she'd bounced around, four different families in three different towns. Her latest family was listed as the Tyners, in Reseda. There was no mention of what had happened to Cyndra's mother.

Dead center on the final page was a black-and-white photocopy of a color picture, two inches on each side, like a passport's. Cyndra's face, long and snub-nosed with big light-colored eyes. Blue, maybe, like her dad's. She had straight brown bangs and the rest of her hair was pulled into a tight ponytail. The photo was out of date. Probably taken when she'd gone to the Tyners at age ten. She was pretty in the way that all kids are before adolescence starts to wreak havoc.

"I considered tossing the pages to the seagulls," said Hollis.

Cyn's expression in the photo was resigned, with a dash of hostility. Or maybe that was just me, projecting.

"But I figured you'd want to know," Hollis continued.

I returned the papers to the folder and walked across the bridge to set them down on the dash. Much more deliberately than I had the coffee mug.

"So," I said. "We know why O'Hasson's got a head of steam. He wants to leave something behind for the kid."

Hollis made a thoughtful hum. I glanced down at the folder. Caught myself before I picked it up again.

"It explains the guy a little," I said. "It doesn't change anything."

We both drank some coffee and watched the water. Whenever the wind picked up an extra knot, the top of each gentle swell shimmered and rippled, like the wavelets were trying to break free.

"Maybe this whole situation is a gift," Hollis said, toasting me with his mug. "Whatever's inside O'Hasson's safe is just a penny lying on the sidewalk."

I made myself smile. "Finders keepers?"

"It's one perspective. I need a refresh. You?" I shook my head. He climbed down the ladder, agile as a gibbon, and disappeared into the cabin.

I watched the boats and the water and thought about Cyndra O'Hasson. Twelve years old. County shelters and foster families for half of that. Her father in prison since she was in kindergarten. If she'd seen him at all since then, it had been in a visiting room.

I knew exactly what that was like. No physical contact. Nothing passed between visitors and inmates. Even emotions were tamped down to the minimum.

"Lucky penny," I said to myself.

AGE ELEVEN

Granddad turned the key and nudged our front door open with his boot, and I swear the air rushing out made a sound like when they open the mummy tombs in movies. The door hinges even creaked a little.

"Home," he said.

It was. I was so stoked to see it, I didn't care how creepy it suddenly felt.

The four digits Granddad tapped into the alarm keypad were the same code I remembered. Which made sense. Neither of us had been around to change it, or the clock on the glowing display. It read half past eleven, and for sure we'd passed midnight while having burgers at Beth's.

Daylight savings time, I realized. Since Granddad had gone to jail, there had been two falls back and only one spring forward.

He walked down the dark hall just as if all of the lights were on. I peered into the shadowy foyer and the front room. They looked the same as when I'd last seen them. Didn't smell the same. The air was hot and it stank like peat moss.

"Damn that woman," Granddad said from the kitchen. I guessed he meant Paula. Paula had been Granddad's girl-friend or whatever when he'd been busted. I dropped my bag and his leather jacket—mine now, by rights, since I'd kept it the whole time he was away—and went to join him. After turning on the hallway light.

He was hunkered down, looking at a white trash bin I didn't recognize. I was still getting used to how much jail had changed Granddad. His chest and arms strained at his shirt now, because of all the weight lifting in jail. Mostly it was his beard, ashy black and unkempt, like one of the pirate captains he was always reading about.

I was still wrapping my head around everything tonight, really. Granddad had picked me up from the Rolfssons' just a couple of hours ago. A complete surprise, I hadn't even known he was out. The past couple hours felt a little like a dream I was going to wake up from and be bummed that it wasn't real.

A ragged hole had been gnawed through the corner of the trash can.

"We've mice," Granddad said. "Check your room for droppings."

Ugh. And also, cool. I could snag one as a pet. Never had a pet before, but maybe the rules had changed and I could keep a cage for it in my room.

My room. Not just a place where I crashed every night, shared with other foster kids or even with babies put up by the same family. Mine.

I ran upstairs.

It was weird. The same, but weird. Maybe weird *because* it was the same. The square card table I used as a desk was covered in stuff, like little rocks, and a baseball I'd sawn in two to see if the inside really did have poisonous gunk in it, and a bunch of padlocks, two of which I had also taken apart—more carefully than the baseball—to check out how they worked. All of it looked just like I remembered. Except that I'd also forgotten about all of it while I was away. That was a strange feeling.

We definitely had mice. The bottom edge of my Ken Griffey Jr. poster had been gnawed halfway into the words THE KID, which meant the rodents had been running around on my dresser.

I opened the drawers to look for mouse crap or other damage. My clothes looked okay. Well, unchewed. But embarrassing. I still had an Animaniacs t-shirt, which I wouldn't wear to school now for a thousand dollars.

Speaking of. I pulled my chair over to the closet and

stood on it to loosen the bulb cover screws with my finger-tips. The glass cover was dusty, but everything in the house was dusty, so who cared? I set the cover aside and reached up to find the wad of money in the hole in the ceiling. When I'd last been here, the woman from Social Services had been watching me like a dog on a pork chop, making sure I didn't put any knives or guns or frickin' TNT in my bag, whatever she was imagining. So the money had stayed. At least I had managed to pass off Granddad's jacket as mine. I'd worn it almost every day, to keep it safe.

Thirty-three bucks. Sweet.

Downstairs, Granddad was probably checking his own hiding places. He had shown me how to open the one behind the shelves in the pantry—it was deliberately tricky—but there were others that I knew about, and I was pretty certain that Granddad didn't know that I knew. Like behind the kitchen baseboard, where I once found a pump shotgun, and under the eaves outside, where he kept his burglary kit.

"Strip the beds," he called from downstairs. "Nobody's touched the linens in a year."

"I thought Paula was looking after the house," I hollered back.

"She had been."

"Did she ever visit you?"

"Get the sheets." Which meant *Don't push it.*

I yanked my blue flannel bedclothes and the pillowcases off and dumped them by the stairs on my way to Granddad's room.

His room was the largest of four on the second floor, and the one in which I'd spent the least amount of time. I wasn't allowed inside at all when I was a little kid. It still felt like I was committing a felony just stepping through the doorway, even though Granddad had just told me to.

Not that his room was at all cool. In the spare rooms we had loads of tools and interesting junk that wouldn't fit in the hobbit-hole garage carved out of the hillside below the house. Granddad's room just had a wardrobe (kinda okay, but nothing in it but clothes) and a closet (more clothes and more junk) and a TV (channels preset to soccer—sorry, *football*—and news, same as he watched downstairs) and a stupid amount of books. Not like stories, but history and stuff. Some of the books were so old they were from when *he* was in school. I knew because he'd use them to show me how words were spelled in Irish, and then of course he'd quiz me.

I guess part of the reason Granddad made me stay out was because of the pistol that was usually in his nightstand, but even as a kid I knew to stay far away from that, and he kept it unloaded anyways.

Thumps of Granddad's steps down in the front room, and musical scrapes of furniture being moved. Maybe he was settling into his favorite leather chair after so long away.

It would be safe for me to have a quick look in the drawer. I inched it open.

No gun. Good. Granddad had been busted—and jailed— for having a gun in our truck, which as a convicted felon he can't do without catching some serious shit.

The phone rang downstairs. It took me until the second ring to recognize the sound. We only had one phone, the green one hanging on the wall in the kitchen, and hardly anybody called us on a landline anymore.

I slipped out to the top of the stairs to listen. The wooden planks had creaky spots, but I knew where to step. Crouched where I wouldn't be visible from the ground floor. The springy phone cord was long enough that Granddad could walk as far as the foyer if he chose.

"Yeah, I'm out," I heard him say into the phone.

I couldn't tell whether the caller was a man or a woman.

"No," said Granddad. Then after another moment, "I don't give a damn what he said."

Now I could hear that the caller was a guy. I faded back an inch, thinking Granddad was coming closer. But no, the guy was just getting louder. Insistent.

"You're a fool," Granddad said. Cold as anything. His Belfast accent came on stronger when he was mad, or especially pleased. He wasn't pleased.

The voice lowered—Granddad had that effect on people— but kept talking. I heard him pacing the kitchen and into the dining room.

"Shut up," Granddad finally said. The voice seemed to obey. "You won't go there again. And you sure as God's own hell won't take him there. If there's anything to be done, I'll decide. You follow?"

A very short moment of quiet. Maybe the guy on the other end of the line was holding his breath, just like I was.

"Lose this number," Granddad said.

His footsteps traced a line to bang the phone back onto its hook, and then out the back door. I stayed very still.

I had forgotten *that* during the past year and a half, too. Just how scary Granddad could be.

Better get the sheets done. I gathered up the pillowcases from his room and brought the armful of linens downstairs. Our washer and dryer were in a closet behind the kitchen, so I had to tiptoe past the big window that looked out onto the backyard. Granddad stood on the wooden steps leading down from the porch, his back to me, apparently staring at the lawn and the bushes. Which were so overgrown and weedy now it was hard to tell where one became the other.

I stopped to watch. He didn't seem to be looking for anything. He wasn't smoking. He didn't really smoke, not since I was real small, but when he *had* smoked Granddad would hang out in the same place on the porch, which made me think of it. Tonight he just stood there, a big dark shadow blocking other big dark shadows behind him.

"I have to go out," he said. Knowing all along I was there behind him. Jeez.

Wait, what?

"We just got here," I said.

He didn't reply. I dropped the laundry on the floor and went out to join him on the porch. He'd left the back door wide open, so I did too.

"Where are you going?" I said.

"It won't be long."

"But we need to clean."

"You know how to run the machines. I'll be home before the sheets are dry."

"We just *got* here."

"*A mhaicín,*" he said, fixing me with a stare. *Boy*. He calls me that, and I know the next thing coming is trouble.

"Fine." I walked back into the house and grabbed the wad of laundry and went to stuff it all into the washing machine. Fuck the different colors. The powdered soap had crusted solid. I banged the box on the washer until a chunk of it came loose and tumbled to explode into granules against the center post. I let the lid fall with a clang—much louder than the slamming phone had been—and twisted the start knob so hard that it popped off and I had to force it back on.

Granddad walked out through the front door. I heard his boots clomp down the stone steps to the street, before the washer kicked in.

Was he working? This soon? He'd told me earlier tonight he was going to take it easy. Nothing big or risky, so we could stay together. Did he have to start now?

Had he taken a gun?

I ran to the pantry. Paula or somebody must have tossed all the food before it spoiled. I didn't have to move any cans or flour sacks aside to twist the support and move the bracket and open up the little hidden door cut in the drywall.

No gun. Some ID cards and a cheap cell phone still in its plastic blister pack, but no gun. Granddad must have taken it.

He *promised*.

Wait. There weren't any boxes of ammunition, either. There would have to be some bullets left around if there had been a gun, right? Maybe Granddad had played it safe and had Paula remove every gun in the house, even the hidden ones, in case the cops came through with a metal detector or a gun-sniffing dog or something. I didn't know what they could do.

Okay. Granddad was angry, and it was for sure he wasn't just going out to buy beer. But he wasn't carrying. That was good.

I had asked him, over the burgers at Beth's—the first meal we'd shared since my tenth birthday—if we could work together. Told him that I'd been training myself with locks, which was true. I'd have to learn more.

The green light on the alarm panel blinked. That was tempting. I could try bypassing it; I'd seen Granddad do that with other systems, and this one couldn't be too different, right? No matter what improvements he'd made?

Of course, if I did it wrong, the whole neighborhood would suddenly learn that we'd come home.

I checked that the washer wasn't overflowing and went upstairs. To my room. Sat at my table, with my things. Picked up one of the stripped padlocks. It was an older Yale, five pins, springs a little soft from use. Easy for me now. The Brinks discus lock would be tougher.

The picks I had crafted last year out of hacksaw blades were still under my shirt, in their cloth eyeglasses case. I'd kept the case taped behind a drawer at the Rolfssons'. While packing my stuff earlier tonight, I'd stuck the little packet to my ribs. Just in case anybody checked my bag.

I laid all the lockpicks out in one neat row on my table and started practicing.

FOUR

I SPENT THURSDAY NIGHT IN my studio apartment off Broadway. The apartment wasn't cheap, but it looked it. It had three bare walls and a sliver of a kitchen and a three-quarter bathroom. Twice as much space as I needed to hold a couple of stacks of clothes, a minimum of thrift-store furniture, and enough tools to build or break damn near anything. The tools filled the shelves I had built in the single closet.

I'd cooked pork chops and rice for dinner, leaving half my plate untouched. Drank a bottle of Georgetown Porter without tasting it. I sat on the edge of my bed and gazed out the window, as the waning sunlight leached color from the brick wall of the third-floor yoga studio next door. From outside, I heard the occasional snaps and whistles of tiny explosions on the street. People eager for the holiday to come. The question of O'Hasson and his gold turned over in my mind so many times that it might have been bit of paper from one of those burst fire-crackers, spinning in the wind.

Taxes were due, if I wanted to keep the house. Or I could sell the scorched land and pay off the county and be free of the whole mess. Near thirty years old, starting from scratch. I could handle that. But if

I helped O'Hasson find his pot of gold, I'd have the land and plenty of cash to rebuild.

And his kid, Cyndra, might get a better shot in life. She'd been shuffled through four homes in six years. She'd probably see a few more, before they kicked her out of the system at eighteen. If she made it that far. Half the kids I'd known when I had been a ward of the state ran off, or wound up in Juvie, or both. I could improve her odds.

Call a thing by its name, Dono's voice said, *or don't expect it to answer.*

I wanted the money.

That was enough.

I picked up my phone and yanked Jimmy Corcoran away from his television to give him a shopping list. Then I called O'Hasson with the news. He whooped and started to ask questions. I told him the time and place to pick me up the following night, and ended the call before he could say another word.

O'HASSON MET ME AT the corner of 5th and Bell in a rattletrap blue Honda he had boosted from a long-term Park 'n Fly. His seat was as far forward as it would go, so he could reach the pedals.

A sharp crackle echoing off the downtown buildings made him jump. "What was that?"

"Fireworks," I said. "Up at Lake Union." As if in confirmation, a deep bang made the Honda's loose windows tremble.

"Shit, I forgot. At least everybody's having as much fun as us, right?"

We drove south on Highway 99 into lower King County, enjoying plenty of distance from the scattering of other late-night drivers. That was for the best. O'Hasson fidgeted so much, it was a small miracle that the Honda stayed between the white lines.

I directed us to a Target that was open until midnight even on the holiday, where I handed him cash to buy a car battery. He stuffed the bills into the pocket of his jean jacket and wedged a rigidly new Seahawks cap on his head to hide the surgical scar.

"Twelve-volt," I reminded him.

He chuckled. "After tonight, you can buy the rest of the Maserati to go with it."

While he was inside, I opened the duffel bag O'Hasson had tossed into the backseat. He'd brought basic tools, along with a few of the same electronics I would want for a break-in, and a large bundle of what looked like cheap glow sticks, if we needed extra light.

No gun. Good.

Back on the road and off the highway, O'Hasson took a long circuitous route into a commercial neighborhood. The area grew progressively lower in rent the farther we drove, until it was clear that hardly anyone was renting at all. Vacant lots and shuttered businesses lined the streets. A jetliner coming off a SeaTac runway thundered overhead as it fought for altitude.

"There. There," he said, pointing with a gloved finger. A six-story tower loomed over the closed teriyaki joints and nail salons filling the rest of the block. Stuck on the outside of the building was a big wooden NOTICE OF PROPOSED LAND USE ACTION sign. The few words on the sign not obscured by graffiti mentioned a mixed-retail commercial usage property, whatever the hell that was. At the bottom of the sign, the date of demolition was filled in with thick black marker, the last day of August.

"See? The place is ready for the wrecking ball," O'Hasson said.

"It'll still be here tomorrow. Stop for a second."

He squirmed impatiently. There were no lights on inside the building, on any floor. Through the scarred glass of the entrance doors I could make out the first few yards of lobby. The space was completely barren of furniture. Bare patches where reception desks had recently stood showed as clean white rectangles on the old tile. Shiny exposed bolts poked out like stubby fingers from the walls of the entryway, marking where security cameras had once been mounted.

"Looks good, right?" said O'Hasson.

It looked stripped to the bones. An unlikely home for a petty cash box, much less a safe full of gold.

"Let's see the back," I said. He touched the gas and we drifted around the block. A large portion of the building's empty ground floor had been occupied by an urgent care clinic. The clinic's sign had survived the purge, though its red cross had faded to pink.

The rear entrance was a mirror image of the front. O'Hasson craned his neck to see out my window. A few shops still survived on this road, but without so much as a neon sign glowing behind their steel gates.

"Look at this." O'Hasson grinned at the street like it was an amusement park. "We could blast our way in with a cannon and nobody would hear."

He was right. No signs of life nearby. Not even tents of homeless camps in the alleys. I pointed to the curb. O'Hasson pulled over and the engine ticked weakly into silence.

"Let's go," I said, stepping out of the car.

O'Hasson scrambled to catch up. "Sweet sugar."

I opened the Honda's trunk. The backpack I'd stashed inside was so heavy that I had to lift it with two hands.

"You catch the utility box?" I said.

He nodded. "On the corner. I got it." He snatched his duffel from the backseat and scurried off to the green metal housing with its PSE logo.

I shouldered the pack and clipped the straps of its aluminum frame around my chest. The frame would support at least a hundred pounds, about as much weight as my old combat gear plus a ruck, once I ditched the equipment I'd bought from Corcoran. If O'Hasson's miracle treasure really existed, we couldn't walk away with gold kilobars stuffed in our pants pockets.

An emergency exit door on the side of the building had a deadbolt that might be an imitation Schlage. Two minutes' work, so long as we didn't have to deal with an alarm.

I grabbed our new car battery and joined O'Hasson at the utility box. He had cut open the plastic housing of the main cable and was methodically stripping and testing each power line with a multimeter. His work was clean, and his fingers moved rapidly. The cancer hadn't eaten away his skill.

"It's cherry," he said. "The power's completely off on this side of the block."

"But no phone lines in this box." On the narrow chance the building still had a working alarm system, it might run through telecom jacks.

He shrugged. "You want to search for them?" I knew what O'Hasson's vote would be. He shifted his weight excitedly from foot to foot, like a kid on hot sand. I wondered what medication he was on for the tumor. And what he might be taking on top of it.

The block was quiet enough that I half expected a tumbleweed to blow through. We could burn half an hour finding the city box that held the fiber optics for the building, and another half to check every line. It was nearly midnight. I wanted to be gone within four hours. One glance at the safe would tell me if that timeline was possible.

"We go," I said. "You'll watch the street."

He brightened and eased the metal lid of the PSE box shut.

I used Dono's old set of lockpicks on the emergency exit deadbolt. A pick gun might have been a little faster, but call me nostalgic. It was a way of having the old man along for the ride.

The bolt drew back with a click and the door swung open. To silence.

"Good start," O'Hasson said.

The door led to a long interior corridor. Once we had slipped inside and shut the door behind us, the blackness was complete. I turned on my small flashlight. Its halogen beam petered out before we could see where the corridor ended.

"Find the stairs," said O'Hasson. "Office 501."

I put a hand on his shoulder, stopping his forward rush.

"You said the safe was under the floor," I said. I shone the flashlight upward. "Ceiling looks like drop tile and plaster. That's not going to hold any weight."

"Hey, I don't know every detail. The senile geezer said his office was number five-oh-one. Like the denim jeans."

I let O'Hasson take point, following the narrow ray from his own penlight. The nearest stairwell was halfway down the hall. Dust coated the railings and grit crunched underfoot on every step. The air was muggy. I guessed no one had been inside in weeks, maybe since the building had been stripped. O'Hasson sneezed. The sound echoed up and down the stairwell shaft. We pressed onward and upward, through the stifling black.

"Here we go," O'Hasson managed to say as we neared the fifth landing. He was wheezing.

"You all right?"

"Don' worry 'bout it."

There was no Office 501 on the fifth floor. There were no offices at all. Every wall and door had been torn out, leaving only a huge empty space with exposed vents and a patchwork of carpet and wood flooring where rooms had once existed. It felt as wide as a football field. An uninterrupted span of windows glowed faintly at the far edge of each horizon. The rest was a dark void.

"Jesus," said O'Hasson. The shadows cast by my flashlight beam made his distraught expression grotesque. "What happened to the office?"

I unclipped the backpack and set it down. The thump released a stink of mildew into the stale air. From the pack's depths I removed a thick black tube that looked like an overfed nightstick.

"What the hell is that?" O'Hasson said.

"Metal detector." It was a variation on the handheld wands TSA agents used in airports. This one had been enhanced—courtesy of Jimmy Corcoran—to focus its magnetic field to a narrow range that could pierce walls.

I guessed that 501 would have been at one end of the building or the other. Maybe an executive suite. I flipped a mental coin and started with the east corner. O'Hasson followed me so closely I might as well have been carrying him piggyback. I bent low to sweep the tip of the detector above the carpet.

"Can't believe you thought to bring that," he said.

"You told me the safe was hidden. Did you want to pull up the whole floor?"

"Look," he said, poking his nose in front of the gauge as it wavered. The shine from his jittering penlight put spots in my eyes.

"Any heating vent could make it tick. Go check the street."

He sulked but didn't argue. The little burglar had been surprisingly agreeable to any task I gave him. Maybe that was why he and Dono had gotten along. My grandfather had never brooked much argument about who was in charge. O'Hasson retreated to the windows and split his attention between me and the road below as he paced.

I traced a line out from the wall and back again, like mowing an invisible lawn, until I'd covered a square forty feet on each side. Nothing under the grubby carpet bumped the needle more than halfway.

"North corner," I said. I walked across the building to repeat the pattern. O'Hasson hurried along the windows, keen to stay close.

On my third pass, twenty feet out from the wall and smack in the middle of a swath of stained brown carpet, the needle pegged itself firmly against the far edge of the gauge.

I tried a few feet to the left, then the right. Up and down. Anywhere within a square yard, the detector was insistent. O'Hasson was immediately at my side.

"Look for a seam," I said, kneeling down and feeling the carpet. He dropped and followed suit.

"Here," he said, digging his thin fingers into a gap. We pulled and the carpet peeled back grudgingly, leaving rubbery chunks of its underlayer stuck in yellowed glue to the fiberboard floor beneath. I held my breath to keep from inhaling puffs of mold spores. O'Hasson dumped half the contents of his duffel out to find a linoleum knife in the jumble of tools and wires. He sawed at the tough strands until we could throw the loose pieces aside.

There was a recessed iron ring pull set into the floor. I could just make out the edges of a square hole cut in the fiberboard. Beside me, O'Hasson inhaled.

I grabbed the ring and pulled. The square tilted up on inset hinges, the dry wood crackling in protest.

"Yes," O'Hasson whispered. "Yes."

It was there. A Durman combination safe, two feet by three. I knew the brand well enough to identify it from the bits of its stenciled name still visible under a layer of dirt and chalky dust. The box was face-up, door and dial pointed toward the ceiling. Shining my light down along the edges, I could see a lumpy line of solder where someone long ago had welded the rear side of the Durman to a steel crossbeam underneath.

"Can you open it?" O'Hasson said, so quietly I knew he was dreading the answer.

"Go get the pack."

He scuttled away for it.

I knelt to brush the dirt aside and gave the dial an experimental twist. A little crunchy, but it moved. I grinned. The faint tick of each number sounded like a drummer, tapping out the beat before the music started.

We unloaded the backpack. O'Hasson's breath was short, and his hands trembled slightly. I hoped I wouldn't be carrying him out of here before the night was through.

It took only a minute by the beam of his flashlight to set up my gear. I'd modified the handheld drill's electric cord to take juice through jumper cables. The car battery would power the drill all night, if we needed it to.

The abrupt shriek of the drill's motor made O'Hasson jump. I aimed its whirling diamond bit at the edge of the dial. Gave it a bit of pressure. A high banshee keen, and curlicues of metal spun away as if in a panic.

It was a tough position to work from. I concentrated on keeping the drill perfectly steady. Too shallow an angle and I'd miss the inner lock. Too acute, or too deep of a hole, and I might fuck up the lock entirely. Then we'd have to try brute force, using the heavier tools in my pack. Bad odds on that method.

After five minutes I turned off the drill to wipe sweat from my face with the back of my glove. "Pass me the scope."

The handheld scope was a simple illuminated magnifier, not much different than the kind used by optometrists to check a patient's retinas. I swept the dirt away and lay on my stomach to stick my face down next to the safe. Its steel smelled like fresh water. With the tiny fish-eye lens against the drill hole, I could see the smooth sharp edge of the first lock gate, as clear as dawn and just as beautiful.

O'Hasson edged closer, trying to see around my head. I turned the dial until the gate budged. Get all the gates lined up like good little soldiers, and the lock would be open. If it still worked.

"Check the street," I said to O'Hasson. My breath fogged the lens for an instant.

"Come on. If an alarm had gone off—"

"I have to look, and I have to listen. And right now all I can hear is your skin vibrating. Go over there."

He backed away. Not all the way to the windows, but far enough.

First gate open. I looked at the dial and marked the number as 37. I turned the dial slowly until the second gate quivered a little, then a little more. The lens only let me see an inch or two into the lock. The dial showed 12. Call it somewhere between 10 and 14 to open the second gate. That was as far as I would get with the scope.

Safecracking was often about reducing permutations to a workable number. I backed off, spun the dial, and started experimenting. Sixty numbers around the dial. I tried 37-10-59. Then 37-10-58. Steady pressure on the door handle as I turned the dial through every tick. I hardly used my eyes. My fingers could keep track on their own.

It became a rhythm, left and right and left again, through each combination. It felt good. It felt right. I'd known I could beat the Durman the instant we'd seen it. That I could drill the pilot hole just so. That I could work the gates and open the lock.

Call it by its name. It was *fun*.

I got all the way down to 37-10-0, without any telltale give in the handle. I took it from the top, bumping the middle number from 10 to 11.

At 37-11-24, I felt the handle tremble. Just a little. No more than if a small bird had alighted on its silver surface.

O'Hasson caught the shift in my posture. "You got it?" he called.

I turned the dial one more tick. The handle clunked. Answer aplenty.

"I told you!" he shouted, running to meet me. "I said it, didn't I?" He was right on top of me as I swung the safe open.

The jumpy little son of a bitch had said it.

And he was absolutely right.

Slim golden bars glittered from the black interior of the safe. Dozens of them, each about the size of a pack of cigarettes, and arranged in meticulous stacks, with their minting stamps and serial numbers all facing the same way. As merrily brilliant after their long airless confinement as if they'd been polished yesterday.

O'Hasson whooped and shouldered past me to reach for the bars. I let him. He'd found his treasure.

"God. God. More than I fucking imagined," he said, gasping. Stray bars fell from his grasping hands to thump heavily on the floor.

I picked one up. Its density was surprising, even though I'd been prepared for it. I clicked open my knife and dug the blade into the edge of the bar. The soft metal parted.

It was real. I'd kept myself from fully believing it until that moment. O'Hasson had caught my smile. "How much is here?" he said.

I made a quick count. At least a hundred kilobars in the stacks. If they were as clean as O'Hasson claimed, we could clear forty grand per.

"Four million dollars," I said. "Conservatively." I might have been a little breathless myself.

"Holy mother," O'Hasson said.

A heavy mother, too. "I can make this in one trip," I said, "if the pack doesn't rip. But it will be slow."

He shrugged exaggeratedly. Happy enough now to slow down and enjoy his moment of victory. "I'll carry what I can."

I tossed the circular and reciprocal saws out of my pack to make room, and began loading the bars. The challenge wasn't size—all of the bars together would make a bundle smaller than two shoeboxes—but weight. A hundred bars added up to 220 pounds, more than I weighed myself. I was in for some exercise.

O'Hasson loaded fifteen or so of the bars from the safe into his half-empty duffel and hefted it, first with one hand and then quickly a second, grunting with the effort. "That's enough."

"Go get the car. Bring it around to the door." I didn't want to lug the loaded pack any farther than I had to.

The little burglar tottered off to the stairs, listing steeply to one side under his load.

Four million dollars. I mean, god *damn*. Even a third of that could let me rebuild the house as a freaking castle, if I chose.

I scooped up the bits and pieces of O'Hasson's electronics that he'd left on the floor and stuffed them into my pockets. My own tools were untraceable to me, but I wouldn't count on my accomplice to have taken the same care. The shining kilobars went into the main compartment of the pack, down at the bottom where the massive weight wouldn't crush my spine once I'd shouldered it.

As I reached down to grab the last two bars, my latex-gloved fingertips brushed the bottom of the safe.

It was softer than it should be. I prodded at it. Hard rubber.

A pressure plate.

A howl sounded in the back of my mind. The atavistic internal cry of danger, even as my higher intellect started calculating just how much trouble we were in.

The pressure plate was jet black. It would be next to invisible even under normal light. Hooked to an alarm, no question. Wireless. Very twenty-first century. Definitely not something abandoned twenty years ago.

We'd walked into a trap.

FIVE

I SPRINTED TO THE WINDOW, checked the road below. It was clear. For now.

Who would be alerted when the alarm was triggered? Had the alarm gone off when we'd moved the very first gold bars, or when the weight tipped over a certain point? There was no way to tell.

I ran to the opposite side of the building to see the street in front. No movement there either. But someone might already be on the way.

Time to run.

The pack was sitting up on the floor, like an obediently patient dog. I sat down and hurriedly clicked myself into its web of straps and belts, and used the open safe door to haul myself and the crushing load up to my knees. It felt like I was trying to drag an anchor through sand. One foot under me. Two. Push. I was up, and taking one thudding step at a time toward the stairs.

Descending the pitch-black stairwell was a nightmare in slow motion. I gripped the railing with both hands to stay vertical. Stepping sideways. Left, right. Acutely conscious that a bad step might destroy my knee, or send me and two hundred extra pounds of metal into a fall that would likely snap my neck. Right, left. At two floors, my thighs were quivering. After four, sweat blurred my vision—not that there was anything I could see in the stygian dark—and the shaking had expanded to my chest.

When I reached the corridor at the bottom, I stole a moment to take a long unsteady breath before lurching toward the exit. I was counting steps. Thirty to the exit, maybe another twenty to O'Hasson's stolen Honda. Then relief. I yanked the door wide and looked out onto the street.

The car wasn't there. Neither was O'Hasson.

Dammit. Where was he? I cursed him as I leaned against the wall of the corridor, sliding clumsily down to my butt, and freed myself from the taut straps of the pack. Had he gone back upstairs? Had the wreck of a car not started?

I wasn't going to be as lucky as that. Something was wrong. Maybe the sick man had collapsed under the strain. Or become disoriented in the dark building.

Standing up gave me a lightheaded rush, like I had landed on a different planet with weaker gravity. I took a pry bar from the pack and left the heavy bulk leaning against the wall, and found a passage that led from the corridor toward where I knew the central lobby would be. If O'Hasson was on the opposite side of the building, that would be my fastest path.

I had just reached the span of the main reception area when someone yelled incoherently from the upper floors, the cry echoing down the central flight of stairs that wound around a small atrium at the ground level. Was that O'Hasson, calling for me? I began running up the flights, leg muscles objecting.

The yell didn't repeat, but as I rounded the third landing a door slammed on the floor above me. I stopped. Listened. When no further noises came, I moved silently up the stairs.

The fourth floor hadn't been fully gutted like the fifth, where we'd opened the safe. I was looking at a hallway, or at least the portion of it I could make out in the dark. No telling which of the doors down its length had slammed.

Not O'Hasson. Instinct told me, before my senses had solid evidence. We weren't alone here.

A heavy thump, from the top floor. I dashed up the last flight, safe in the enveloping blackness.

My boot sole skidded on something. I peered down at it in the gloom. A small tube on the tiled floor of the landing.

No, a dart. Two inches of hollow white syringe with a billow of red strands at one end and a needle on the other. I picked it up. The steel needle glinted wickedly where it was still clean. Its tip was dark, and wet.

What the hell was happening?

Without the help of a flashlight, the empty fifth floor was a cave, with only the narrow ghostly glow of the city light coming from outside to interrupt the black. I felt exposed, and automatically dipped low to where I wouldn't be silhouetted against the windows. I moved around the edge of the room, listening. Someone was here. I could almost hear them breathe.

As if in answer, the tiny figure of O'Hasson abruptly appeared in the middle of the vastness, still carrying his duffel bag. He must have stood up from the safe. Maybe what I'd heard had been the weakened man falling down. I started to call to him, when more silhouetted figures emerged from the shadows, far off at the end of the building.

O'Hasson saw them, too. He yelled again, a guttural, desperate sound of fear, and broke something in his hands with a loud snap. One of his glow sticks, I realized.

He hurled the sticks to the floor. Fire burst into life, globs of some burning gelatinous substance splashing up like a tiny volcano from the carpet.

I hit the deck, catching a glimpse of white men's faces on the dark figures as I dropped. O'Hasson broke a full handful of the sticks. The men shouted. He hurled the firesticks into the mound of carpet remnants between him and the men. The flames surged to life in a flash that blinded me. An instant bonfire lapped at the ceiling and engulfed the heap of desiccated fabric and the floor beyond. The figures retreated, as a sudden wave of heat made me shield my eyes.

The fire was already rolling in a wave across the carpet toward me. Whatever the accelerant in O'Hasson's homemade Molotovs was, it was volatile as hell itself.

Through watering eyes I saw O'Hasson on the other side of the fire, staggering toward the main staircase. He wasn't going to make it. The men were right on his tail.

I jumped up and raced in the opposite direction. There would be another set of stairs at the far end of the building. There had to be. Behind me, the crackling roar pursued.

At the south wall I slammed against a door, making its push bar bang like a pistol shot, and emerged into an unlit stairwell. I ran down the stairs as fast as the dark allowed. My hands swept every speck of dirt off the stairway railing. The hungry growl of the fire grew louder, even as I descended.

The stairs ended at the lobby. I couldn't see enough of the street to know if it was clear. I'd have to chance it. A heavy padlock and chain sealed the rear doors. I thrust the pry bar into the lock shackle. It was a clumsy fit. I couldn't get leverage, and the lock resisted every attempt to snap it. Acrid fumes began to fill the room. I jammed the tip of the pry bar into the handle of the door instead, and threw my back into it. The screws gave with a screech. My eyes were blinded. I pushed harder. The handle burst from the door, the chain falling away. Choking, I felt for the top and bottom bolts, yanked them open, and lunged out onto the sidewalk.

I'd lost direction. Which way had we come in? Had O'Hasson made it out?

No time to dwell on his fate. A sharp crack and a flash of yellow light high above the street made me flinch, as a swift rain of glass jingled down onto the asphalt. The car battery had blown, adding to the inferno. I could see the windows on the middle floors warping with heat. It wouldn't be long before the entire structure was ablaze.

One distant moan of a fire engine was soon joined by a second. Cops would be close behind. I needed a car. Or I'd have to hide in one of the boarded-up shops. Walking out in the open in this neighborhood would be as good as signing a confession.

The dented blue Honda was right where we'd left it, the street quiet. Without the approaching sirens, I could have believed myself the only person in a square mile.

No time to question my good luck now. I dashed for the Honda and yanked the door open, ducking as the first hook-and-ladder howled past, headed toward the front of the building.

I kept my head down to strip the ignition wires and tap them together. The second the fire truck rounded the corner, I hit the gas and got the hell out of there.

Run as far as you like. Dono's voice in my head, both mocking and disappointed. *It won't matter, will it now?*

It wouldn't. O'Hasson and I had stumbled into a snare. As elaborate as anything laid by hunters for a jungle cat. I looked at the tranquilizer dart. It bounced minutely on the passenger seat as I made the aged Honda's pistons whine.

We'd screwed with somebody's carefully laid plans. Mick O'Hasson might already be bagged and tagged. Or worse.

And now the hunters would be on my trail.

SIX

At the first touch of morning, the huge marina at Shilshole looked diminished. Elongated shadows shrunk the luxury cruisers and tall masts into so many toys set in orderly rows, waiting to be tossed into a child's bathtub. I parked my truck where I could see the road that ran alongside the vast and mostly vacant marina lot, and watched to see if anyone turned in after me, or slowed on their way past.

I had been a short hop away from full paranoia since fleeing the scene of the fire in O'Hasson's stolen Honda. Even after I'd ditched the car and caught a train at the next light rail station to retrieve my truck, I kept doubling back, looking for signs of pursuit. No one was chasing me. Not yet.

My speedboat was moored two docks over from Hollis's *Francesca*. The Stingray had been my grandfather's, registered under one of his many assumed names. It was a deliberately dull vessel. Gray hull, gray trim, with no name painted on the transom. But it had a spearhead shape and a 300-horse engine that could make it lunge like a hungry shark.

I reeked of dried sweat and chemical smoke. Like Dono had before me, I kept a change of clothes and a few emergency provisions in the boat's tiny cabin. A rag and the dock's water hose would serve to wash the worst of the grime off of me. I stripped to my boxers. The icy spray crushed the air from my lungs on the first blast. Also the second.

As I was dunking my head under the freezing stream for a final time, the gate at the end of the dock banged shut. Hollis, dressed in madras shorts and a red-and-white-striped Derry City FC shirt, trundled noisily down the ramp.

"I was gonna knock on your door," I said through slightly chattering teeth as he drew closer, "once the sun was higher."

"And once you had some pants on, I hope. What the hell happened with you?"

I twisted the faucet closed and dropped the hose over the dock edge to drain. "Bad night."

I filled him in on the past few hours. By the time I got to the part about not finding O'Hasson or the shadowy men on the street before the fire trucks showed, I had dressed in a t-shirt and frayed jeans and we were sitting together in the cockpit of the speedboat.

"No chance he got away?" Hollis asked, his voice uncharacteristically somber.

I thought of my last sight of O'Hasson, barely on his feet as his pursuers closed in. "No. He couldn't have made it out on his own. Either he collapsed and died in the fire, or they have him now."

"Like an arrest," Hollis said.

"Like big game." I handed Hollis the dart I had picked up off the stairway landing. "Don't touch the tip."

"No chance there. Evil-looking thing."

It was. But it gave me some small hope that O'Hasson was still alive. If the hunters—I kept thinking of the men at the building as that, with their trap and their trank gun—wanted to kill outright, they could have gunned O'Hasson down the moment they saw him.

There was a flip side to that hope. O'Hasson might have given up the name of his partner in the fiasco at any moment. The next dart could be coming for me.

Hollis brushed his broad thumb over the red plastic hairs on the tail of the dart. "Who would care enough about that little man to shoot him with this?"

"They came ready to take down whoever opened the safe. A dying ex-con wasn't exactly who they were expecting, I think."

"And he brought you."

I leaned back against the cowling. The sun was already hot and promising to get nasty before the day hit noon.

"I should be more pissed off at the son of a bitch. He burned down the whole building, and could have cooked me right along with it. I thought he was just carrying glow sticks. Break the damn things and they become instant Molotovs." I whistled at the memory of the roaring heat. "But if O'Hasson hadn't torched the place, maybe I'd have wound up wherever he is now."

"And the gold?" Hollis said. "You said you left it all in the backpack, by the exit?" His antennae were out, feeling the air for the scent of possible profit.

"The fire wouldn't have hurt it. Either it's still there, waiting for the arson investigators to come across it, or"—I shrugged—"the hunters found it and took it while I was busy saving my own ass."

"You don't suppose we could, well, have a quick look? Just to see?"

"I'm not getting near the place. It'll be swarming with law. And maybe the hunters have the same idea. If they were after the real owner of the gold, they might be hoping he shows up to see if the safe is still there."

Since the train ride from South Seattle, I had been wondering about Office 501, and who had been leasing it before the building was sold. And thinking about that gave me another notion that made me sit bolt upright.

"What's the matter? You look knocked for six," Hollis said.

"The building. It was scheduled to be torn down."

"Sure. You said that was why O'Hasson couldn't wait for his partner to be released from Lancaster."

"Right. O'Hasson had to crack the safe now. And the hunters knew somebody would be coming soon, for the same reason. It can't be just random chance that the building was sold and empty when they needed to set their trap." I shook my head. "Too big a coincidence. The building being demolished had to be part of the lure."

Hollis stared. "What are you saying? That the bastards actually own the building?"

"Or they bought it, just to gut the place and wait. Think about it. If you want to catch a tiger, you set fire to the tall grass and flush him out. If you want to make someone hurry to open a secret safe—"

"Then you make it look like the safe is about to be discovered. Christ Almighty."

Hollis stood and stepped out onto the dock. Fifteen minutes sitting in one place might have been a new record for him. His sandals slapped against the planks as he paced.

"How much money would that take?" he said. "Hundreds of thousands, surely."

"Or more. Enough that I wonder if the gold—wherever it came from—wasn't what the hunters were after. Not entirely. Maybe they set the alarm themselves, or maybe they just took advantage of an alarm that was already installed. Waiting to see who showed up."

"And as you said, that wasn't supposed to be O'Hasson."

"No."

"So they don't have much use for him."

I didn't have to say anything for Hollis to know that I agreed. O'Hasson's attendant in the prison infirmary had sold him on the idea of the safe, and the gold. Once the hunters wrung a little information out of him, O'Hasson would be expendable.

"Bad way for a man to check out," said Hollis. "Even if the poor bugger didn't have much time left to him."

Maybe especially if that. Days had more value when there were fewer left. I wondered about O'Hasson's kid, Cyndra. Where would she be when she learned about his death? If he simply fell off the end of the earth, his body never found, would she think he'd left her?

That idea disturbed me. Almost as much as thinking that people with enough resources and determination to buy a whole building might come looking for me, now that O'Hasson was gone.

I took a long breath and stretched. My muscles creaked, my body finally daring to relax after hours of tension. I knew the feeling. Aches and twinges sprang up after every mission with the Rangers, no matter how short. It was more than simple physical exhaustion. It was the hangover from the rush.

Hollis must have read my fatigue. "You'll want food in your belly. Come along to the boat with me, I'll show you something."

I locked up the speedboat's cabin and joined him. The seawater smell coming off the dock pilings was strong, with salt and bits of kelp left by the retreating tide baking slowly in the heat. We walked without haste toward the gate. It gave me time to think about my next move.

I wouldn't sit and wait. If the hunters really had bought the building, maybe I could follow the money. It would be much better if I knew who might be coming after me.

Hollis led me down his dock and its array of large luxury powerboats, and on board the *Francesca*. Surprise made me stop short at the door.

The main cabin was partly dismantled. Hollis had removed the built-in settee and the lockers underneath, and some of the wall behind on the starboard side, exposing the curve of the inner hull. Large pieces of teakwood and molded fiberglass lay scattered around the room. A pile of nuts and bolts and brackets and screws took up half of the chart table.

"You've been busy," I said.

"A little project. I want to be able to take out the whole side here and put it back at short notice, whenever I require."

I took a closer look. Despite the clutter of tools and bits of furniture, the removal work had been very carefully done. The seam where the settee had met the floor was cut as straight as a guitar string. "Just because."

"Well, there's a particular need I have in mind."

"No kidding. You wanted me to see this why?"

He sighed. Hollis did not play cards, should never play cards. He could look a cop in the eye and swear that the stars were made of popcorn without blinking, but dissembling with friends was something he'd never mastered. For a crook, he was shockingly honest.

"Call it advance planning," he said. "So you can do me a favor, if there's reason."

I looked at him. "In case you're not around?"

"Not that way. I'm not expecting any trouble on this little venture. You know I like to keep my life less exciting. Unlike some young fools."

"Don't change the subject."

"It's a timing thing. I might not be able to retrieve whatever items I've placed inside this handy little compartment promptly. If I'm delayed, I thought perhaps I could get word to you, and you'd know how to open it up and take what's inside elsewhere."

"Before what happens? Cops coming with a warrant? Or worse?"

"Let's say police."

"And the reason you're talking in circles around whatever you're hauling is because you think I'll faint dead away."

"Some art pieces. They're from Japan." When I didn't respond Hollis filled the awkward silence. "Carved posts, each about eight feet long. Which is why I need such a long space to hold them. See, they'll run along the hull, behind these panels here."

"Posts."

"Bedposts, really."

Bedposts. "Carved with what?"

Hollis actually blushed. And I started laughing.

"It's just business," he said.

"I'm glad it's not pleasure."

"The damn things are worth as much as a house. Japanese take their smut seriously. The posts have pearls and jade laid in them."

The word *laid* made me laugh even harder. After the long night of fear and felonies, I welcomed it. "Great, Hollis. A niche market."

"To hell with you, then." But he was starting to break up, too.

When we'd finally stopped snickering like a couple of eighth-grade boys, Hollis showed me how he was going to reconstruct the pieces of the cabin, and where he was going to install bolts and thumbscrews to allow someone to access the space beneath. You could take the whole section apart and reassemble it again within twenty minutes. It was ingenious.

My cell phone buzzed as Hollis was describing how to reattach the final pieces. A voicemail. I must have missed the call while I was giving myself an ice bath.

Van, I'm sorry to call so early. Addy Proctor, my elderly neighbor. She didn't sleep much, and I received calls at strange times. *I have to move the washing machine today to get the window replaced.*

Shit, I had told Addy I'd come by yesterday. I'd gotten distracted with preparations for the safe job. *The man will be here around ten, I think. They are maddeningly unspecific about times. Could you*—I ended the voicemail.

"A rain check on the meal," I said to Hollis. We'd set one of the larger teakwood panels against the cabin door during Hollis's little master class in smuggling, and I handed it back to him. "Hell of a job. Dono would have been impressed."

"You think? Your man was a hand at the tricky carpentry himself." Hollis flushed again, this time with pride. "Was that the one from down your street?"

"Addy. Yeah."

"Give the old bat my love."

On the way back to the truck, my eyes making a careful survey of the road and the parking lot, I hit Contact to call Addy back.

"I'm on my way," I said on the tail of her hello. Her dog, Stanley, woofed in the background.

"He hears you," Addy said.

"You want donuts? I'll bring donuts."

She hesitated. "What's the matter?"

Jesus, Addy knew me a little too well. She'd been there during the hellish time when Dono was dying. I'd even crashed on her couch for a couple of weeks after the house had been destroyed and Luce Boylan and I had broken things off. I had been smart enough to find an apartment before Addy and I started snarling at each other. Both of us were used to having our own space, and two stubborn adults and one dog the size of a Harley-Davidson outstripped the sanity limits of her orderly little house.

"Long night. Tell you about it later," I said.

I wouldn't, and she probably understood that, and she would probably let it go. I knew her pretty well, too.

SEVEN

I BEAT THE MORNING RUSH to snag half a dozen jelly-filled and apple fritters at Top Pot, and made it to the east side of Capitol Hill before the oily condensation had soaked through the bags. The last time I'd been on our block, I had met O'Hasson. Half a week and a lot of grief since then.

Before drawing near, I circled the block to pass the street on both ends, looking for anything out of place. There were no strangers hovering around my little plot of land with its skeletal house frame. No unfamiliar cars parked nearby. I knew all of my neighbors' vehicles, and their regular visitors. Long practice, from when Dono had been alert for any change on our hill that might signal trouble.

The block looked safe. But O'Hasson knew my address. If the hunters had spotted me during the chaos of the fire, if they had forced O'Hasson to tell them who I was, then this would be where they would try to pick up my trail. I would have to prepare for that.

I left the Dodge on the next block—O'Hasson knew my truck, too— and walked around the lower corner to Addy's place. Addy opened her front door, and Stanley, her huge white pit-bull-maybe-mastiff-maybe-rhinoceros mixed breed came bounding out. His catcher's-mitt paws slapped loudly on the paving stones as he ran to meet me. I tore off a piece of fritter and hook-shot it over the picket fence. Nothing but throat.

"Thanks for this," Addy said. "The washer, I mean. Not for teaching my dog bad habits." She was already dressed for the day, in brown jeans and a silver-gray wool sweater that wouldn't have looked out of place on a sailor from Melville's time. The sweater matched Addy's spiky hair and came down almost to her knees.

"I want a favor in return," I said.

"Fine."

"Wait until you hear it."

Addy's house always reminded me of a kid's storybook, waiting for a cartoon mouse to move in and start baking. Yellow walls with blue stenciled flowers along the ceiling and floor brightened the living room where she spent most of her hours. Knickknacks from vacations Addy and her late husband, Magnus, had taken to his native Sweden were set high on built-in shelves, safe from Stanley's swiping tail. The dog and I followed Addy to the back of the house, jostling for position around her overstuffed furniture.

I unfastened the washer hoses and wrestled the machine into Addy's project room. The twelve-by-twelve space was overflowing with what looked like old reference books. One stack fell over as I nudged it aside with my foot.

"New hobby?" I said. Or grunted. The washer wasn't light.

"The books? Homework. I've got an event coming up, and I want to recognize the names, even if the faces have wrinkled and creased and generally collapsed."

I picked up one of the volumes. An annual industry directory for *AM Radio in the Western United States*, 1968. "You used to work in radio?" I couldn't keep track of Addy's latest pursuits, much less her tangled job history.

"My first husband was a jazz musician, when he could be. I hung around nightclubs long enough that I picked up this and that and eventually talked a station into giving me a show, spinning records."

"Addy the D.J. Damn."

"Well, there wasn't any sampling or scratching involved with it. Yes, I'm aware of the terms, don't give me that look."

"I'm just impressed."

"Impress the washer back into the corner there. Then we'll get to your favor. I assume coffee is in order."

"God, yeah."

While Addy was brewing the pot, I squeezed into the chair at her tiny secretary desk in the living room and used her computer to pull up the address of the office building—*former* office building—on a city map. The search also pulled up breaking news links from the local affiliates. The KIRO story conjectured that transients may have been squatting in the building and that the fire may have been accidental, caused by cooking or fireworks. No bodies were reported found, and no firefighters had been injured battling the blaze. I let out a breath I'd barely realized I'd been holding.

The accident theory wouldn't survive an arson investigation. They'd identify O'Hasson's accelerants and find my charred tools by the safe, and then the SPD would quickly take the reins.

Addy brought a cup of coffee to the desk and peered over my shoulder at the screen. "What happened there?"

I pointed to the address. "I need your research mojo. Do you think you can run down the records for this property?"

Addy had once been a librarian, and worked at a newspaper. While I'd been struggling with the aftermath of Dono's death and his various properties, I had learned that the elderly woman had an almost preternatural ability to navigate bureaucracy and official documents. Her casual network extended to retired professors, reporters, and I swear I'd once caught her flirting on the phone with a former governor.

She was still looking at the news story as a video loop of firefighters pumping water into the smoldering wreckage ran mutely at the top of the brief text.

"I might help," she said, slow as syrup. "Did you have anything to do with what I'm seeing here?"

"I didn't set the fire."

"Master of the half-answer."

"See if you can learn what company managed the commercial leases on this building when it was open. And who owns it now, if it's not the same people."

"So you know it was sold," Addy said. "Is the fire some sort of insurance scam?"

"No."

"And if someone should ask *why* I'm calling the county Recorder's Office about the history of a five-alarm calamity?"

I tapped the screen. "Say you're a freelancer. That retirement bored you and you're interested in writing for these new things called blogs."

"That's terribly ageist," Addy said, although she didn't sound offended.

"The more you play the doddering senior, the better. Less attention that way."

"Good Lord, you really think I'm past it, don't you?"

"Think of it like a radio play, with Foley artists and everything. Yeah, I know the term."

Addy stopped my hand on its way to the coffee mug. "Are you in trouble here? Because it wasn't so long ago you were having a lot of conversations with policemen."

"Polite conversations."

"Some while in custody."

"I won't be asking you to post bail, Addy."

"That's hardly my point. You didn't much care for being on that side of the table. And history repeats itself, unless you pay attention."

I frowned. "Okay. I'll pay attention."

"And I'll mind my own business now. There's another lemon left. Somehow the fritters have vanished."

I grabbed a donut and Stanley followed me to the backyard, where he managed to talk me out of a couple bites while I tossed a lacrosse ball for him to fetch. Addy's house was on an eighth of an acre and the backyard wasn't much more than a patch of torn-up grass half the size of a tennis court. I was careful not to throw the ball too close to the fence. Stanley might have run right through the thick wooden planks without noticing.

Dono had been neighborly with Addy, but my grandfather would never have shared details about his criminal life with her. The old woman and I had a different kind of friendship. She knew I had occasionally skirted the line between what was right and what was legal.

This job with O'Hasson was one big parade march step over that line. I had made my choice, and it had all gone to shit. Addy would have said that was just deserts. She might even refuse to help me, if she knew the whole story. I didn't like lying to her, even by omission, even if keeping her in the dark would keep her legally protected. But I needed her help. If Addy could find out who bought the building, that might give me a line on the hunters.

The hunters had the little burglar now. But who had they really wanted? Who was worth so much to them that they would sit on four million dollars in gold and wait patiently for the alarm to sound? Was the gold just a fraction of a larger fortune they were after?

Find the hunters, and maybe, if I was very lucky, I could find Mick O'Hasson.

Because I couldn't leave the man to his fate. Not until I knew for sure there was no way to save him. It wasn't because he was sick, or because he had a kid.

It was because O'Hasson had fought back, and maybe he'd accidentally saved my ass in the process. He might not know it—he may never know it—but I owed him.

AGE TWELVE, DECEMBER 17

One minute to go. I willed the big hand on the clock to make the soft tap into ten past eleven. Jon Bower in front of me was watching, too, and being so obvious about it that I knew Mr. Brameley was going to tell us for the hundredth time that the *bell* doesn't dismiss you, *I* dismiss you. It might not do much good. Not today. I could feel Susanna behind me leaning toward the door, the pom-pom on her elf hat dangling to the right. Last day before vacation, they let us wear holiday shit like that.

In front of the class, Mr. B. was saying something about our reading assignments and how we should write that down so we don't forget. But we all had our books and stuff shoved into our bags already, so nobody was writing anything, except for a couple of the real sticks, trying to suck up.

Susanna poked me in the back with her sky blue colored pencil. I knew it was sky blue because it was always the same one. I would see the bright little marks on my shirts every day when I got home.

"Van," Mr. B. said.

I nodded. Not sure what at.

"Go ahead," he said.

Half the class turned to look at me. What? The bell rang. Everybody jumped. And now they were waiting for me.

Right. The pledge. Every Friday. It was my turn.

"To praise people . . . To notice and speak up about hurts I've caused . . ."

I rattled through the list, feeling everybody getting annoyed now that it was after the bell. It wasn't *my* fault. I thought we'd be done with stupid stuff like this when we got to middle school.

". . . To right wrongs . . ."

Susanna poked me, one last time, and I almost broke. That got Jon Bower and Samuel laughing, and I barely finished.

"Okay, okay," said Mr. B. "Have a good holiday break, everyone."

We were out of our seats before the second *okay*.

On the way to the bike racks, Davey came running around the corner of the gym building at top speed. Behind the gym was where he and some of the other A.R.s would hang when they could slip away. A.R. for At Risk. The term had tagged along with Davey—and me, too, I guess—from elementary school.

"Dude, did you skip?" I said.

"Just the last period."

"It's a half-day."

Davey could be an idiot. Pick a tough day, a day with tests, not a day where we would read half a chapter and spend an hour on art.

He shrugged. "Marcus Bo stole some chew from his dad. Enough for us to try some."

I made like I was hurling up my lunch. Two eighth-graders passing us jumped aside, in case I wasn't fooling.

"Like you've done it," Davey said.

"Like I'd want to. When do you guys leave?" I used a key to take the chain lock off my bike. If I'd been alone, away from school, I might have tried to pick the cylinder lock on it—nearly had it beat just yesterday.

"Christmas morning. But Mom says I have to help clean up the house today."

Davey and his mom and little brother Michael were spending half the holiday vacation with friends of their mom, way down in Kelso or Longview or some other place who knew where.

"Can you come over?" he said. "You could chill while I pack."

"Last time your mom made me mop the kitchen."

"Come *on*," he said. He grabbed the cloth-covered chain and snapped it like a whip.

"I'll ask Granddad," I said.

"So that's a no. He hates my guts."

"Does not."

"He hates everybody, 'cept maybe you. Fuck it." Davey was one of the few guys I knew who would use that word every day. Granddad would have tossed me into the garden shed with the spiders for a week.

"I'll come over later. For dinner."

"'Kay. Catch you." He sprinted off to catch up to Jake Schroeder, who probably had cigarettes.

I wound the chain around the seat post, jumped on my bike, and hauled ass, the pedals rocking *good-bye good-bye* to Louise Hovick Middle for two whole awesome weeks.

Getting home, the last part was the toughest part. I could either coast down Madison and cut across to come in at the bottom of the block. Then I'd have to pump hard in low gear until I reached the top of our hill, red-faced and sweaty (embarrassing), walk the bike up (worse), or I could grind my brakes down two steep blocks and then dodge traffic on 23rd until I reached Roy Street. That could be scary. Today I picked scary.

When I got to the house, Granddad's pickup was at the curb. Our garage was way too small to hold a truck, so I always knew when he was home, or at least not out on a contracting job. I tossed my bike in the garage and ran up the stone steps. I'd ask him about Davey now. If I waited, he might start giving me chores to do, and then I was screwed.

Coming through the front door, I heard a crunching sound from the back porch. Then a man's voice. Not Granddad's. I took one big step forward to the coat hooks on the wall, where I could lean around the hanging sweaters and other clothes and see through the picture window to the yard.

My wrist whacked painfully against something in Granddad's barn jacket. I felt in the pocket, and pulled my hand out like I'd touched a snake.

It was a gun. Granddad was carrying a gun now. He *never* did that.

I pushed the clothes aside—more carefully this time—and peered around the doorframe.

Granddad stood on the porch with two men. The first man had bushy red hair and so many freckles that his skin was half pink, half brown. He was at least as tall as Granddad, a couple of inches over six feet. As he talked he made sweeping gestures with arms like the wingspan of the heron birds we read about in ecosystems class.

The second man sat on the porch railing. He was a little older and grayer, and his wiry neck thrust forward over a white waffle shirt as he hunched. His face was pinched like he'd bitten into something rotten. If the redheaded guy was a heron, the other man was a vulture. A crushed can of Rainier sat on the railing next to him; that must have been the crunch I'd heard.

Granddad leaned with his arms crossed against the round porch post. If you didn't look closely you'd think he was totally relaxed, just listening to the redheaded man talk. I knew better. Something about the way he kept both men in view, and that he could move any direction he wanted with his feet like that.

I slipped into the dining room and sat on the side of the window where I could hear.

"—no chance they got their own guards," the redheaded man was saying. He spoke as fast as his hands flapped. "Ain't a gate on the driveway or any patrols driving around the property."

"What about inside?" Granddad said.

"Well, we figure it's wired."

"No shit. Besides that. How do you know they don't have security people hanging around?"

"You're right. We aren't sure." That was the second man, the vulture. "So let's get sure."

It must have been a question, because there was a pause. I almost bolted, believing they were coming back inside through the kitchen door and I'd be caught.

"We'll need to case the house," Granddad said. "Somehow. Anybody out of place in that neighborhood is going to attract attention very damn fast. You know anybody who's worked there before?"

"We could find one," the vulture offered.

"Forget it. I'll look for myself."

"So you're in?" said the redhead.

"I'll look," Granddad repeated.

The conversation was coming to a close, no matter what the other guys might think. Time for me to leave. I crawled out to the foyer, retreated all the way down the steps, and made a lot of noise slamming the garage door. By the time I ran back up the porch, backpack slung over my shoulder, the men were making their way inside.

"Hey," said the redheaded guy. "Who's this?"

"Somebody who should be in school," Granddad said, giving me *that* look.

"Half-day," I said. Breathing a little hard, like I'd just come off the bike. "It's on the calendar."

"All right, early Christmas." The tall redhead grinned.

"We gotta go," said the vulture. He looked less bitter, more uncomfortable as we all stood in the kitchen-slash-dining-room. Two big guys, one regular-sized, and me. There wasn't a lot of standing space.

"This your kid?" the redhead asked Granddad. That was typical. My mother had been sixteen when she had me, and

I don't think Granddad was much older than that when he'd had *her*. So everybody always guessed he was my dad.

Granddad put a big hand on my shoulder and steered me as smoothly as if I were a vacuum cleaner toward the stairs.

"Do your homework," he said.

There was no homework, not over vacation, but I shut up and ran to my room anyway. I threw my backpack under the bed—no need for that thing for two weeks—and turned on the radio. The sound of Veruca Salt blaring out of KNDD covered my careful steps into Granddad's room to look out the window to the street.

Granddad never had guys like that in the house. Hollis didn't count. Or Jimmy Corcoran or even Mr. Willard. I meant guys I hadn't met, and who Granddad didn't want me to meet.

And he was carrying a *gun*. Jesus.

A couple of minutes later both men walked down the stone steps. The redhead tapped his keys and a green Ford Taurus parked across the street chirped. As they drove off, I could see a maroon bumper sticker on the Taurus with the Balewood School logo. I knew Balewood. It was a private school, just a few blocks away. All girls.

"Hey."

Shit. Granddad, calling from what I hoped was the dining room and not right at the bottom of the stairs. I dashed out of his room and back to mine, and turned down the radio.

"Who were they?" I shouted down the stairs.

"Work. Since you're home early—"

"Can I go to Davey's tonight? I don't have homework, and it's vacation. And he's leaving."

"Don't interrupt."

I knew he was waiting for me to come down, so I did. "Can I?"

"Did you clean your bathroom?" He'd have already looked, of course.

"I was going to tomorrow. I've got all day."

"Do that first."

"What kind of work is it? With those guys." I wanted to ask him why the gun, but knew that would be a seriously wrong move. Instead I offered a step toward the washer closet where we kept the cleaning brushes and Bon Ami in a carry tray. "Can I work with you? You said."

He thumped his hand on the banister. Not mad-like, just fed up. "I did say it and I meant it. Not this time. In fact"—he coughed, almost a growl—"I want you to keep an eye peeled for those fellows. Around the house, and away from here, too."

"But who are they?"

"Get your ass in gear. Do a proper job and you can go to Davey's for dinner. And take this."

He handed me a flip phone.

"To keep?" I said. Hoping.

"For you and me to stay in touch, no one else. You follow?"

"Yeah. Business."

All right. My own phone. Davey would spit.

EIGHT

By LAST CALL, THE patrons at Bully Betty's had winnowed down to two distinct groups. People too drunk to get home on their own, and those too invested in finding company for the night to give up now. Quiana the bartender would start calling Uber soon, rallying cars to rescue the first group. The second bunch, the hopeful players, had to fend for themselves. So long as they weren't preying on the drunk or distraught, we'd let them try their luck until we tossed them to the sidewalk.

Betty had commandeered the Mac under the counter to start NTS Radio streaming live from London. A rapper from Morocco threw out what I guessed were rhymes and dared a techno beat to keep up with her. Quiana swayed to each line as she drew a round of red ales from the tap. The late show at The Egyptian up the street had ended over an hour before, and a handful of their ticket buyers had continued their dates at Betty's. I'd caught a little of their conversation. Picking apart obscure documentaries made for a weird kind of flirting.

I hauled cases from the storage room and began refilling the stock on the mirrored shelves. It took more time than it should, edging each bottle around the strings of purple and white Christmas lights that were the bar's main illumination after midnight.

"You got some extra quiet in you tonight," Betty said. "Which is saying something."

"Just thinking," I said.

O'Hasson. His abductors. The safe. I had been tossing the details like juggler's clubs in my mind all night, one and then the next, spinning them around and around in search of anything I had missed. Instead of yielding new insights, it felt like the whirling facts were taking turns clocking me on the skull.

But there wasn't much else I could do right now, except keep my head down. Betty paid me under the table. No paper trail that could lead the hunters here. I didn't know what they were capable of, or how determined they might be to find me, but if they really had bought an entire office building, I wasn't taking many chances. My apartment was leased under my name, so it was too risky. I could sleep in the speedboat. Spend my days on the move, until Addy turned up some names from city records and I had a trail of my own to follow.

"When Shy's thinking, she hardly stops her talk," Betty continued, counting out the bills from the register. "Thoughts just flood right on out her mouth, even if I'm all the way across the house."

Betty probably weighed about the same as I did, but in a radically different configuration. Six fewer inches of height, and a lot more bam, as she put it. Indigo tattoos wound under every inch of her dark skin, from wristbones to jawline. She claimed to be part Aztec. You could squint and see it in the broadness of her face and the dark slashes of brows set far apart, like quote marks around her eyes. Her head was as bald as Jimmy Corcoran's.

She watched me open a bottle of Black Seal and pour the half-shot trickle from the old bottle into the new. "How many left in the back?"

"One case of Bacardi. This is the last of the dark."

"The season for beach drinks. You know you can always pour the last drops for yourself, bottle's that low."

"Thanks."

"Not tonight, huh?" She thumped the cash drawer shut with her substantial hip. Betty didn't really need my help to toss the occasional asshole out of her bar. But she felt that having the big scary-looking white boy on the door stopped trouble before it began.

As if to balance Betty's bare scalp, a large knot of dreadlocks in various shades hung above the cash register. One of many such clumps. It had started as a charity drive—wigs for cancer patients—only the charity couldn't take dreads, so Betty offered three bucks an inch for every dread her customers sacrificed. With the Broadway hipsters and SCC campus just up the street, she had the makings of a bountiful harvest. The movement took on a life of its own, and now the back of the bar was festooned like an Iroquois tribe had won a major victory against Rastafarians.

"Closing up," Betty hollered. A couple of students drifted toward the bar to retrieve their credit cards. My phone burred in my pocket. Hollis.

"Your boat is ringing," he said.

"Try that again."

"Ringing," he said. "I walked over to tighten the lines—wind's coming up—and there's a digital something-or-other chirping away like a wounded parakeet from inside the cabin. It stopped after a minute."

There was a VHF radio in the speedboat, but I knew it was turned off. Depth sounder, too. Nothing that could—

I had a quick mental flashback of shoving O'Hasson's scattered pieces of small electronics into my jacket pockets, by feel more than sight in the black cave of the office building. Everything I could grab, as fast as I could grab it. The sense memory of a tangle of wires and alligator clips and tiny jeweler's tools, and a small plastic object in my palm. O'Hasson's cell phone.

Someone was calling it, trying to reach him.

If the hunters had the resources to buy a building, could they trace a cell signal?

"You good here?" I said to Betty, already moving around the bar.

She said yes. She may have started to say more, but she was slower than the street-side door slamming closed behind me.

HOLLIS HAD THE PIECES of O'Hasson's cell phone laid out on a towel in the speedboat cockpit, in one orderly line like instruments in an operating room. The body of the phone, its back cover, the battery, and the SIM card. While driving from Fremont, I'd told Hollis to unlock the cabin, find the phone, and take it apart.

The small cabin doors were flung open to let the interior light shine out, adding marginally to the beams from the stubby lampposts on the dock. At two in the morning, Hollis and I were the only things moving in the marina.

"Is it defanged?" Hollis said, prodding at the phone's guts.

"He was smart enough to find an old one." It was the same Ericsson O'Hasson had been using at the bar. We wouldn't have to worry about the hunters tracing it through false signals. With newer models, a topnotch tracking device could force any phone to give up its identity and location, just by mimicking a cell tower. It didn't matter if the phone was turned off. The trackers could be mounted on anything from cop cars to aerial drones. Harder and harder to be off the grid these days.

I picked up the tiny gold SIM card and plugged it back in, and the battery, too.

"Hey," said Hollis. "You just had me dismember the damn thing."

"Damage is done," I said. "I need to see who's been calling."

Hollis sat down quickly. "Jesus. Could it be police?"

"You're a bystander. Just my friendly neighbor in the marina."

"With a few acquired items in his boat"—Hollis's voice had lowered to a whisper—"and a shitload of new renovations to the interior. I'd rather not have anyone official looking in my windows right about now."

"Head back to the *Francesca*. I'll meet you there."

Hollis didn't argue. He walked quickly back to his own dock, looking a little like he was hiding one of his stolen bedposts where the sun wouldn't fade the varnish.

I turned on O'Hasson's phone. The battery was so low, I began pressing buttons as fast as I could. I checked the contacts. Nothing there. No messages either. In the list of recent calls, one number appeared a dozen times. Every couple of hours, since last night. An 818 area code. Was that California?

I pressed Redial. The space between each ring felt a lot longer than the usual four seconds. Then the ringing stopped.

The call hadn't gone to voicemail. The line was open. I could hear movement, and maybe an inhalation of breath. Whoever was listening might have made out the faint sounds of the marina in the background. The wind, and the cry of a gull, far off.

She broke first.

"Dad?"

A girl's voice. O'Hasson's kid, Cyndra. I pictured her grave face from the Child Services photo, all bangs and wary antagonism.

"You there?" she said. "Dad?"

I wanted to answer. To tell her what was going on. She'd called her father practically every hour since last night. Maybe they were supposed to talk at a certain time, and he'd missed it. Or maybe she had expected him to be back in L.A. by now. It had been a full twenty-four hours since we'd cracked the safe.

Someone else could be listening on her end. I stayed quiet, and so did she. After half a dozen breaths she cut the call, beating me to the punch.

HOLLIS'S NERVOUSNESS ABOUT ANYONE seeing the *Francesca* had been an overreaction. He had the interior fully reassembled. The only thing that looked wrong about it was the uncommon tidiness. For anyone who knew Hollis Brant well, that was a dead giveaway.

"What'd you find?" he called from the galley as I opened the sliding glass door. I smelled meat frying.

"O'Hasson's daughter," I said. "Cyndra."

He set down something with a sharp clang on the stove element and stepped out into view.

"You talked to her?"

"Not exactly." I fingered the sharp edge of the phone's SIM card. "She's been trying to reach him."

"Ah." Hollis wiped his hands on the dish towel he was holding. "And of course she's worried. Do you suppose the girl knows why he came here?"

"If you had a twelve-year-old kid, would you tell her about your plans to commit grand larceny?"

He curled his lip, slightly aghast at the idea. "If I had a child, I'd likely put her high in a tower. Keep her away from the whole mad world."

O'Hasson had been in prison half of Cyndra's life. But he had given her the number of his burner phone, and she called him Dad. She might at least guess why he was out of town. Did she also know about me?

I parked myself on the settee. Hollis went back into the galley and returned with Canadian bacon and eggs. An ingrained habit of hospitality. He would have offered me something even if I were jogging past on the dock.

"Dono would have told me," I said, "at that age."

He shook his head. "It's not the same. You might have been right alongside Dono at the safe, helping him hold the welding torch or some such."

"I know that."

"She's just a girl in—what? Sixth grade?"

In other words, I had no idea what it was like to be a regular kid. I'd been six years old when I came to live with my grandfather. Dono had trusted me with small shared confidences—where he kept the spare change, how to open the door on the old Cordoba without a key—and watched, I'm sure. When he saw I could handle it, that I wasn't the kind of kid who had a lot of close friends, or who chattered about every tiny thing that passed through his brain, he stepped up the importance and potential consequences of the secrets he shared.

I couldn't recall the first time Dono had confessed where our money came from. His real money, not from general contracting work, or whatever meager dollars his bar might have squeezed out. The bar had mainly been a handy way to launder cash. Maybe Dono never actually said the words out loud. He just introduced me to using lockpicks and greasing alarm systems the same way other children would learn how to make their own oatmeal in the morning.

And when Dono got busted and I went into foster homes, I had kept practicing. Half because it was a way to pass the time. Half because if

I got good enough, maybe that would ensure, somehow, that he came back.

So what if I could relate to Cyndra Ann O'Hasson? At least half the kids in the fucking system had a parent in jail, just out of jail, or about to get their ass chucked back inside. It didn't mean she and I were anything alike.

Hollis sipped his coffee. "It's hard for the girl, sure. But it could be a hell of a lot worse."

"You're right. We're not the same."

I tapped on the wall, somewhere behind which were Hollis's Japanese bedposts, wrapped in linen sheets. "When is your adventure in furniture moving? Do you still want me on call?"

"What's today? Barely Tuesday? Then it'll be Thursday night, Friday early morning, depending on the tides."

"Which tides?"

"Figure of speech. There's a ship coming in which I aim to meet. If you could keep one ear on your phone until then, I'd appreciate it." He shrugged. "Worse comes to worst, you might be swinging by here and moving the posts to your little boat. They'll fit; I took the liberty of measuring your cabin while I was waiting for you."

"How heavy are they?"

"Well, if an old barnacle like me can lift all four in a go? Barely exercise for you."

"Done." I paused before diving into the eggs, which had grown cold during my musings. "You'd tell me if you needed backup."

"I've done business with these boys before. Everyone's civil."

I nodded. "Good to work with professionals."

"Isn't it just?" Hollis said.

NINE

SLEEP CAME FAST, AND left the same way. I'd crashed in the berth at the bow of the speedboat, wondering whether O'Hasson might still be alive somewhere, and I went right on wondering it when my eyes popped open to see the underside of the foredeck, eighteen inches above my face. The berth was a thin wedge-shaped mattress, short enough that my feet dangled over the edge, narrow enough at the tip that I could hear the faint echo of my own breathing on the hull. A more claustrophobic person might have been reminded of a coffin.

A buzzing sounded from my phone, and I shimmied my way down and pushed open the little cabin doors with my foot. Cold air rushed in, making my skin prickle. Day was still getting a firm grip on the sky.

Addy had sent me a text message. Up and having her single cigarette of the day, probably. I called her back.

"I have news," she said.

"That was quick."

"I outsourced it. Some of my friends in the library system know far more about real estate and finances than I do. Enid dug up the county records almost before we'd asked her. The building was owned and managed for many years by a"—I heard Addy leaf through papers—"PNW Commercial Realty, that's the name. Then two months ago, PNW sold the building to another company called Radius Properties, in Los Angeles."

O'Hasson was from Los Angeles. I wondered if that was just coincidence.

"PNW," I said. "A local outfit?"

"They have a Washington license, of course. And a leasing office. It's down in Burien." She gave me the address and the phone number. "Should we call them?"

"Better if I talk to them in person." I found an olive Henley shirt in the bag of spare clothes and pulled it on over my head as we talked. "Did Enid find anything more on Radius Properties?"

"It seems to be a subsidiary, owned by other corporations."

Which in turn were probably owned by others. Shell companies to hide the real players. If the hunters were behind Radius, I doubted that trail would lead me anywhere useful. Forensic accounting was well beyond my skill set.

But an idea struck me, sparked by all of the property paperwork I'd had to wade through with Dono's legacy.

"Do those records tell you Radius Properties' insurance company?" I said. "That has to be listed as part of any real estate sale, right?"

More page shuffling. "Safehome Insurance. I have my auto coverage with them."

"Thanks, Addy. I'll take Stanley out for a run later this week, give you a break."

"Radius Properties is a strange one. They don't seem to have existed before this year. I'm curious."

"Don't get too curious, right? Stick with the public records," I said.

There was a moment of quiet. "You think Radius is criminal?"

"Or close enough. I don't want you or your friends anywhere on their radar."

"Aren't I supposed to be the one cautioning you?" she said.

"Indulge me."

I MADE TWO STOPS on my way to PNW Commercial Realty. A copy center, where I bought a couple of manila folders and used their rent-by-the-minute iMacs to print some application forms and policy examples written in very fine print off of the Safehome Insurance public website. Thick and detailed enough to glaze anyone's eyes.

My second stop was a thrift store. I rummaged in the racks and fished out a white button-down and some navy trousers without obvious cigarette burns. Rescued a cornflower blue tie from a serpentine tangle in a plastic tub. Finding dress shoes was tougher. My best option was a black pair of oxfords two sizes too large.

The narrow fitting room mirror threw back a head-to-toe slice of my new ensemble. I still didn't look much like an office worker. I tried on a reassuring smile, the one that didn't frighten children. Better. Not great, but better.

I left the shoes off while I drove.

PNW Commercial was a stone's throw off of Sylvester Road, in a two-story strip mall designed in Spanish mission style. Sport utilities and hybrids crowded the lot, thanks mainly to the mall's top dog, a Starbucks on the lower corner.

PNW held the first spot at the top of the stairs. I walked up, shoes flopping and manila folders in hand.

The office was wide and glass-fronted. I could see one desk with tiers of neatly stacked files just inside, and another past a cubicle wall farther back. There were healthy-looking plants on the shelves. The carpet showed the lines of recent vacuuming. Painted letters on the window proclaimed expertise in warehousing and industrial and retail spaces.

I knocked on the glass door and pulled it open wide enough to stick my head in. "Hello?"

Quick steps from the back room and a slim woman with long white hair in a braid leaned into view, her angle mirroring my own. Her rose-colored polo shirt blended well with the lush plants in the room. She looked around sixty years old, and capable of running a full marathon without her tight braid unraveling.

"Hi," I said brightly, "I'm Jake. From Safehome?" I gave her a glimpse of the insurance policy on top of the manila folders.

"Hello." She nodded, all puzzled politeness, both hands wrapped around what might be her first cup of tea of the day.

"Did Sarah from our office call you?" I said. "About the property at—" I flipped quickly to one of the pages in my hand and read her the address of the torched building.

"Oh!" she said in recognition. "No. No one called."

"Well, we've been moving pretty fast. We hold the policy for Radius Properties, and unfortunately the sale is so new that our branch office doesn't have all of the information we need to process the claim. You heard about the fire?"

"Yes, of course. On the news. How terrible." Her eyes lit up, and she came into the room and sat at the first desk, the one with the precise clutter of stacks of files and family pictures. A wood veneer nameplate, pushed aside and half-hidden by the stacks, read MARTINA DEVI, OFFICE MANAGER. "No one was hurt?"

"No, just the building. I told my boss I'd drop by your office on the way in today, save him a long email."

"Well, I'm grateful." She smiled, seemingly delighted to have permission to talk about the disaster. "When Lou and I walked in the door yesterday, it was the first thing we both said: 'Did you hear?' We managed that property for *years*. I lost a whole hour looking at the news film of the fire online, I don't mind telling you. We're just so grateful that none of our tenants were still in the building. Do they know what started it?"

"There's no official report from the investigators yet. It was your tenants I wanted to ask you about."

"Yes? Are they on the claim?" When Martina set her mug down, her polo sleeve edged up to reveal a rainbow band of dancing Deadhead bears.

"No, but the fire started in one of the upper offices," I said. "Harrison Community needs to make sure that all possessions were removed prior to the fire. In case there's a cross-claim or a lawsuit down the road for unacknowledged or disputed losses, you understand. Could you tell me who leased the office in the northwest corner of the fifth floor? Number 501?" I showed her one of the few legit pages I had printed, a

Google Maps overview of the nearby streets, with the proper corner on the building circled.

"Oh!" Martina tapped the page abruptly, like she was capturing a gnat under her fingertip. "That's Claudette's office!"

"Claudette?"

"Claudette Simms. She leased that space for—well, at least eight years, since I started working here after my divorce. Terrible."

"The divorce was terrible?"

"Well, that too, but I meant what happened to Claudette. She died, just earlier this year."

The stiff paper of the folders crackled in my hand.

"I'm very sorry. Was she sick?" I said.

Martina shook her head. "She had a heart attack. Lou and I were very upset."

"You knew her pretty well?"

"I wouldn't say that. Only small talk in between taking care of the accounts. I talked her into letting me buy her lunch once—we try to get to know all of our long-term tenants—but she turned me down every time after."

"She wasn't a Jerry fan?" I nodded toward Martina's tattooed arm.

She returned my smile. "Claudette was a very shy person. I think perhaps a bit stunted, socially. She didn't talk at all about herself."

"Ms. Simms's business must have been successful. What did she do?"

"Trucking. Isn't that funny? Pacific Pearl Freight Company, that was the company name. She wasn't a driver herself." Martina permitted herself a small laugh. "At least I don't think so. The space she leased from us was just their business office."

"What happened to the space after she died?"

"We had all the mail forwarded to their freight location in South Seattle. Claudette's was the only name on the business office lease. I had thought someone would call us about taking it over. Then we got an offer for the building, and sold it almost immediately to Radius Properties. And honestly"—Martina pinged the rim of her coffee cup with a flick of her nail—"we had very few tenants remaining in that building.

It was reaching the point where we'd have to invest heavily in renovation, or sell outright."

"Who was your contact at Radius? I might be able to close the books just by letting them know about Ms. Simms."

"I have an email address for the company. But we never worked directly with anyone, it was all very formal. Not that I minded."

"They offered a good price." I said it like I already knew the answer.

"Oh, absolutely."

So good that there would be no question of accepting, I imagined.

Martina wrote down the email for Radius, and at my request the address of Pacific Pearl Freight's shipping office.

"Perhaps someone there can tell you more about their business," she said.

My thoughts exactly.

"I'm sorry again about Claudette. And the building, too."

"Bad luck," she said. "If it comes in threes, we'd all better watch out."

I JOGGED BACK TO the truck, already typing Claudette Simms's name into my phone. The first link was to a *P-I* article from April.

MOUNT BAKER WOMAN DROWNS IN BATHTUB

Claudette Simms, a 49-year-old woman, drowned in her apartment bathtub sometime during the weekend after being struck by an apparent cardiac arrest, the King County Sheriff's Office said in a news release Wednesday.

Police responded after getting a 911 call on Tuesday from the apartment manager, who had found Simms's cat wandering the complex property in southeast Seattle.

When Sheriff's deputies arrived on scene, they had the landlord open the apartment door and discovered the body of Claudette Simms in the bathtub. She was taken to Pacific Medical Center, where she was pronounced dead. The King County medical examiner has confirmed drowning as the cause of death, likely as a result of the heart attack. Police are seeking next of kin.

There was another article on KING-TV's online blog, with an over-exposed photo from what might have been a DMV shot. Claudette Simms had a broad, heavy face made wider by a mass of curly ash blonde hair pinned into rough order atop her head. She had very dark brown eyes, and wore makeup and a black blouse. She stared down the camera with an expression more suited to a mug shot than a license picture.

The second article didn't tell me any more than the first. There were no follow-up stories. If the cops suspected there was more to her death than an accident, they weren't saying.

I sure as hell suspected it. The sudden death of the tenant who leased an office with a hidden safe, followed by the immediate purchase of the same building? It had to be connected. Maybe even pre-meditated.

I FOUND PACIFIC PEARL Freight's shipping location south of the stadiums, on a sparsely developed stretch where one of the old railroad lines crossed under the sleek elevated light rail track. The nineteenth century meeting the twenty-first. There was no sign to identify the company on the low-slung building, or on the fence around it. I checked the address against the map on my phone as I coasted past to make sure I was looking at the right place.

Fifty yards down the road, a dotted line of parked cars connected a martial arts gym and a concrete paving business. I reversed into an open spot, giving me a good view of the Pacific Pearl building without having to stand out in the open.

The freight company was a small operation. I could have tossed a baseball—without giving it heat—from one side of its property to the other. A single L-shaped building of brown cinder block squatted in the center of a fenced lot like a toad in its cage. Razor wire topped the fence in long, sagging loops.

The long side of the L had two loading bays. A twenty-foot refrigerated Ford box truck had been parked sideways, blocking both rolling doors. An identical Ford waited flush against the western wall. The trucks were Class 4 or the low end of Class 5, fine for day runs and city deliveries but nothing like long-haul cargo. A dozen years of dings and scrapes stood out starkly on their white aluminum siding.

I couldn't see any other evidence of what kinds of freight Pacific Pearl handled. I had wondered if Claudette Simms might have been embezzling, slowly amassing the fortune in her safe. But this wasn't a company that could possibly generate enough revenue to skim four million. Empty wooden pallets made a pile like a stack of splintered pancakes outside the bay doors.

Maybe Pacific Pearl was defunct. Claudette Simms had died in April. If she were the sole proprietor, it wasn't out of the question that their freight location might have been shuttered after her death.

I tried to put myself in the hunters' place, from what little I could guess about their motives.

Claudette Simms was dead. Maybe even murdered by the hunters themselves. She had rented an office in the aging building, and she had installed a safe to hold a fortune in gold.

And instead of simply breaking into the safe to take Claudette's gold, the hunters had set a trap. A trap that ensured anyone who knew about the hidden safe would come running.

So maybe the socially-stunted Ms. Simms had a partner, and the hunters wanted to catch that individual. They'd gone to huge effort to make it happen. Maybe the partner could lead them to another score, large enough to make even four million in gold kilobars look like the penny on the sidewalk Hollis had described. The hunters had been watching Pacific Pearl's business office closely enough that they were on top of O'Hasson and me only minutes after we set off the alarm.

Were the hunters also watching the freight yard? In case the partner showed up here? I stepped out of the truck to get a different angle on the place.

The light rail train hissed overhead, flying toward downtown. Sweat beaded on my scalp as I walked under the elevated tracks. Two men came around the corner of the MMA gym, already drenched from their workouts. They grimaced and shielded their eyes from the sun as they hurried to the shelter of their cars.

I looked around the squat Pacific Pearl building, and the handful of neighboring businesses. Thought about how I might keep eyes on the place, if it were me.

It might be possible to set myself up somewhere with a direct view. The closest window with any vantage point on Pacific Pearl was nearly a hundred yards off. I already suspected the hunters had bought the office building we'd burned down. If I were right about that, then it was feasible, if improbable, that they had also bought out a nearby business, simply to watch the freight building. But the sightlines sucked.

That left a rooftop post, or finding a way to hang around outside in the summer heat without attracting attention. Even less likely.

Occam's razor. If the hunters couldn't easily watch the Pacific Pearl yard in person, maybe they had installed a little electronic help, to make it simple.

I made another scan of the area, this time looking higher. When I'd seen all I could see, I walked another few yards down my path under the light rail track and tried again.

When I finally spotted what I was looking for, I was almost directly underneath it. A rectangular metal box, nestled under the overhang of one of the elevated track's octagonal support pillars. Almost twenty feet up from the gravel and directly across from the freight yard's loading docks. The box was the size of a large loaf of bread, and painted a flat brownish-gray to match the support pillar of the elevated track. I edged out a few steps, just enough to see the smaller side of the box, the side pointed toward Pacific Pearl. Not so far that I would be exposed.

The front end of the box wasn't metal. A pale scrim, maybe. Enough to block dust and dirt, but not enough to obscure the camera I was sure was inside.

It was a good camouflage job. I would bet that even regular workers could pass by every day for a year without spotting the small addition to the pillar, as high and unremarkable as it was.

At the back of the box I could see what looked like a stubby rubberized antenna, in similar dirty beige. The camera was sending its feed somewhere. And with the office building burned to the ground, maybe the hunters were more alert than ever to what this camera showed.

I would come back tonight. I wanted a much closer look at Pacific Pearl.

And I had a notion on how to make one of the hunters' clever little traps work for me, for a change.

TEN

Iᴛ ᴡᴀѕ ɴᴇᴀʀɪɴɢ ᴅᴀʀᴋ when I raised a hand to knock on Addy's door. She swung it wide before my knuckles connected.

"We need to talk," she said, pruning every syllable with shears. She was in her habitual evening loungewear, a black cardigan over a t-shirt and black silk pants.

"What's going on?"

"There's a girl out back. A young teenager. She'd been sitting in front of your house, on those stone steps, since this afternoon."

A girl. I had a premonition of exactly what kid Addy was talking about. My luck was running just that thin lately.

"In front of my house. And you invited her in," I said.

"Once I realized she wasn't some addict who'd wandered too far from Broadway, I walked up the street to talk to her. The first thing out of her mouth was to ask if I knew who owned your place."

"Did you tell her?"

"I said that I would call you, but only if she came inside. It took a lot of convincing. My offer of food finally tipped the scales."

"It would have been better to let the kid sit."

"You didn't see her. She looks like she hasn't slept in days. And she's clearly been crying."

"Terrific."

"Van, what on earth is going on? This child is so determined to see you, I think she would have stayed on those filthy steps until she froze."

"It's July. Sunstroke would have got her first."

"Don't joke."

"It's about all I can do anymore. Come on."

She led me through the small house, into the relative cool of the back porch that overlooked her plot of grass.

Stanley was lying on the porch, panting softly. Sitting on the slats behind him, petting his thick neck, was Cyndra O'Hasson.

Even with two years of growth on her since the photo I'd seen, Cyndra was still undersized and gangly enough to be mistaken for younger than twelve. Her bangs were gone, the remaining hair buzzed down to a stiff half-inch and dyed to match the gloss of a young raven. She had a snub nose dusted with freckles—her father's gift—and the same blue eyes, which glared up at me with suspicion.

Addy was right. Cyndra looked drained. The dog did most of the work keeping her vertical. Her white V-neck tee reading RANDOM GRAVITY in huge cracked green letters looked as soiled as if she'd been wearing it for days, which maybe she had. Jeans shorts and low-top black Converse completed her grubby ensemble.

"Cyndra, this is Van," Addy said, as if we were meeting at a garden party.

"Addy says you want to talk to me," I said.

She nodded, while her eyes examined my face from hair to chin. Not the morbid curiosity some young people had about my scars. A look that said she wondered if she knew me from somewhere.

"I'm here." I sat down in one of Addy's aluminum porch chairs, the kind molded as one piece and designed to be stacked. The thin metal creaked under my weight. Stanley reached out and tapped my shin with his snout. "Talk."

"Do you know my dad? Mick O'Hasson?" Cyndra said. Her voice was high but not without strength.

"Should I?"

She didn't reply.

"But you know my house," I said. "How?"

More silence.

"Look," I said. "We can play Jay and Silent Bob all night. I don't care. You're the one who came to my doorstep. So tell me something, otherwise I'm going home and Addy will put you out for the trash pickup."

I caught Addy's frown in the corner of my eye. It promised that Cyndra might not be the only one out on the curb soon.

"Why do you think I might know your dad?" I felt like a cop, grilling her for answers I already had. But like a cop, it was the easiest way to know whether she was trying to feed me a line of bullshit. She might take after her father in that regard.

"He looked up directions to your house from the airport, like, on my computer," Cyndra said. "He tried to erase the history, but I could still find it." A hint of pride.

"Doesn't explain why you followed him," I said.

Cyndra hugged Stanley tight enough that he whined a little. "He left for Seattle on Tuesday. He should have come back by now. I have a number, but he doesn't answer. For like, days."

"Left from where?"

"Reseda. That's by L.A."

Addy had reached the limit of her quietude. "You came here all the way from California? How?"

"On the bus," said Cyndra. A frayed Bauer backpack, packed so full it was straining at its loose seams, leaned against the railing within her reach. The pack pinned a skateboard with peeling grip tape to the porch.

"They let you buy a ticket?" Addy said.

"Forget how, get to the why," I said.

"There was another address he looked at in Seattle. Down south somewhere."

Shit. I knew exactly the building Cyndra meant. Or at least the huge charred spot where a building used to be.

"When Dad didn't come back, I looked for it," she continued, "and it was already on videos on YouTube and everywhere. There was a big fire. I thought Dad might come back, after that. But he didn't. And then—"

Her voice stopped before it broke. Tears crested like tiny waves and she wiped them away angrily before she buried her face in Stanley's neck.

God damn it. The girl thought her father might have died in the inferno. The worst part of it was, that fate might have been more merciful.

"Oh, honey," Addy said, and knelt down to hug the girl. Cyndra let her. Stanley looked at me, vibing on the emotions and not knowing what to do. I was no help. I left the females—one weeping, one murmuring softly—and went back inside the house.

Addy would make tea, or something, in a situation like this. I rooted in the refrigerator for cans of soda.

Cyndra knew a hell of a lot more about her father's plans than I liked. If complete ignorance was a zero, I put her loose information to tie me to O'Hasson and to the break-in and fire at somewhere around a six, with ambitions. It might not be legal proof, but it could sure as hell spark the interest of any investigators. My past week would be under the microscope. Hell, the cops might be looking for the kid right now, if her foster family had made enough noise.

I found two 7-Ups and a Coke that might have been in Addy's fridge since my homecoming over a year ago, and carried them to the porch. Stanley had freed himself from Cyndra's grasp and was trotting around the yard. The kid's face was red enough to match her freckles, but her eyes were dry.

"They'll be worried sick for you," Addy was saying to her.

Cyndra sniffed through her plugged nose. I took that to mean that her foster parents were something less than involved. I'd been placed in houses like that myself.

I handed the 7-Ups to Addy and Cyndra and sat down on the steps.

"I don't know where your dad is," I said, "or if I can help you. But I can't find him unless I have the same facts as you. Yeah?"

Cyndra nodded cautiously.

"What did Mick tell you about his trip to Seattle?" I said.

"Just that he was sorry he had to leave, and that he'd be back in like a couple of days. I could tell it was something about money. He wasn't lying about being sorry, but he really wanted to get going." She made a sour face. Maybe Mick's leaving had turned into a family squabble, so soon after he'd been released. "All excited."

"You know what your dad does?"

"He steals shit." She said it so matter-of-factly, it startled me a little.

"Did you always know that?" Addy said.

"He got out of prison, like, a couple of weeks ago. And—I know that he's sick. I think he wants money so he can get better."

Getting better wasn't in O'Hasson's prognosis. The money was all about Cyndra's future. Not that he would have told her that.

"What happened in Reseda?" I asked. "Why didn't you wait for him?"

Cyndra took a long, shuddery inhale. I thought the tears would come again, but when she spoke, her voice was steady.

"Two men tried to grab me," she said.

Addy and I exchanged glances. My expression couldn't have been much more dumbfounded than hers.

Cyndra kept talking, her eyes on Stanley as he sniffed around the fence. "I was walking to Farrah's. That's my friend. She called and said could I sleep over, and I said sure, 'cause Tachelle doesn't give a shit when I come and go."

Addy started to ask a question, before I shook my head no. The girl was finally talking.

"It was nighttime and Farrah only lives a little ways," Cyndra said. "I took a shortcut down the alleys. This van followed me. Like, I didn't know it was following me, I thought it was just going the same way I was, you know? But it didn't pass, and then this big swole-up creepy guy started walking towards me, from the other end. He was staring at me. I heard the van start to go faster."

Cyndra took another long inhale. "And I ran. The big fat guy reached out and almost grabbed my bag, but the van got in his way, and then he was chasing me. I can go fast as shit, okay? I climbed a fence and ran across a couple of people's yards and I hid. I thought they would give up, but they both came after me."

"My God," said Addy.

"I lay down on the ground, in some bushes. They walked around for a while. I could hear them whispering in the dark. Nobody was home in that house. I could have screamed a whole bunch. But that doesn't always help, where we live."

I nodded. "So you stayed put."

"Uh-huh. Like a long time. They knew I hadn't gone far. Then one of them stopped right near where I was. Really, really close. He was listening, I think."

"Did you get a look at him?" asked Addy.

"No," Cyndra said. Then she turned to me, and the touch of self-confidence was back. "I got pictures."

Addy gasped, distracting Stanley from whatever he was nosing in the dirt. "You took photos?"

"Well, I thought I would call, like, 911 while I was running, before I had to hide. And then the guy was right there, and I thought, 'Shit, if I get some photos maybe I can throw the phone where somebody else will find it.'"

"Damn, kid," I said, almost reflexively.

Cyndra took out an older-model iPhone with a crack splitting one corner of the screen and tapped it to bring up the pictures. She swiped to show me there was a whole series.

The photos weren't great. They weren't even good. With no flash at nighttime, half of it obscured by leaves and twigs, the figure was barely identifiable as an actual human and not a lawn statue. Plus, he had been facing away from her. Very wide body. Short matted black hair over an orange sleeveless shirt, showing off arms that had seen a lot of heavy reps. Light brown skin. Those were the clearest features in most of Cyndra's hasty pics.

But the final shot caught his face in profile. More outline than details. I enlarged the photo. Low hairline. A nose that had been flattened by more than genetics, and the ear was puffed with cartilage. Maybe Latino. Definitely a fighter.

"Do you know him?" I asked Cyndra, still peering hard at the dim images.

"Nuh-uh." Her face was less buoyant as she looked at the thug in the photo.

I remembered how she had given me a close examination. "Did you think I might be one of these dudes who came after you?"

She nodded. "But you aren't. Not even the other guy from the van. He was a lot shorter, and he was blond. But you're kinda like—" She stopped, not sure of the words. Or not sure if she should tell me.

"He's the same type," Addy said. "Tough."

Mean, I thought. The dude looked mean. Just the kind of asshole you could picture snatching a young girl out of an alley at night.

"What did you do then, dear?" Addy said, maybe to get Cyndra's mind off the man's face.

Cyndra shrugged. "Just waited until I heard them drive away. I stayed in the bushes for like an hour. When I got home, I saw their van parked way up on the next block. So I went in through the bedroom window and took my stuff and a bunch of Tachelle's money—she has all these hiding places she thinks are so smart—and then I got Farrah's sister to buy me a bus ticket."

Addy tsked. "Honey, you should have called the police."

That advice received another sniff from Cyndra.

There was something else in the last picture, something that I had missed in my concentration on the meathead's face. A tattoo bridging his bicep, half in shadow. Red or orange or brown ink, it was hard to say. The crude illustration looked like an axe or a short sledgehammer. Instead of a maul for a head, the tattoo had a clenched fist.

"You'll sleep here," Addy said. I looked up to catch Cyndra's head bobbing. Now that she had found me, the fumes she'd been running on were burned clean away.

The kid didn't protest as Addy helped her up and into the house. Stanley followed. I stayed on the porch.

Were the two men in Reseda the same ones who had grabbed O'Hasson? Had they driven all the way from Washington to Southern Cal just to find Cyndra? The creep in the picture didn't look like the type to set sophisticated traps or use tranquilizer darts on his victims.

More like he'd hit them with a steel pipe, and if they didn't wake up afterward, that was just too damn bad for them.

Kidnapping Mick O'Hasson might have been a case of mistaken identity. But Cyndra had been the deliberate target of the two lowlifes. She'd just been smarter, or luckier, than her old man.

Addy came back ten minutes into my musings. "She dropped off immediately, poor child. So much terror."

"She's holding up better than most adults would," I said.

Addy made a noise that wasn't too far from Cyndra's derisive sniff. "She's putting on a face, can't you see that? So exhausted that she forgot to ask you the real question. Her father, Mick, came to see you. Did you meet him?"

"Yeah."

"And you know what happened to him?"

"I don't know where he is now. Dead or alive."

"That's not a direct answer."

"No. But it's already more than you should know."

"Don't even imagine that you're protecting me, Van Shaw."

"Addy," I said, "I need you to go with me on this. Whatever happened to Cyndra's dad must have some connection to those thugs showing up in Reseda and going after her. If it goes sour, and I get busted, you could be an accessory after the fact just from whatever I tell you. And for not calling Cyndra's foster family."

Addy's apple cheeks went pale. "We're not calling the police?"

"I can't stop you if you want to. But if she goes back to Reseda, maybe the goons in the van try to kidnap her again. Even if we tell the cops her story, and they watch her for a day or two, she's vulnerable the minute they've gone."

"But surely there's protective custody."

"From what? I could spill everything I know about Mick O'Hasson, it still doesn't help his kid."

"And you would be arrested. Is that accurate?"

"Yeah."

"Do you deserve to be?" Addy's tone made Stanley whine from inside the screen door. She was angrier than I'd ever seen her, and Addy Proctor was not a woman who hid her temper.

"Probably," I said, "but me waiting on a bail hearing isn't going to do Mick O'Hasson any good. Or his daughter."

"So what do I do?"

"Buy some junk food. Convince Cyndra that we're on her side." I had to grin, even though it would piss Addy off even more. "And lock up your cash and your silver. The kid inherited more than freckles from her dad."

ELEVEN

FOR MY MIDNIGHT RETURN to Pacific Pearl's freight office, I had brought a few items not normally in my tool kit. A boat hook borrowed from Hollis. Its aluminum pole could telescope from five feet to nearly twelve in length. A handful of rubber bands. And a short tree branch from my own property, its twigs sagging under the green weight of thousands of height-of-summer pine needles.

I circled the surrounding blocks and stopped up the road, on the far side of the railroad tracks. Spent half an hour scoping out the shipping yard and the street nearby. Except for the occasional train passing on the elevated tracks, nothing had moved. When I was sure I wouldn't be interrupted, I drove the truck around the block once more to come up behind the camera I had spotted earlier, high up in its nest on the support pillar.

While sitting in rush hour traffic on my way to Hollis's, I'd considered what to do about the camera. I didn't want to simply trash it. That might clue the hunters that their surveillance of Pacific Pearl was blown. They might never come near the place.

And I wanted them here. Get them close enough for a visual, and follow them. With a little luck, right back to where they were holding O'Hasson.

So instead of just putting a bullet through the metal box housing the camera, I'd let my tree branch do the dirty work.

Standing on the canopy of my truck, I could reach the box with the very tip of the extended boat hook. I fixed the branch to the end of the long pole with a few of the rubber bands. The branch drooped heavily, and it took some muscle to lift the hook skyward and drape the branch over the box, its curtain of needles covering the camera lens. A twist or two, and the rubber bands snapped, leaving the branch right where I needed it.

There weren't any trees around, but the branch could conceivably have been blown from the tracks above. For good measure, I gave the rubber antenna on the camera box a solid whack with the boat hook, as if the falling branch had struck it.

I could imagine my grandfather shaking his head in disbelief. Then again, I'd seen Dono shrug and kick open more than one unalarmed door during our time together, so I knew he hadn't been opposed to a low-tech solution when it presented itself.

And speaking of breaking and entering, I wanted a closer look at Pacific Pearl, while the hunters wouldn't be watching. I moved the truck back up the road and put on the thin cotton gloves from my burglar kit.

The shipping yard looked like strawberry pie and ice cream. A tired Masterlock padlock secured the gate, loose enough to pop open with a twist or two of the tension bar. My careful casing earlier had revealed no motion sensors or security cameras under the rusty doorway awnings. I locked the gate behind me and jogged to the building, slipping between the closest refrigerated truck and the grimy bricks. No entrance on this side. The loading bays were shut tight. I edged around the corner.

Pacific Pearl held a few surprises. The rear door was a serious step up in security from the gate. Inch-thick steel, with a heavy strike plate protecting the bolt. A Medeco electronic cylinder lock, too. Good choices, but bad placement. The rear door was out of sight from the road, giving me all the time in the world to beat the complex lock. It took four minutes.

Inside, my eyes slowly adjusted to the tiny bit of light pushing its way through the yellowed windows into the large room. Large, but meager. An office space, not much more than roller chairs and rough tables and steel shelves. The loose carpet smelled of mildew. A doorway in the sheet metal wall directly across from me led to the loading bays.

I clicked on my penlight and leafed through the handful of papers left on one of the tables. Cargo manifests. A consignment of melons and other produce, received from a distribution center in Spokane and delivered to multiple independent groceries on this side of the mountains. Normal enough for a company with a fleet of refrigerated trucks.

The manifests were dated from one week ago. It seemed Pacific Pearl was still operating after Claudette Simms's death, if not exactly overwhelmed with work.

I walked through the doorway into the broader expanse of the loading bays. My footsteps, light as they were, seemed to echo off the big steel rolling doors.

The bay walls were packed close with a jumble of empty plastic crates and more shipping pallets and one plywood workbench with a band saw. A rack of bulbous aluminum tanks dominated the east wall, looking like bluish-white eggs from some big prehistoric bird. The penlight beam revealed their labels: 134A TETRAFLUOROETHANE. Refrigerant for the cooling systems on the trucks.

The surface of the workbench was strewn with metal shavings from the saw. Some of the tiny curls were stuck in patches of dried paint, which matched the color of the coolant tanks. Curious.

A steel tool cabinet next to the workbench was locked. I opened it with my pick gun. Inside, on a shelf below a few battered tools, I found one of the tanks, cut into two. The top had been sheared off neatly enough that the two pieces would fit back together with only a narrow seam. In a cardboard box I found quick-dry epoxy, spray paint in the same color as the tanks, and warning stickers for toxic contents.

Hello, Claudette. I was starting to understand how the dead woman made her fortune.

A smuggling trick. That's what I was looking at. Put whatever you wanted to transport inside the empty sphere, then glue the pieces back together, apply a coat of paint and stickers to disguise the seam, and scuff some dirt on to look just like the others. Hell, maybe they could even fill the false tank partway with coolant and complete the illusion by hooking it up to the refrigeration system.

The usable space in the false tanks wouldn't be enough to hide anything bulky, but I could imagine the trick working over and over for regular runs, making a steady profit off of gallon Ziploc bags stuffed full of meth or prescription Oxy or kilos of heroin.

Pacific Pearl was a front. And their method was pretty slick. I'd have to ask Hollis if he had seen anything like this before. He knew just about every trick used to move contraband since biblical times.

The loading bays gave way to the shorter side of the L-shaped building. In a more successful shipping business, the space next to the bays might have been used for packaging or cargo storage. Instead, the room was some sort of oversized employee lounge area. A big wooden cable drum had been set on its side to make a table and rickety chairs. Two open cans of Pabst and a thousand stains decorated the surface of the round table. One fridge, a water cooler so dry there might have been dust inside, and an emergency exit beside the building's fuse box. If I worked in this dismal place, I would be tempted to run straight out that exit every single damn day.

Time for me to leave. The hunters might show up at any time to see what had happened to their disabled camera. Maybe they were here already. Instead of retracing my steps out the front gate, I ran to the back fence and climbed over it in a spot where the razor wire hung uselessly low.

Working my way through the bramble bushes lining the railroad tracks, I came out on the far side of the block of buildings that included the MMA gym. The road looked clear. I looped around the building and angled toward where I had left my truck.

Before crossing the road, I hesitated for a long moment at the corner, where the light shining on the painted sign for the gym made shadows deep enough to hunch down and watch for any movement nearby. The branch was still draped over the camera, high on its support pillar. No new cars had appeared. I took another last glance at the gym, then ran to the truck.

It was close to two o'clock in the morning. Over three hours until sunrise. Plenty of time, if the hunters wanted the cover of darkness.

Of course, that was only my guess. Maybe they had stopped using the camera weeks ago. Maybe the camera had nothing to do with the hunters, and it had been installed by Claudette or her silent partner as some sort of security measure. Shit, maybe I was even wrong about there being a camera in the damn box.

If no one showed tonight, tomorrow I would buy a tall enough ladder to let me verify my guess. But for now, I would have to go with my gut.

Stakeouts were tedious. I'd done my share of guard duty as an enlisted man, and more than a few reconnaissance missions in the Rangers that had amounted to little more than lying in the brush and waiting for something to happen. There was no way around the monotony except to keep your eyes and brain both moving.

I thought about the smuggling operation at Pacific Pearl. Mick O'Hasson's infirmary attendant had told him that the gold in the hidden safe had been bought with the profits from drug running up and down the West Coast. At least part of that story looked to be true. O'Hasson had mentioned a name. Karl Ekby, that was it. A power player, back in the day. I wondered whether Claudette Simms had any connection with a dead kingpin.

As the digital clock in the truck ticked 4:07 A.M., headlights appeared at the far end of the road. A large white truck. It cruised steadily down the street, slowed, and turned to stop right under the support post with the camera.

My first thought was *Bingo.*

My second was *What the hell?*

Because the truck wasn't a civilian vehicle. It was a full-sized service rig from the Viridian cable company, including a row of storage lockers and even a damn cherry-picker lift folded over the top. The green-and-orange Viridian logo made a neon splash across the passenger door.

Had I made a mistake? Was the box on the support pillar some sort of legitimate cable company installation?

As I watched, the driver got out and came around the truck. A woman, dressed in what looked like company-issue dull brown work togs. Her matching cap shielded her face from my view, but couldn't tame a mass of brown curls that fairly exploded out from the back. She had fair skin and stood maybe five and a half feet, in her sneakers. Moving like she was in a hurry, the woman opened the passenger door and slung a tool belt around her hips.

Could she be one of the hunters? The truck was real, and given how fast the woman had gotten here—and how quickly she was releasing the safety locks on the cherry picker—I had to assume she was a real Viridian company employee. It wasn't impossible for her to be both.

By the time she had climbed into the cherry-picker bucket and started the machine lifting her upward, I had decided something was off about the woman and her sudden visit here. She had kept all illumination to a minimum. No headlights, no blinking hazards. She hadn't even shone a flashlight toward the camera box to examine it from the ground.

And besides, what kind of cable repair reacted instantly in the dead of night to an unreported outage? Viridian ran my apartment wireless. I was lucky if they responded within a week.

I could stick with the plan. Follow her wherever she led. But the odds of her driving the cable truck to wherever O'Hasson was held seemed like the longest of shots. Maybe there was another approach.

The woman had reached the camera box. She tossed the branch aside to fall to the ground, and began examining the box with a pencil flashlight. I left the truck and made my silent way along the line of support posts, toward the Viridian truck. Someone had tossed a trash bag out of their car to burst open against one of the posts. I fished an unbroken beer bottle from the refuse, and as I neared the truck, I put a little stagger-swagger into my walk.

"Hey," I half yelled. "Whayou doin'?"

The woman nearly jumped out of the bucket. She looked down at me, where I listed precariously against the rear of her truck.

"Sir?" she said.

"I see you," I replied. "Not supposed." I sat down on the bumper.

"I'm on a service call, sir," she said. This close, I could see that she was in her twenties. And edgy. "Please don't sit on the truck."

"Middle of the nigh'. Sleeping."

"I'm sorry if I woke you. I'll be gone in a few minutes." She looked around, trying to see where I might have emerged from. Or if my noise was attracting anyone else.

"'Erz your work order?" I said as if I hadn't heard her. "Gotta have work order."

"Sir, if you'll just let me fix this, I'll be on my way."

"Call'n the cops on you," I said, taking my phone from my pocket. I feigned obliviousness, but I was watching the woman very closely. If she were with the hunters who had ruthlessly grabbed O'Hasson, it wasn't a big leap to imagine her putting a round through my heart before letting me make that call. The cover of the big truck was only a step away, if her hand dipped out of sight.

"No," she said. "You don't have to. I'll leave right now." And the cherry picker started to lower.

A real worker, on a real call, would have welcomed the cops rousting the large, aggressive drunk. She was willing to risk coming down to street level with me rather than have the authorities around.

Gotcha, sister.

"So what is it?" I said, abandoning the act. "The thing in the box?"

The cherry picker stopped. The bottom of the bucket was about eight feet off the ground.

She looked at me, more uncertain than ever. "It's—just a base station. For cell phones."

I shook my head. "Try again."

"Sir, I don't know what you want from me, but—"

"I want to know what that box is. I want to know who hired you to put it there, and why. I want you to tell me all of that in the next five minutes, or I will call the SPD and tell them everything I saw tonight. Pictures included." I showed her my phone, at the ready. "You want to keep bluffing?"

She didn't. Her face might have been pretty when it wasn't tight with anxiety.

"Who are you?" she said.

"The guy asking the questions. Talk."

"It's only a camera," she said. "That's all."

"For who?"

"I don't know." Off my disbelieving expression she said hastily, "I was hired over the phone. A man. He knew I had done some other work, and he told me what he wanted, and I picked up the camera from baggage storage at Union Station the same day."

"When was this?"

"Start of May, I guess."

Right about when the building had been sold, after Claudette Simms's death. "What other work? How did he learn about you?"

"Look, I don't know anyth—What are you doing?"

My camera's flash captured the Viridian truck vivid and clear. "You can be in the next one. Want a selfie?"

"Stop. Please. I hire out sometimes. To private security firms. P.I.s. Stuff like that. He wouldn't say who referred him to me. That's happened before."

"Wiretapping," I said. "Bugging places. Those kind of jobs?"

She squirmed. "It's mostly just companies trying to get an edge on the competition. Just information." She glanced around. "We can't stay here."

"How does your deal with him work?"

"Come *on*. It's a blind job. I never see him."

"Fix the camera. And keep talking."

Now she was the one who looked skeptical. "Why do you—"

"You're the one who wants to leave. Get to it."

She stared for another moment, and then the cherry picker began to rise. While she started removing the side of the metal housing with a power screwdriver, I checked the front of the truck. Her purse and a laptop in a carrying sleeve were stashed between the seats.

"Hey," she said, noticing where I was.

"You were telling me how the camera works," I said while I went through her purse.

"It—it sends a picture every few seconds."

"Sends it where?"

"To me," she said. "I go through the pictures every day and send any photos of people working here to a shared website in the cloud. The man gave me the password." Now that she was absorbed in repairing the camera's antenna, she seemed to be losing her nervousness about speaking. Or maybe she'd just given up. "The camera's very high resolution. It shows faces very clearly."

The hunters could afford the best. I already knew that.

Juniper Adair. That was the name on her license. She was twenty-eight and lived in the Ravenna area. Her Viridian company ID read *Sr. FiOS Technician* under her name and smiling photograph. There were other photos in the purse, snapshots of her and a boy of about four with the same mop of curly brown hair.

"So he wants pictures of people," I prompted. "Every day. How many pictures is that?"

"I have to look through hundreds. But he only wants one or two of each person. Unless there's anyone new. Then he wants me to send him everything I have."

Looking for someone specific. That jibed with the trap at the safe. Their hunt wasn't about gold, not entirely. And if Juniper was still sending the pictures, then they hadn't found their prey yet.

"Have you spoken with him since he hired you?" I asked.

"No." Juniper finished with the antenna and began reattaching the housing plate to the box. "I just send the pictures and he wires me payment."

"How much? And how do you know when to stop?"

"I stop when he says so, I guess." She started lowering the cherry picker.

"And the money?"

Juniper wouldn't meet my eye as she climbed out of the bucket. Knowing I was going to put the bite on her. "It's fifty a day."

I figured she was lying, so that if I demanded half or even all of her daily rate, she'd still come out ahead. But it didn't matter.

"Here's the new deal," I said. "You keep sending your guy the pictures. You keep getting paid. Same as usual, with two new steps. The first is that you're going to give me every face you've given him. I want to know everyone who's gone near Pacific Pearl since that camera started clicking. Right?"

Juniper nodded hesitantly. If this wasn't an extortion squeeze, she was back on uncertain ground.

"Next, you don't send your guy anyone new. If anybody shows up that you haven't seen before, you will call me. Immediately."

Her eyes went wide. "Wait, no. That's too much. If he finds out—"

"He's not what you should worry about, Juniper. I have evidence of you working in the dead of night on an unknown box placed on a support column of city infrastructure. Imagine what kind of hell Homeland Security will rain on you if they learn that. The fact that it's just a camera in the box won't mean shit. You'll be lucky to see your kid before he graduates college."

"Please," she said. "No."

"Then do what I say. No one needs to know you were ever here."

She nodded, first slowly, then with increasing vigor. Committed.

She had the pictures on her laptop, and I snapped shots of each face with my phone. There were only a dozen or so individuals. One was the huge Latino thug who had chased after Cyndra O'Hasson. I was not overly surprised to see him. There had to be some connection between the gold in the safe at Pacific Pearl's business office and the two men who'd tried to kidnap the daughter of the burglar sent to steal that same gold. I didn't know exactly what that link was, but now I had one more clue.

I gave Juniper Adair the number of my burner phone. She nodded again, glumly. She'd hardly said a word while I'd scanned through the faces and she locked the cherry picker back into place.

The sun was coming up. I handed Juniper back her laptop. I'd wiped my fingerprints. "Keep your head down. This will be over soon."

"What are you doing here?" she said. "Can I at least ask that?"

I walked away. Behind me, I heard the Viridian truck start up and drive away, not slowing a hair at the stop sign. Desperate to get some distance from me.

Brutal, I knew. I could justify coercing Juniper with custody of her kid. Tell myself that if she did find the person the hunters were looking for, the technician might unwittingly step from illicit surveillance to accessory to murder.

But that would be a lie. I saw the woman's jelly spot, and I used it. I wouldn't hesitate to do it again. Even if I didn't like myself much in the moment.

On the way back to the Dodge, I took one more moment to examine the martial arts gym down the road from Pacific Pearl. I owed Juniper Adair at least one thing: I might never have taken a close look at the western side of the place without her little side occupation.

The gym used to be a warehouse, I guessed. Corrugated walls, with black paint faded enough that the rust that bled from each metal bolt looked almost artful. The glass entrance doors were up a short flight of wooden stairs, and above the doors was a sign. SLEDGE CITY GYM, it read in caps. Below that: HOME OF CHAMPIONS—MMA—BOXING—THAI.

The letter I in CITY was dead center on the sign, large and red and distinctive.

A clenched fist, on top of an axe handle.

The tattoo on the thug who'd tried to kidnap Cyndra.

TWELVE

THE MORNING WAS WARM and the rain, if anything, warmer still. A rare enough event that Corcoran and Hollis and I sat out on Corcoran's small balcony, under the shelter of the overhang, feeling the air while we sipped at lemongrass iced tea, a glass bottle of which Corcoran's wife, Nakri, had left for us. I placed the highball glass idly against my lips, less drinking than absorbing. I was too deep into my head to be concerned with taste or other senses.

"I think Mickey O'Hasson might be alive," I said.

"So where is the prick?" said Corcoran.

"Stuck in a room without any windows, most likely." I tapped the glass, watching the amber liquid ripple.

They exchanged glances. Hollis's frown almost matched Corcoran's.

"Who would want the man, lad? He's got nothing."

I shook my head. "He's got value. Just by continuing to exist. Because to his prison buddy, it looks like O'Hasson ran off with the gold."

"You make less sense than my kids on that energy drink crap," Corcoran said. His wife and high-school-age children had gone out for the evening. Thinking of Jimmy Corcoran as a family man, even by a late-in-life marriage, was one of those pieces of reality too dissonant to be conceivable.

"I've had to stack some guesses on top of what I know for sure," I said. "A woman named Claudette Simms ran a small freight company called Pacific Pearl. The company was—maybe still is—a front for smuggling of some kind. Over time, Claudette bought gold kilobars and stashed them in her hidden safe. O'Hasson's attendant had told him the gold came from drug running. That might be true.

"Around two months ago, Claudette had a heart attack and drowned in her tub. It might have been random chance. Or someone could have killed her and made it look like an accident. Either way, her death set things in motion. Very soon after, the building with her office is bought and gutted. Another group—the hunters—was laying a trap with Claudette's safe as the bait."

"A trap for who?" Hollis asked. "The woman's dead."

"I'm assuming Claudette Simms had a partner in Pacific Pearl. A partner who might know or suspect she had gold squirreled away in the safe. The hunters were hoping that the partner would show up to take it. Instead, they got O'Hasson. And me."

Corcoran sucked at his teeth. "Two morons for the price of one."

I ignored him. "O'Hasson's attendant in the prison infirmary was the one who sold Mick on the story of the fortune in gold. He said that the gold was abandoned long ago. That part, at least, was a lie."

"Mick O'Hasson is an even bigger sap than you, Shaw," Corcoran said.

"No," Hollis said, realizing. "He's a burglar. Who's dying, and maybe desperate for money. He's a patsy."

I nodded. "In Iraq, the locals would rub sticks with rotten meat, and throw the sticks into fields where they suspected mines were buried. The scent would attract wild dogs."

"Boom." Corcoran grinned. A sight even scarcer than warm rain, and a lot less pleasant.

"Mick O'Hasson is somebody's minefield dog. Sent in to find out if Claudette's office was dangerous," I said.

"'Cept it was the building that blew up."

Hollis grunted. "And Mick got himself shot with a tranquilizer. Now the hunters have a dying burglar instead of the man they wanted. Whoever that is."

"I'm still in the dark about that," I said. "I don't know what the connection is between O'Hasson's prison attendant and Claudette's silent partner in Pacific Pearl. I have to guess that they aren't the same man, since the attendant has been locked up in Lancaster Pen for years."

"Another reason why he sent Mick to take the risk," Hollis mused.

My glass was empty. I took the half-empty bottle of tea from Corcoran. The screw top came off with a twist of my fingers and I poured another inch, more lost in my head than thinking about the motions.

"I also don't know who the hunters are, or why they are so hell-bent on catching Claudette's partner," I said. "It's possible that they murdered Claudette after forcing her to tell them about the gold, to get to him. They've spent weeks, and maybe hundreds of thousands of dollars, trying to trap him at the safe. They've installed a camera at Pacific Pearl to watch for people coming and going. They're still watching now." I shook my head. "It's not about the gold. Not for them."

"What if," said Hollis, brightening, "the four million is just the tip of the mountain. Some of those big drug operations spend that much on bribes. Maybe there's a huge pile of the lovely stuff somewhere."

"Also possible," I said.

"Still doesn't explain why Mick O'Hasson isn't fertilizing a field somewhere," Corcoran said.

"What would you do?" I offered. "If you were the hunters? You lost your trap at the safe, but gained O'Hasson."

"I might try to use Mick as the new bait," Hollis said after a moment's thought. "Pretending to be him."

"Uh-huh," I said. "O'Hasson is the hunters' best bet to lure Claudette's unknown partner out in the open."

"Screw that," said Corcoran. "O'Hasson put a match to the building, didn't he? And then disappeared. That's gotta look hinky. If I were the dead woman's partner, sure as shit I wouldn't be sticking my neck out right now."

I nodded. "He's playing it safe. But he *does* think O'Hasson has his gold."

Hollis was keeping step with me. "The girl."

"Mick's daughter, Cyndra," I said. "Two meatheads—one of whom works at Pacific Pearl—tried to grab her in Reseda. Somebody gave the goons orders. Maybe the partner, maybe the prison attendant, or both. Grab Cyndra, and they think they can force O'Hasson to give them their gold back."

"Shitbirds," Corcoran said. "I'd fucking kill 'em, it was my kid they went for." He spat with surprising distance, the gob arcing over the rail and joining the other precipitation. I made a mental note to wear a hat walking past Corcoran's building in the future.

"Cyndra's with Addy now," I said. "She's safe. And the hunters are at a stalemate. O'Hasson is useful bait, but the silent partner is too gunshy."

"Entertaining as all this crap is," Corcoran said, "why do you give a rat's ass? Nobody's offering to trade you for nothing."

Hollis looked at me, blue eyes shining with amusement. "You don't want the little fellow to get killed, now do you?" he said.

"You're shitting me," Corcoran said, staring. "He tried to cook you."

"Not me," I said. "The hunters."

"Oh, well, that makes it okay."

"It's the girl, Jimmy," Hollis said. "Van can't let the girl lose her father."

Corcoran threw up his hands. "The moron's dying anyway."

"All the more reason," said Hollis.

"Fuck that. And fuck you, Shaw. Your priorities are seriously out of whack." Corcoran got up and opened the sliding glass door. "Dono would never be such a chump." He slammed the door behind him.

Tiny beads of rain trickled down the cap of the balcony railing, collecting into fat drops that hung for an instant before falling and breaking apart on the next rail down, repeating the cycle. Hollis tilted his glass high, waiting for the last drips to finish the journey.

"You know," he said after a moment, "it's always a shame when Jimmy's right."

I kept watching the rain.

"A week ago you were hemming and hawing over whether to stay on the straight path," said Hollis. "Not something I'd fret about myself, but okay. We all make our own choices. Now you're all knotted up inside about O'Hasson, who has no one to blame but his own self. The way I see it, you dodged a speeding train, and you should give thanks and be done."

"Jimmy meant I should be focusing on the money, not the girl."

"I know what he meant," said Hollis.

"I agree with him."

Hollis stared at me, and I met his baffled gaze.

"Four million in gold," I said. "That's the key. Before long, both sides—hunters and the silent partner—are going to risk a meeting. And the gold has to be right in the middle, or nothing happens. Somebody's going home with it."

Hollis straightened in his chair. The white hairs on his arm popped with goosebumps.

"What are you thinking?" he said.

The screw top of the tea bottle was still resting on the plastic tablecloth printed with magnolias. I tilted the little disk of metal on its side and flicked it with a fingertip, sending it spinning across the table.

"I'm thinking we need to crash the party," I said.

For once, I didn't mind taking out the trash. While hauling the heavy load out to the bins, I spotted the bright yellow coffee cups smashed against the taut plastic of the Hefty bag. I knew those cups.

I pulled the drawstrings loose, letting out a swampy waft of wilted vegetables. There were three twelve-ounce cups in the bag. All from the same coffee shop called Armond's, up on 19th. All three brought in from Granddad's truck, one each day during the past three days. He'd been going out at weird hours, really early or really late, always telling me it was contracting work. Not a chance.

He was staking someplace out. Maybe the house he and the two men were planning to burgle.

Burgle was the word, I hoped. Not rob. Robbery meant guns, or at least something violent and threatening, and that was exactly the kind of work Granddad had promised me he wouldn't do.

But he was still carrying the Colt. I'd checked every night, while he was reading and I was mostly watching TV downstairs. The small automatic was always in the right-hand pocket of whatever jacket he'd been wearing that day.

A house job meant burglary. That would be okay. But there were plenty of businesses around 19th, too, and I guess some of them might have enough cash to make a robbery worth it, especially around Christmas. Would Granddad really hit a place so close to home? He hardly liked working in Seattle, much less on the Hill. I wasn't sure.

I'd have to see for myself.

Armond's coffee shop was across the street from an elementary school, and the playground made a good place for me to hang out with my bike. It was so early that the sun wasn't up yet. I was barely up myself. Only the cold kept me awake. I tried sitting on the merry-go-round, but its metal was so freezing my butt got numb in like a minute. Instead I got up and walked around the play structure, gloved hands shoved into my pockets and head squished down into my collar. My breath made white puffs in the air, even through my scarf.

I'd worn my darkest coat and sneakers to stay over at Davey's the night before, and told Davey and his mom that I had to leave super early to join Granddad on a construction job. Davey's mom fussed but told me I should be proud of helping out. Davey made faces at me from behind her. He and I had stayed up late—too late, it felt now—messing around with *Mario Kart* on their Nintendo.

Granddad might not buy coffee at Armond's again today. But people had patterns, and they liked to stick to them. That's what he had said when he was teaching me what to look for when casing a place, to see when it would be empty. I guess this would be ironic or fitting or something, me now watching for him.

But *man*, it was cold. I hoped he'd hurry up. The lights had just gone on at Armond's, and the store glowed like a fireplace. Bet they had hot chocolate.

I didn't have to wait much longer—twenty minutes of frostbite creeping into my toes—before our black Chevy pickup came down the street. I ducked behind the play structure, near my bike lying on the ground like a dead dog. Granddad pulled up to the curb and got out and went into Armond's. He was wearing his barn jacket and blue jeans and sneakers that were a big pair of the ones I was wearing. We'd bought them at the same time at the Payless, the week after he'd brought me home from the foster house.

I grabbed my bike and coasted to the gap in the fence. The school was closed up for the holidays, but the gate was only attached with a little click-lock, the kind I'd learned to beat even before Granddad went away. I wheeled the bike through and relocked it, and ducked behind a parked car.

Granddad came out, fresh cup of coffee in his hand, and got in the Chevy and pulled away.

Here came the tough part. Following the truck without him seeing me. The sky was brighter now, and the roads mostly quiet. I leaned in and pumped hard on the pedals and the bike sped down the sidewalk.

I was going to lose. In the first block alone, Granddad made twice the distance I did. If he hadn't stopped for a few moments at a five-way intersection, I'd have given up already. He angled to the right, out of view, and ten seconds later I flew through the same stop sign without hesitating.

We were running alongside Interlaken Park now. The sidewalk was cracked and every couple hundred feet there was a telephone pole just waiting for me to smack into it. I'd lost the Chevy. I pedaled harder. Up ahead, I saw his lights as the truck turned left, following the edge of the park. A Roto-Rooter service truck was in my way. I swooped around and in front of it to cross the street. Its brakes squealed, but I was already zooming after Granddad.

The road was just a single lane. Houses on the right, and a thick wall of trees and brush leading down into a small ravine that bordered the park on the left. Cars parallel-parked against the single shallow sidewalk made the road even tighter. I used them for cover, half coasting and half kicking it down the easy slope, hoping no one would come backing out of their driveway to mash me.

Granddad's Chevy, just fifty yards ahead and brake lights flashing. I skidded to a stop, my rear tire leaving a black streak on the asphalt.

Oh shit, he was backing up.

No time to jump off the bike. I let it fall and went with it, my shoulder thumping painfully into the pavement.

Had he seen me? If so, I was going to look pretty stupid,

lying on the sidewalk behind a parked Corolla. And then one hellacious storm would follow.

Twenty seconds passed. The Chevy didn't appear. Instead, I heard the sounds of shifting gears and, faintly, the truck's engine turning off.

I risked a peek above the Corolla's hood. Granddad hadn't gotten out of the truck. He was just sitting there, parallel-parked at the curb.

Okay. Was he casing one of the houses? They were nice houses, sure, at least as good as ours and a lot newer. But not nearly the kinds of places that would have security guards, like Granddad and the two men at our house had been talking about. The most they would have to worry about here would be a family dog.

I picked up the bike and, still hunched way over behind the line of cars, wheeled it back up the road. When I was around the bend, I sprinted with it across the street and into the first line of bushes at the ravine.

Hiding my bike was easy—just lay it down in the clumps of ground ivy and scotch broom and it was invisible. It was a lot harder to make my way back to the Chevy through the trees. I had to go ten yards down the ravine's slope to where the brush thinned out to even start. Brambles caught my pants on every step, but at least I couldn't be seen. Granddad would have kicked my ass for spying on him.

At last I had gone far enough that I guessed I was near the Chevy and I could climb back toward the road, pushing the hanging evergreen branches aside. When I finally saw it, the big black truck was shockingly close. Granddad's dark head *right there*. I dropped flat on the wet ground.

He was just watching the road, it looked like. Waiting for someone to leave? I edged another yard forward to get a view of the houses down the road. The grass smell made my nose run.

I didn't know any of the houses. But I did know one of the cars in one of the driveways. A green Ford Taurus, with a Balewood School bumper sticker.

The redheaded man's car.

Granddad sat there for two hours. My pants had soaked through from the wet ivy and mostly dried again with the heat from my body. Ten times I thought about inching back into the trees and leaving, but I wanted to know. Even the shivering didn't make me quit. He might be proud if I could ever tell him.

Like all the houses on the narrow road, the redheaded man's home—if it was his home—was close to its neighbors and elevated a little bit from the road. Not as steeply as our house, which was on top of a rise, but enough so there were stairs leading from the driveway along a rock wall that faced the sidewalk, curving upward to meet its front door. The house was brown and two stories and partly sheltered by a couple of leafy trees on the small slope of its front yard.

Just a house. Nothing unusual. So why was Granddad so intense about it?

The redheaded man came down the steps from the side of the house, got into his car, and pulled out of the driveway. Granddad had ducked down in the truck. It was kind of funny, me hiding from him hiding from the redheaded man. The Taurus drove down the road, and a moment later, Granddad and the truck did, too.

I stood up and brushed myself off and fought through the last of the brush to the road. It felt great to finally be standing. I wiped my nose on my sleeve, for about the hundredth time.

So Granddad was following the tall redheaded guy. Or staking out his house, or both. I had thought they were partners.

"Hey," said a girl's voice from across the street. "What're you doing?"

Ah, crap. I hadn't seen her standing behind the trees in front of the house.

"Uh," I said.

The girl came down the steps. She looked about my age, maybe a little older. Definitely taller. Her black t-shirt had a picture of the Tick and the word SPOON in red letters that were flaking with age. It was cool.

Then I noticed that her hair was the same color as the redheaded man's. Not cool.

"A snake," I said quickly. "I saw one." That would scare her off.

"Yeah?" She hurried across the road. "Where?"

Dang. "Uh. Back there. It went this way."

"What kind? A rattlesnake?"

I didn't think there were rattlesnakes in the city, though whenever we drove out to the woods to shoot, Granddad had warned me to watch my step around logs and rocks. But I didn't want to look dumb if the girl knew for sure. "No, a garter snake. Black and green."

"Oh." Clearly disappointed. She folded her arms—no coat on and it was still crazy cold out—and looked around at the grass and ivy. Her orange hair fell in her face and I realized she was wearing slippers instead of shoes, which were getting wet.

"I think it's gone," I said. No reason she should stand around waiting for a fake snake.

"Okay," she said, but didn't move.

"Well." I shrugged. "Bye."

"I'm Kassie," she said before I'd taken two steps.

"I'm Van." Shit, I should have lied. Didn't matter. I wasn't going to see her again.

"Do you live on this street?"

"No. Just riding around."

Kassie nodded like she'd expected that. "I'm the only one, I think. It's boring here during vacation."

Wait, maybe the house wasn't hers, or the redheaded man's. Maybe they were visiting or something.

"Do you go to Balewood?" I said. "I saw the bumper sticker."

Kassie nodded again. "What school's yours?"

"Hovick. Middle School," I added in case she thought I was a fifth-grader.

"Do you want to watch TV?" she said, looking at her feet. "Or I got a PlayStation."

Really? I didn't know anybody who had one of those yet. I didn't want to play, not really. But it would let me see inside the house. Maybe the redheaded man had something lying around that would tell me what score they were planning. Or why Granddad considered him a threat.

I'd have to be gone before he got back. The redheaded man knew who I was.

"Okay," I said. "But then I gotta go home."

"Cool," said Kassie, smiling. We walked across the street toward the house. "What's Hovick like?"

"Like hitting your head on the desk all day," I said.

Kassie laughed. Which made me happy, somehow.

THIRTEEN

ADDY CAME OUT ONTO her porch before I had turned off the truck's engine. This was getting to be a habit, her dashing out to meet me. She shifted her weight anxiously from side to side, causing Stanley to rock with her like a dance partner. If the rain hadn't been pelting down, she might have come right up to my window.

"Cyndra's run off," Addy said as I came up the walk.

"Just now?"

"I came home from the grocery store and found her gone. Her backpack, too."

"That pack has everything she owns. She wouldn't let it out of her sight, even if she were just walking up to 15th for a Slurpee. Did she steal anything?"

"Not that I noticed."

"So she's not burning bridges. She'll be back."

"I don't like it," Addy said.

"Me either. But we can't tie her to a chair."

Still, my previous worries came creeping back, about what sort of trail Cyndra might have left on her journey to Seattle, and maybe to my address. I was sure there was more that the clever twelve-year-old hadn't told me about her father's plans.

I went back to the truck and retrieved one of my burner phones from the glove compartment. Stanley came with me and bruised my thigh with his head on every third step, asking for attention.

"A new toy of yours?" Addy said when we rejoined her. I was already thumbing through menus.

"Congratulate me, I'm a father. Great apps for parents these days." I found the map portion of the controls and pressed Locate.

"Did you install something on Cyndra's phone?" Addy looked aghast.

"She'd spot that. She's probably smarter than I am about tech. I just hid a different phone in her backpack." Way down in it, taped near the bottom. I could probably have hidden a soccer ball in that mess without her finding it. "Last night, while you guys were asleep."

"You worry me sometimes," Addy said.

"It's not satellite positioning, but best I could do on short notice."

A red digital pin appeared, a block off Pine. I showed Addy. "She's on the Hill. Probably walked there from here."

"Thank heaven."

"I'll check it out."

"Watch yourself on the road. Drivers in this storm—"

"Your maternal instinct is in overdrive, Addy."

She reddened. "Fine, then."

I'd hit a nerve, though I wasn't sure why or how. "I'll take Stanley. Maybe it'll grease the skids with the girl."

"Do that."

Stanley did a good job of getting every inch of the backseat wet while I drove up and over the hill, musing on how I'd managed to tick Addy off. Sometimes the fact that I'd only known the formidable Ms. Proctor for a tiny percentage of her life slapped me upside the head. She wasn't all that forthcoming about certain parts of her history. I was supposed to be the one with secrets.

The pin on the phone's map hadn't moved. I found a space at the curb by Anderson Park, threw on a Sounders cap, and clicked Stanley's leash in place before letting him lunge out of the truck into the down-pour. We walked through the sidewalk puddles, me with one eye on the map. The leash was mostly symbolic. I was pretty sure Stanley could snap the leather in half with a bite and a twist, and I was very sure he could yank me right off my feet if he set his mind to it. Addy had broken him of the instinct.

I looked at the stores. A Brazilian churrascaria, a chain drugstore, a thrift shop for hospices, and a coffee roaster all had their lights blaz-ing bright to ward off the gray of the day. I tugged Stanley away from what he thought was a very intriguing signpost and headed toward the coffee shop.

Cyndra was sitting on a tall stool in the window, looking straight out onto Pike. Her stuffed pack and skateboard lay on the floor under her feet, and she cradled a bowl-shaped mug half the size of her head in her palms.

She spotted me through the window and jolted out of whatever reverie had had her in its grip. A frown followed quickly.

I brought Stanley with me into the shop, pausing in the doorway for him to shake the rain from himself with happy violence. The storm had cut into the shop's business. The kid and I doubled the place's cli-entele.

"That much latte," I said, "you'll be awake until Tuesday."

She wore a hooded yellow rain slicker that was voluminous enough to fit over the backpack and still come down to her knees when she was standing. Seated, it looked like a cape. The slicker was unzipped to show denim overalls and the same stained white V-neck as before.

"I'm not leaving," she said.

"I didn't ask."

"I mean it. Touch me and I'll scream for help."

"Could make a rough day for both of us. You really want to talk to the cops about where you live?"

Cyndra folded her arms tightly against her body. "How'd you find me?"

"Stanley's part bloodhound. What's so fun about this place?" I looked across the street. One of the offices on the second floor had signs of movement. So did the drugstore.

The kid's father was dying. With every other piece of madness swirling around me lately, it was easy to lose sight of that.

I looked at her. "His prescriptions?"

Her lips got white. She watched the store fixedly. The first time we'd met, Cyndra had been exhausted from stress and a long journey. She'd cried. Maybe she was embarrassed at that, or angry, or both.

I took the stool next to her, setting my wet cap on the narrow strip of table. Stanley lay down and started sniffing at Cyndra's pack.

"How do you know this is the right pharmacy?" I said.

She stayed immobile, her thin shoulders hunched like the wing bones of a sparrow over her back.

No harm in my guessing. "Your dad used your computer, like he did to find my house. To see where he could get his meds in Seattle. It's a twenty-four-hour store. Did Mickey actually place an order here?" If so, O'Hasson might have used an alias, which would be useful to know.

Cyndra fidgeted. I took that as a yes.

"Okay. No way to tell, so you're waiting. Is that it?"

She continued to stare at the store.

A man in a burgundy apron approached us from the counter, a fussy apparition in the window's reflection.

"Sir. We can't have dogs in here. Unless they're service dogs."

I turned to stare at him, stone-faced.

"Oh," he said. "Um. Okay. Sorry." He retreated.

I spun the stool back to the window. Cyndra glanced my way, and I winked without looking at her.

"Sometimes scars are useful," I said.

She didn't reply, but contemplated me in the window before resuming her surveillance of the pharmacy.

"Addy got worried when you took off," I said.

Cyndra shrugged. "So?"

"So, when Addy's upset, she calls me. And I have to answer, because she's my friend and I owe her, in that order. Then she gives me marching orders to make sure you're not lying in a ditch somewhere."

"Tell the old lady I'm fine."

"I will do that. It might even keep that particular old lady off my back for a whole hour."

"That's dumb. I don't need a babysitter."

"Neither do I. It doesn't keep Addy from fretting about me."

"Just leave me alone."

I waved a hand at the street. "Stay here until you grow mocha-colored roots. I don't give a shit. But if I have to go looking for you, that's time spent not looking for your dad. So keep Addy posted, or we both lose."

Stanley nosed at Cyndra's shoe. His head came up high enough that she could reach down and scratch his ear without leaning far.

"I'm not stupid," Cyndra said. "I know Dad's probably not gonna be here." She shrugged again, like the truth of it didn't matter. I got what she meant. It was something to do, other than sit and stew in her own fear at Addy's.

We observed the street. People went in and out of the drugstore. None of them was O'Hasson. Cyndra's coffee mug was empty, but she still held it as carefully as if it were brimming.

"I met your dad," I said.

Cyndra looked at me.

"He came to Seattle to see me, like you thought. I don't know where he is now. I'll try to find him, because both of you deserve that. But there are things I'm not going to tell you. For him, and for me. You get why?"

"Incriminating," she said.

"That's right."

"Is Dad in trouble?"

I took a breath. "Yeah."

She turned back to the window. Not watching the people on the street anymore. Just staring. The rain eased, allowing a minute of weak sunlight before the next sodden cloud would roll overhead.

"I think those men in Reseda tried to grab you so they could make your dad do what they wanted," I said. "That's a good sign that he might be okay."

"But you don't know."

"I don't."

"So what do I do?" she asked, her anger suddenly boiling over. "If I can't ask you, and he's out there, and those guys—"

"You can do at least one thing, for now. Tell me what else you know about your dad and Seattle. No more secrets like the pharmacy."

"I don't *know* any more."

"Mick didn't use your computer to look up anything else? Websites? Flight reservations? Rental car?"

"*No,*" she said.

"Calm down. I'm spitballing."

"He didn't tell me *anything.*"

We were attracting more attention from the barista. "Rain's slacking off. Let's walk." I stood up and handed her the battered backpack before she could argue. Stanley leapt to his feet.

Cyndra pulled her slicker hood up against the rain. Stanley happily lapped from every puddle we passed. On our way down the gentle slope of Pine Street, Cyndra stopped short.

"Dad talked to somebody," she said, "like the day after he got home."

"Who was it?"

"Someone from jail. I know because we had to wait at home to take the call."

Phone privileges. Unless O'Hasson's caller had access to a contraband cell phone in Lancaster, he would have had to make a collect call to a landline, during the hours allowed.

Cyndra was deep in thought. "I heard the name. The phone was loud, I heard the robot voice ask if he'd accept the call before he made me leave. Wait," she said before I could press her. "Wait."

I bit my tongue and let her think. If the caller had been O'Hasson's prison attendant—

"Gar Slattery." Cyndra nodded her head. "That's it."

"Slattery. You're sure?"

"Yes. I have a very good memory. I got tested once. Try me."

I looked at her. "Okay. What was I wearing yesterday when we met?"

She considered it. "I hafta make the picture in my head," she explained, and after a moment said, "Adidas. And—black jeans. And a

green shirt, with buttons down to here and the seam ripped up here."
She pointed to her chest and her shoulder, describing the Henley.

I put up a hand, and Cyndra high-fived it before she realized that
probably wasn't considered cool.

"You hungry? I need food," I said. Stanley heard the magic word and
became very attentive.

"Okay," Cyndra said.

"We can walk up to Dick's. Burgers."

She nodded acceptance and we resumed our walk.

Gar Slattery. The name might be nothing, just a cellmate or another con, marking the time by calling his buddy Mick. But I didn't
think so. O'Hasson had been obsessive about the gold. If he had talked
to anyone in Lancaster the day after he got out, it would be his infirmary attendant.

We waited in the ever-present line—a rainstorm would never keep
customers from Dick's; the line would survive the apocalypse—and
I bought enough Deluxes with relish to feed a family of six. Cyndra
tossed fries into Stanley's waiting maw on the drive back to Addy's.

After we had eaten, I slipped away to search for the name Gar Slattery online. I found a few Garfields and Garretts. The one I wanted was
Gareth. I knew the instant I saw the link that read *Man, 31, charged with
murder in killing of accomplice* . . .

The link led to a brief *L.A. Times* article in the paper's archives, eighteen years ago, which described the formal charges filed by the prosecutor against Gareth Slattery. Slattery was noted as having a long history
of arrests, most of them for violent crimes. There was a follow-up article covering a conviction of fifteen years to life for second-degree murder after the court accepted Slattery's plea bargain.

Another thread, starting to weave together with what I'd learned.
Slattery had been into drug trafficking. I was ninety percent sure Pacific
Pearl was a front for same.

There was nothing more online for Gar Slattery. He had been inside
prison walls while the Internet was still tightening its grip on the rest of
the world. I could see if Hollis's contacts might pull more on Slattery's

history. But that would just give me the official record. I needed the local view.

Both of the articles had the same byline, Calvin Lorenzo. A search on Lorenzo's name popped up more crime reporting, most of it from when I'd been in grade school, and one email address for the man.

Addy and Cyndra were in the living room, absorbed in the television. They had discovered a shared love of the kind of science-fiction shows where the ideas were big and the budgets low. Before I left them to their rerun of *Doctor Who,* I fired off an email to Lorenzo, asking him to contact me if he could recall more details on Gar Slattery.

I drove the Dodge down MLK Way, aiming for Beacon Hill and a zigzagging route back to a road I was coming to know very well.

Had Slattery used O'Hasson as his pawn, selling him half-truths about drug runners and hidden gold? Just enough facts that the story held up to whatever O'Hasson could check. Until the dying man was in a frenzy, dreaming of a rich legacy for his daughter.

So dazzled by that dream that maybe O'Hasson had missed the obvious. Gar Slattery was a killer. If O'Hasson succeeded in rescuing the gold from the safe, my guess was that the little burglar was a marked man.

The poor son of a bitch had it coming and going. Steal the gold, become a target. Spring the trap, get abducted. Or just wait, as that tumor tightened its grip in his head.

Hang on, Mick. If you're still out there, hang on. Just a little while longer.

FOURTEEN

FIGHTING GYMS HAD PERSONALITIES. They could be blue-collar unions or boisterous frat houses. I'd known a gym in Georgia that was practically an ongoing family reunion, and another near Bergen-Hohne in Germany that had been as solemn as a monastery.

When I stepped through the door at Sledge City, my gut reaction was *Savage*.

It was late. The outside lights were already off. I'd been aiming to catch the gym owner or one of its employees closing up and wheedle some information about the big tattooed thug who'd tried to kidnap Cyndra. But a handful of men remained around the single boxing ring, like moths attracted to the bright tube lights at the far end of the long room.

I wouldn't have to talk to the owner to find Cyndra's attacker. The son of a bitch was standing right in the center of the ring.

The fleshy heavyweight faced off with a blond who couldn't have tipped the scales at more than welter. They wore shorts and fingerless fighting gloves, nothing else. The heavyweight, unsurprisingly, was beating the crap out of his smaller opponent. Four other men around the ring were cheering the fight on.

"Don't let him out," one of the onlookers hollered, as the welterweight ducked and tried desperately to move out of the corner the big man had herded him into. The heavyweight put out an arm and tossed him bodily back into place.

"Yeah, Bomba!" yelled another of the spectators. He was ready for the beach. Mid-twenties, ripped, hair piled up into a topknot and looking like he lived 24/7 in board shorts and a tank.

The welterweight landed a kick on the thug's meaty thigh and was rewarded with three clubbing right hands, graceless and thunderous, that smashed him to his knees. Howls erupted from the men. The blond spat. A tooth, blood fluttering behind it like a tiny comet's tail, bounced once before coming to rest on the canvas. No shirker, the welterweight got his feet under him. An uppercut lifted him up on his toes and he slid down the turnbuckle to the canvas again.

"Enough," said a high hoarse voice from the back of the room. The command stopped the heavyweight, who had been rearing back to deliver another haymaker. "He's had enough, goddammit."

The older man who belonged to the voice was sitting on stacks of rubber matting, in the back half of the gym where the overhead lights were turned off. He grumbled as he stood. He was followed by a younger guy who walked with the languid ease of a bored leopard. Six feet tall, lank hair, sleeve tattoos of dragons and blue fire covering his sinewy arms. He looked just as unimpressed by the one-sided bout as the older trainer.

"Miguelito, get Roddy some ice," the trainer said. A teenager by the ring hustled off. "The rest of ya get back to work."

Bomba ducked his head under the ropes to climb out of the ring. He was the first one who paid any attention to me, in the form of a heavy-lidded glower. As he stomped away to grab a water bottle, the beach bum clapped him on his sweaty back in congratulations.

"Help you?" said the trainer, coming to meet me. He was somewhere past fifty, hard to estimate how far, thanks to a long history of wreckage and cheap restoration to his face. Steady punishment, one punch at a time. His cheekbones had been reset at some point, not quite identically. Scar tissue thickened his brow and eyelids. Age may have stooped him, but in his prime he would have matched Bomba for size.

I nodded to the ring, where the welterweight Roddy was still sitting, leaning against the corner post as Miguelito held a produce bag of chipped ice to his jaw. Now that he wasn't ducking and dodging, I recognized Roddy from the surveillance camera photos Juniper Adair had shown me.

"Saw the fun through the window," I said.

While I'd been sizing up the trainer's face, he'd been doing the same for mine. "You fight?" he said.

"Not professional." I tapped my left profile, where a good portion of the bone structure was bioglass beneath the white furrows that divided my cheek into three uneven sections. "Car accident. When I was a teenager."

"Ah." He smiled. The row of teeth that gleamed from out of his grizzled whiskers was unnaturally even. Dentures, probably. "Well, if you're looking for a gym, this is the best around. They got some serious warriors."

"I noticed."

He followed my eyes to the welterweight being helped to his feet. His hay-bale hair was dark with sweat and the left side of his face was already puffing, ice or no ice.

"Yeah, that," said the trainer. "That shit ain't a regular thing, far as I know."

The surfer dude with the topknot spoke up from where he'd been practicing elbow strikes on the heavy bags. "Roddy fucked up," he said, dancing in his fringed boxing shoes. "House rules."

"He piss on the seat or something?" I said.

Topknot grinned. "Wadja do, Roddy?" he called.

Roddy glowered at us through his unswollen eye. Topknot laughed.

"He won't tell us," said Topknot, "but he knows, and Bomba knows, and that's enough for Roddy to pay the bill."

Cyndra had said that the second man who'd tried to grab her in Reseda was blond, and short. The welterweight fit both criteria. Perhaps Roddy had been the scapegoat for their failure to grab Cyndra.

"Gimme the tour," I said to the trainer.

He nodded, maybe glad I hadn't bolted for the door after the show.

"I'm Orville," he said, holding out a broad hand. As we shook, his crooked pinky finger didn't bend at the knuckle with the others.

"Zack," I said, randomly picking the name of one of the staff sergeants from my last platoon. At least I hadn't reflexively told Orville my name was Wilbur. "You run the place?"

"Nah. I mean sometimes I help out, when I'm not on the road. When I'm in Seattle, I mostly work with Dickson." He nodded toward the guy with the blue sleeve tattoos, who leaned lazily against the largest heavy bag, talking to Bomba.

"A contender?"

"Gettin' there," Orville said, pointing. I belatedly noticed the large fight poster on the wall behind the ring, hyping an event from last year in Mexico City. The blanket-sized print allowed plenty of room for headshots of the main matchups, including a sneering picture of the fighter currently shooting the shit with Bomba. Dickson Hinch, the poster read under his photo.

"Ranked number eight now, light heavy," Orville continued. "He's coming up. You watch."

"And Bomba? Is he one of your fighters?"

Orville's face twisted in disgust. "Not with that gut. He's just Dickson's buddy from the day job."

I took that to mean that Hinch worked at Pacific Pearl, too. His face hadn't been in the photos from Juniper Adair. I'd come in to track down Bomba, and discovered an entire faction of Pacific Pearl employees here at the neighborhood gym. Dickson Hinch and blond Roddy, along with Bomba. I wondered how many others at Sledge City were included. And how many knew that Pacific Pearl ran more than lettuce and carrots across the mountains.

The gym might simply be a convenient place for the freight company employees to work out. Or the link between them could run the other direction. Pacific Pearl had to find their drivers somewhere. Recruiting muscle out of a nearby MMA gym was an easy leap.

Orville led me around the wide space of the converted warehouse. The equipment was the same scattering of a dozen makes like Everlast or Reyes or Title you'd find in any gym. A thousand pictures and flyers covered the walls, most from fights long past and fighters who'd never made it big. Duct tape reinforced somewhere between five and ninety percent of all gear.

Mostly, the smell was the same. Its strength varied with the frequency of cleaning, but it was always the same mix of old sweat and new sweat layered over leather and vinyl and ammonia. The odor should be bad, but rarely was. I'd spent too many hours in gyms not to have positive associations with it, even in a dog pit like Sledge City.

I kept half an eye on the fighters while Orville talked. Dickson Hinch and Bomba were clearly cocks of this particular walk. The other fighters made way for the pair, even if it meant interrupting their flow as they drilled on combinations.

Nobody acknowledged Roddy as he came out from the bathroom, his raw face dripping with water. Still a pariah, even after Bomba's punishment.

Orville noticed my glance at the walking wounded.

"Uh," he said, "you probably didn't get the best first impression, okay? It's after hours, kind of, and Bomba and Roddy had a personal beef, I guess. It ain't acceptable. Where you from?"

"Georgia. Most recently." Which was true. I'd been discharged out of Fort Benning six months earlier.

"Well, great. You want training, the gym's got some guys who know their way around."

"Who's the owner? I'll look at the contract."

Orville shrugged. "He's signing some guy up in Quebec, I think. Fight promotion. Makes him go where the work is, just like me. Nobody cares about paperwork."

I didn't want to press Orville for more. It might make the conversation too memorable. Sledge City was enemy territory; I'd sensed that the instant I'd crossed the threshold.

But I was very curious about the gym's absent owner. If Claudette

Simms really did have a silent partner like I suspected, that made two businesses on the same road with unseen bosses.

Orville read my hesitation for reluctance.

"First workout's free. And you should see the girls who come in from downtown. Come by whenever."

"Take you up on that," I said.

Orville and I shook hands again. Hinch and Bomba were still close in conversation, their words lost in the thuds of fists and shins on heavy bags from the other fighters. Bomba cast me another malignant look. Maybe just heavyweight posturing, staring down a potential rival. Or maybe something more.

Roddy sullenly tossed his gloves and wraps into a backpack. I went outside to wait.

RODDY WAS EASY TO tail. He kept his eyes on the rain-wet pavement ten feet in front of him, as his legs trudged a path that didn't require thinking. Every hundred yards he'd hock a gob of equal parts spit and blood onto the sidewalk.

We went three blocks west and three more north. Just when I thought that the bruised welterweight was headed for the nearest light rail station, he turned and disappeared into the red-lit doorway of a tavern. The crimson light came from an old-fashioned glass lamp that hung over the entrance.

So much for following Roddy home right away. I wanted to find out where he lived, maybe toss the place later and confirm whether he'd been in Reseda with Bomba, driving the kidnap van. And see if I could find anything that would tell me the gym owner's name, or at least give me a lead on the man.

I could wait outside the bar and continue to tail Roddy when he came out.

Or I could see if he needed a drinking buddy after his tough night.

The tavern had a train motif, maybe in honor of the nearby tracks. Railroad crossing signs and faux station markers for places like Duluth and Kansas City adorned the walls. Peak hour, most of the tables occupied by small knots of working men or couples getting a start on the night's drinking.

Roddy stood at the counter. Now that the sweat from his fight had dried, his blond locks had curled into a mass of ringlets that looked oddly babyish on his short blocky frame. He shuffled his feet and tried to catch the eye of the bartender.

On an open table by the door was a dead pint, dregs of IPA at the bottom. I grabbed it and took it to the counter like I was looking for my next round.

"Hey," I said to Roddy. "You were at the gym."

He blinked at me. His left eye wasn't completely closed, but I'm sure focusing took extra effort.

"Yeah," he said, not sounding too certain.

"You gave that big guy a bad time, man," I said.

His puffed brow tightened. "You giving me shit? 'Cause I'll show you right here, motherfucker."

Roddy was giving up at least fifty pounds to me and he'd already had his bell rung once tonight. Wounded pride, maybe stirred into a base of crazy.

"I mean it," I said. "Guy that size, I thought sure he'd mash you. But you hurt him some."

He grunted. "Popped his leg. The shithead hates that, he's slow."

"What do you drink?" I said. The approaching bartender glanced at Roddy's purpling face, but kept his thoughts to himself.

"Huh. Red Ale," Roddy said.

I pointed at my empty pint. "Another for me. And give us two shots of Jack. Hey." I nudged Roddy on the shoulder. "Grab that table, man. I got this round."

He scowled but slouched off to the table I had nodded to. The bartender poured the shots. While he waited for the pints to settle, I slipped two crushed tablets of trazodone into one of the shot glasses and swirled it.

If I had any qualms about pouring alcohol and prescription sleep drugs into a guy who might be flirting with a concussion, the thought of Cyndra running from these Sledge City assholes took that hesitation and jammed it down a garbage disposal.

I joined Roddy at the table. Set the pints down and handed him the shot glass.

"Here's to violence," I said as we tossed them back.

AN HOUR LATER, I dumped Roddy's stumbling form into a cracked plastic chair outside his ground-floor apartment door, two miles from the bar. He'd made the journey in the passenger seat of my truck, not that he was likely to remember it. I sidestepped a soup can filled with cigarette butts and chew spit and unlocked his door.

No one inside. Either he lived alone or his roomies were out.

"Hey," I said, but he was already zoned. There was a Chevy key fob on the ring I'd lifted from his pocket, its half-broken plastic reinforced with black electrical tape. We'd passed a Chevy minivan coming up the block. I turned to the street and pressed the button.

A beep sounded, but not from up the street. It came from the alleyway on the closer side of the apartment block. I left Roddy slumped where he was and rounded the corner.

Halfway up the alley, a panel van sat, leaving a scant foot of space on either side of each wall. No license plate on the rear bumper. I opened the back door and climbed in.

Someone had removed the third row of seats and replaced it with a large thick plastic bin, the kind used for storing seat cushions and kids' toys on outdoor patios. The beige bin took up the entire width of the back. I popped the plastic latches. The bin was empty. It looked brandnew. Jammed between the bin's plastic side and the interior wall of the van was a roll of duct tape, a few bottles of water, and a bag of t-shirt rags. They might as well have put it all in a sack labeled *Kidnap Kit*.

No need to search Roddy's home to verify that he was one of Cyndra's would-be kidnappers. I wished that Bomba had knocked out a few more of the fucker's teeth before the fight was over.

Back at the apartment, I yanked the unconscious welterweight more or less vertical and walked him inside. My place off Broadway wasn't much fancier, but at least every surface in my home didn't look coated in grease. I let Roddy go and he fell facedown onto his frayed bedsheets. He was snoring in less than a minute.

I wanted to jam Roddy into his plastic cage and drive the kidnap van into the Sound. But during our hour at the tavern, I'd played the starry-eyed MMA fan and got Roddy mumbling about Sledge City's stable of pro fighters. He admitted, grimacing, that Dickson Hinch was king shit around the gym, a real badass. Roddy's dance partner Bomba had a few serious bouts on his record. But more recently, Bomba was edging into promotion. Right-hand man to the chief himself, Sledge City's owner and Hinch's manager.

"Oh yeah," I had said, playing up the whiskey shots. "Orville tol' me about him. What's his name?"

Roddy rocked his stoned head from side to side. The traz was kicking in. "Fekkete. Fuck it, Fekkete. Thas what I say."

"You met him?"

"Hired me himself. Ta-mas." His lip had curled like he was about to spit another gob on the table. "Not fucking Tom for him. No way. Tamas."

"Hired you at the gym?"

The head rocking turned into a loose shake. It wouldn't be long before his skull bounced on the table. "For drivin'. Hires me, then he goes out of town, fuckin' weeks. I don't hear a damn thing. Then suddenly he's got us running around fucking everywhere. Believe that shit?"

I did. I tapped his glass, and he obediently drank. "Running where?"

Roddy's eyes blinked. Maybe remembering that he shouldn't be talking about that with strangers. Or trying to recall if he was talking at all.

"Don' matter. Suddenly it's hurry up, 'cause now he's coming back like we've been pissing ourselves waitin'. Yeah?"

I believed that, too. Enough that I would let Roddy keep the ability to walk. At least until he could arrange an introduction for me with boss man Tamas Fekkete.

FIFTEEN

THE REPORTER CALVIN LORENZO was either nocturnal or a very early riser. He had sent me a reply at four in the morning. It simply said *Call me today* with a phone number attached.

He picked up on the second ring. "Yeah?"

"Mr. Lorenzo? I'm calling about Gar Slattery."

"Right, right. Hang on." I heard a sharp clunk and then my phone beeped. Lorenzo was changing the call to a video chat. I put my finger over the phone's lens and pressed Accept.

Lorenzo appeared on the screen. Too close and overexposed to the lens, so that the deep lines of his face stood out like a rough sketch—gloomy, elderly, eyes squinting through reading glasses and lips pursed from decades of sucking on either cigarettes or lemons. Then he leaned back and the face became a real face, but my first impression stuck.

"Can you see me?" he said, the speaker adding to his natural rasp. "Nothing on my end. Say somethin'."

"My camera's broken," I said.

"Yep. And you didn't mention your name, either. That broken, too?"

"Zack."

"Okay, Zack." He shrugged, like he was used to people playing games with him. "I might have to ask you to repeat what you say if I can't see your lips move. My hearing isn't worth a damn. What's your interest in Gareth Slattery?"

I decided to serve Lorenzo a thin slice of the truth. "A friend of mine just got out of Lancaster. He knew Gar Slattery inside. Slattery's due to be released soon. If he comes around, I want to know if I can expect trouble."

"Huh." Lorenzo's eyes narrowed in thought. "Gar's getting out? I'd half forgotten he was inside. I only retired eight years ago, but you lose touch fast. How much did your friend tell you about that scumbag?"

"Not enough."

"So you tracked me down. That's diligent." He waved a hand, as if to say, *What the hell.* "Your mentioning Gar brought back a whole garbage barge full of memories. If you saw my articles, then you already know the Slatterys made their money moving narcotics, right?"

"Slatterys?" I said, stressing the plural.

"Oh yeah. Gareth had a twin brother, Joseph. Gar and Joe Slattery. L.A.'s answer to the Krays. You know who they were? Never mind." Before I even started to answer. "Gar and Joe and their kid sister April took over the West Coast pipeline on heroin, back about twenty-five years or so. They weren't importers, you understand. They were transport. From the border, all the way up to Canada. Only white guys to control that since Mickey Cohen. Don't suppose you know who he was either."

I knew. Cohen had served time on McNeil Island. So had my grandfather, decades later.

"So they were smugglers," I said. I had to repeat it before Lorenzo heard me right.

"Smugglers, enforcers. Gar and Joe were scary as shit. That's not secondhand color. I saw Gar myself once, when I was working the court rotation. He was being released on bail from one of his abundant charges, and I swear his reputation alone parted the crowd like water for Moses. He had that feel. Evil."

"Mr. Lorenzo—" I started.

"You might think that's not objective, not *journalism,* but I'll tell you that I knew evil when I saw it. His brother Joe was cut from the same rancid cloth. Joe was the sly one, people said; he and April did all the thinking. Not that it helped them."

"What happened?"

"Joe pissed off somebody or other, and one of their company trucks showed up in Long Beach with a lot of Joe's blood decorating the dashboard. His body is probably still dressed in chains somewhere at the bottom of the harbor."

"They don't know who killed him?"

"Who killed him, you said? My money would be on Gar himself. Maybe even April. Volatile mothers, all of the Slatterys. Gar was probably the worst, but we're talking about a few degrees on a hot day. He didn't last long after Joe got his. I think April was the one who kept the boys focused on profits instead of mayhem. Six months after Joe died, maybe less, Gar put four bullets in some mule's head and the prosecutor made it stick."

Something was tickling at me, and I waited for Lorenzo to take a breath. Maybe I'd been wrong about the cigarettes; his lung power seemed fine.

"Baby sister April," I said. "She skipped town?"

"Ye-ah," Lorenzo said, drawing it out. "Right after Joe. You didn't get that from reading my stuff."

"Give me a minute."

I dug up the KING-TV article with the picture of Claudette Simms, saved the image, and sent it to Lorenzo's email.

"Is that April Slattery?" I said.

His expression told me everything I needed. Claudette and April were the same woman.

"Good God," he said. "Looky there. Where'd you get this?"

"If I tell you, are you going to follow up on it?"

Lorenzo shrugged noncommittally. "I'm retired."

Addy had accused me of being evasive. I was getting a taste of that medicine. And I suspected that Lorenzo was wily enough not to need my help in chasing down the source of that *P-I* photo, now that he had the scent.

"Give me a week before you start fishing," I said. "April left Los Angeles twenty years ago. One more week won't make a difference."

"And in return?" Lorenzo said.

"I'll tell you where April wound up, and what's been keeping her busy the last few years. But I need something else."

He grunted. "'Course you do."

"Gar Slattery's release date. I don't want to be surprised."

"You do not," Lorenzo confirmed. "I dunno how much of what you've told me is bullshit, Mr. Zack. I don't really give a hang. That's one of the many pleasures of being out of the game. But the Slatterys were animals. Cunning, maybe, but still sub-fricking-human. There were whispers about the brothers, after Joe died, when the law was deciding what combination of charges would make the best case against Gar. Bad rumors. Like torturing competitors to death, just for kicks. Both of them beating the living hell out of women. Raping them. I wouldn't ever want to meet a Slattery outside its cage."

"I'll remember that."

"Talk to you in a week. Keep your guard up."

With that cheery thought, Lorenzo ended the call.

April Slattery had fled L.A. right after her brother Joe had died. She eventually settled in Seattle as Claudette Simms, and built herself a new little racket with Tamas Fekkete filling in for her absent brothers. April as the brains, Fekkete as the muscle, bringing his Sledge City gym goons from next door into Pacific Pearl as truck drivers.

Those pieces fit together cleanly enough. But I still didn't know why April had been hoarding gold in the safe. Had she been setting up a big drug deal? Or waiting for brother Gar to be released from prison?

I considered the gold from another angle. Had Fekkete known April was stockpiling kilobars? If he had caught her embezzling, that could explain her murder. He'd been out of town for the past few weeks, if I could trust Roddy's stoned ramblings. Maybe Fekkete was her killer, and he'd fled after doing the deed.

Or Fekkete was worried he would be the next to die. The hunters had moved awfully damned fast after April was out of the picture.

I liked that theory better. The hunters had some grudge against April and Fekkete, and after her death they had set the trap at the safe, trying to lure him back to Seattle. Maybe April and Fekkete had reneged on a drug deal. Maybe they had stolen the gold from the hunters in the first place.

Find the hunters, and I might be able to save Mick O'Hasson. Find Fekkete, and try to figure out how to keep his goons from going after Cyndra again. I couldn't stash the kid at Addy's forever.

SIXTEEN

JIMMY CORCORAN AND I pulled up in front of a small airplane hangar at the far edge of Scobee Field. The face of the hangar was shaped like a semicircle, its curved roof of corrugated steel sloping down to form walls at the sides. A large mud pit had formed along the base of each wall, where yesterday's rain had flowed down the pitted steel grooves to melt into the earth.

"She ain't here," Corcoran said, rolling down the window on his antique BMW.

"We're early." Over an hour early. I was hoping to get this errand done as soon as I could, so that we could get our plans in motion. The faster we moved, the better chance O'Hasson might still be alive to make the effort worth something.

As if he had been reading my mind, Corcoran shifted to look at me from the driver's seat.

"So your idea is to trick the assholes into showing themselves, and follow them back to where they're keeping Mick, yeah?"

I nodded.

"Without getting grabbed yourself. Or worse."

"Or losing them. We're only going to get one shot. That's why I need a better way to follow their car than just tailing them."

"Like that's a problem for me," Corcoran scoffed. "Look here." He reached into his pocket and pulled out a rubberized disk about the size of a thick half-dollar. The disk had paper covering one side.

"Peel this off, slap it onto a bumper, and you're done," he said. "It'll send GPS coordinates right to you." He plucked my phone from my chest pocket without asking, plugged a flash drive into the base with an adapter, and began installing his homemade app.

"That's all?" It wasn't much different than the location service I'd used to find Cyndra at the pharmacy. "What's the range?"

"Effectively unlimited. But the battery, that's the thing. It's small. Enough juice to send a signal two, maybe three times. Then it's toast."

"So I have to cross my fingers and hope they don't stop for dinner."

"You said quick and easy. This is quick and easy. You want to follow them across the fucking country, that's something different."

"It'll work."

"Don't fall all over yourself with gratitude."

"Here she comes," I said, opening my door.

I was assuming that the little red Fiat convertible zooming toward us down the dirt road belonged to Elana Coll. It looked like the kind of car the leggy brunette would drive. Quick, and a little flashy.

I'd called Elana for two reasons. The first was because I needed a car, which was why Corcoran and I were here. The second was because I had been hoping to rope her uncle Willard into helping Hollis and Corcoran and me in my plan to find O'Hasson. I could use the extra man. Plus, Willard was roughly the size of the hangar door. His size and strength could come in handy if things got rough.

Willard was back east for the summer, Elana had said, but she could help me with the car. She'd directed me to Scobee Field and told me to meet her at ten in the morning.

Not just her, I realized as the Fiat came to a stop, and Elana and her passenger stepped out.

She'd brought Luce.

The sight of my ex had always stopped my breath. In the past, that had been a very natural reaction to Luce's looks, and our chemistry. Now it felt more like a sucker punch to the solar plexus.

She looked just as surprised to see me. And just as uncertain about what to do next.

"You're early," Elana said to me. Maybe she meant it to be apologetic.

"Luce," I said.

"How are you, Van?"

I nodded an okay. We both turned to look pointedly at Elana. She waved a frantic hand at our unspoken accusation.

"This isn't a setup. I swear," Elana said. "I was going to check to make sure Willard had the pink slips with the cars. Then drop Luce off before coming back to meet you, Van."

Corcoran chuckled, a burbling sound like a drain suddenly voiding a hairball.

"Open up," I said.

Elana took the out and hurried to unlock the hangar door. Corcoran loped after her, still amused. Luce and I were left alone.

"She's telling the truth," Luce said.

"I know."

"We went out late last night, and I wound up crashing at her place. She didn't even mention you were the person she was meeting later."

Luce looked good. She always looked good, even when she was just in her work uniform of black jeans and a white button-down with her hair forced into a ponytail. This morning she was downright radiant. Sky blue tank top and skirt. Shoulders tan from the summer, accentuating her blonde tresses. That was new. She'd been getting outside. As the owner and taskmaster of her own bar, the Luce I knew rarely worked less than twelve hours a day, seven days a week.

The Luce I'd known, I reminded myself. People changed.

"How's the job?" I said.

"Insane." She smiled. "Tourist season. I hired someone to manage it part-time."

"Suits you."

"How about you? Elana said you were working for the competition."

Teasing me. Bully Betty's dive and Luce's bar, the Morgen, were in different neighborhoods, with different crowds.

"While I work on the house, yeah," I said. "Framing's about done."

"I know," Luce said. She tucked a lock of hair behind her ear. "I drove past the other day. Just to see."

Luce had been there when the house had burned down. A bad night during a bad time. Close to the end, for us.

Wait. She came to see the house? Or to see me?

Corcoran and Elana yanked at the low handles and the hangar door swung up with a rumbling shudder. Inside, a dozen cars and SUVs of various makes were parked bumper-to-bumper and door-to-door. All of them had come off the production line within the last few years. Nothing rare. Nothing garish.

"So you're getting a car?" Luce said, her smile slipping a notch. "Is the Dodge finally dead?"

I shook my head. "Still rolling."

"Ah."

A whole lot of weight in one two-letter word. If I needed a car from Big Will Willard, and it wasn't for personal use, then it would be for work. Willard's kind of work, and Dono's. My playing hopscotch over and around aspects of that life had been why Luce had broken things off with me.

I could explain that this wasn't exactly what Luce thought. That I had good reasons—even altruistic reasons—for wanting a car with a clean history.

But any explanation would just dig that hole deeper. If I wanted a car like a regular citizen, what the hell was I doing here?

Luce made the choice for both of us, and turned away to stride back to Elana's Fiat. Leaving us to our business.

"I like this one," Corcoran said, whacking the hood of an Odyssey minivan. "No cop looks twice at a mom-mobile."

"Do you have the registrations?" I said to Elana. She unlocked a cabinet on the hanger wall and handed me a zippered folder. Inside, the registration cards were in plastic sleeves, as crisp as if each card had been ironed. Probably free of any fingerprints, too. That was Willard for you.

I looked through the names and addresses. A woman in an apartment house. A man with a home in the wealthy Sand Point enclave. No good.

"All of the addresses are real," Elana said. "The names are fake. The cars will pass a trooper check."

"What's this one?" I showed her the card, which read *Hoskins Livery*.

"It's a real business. Here." She pointed to a glossy black Lincoln Navigator with tinted windows.

I had been looking for a car that belonged to an address that would be easy to stake out. I hadn't considered using a car registered to a business.

"Perfect," I said. "I'll have it back to you in a couple of days."

"Take your time," Elana said. "I'm booked solid for the next few days getting ready for the Con."

"What con?" I asked, misunderstanding.

Elana laughed. "EverCon. God, you live in your own world, don't you? Haven't you seen the signs on every lamppost?"

I had, now that she mentioned it. Big green-and-white banners, with a lightning bolt *E*. Some huge fantasy and comic convention in the main downtown center. Traffic would be crappy the next few days.

"I didn't know you were into cosplay," I said.

"Every geek god in the state will be there," Elana said. "Some of those guys were worth seven figures before they were out of high school."

And a long lean girl with flashing green eyes could make friends easy. Elana wasn't a hustler, but higher social circles provided bigger opportunities. Some of those entrepreneurs, especially foreigners looking to avoid taxes and tariffs, dealt almost exclusively in cash.

"We finished here?" Corcoran said. "I got shit to do."

Elana handed me the keys to the Navigator and I backed it out of the hangar. Corcoran pulled the door down and Elana locked it. Luce was still sitting in the Fiat, apparently busy on her phone. Corcoran came over and leaned against the fender of the Navigator, picking at his teeth.

As Elana drove off, Luce finally glanced up. She didn't wave. Just looked at me, until the car turned away.

"You fucked that up real good, huh?" Corcoran said.

"Shove it, Jimmy," I said. He grinned and walked back to his car, delighted to have scored a point.

SEVENTEEN

JUNIPER ADAIR ARRIVED AT the parking lot of the Safeway on 15th driving an aged hatchback the color of a dirty snowball. A big step down from her pristine Viridian truck. She parked. I let her wait, while I watched the morning rush of traffic and pedestrians around the store for a few minutes before crossing the street to join her.

I got into the passenger seat. Her brown uniform was crisp with starch, and so was the woman herself by that point.

"I could have sent these to you," she said, repeating her complaint from our phone call half an hour earlier. "I'm supposed to be out on a repair visit right now."

I didn't say anything. We both knew she was just venting steam. And that she would bend. She fumed for another second before pulling her laptop out of its carry sleeve and firing it up. Its screen brightened into a series of images captured by Juniper's hidden camera at Pacific Pearl.

The images Juniper had shown me two nights previously had been selected and enhanced by her, to better reveal the faces of anyone who visited the freight company. These images were different. Raw material.

One picture, every few seconds, so that the series told a story. A vehicle crosses the yard, a man in a green hooded sweatshirt gets out of the vehicle, walks out of frame and presumably around the building. Then the man returns and drives away. The timestamp said he had arrived at just after six in the morning.

I already knew that. The vehicle was a glossy black Lincoln Navigator. And the man was me.

"He doesn't show his face in any of these," Juniper said.

Very true. But the license plate of the Navigator was as clear as if I held it in my hands.

"Send them to your boss," I said, "like normal."

"That's it? We could have done this in sixty seconds over the phone."

"Maybe next time."

"Now that you know I'll cooperate, is that it?"

"You're late for your repair call." I got out of her car.

She yelled over the revving engine, "If I get fired, I can't help anybody."

Juniper was right, I had wanted to see if she would cooperate. She had called me as soon as she had checked the camera feed and found my visit to the Pacific Pearl yard. One point for her reluctant loyalty. And she hadn't led the hunters to me at the first opportunity. That was two. If the pictures of the Navigator managed to lure the hunters out of the shadows, that would make a hat trick. I'd let Juniper off the hook.

WITHIN THE HOUR, HOLLIS and Corcoran and I had taken our positions around Hoskins Livery. A small fleet of polished black vehicles dominated the lot, with a cramped office and a carport for washing and waxing forced into the far corner. The limousine company anchored the end of a retail business block off Southcenter Boulevard, practically in the shadow of the gleaming Tukwila rail station, the commuter train's first stop after leaving the airport.

The busy boulevard made our stakeout easier than most. Corcoran had invaded an outside seat at a coffeehouse across the four-lane road from the Hoskins lot, bleeding their WiFi for his VoIP connection to keep a string of complaints coming our way. For a misanthrope, Jimmy C. sure liked to talk to people. Hollis and I sat in the front of his Cadillac, parked in the strip mall lot next door with a broken line of ornamental hedges separating us from the Hoskins office.

The plan was simple. Wait for the hunters to show, slap one of Corcoran's trackers on their car, and follow it. I was sure that the hunters would be easy to make. Hoskins Livery wasn't swamped with customers, and anyone who came drifting around—scanning the property for any sight of a Lincoln Navigator or a big guy wearing a green hooded sweatshirt—might as well be wearing a strobe light on their head.

"Shouldn't we be doing this in shifts?" Corcoran said, his voice coming from the speaker on my phone, which lay on the dashboard.

"They'll show," I said. "They've got resources. Once they trace the license on the Navigator, they'll come straight here."

Hollis pressed the Mute button with a thick finger. "Not that I want to take Jimmy's side, but are you as confident as you sound, lad?"

"No."

He shrugged. "Okay then. Just so we're on the same page."

"The hunters have been looking for their man—Tamas Fekkete, I suspect—for weeks. They've spent huge money and even more energy. That kind of waiting can drive anyone batshit. If O'Hasson is still alive, it's because he's a possible means to an end. *End* being the key word. These guys want their hunt to be done."

"So they'll stampede toward any new clue that might make that happen."

I nodded. "We'll wait."

As if he'd heard, Corcoran's voice came through the speaker again. "You're paying me back for all these fucking coffees I gotta buy, sitting here."

I won the debate in the end. They came less than ninety minutes later, and they came in force.

Two Impala sedans, one red and one champagne silver, cruised in tandem past the strip mall. The red one turned into the Hoskins Livery lot. The other made a U-turn around the median and drifted to a stop on the opposite side of the boulevard, a stone's throw from Jimmy C.

The driver and a passenger got out of the red Impala. Both were of a type. White and mid-thirties, clean-shaven and short haircuts, white dress shirts with razor-sharp collars. Suit jackets too, despite the warm day. The driver went into the Hoskins office. His passenger stood by the sedan, looking around the lot. He reflexively adjusted something under his navy blazer. A belt holster, sure as shit.

"Dammit," I said. Hollis didn't reply, but his body slumped a little in my peripheral vision.

I had bet on the hunters making a reconnaissance run. One or two of them at most, posing as potential customers. It would have been simple to use the surrounding vehicles as cover and stick the tracker in place while they were in the office or searching the lot for the Navigator.

That goal was shot. Too many eyes on the scene, too much situational awareness for me to count on luck.

"What now?" Hollis said. "I could wander over, try to get that bastard away from the car. Give you an opening."

I shook my head. I had a fallback scheme in mind. But it was a hell of a lot riskier, enough that I was desperately seeking an alternative.

If we lost the hunters here, they might be gone for good. I couldn't use the same stunt with Juniper's camera again. Dammit times two.

Divide and conquer. That was the only way.

I tapped the phone speaker. "Jimmy."

"Yeah, I see 'em."

"I need you to stall the silver car. Enough to give me at least five minutes' head start on them after you see me drive by."

"How the hell should I do that?"

"Your car's parked in front of them."

It was. Corcoran's little blue BMW had the metered spot directly in front of the Impala.

"Fuck you," Corcoran said, realizing what I was suggesting. "Fuck. *You*. I'm not."

"Up to you, Jimmy," Hollis said. He muted again, and lowered the volume against the torrent of expletives that followed.

I was already climbing into the backseat. "Meet me at the airport."

Hollis glanced toward the ultramodern glass wall and cantilevered roof of the Tukwila station, shining in the distance. "You're catching the train?"

"I sure as hell hope so."

I cracked the back door of the Caddy and slipped out. The Navigator was parked behind the strip mall. Before I started it, I put on the green sweatshirt and pulled the hood up over my head, like it had been when I'd visited Pacific Pearl. Not comfortable, but memorable. I drove the Lincoln around the far side, down a short alley, and around the block. Taking my time. As I rounded the corner and approached the Hoskins Livery lot, the driver of the red Impala strode out of the office. He and the passenger spotted me. I drifted past.

Across the boulevard, I heard a basso thump of collision. Any fainter noise, like headlights breaking, was lost to the rumble of the Navigator's engine as I pressed the accelerator. I tilted the sideview mirror to catch sight of Corcoran, already out of his car, gesticulating wildly at the hunters in the silver Impala. Their car had made it a scant foot away from the curb before Corcoran's BMW had backed into it. It looked like the bumpers might be locked.

A sure bet that Jimmy was telling everyone in sight that the accident was their fault. Probably demanding cash payment on the spot. A smile crept onto my face, which lasted until the red car showed in my rearview.

They were hanging back. Not wanting to spook me. Professionals. They had lucked out, spotting their quarry, and now they aimed to follow me to where they could either stuff me in a bag or figure out who I was.

I turned in to the train station. It was a weekday, the commuter lot crowded, but I nabbed a spot near the station corner as a Volkswagen pulled out. I left the Navigator and strolled toward the entrance as if I didn't have a care in the world.

The passenger from the Impala would already be on foot, following. The driver would have to find a place to leave the car. They would both have to buy passes for the train, unless by weird chance they already carried transit cards. All of that gave me a window of a minute or two.

I jogged up the escalator to the ticketing level, and turned immediately toward the set of stairs that led to the airport-bound side of the station.

The light rail track was built high in this part of the city, to pass over the highways and hills.

At the top, a dozen people were scattered along the fifty yards of platform, waiting for the next train. Bright yellow letters on the reader board shone SEATAC 7 MIN. Plenty of time. No cops or transit personnel in sight.

I didn't hesitate, just jumped down off the platform and walked briskly across the two sets of tracks to the opposite side. One woman said, "Hey," but nobody gave much notice. I climbed up onto the north-bound platform.

Within thirty seconds, the passenger from the red Impala emerged on the airport side, at the top of the stairs I'd just climbed. He quickly scanned his platform, and when he didn't spot me immediately, he began to move at a casual pace down his length of the station, checking if I was standing behind a ticket kiosk or otherwise out of view. He hadn't thought to look across the tracks yet.

I leaned against a post and pretended to be engrossed in my phone as I examined him. Horn-rimmed glasses and prematurely gray hair. His navy blue suit was decent but not fancy. Middle management. In his left hand, he carried a soft black leather attaché case with a zippered top. Large enough for a few legal briefs. Or a tranquilizer pistol.

The elevator doors opened and the Impala's driver stepped out. He was leaner and taller than his partner. A long movie-hero-handsome face, topped with hair the curled reddish-brown of dried tobacco leaves. A gray suit with better tailoring than his partner's. The man with horn-rimmed glasses reversed direction to meet him.

They would be in contact with the other two hunters in the silver Impala. But would all four men converge here to trap me? They wouldn't want to watch helplessly as I stepped off the train at the next station into a taxi, and be stranded without a way to follow. The silver car would hurry to try to intercept me, once they figured out where I was headed. I had to keep them guessing.

The driver with the Hollywood face spotted me across the tracks. His partner looked, too, then glanced away just as quickly.

They couldn't jump the rails like I had. Too obvious. They thought I was clueless, and wanted to keep it that way. Horn Rims broke off to catch the elevator. He would go back down and cross to my side of the station while his partner kept watch. Good. To keep me covered, their team had split from four men to two, and from two to one.

Now the hard part. I pretended to answer my phone, and walked slowly along the platform, toward the elevator on my side. I mimed a conversation, drifting through the waiting passengers. Less than a minute until the next northbound train would arrive. An electric hum began, low at first, growing in volume and pitch as the train neared. Some commuters were already leaning forward, looking up the track in anticipation.

Mr. Hollywood had a fast decision to make. Hurry across the tracks and join me when I boarded the train, maybe blowing his cover, or rely on Horn Rims to make it to my platform on time. He stayed put. My last sight of him before the white caterpillar shape of the train came hissing into the station was him drawing his phone from his pocket. Probably calling the backup team in the silver Impala, telling them I was about to head north. The waiting people pressed forward as the train whispered to a stop.

The elevator doors opened to reveal Horn Rims, black attaché still clutched in his hand. He stepped out. I walked past him, onto the glass and steel elevator, still engaged in my imaginary call. He did an abrupt about-face to join me. I pressed the button for the ground floor.

"Wrong side," Horn Rims explained as if I had reacted to his unexpected move. We were alone in the elevator, the arriving passengers not exiting the train yet. The doors closed.

I spun and hit him. A swinging hook from all the way down at my hip, catching him just below the heart. His head banged the glass wall as he coughed and sagged. His hand moved in the direction of his attaché. I was there first. The grip of the pistol waited right at the zippered mouth, and the weapon was in my hand and out of the case in less than a second.

A long barrel with a wide caliber, like a paintball toy. I pointed it at his thigh and pulled the trigger. The gun made a snapping sound and the red feathers of a dart blossomed instantly against his navy blue trouser leg.

Sleep tight, asshole.

He wilted into the corner and down to the floor. I yanked the dart out and stuffed the gun into my hoodie as the doors opened on the ticketing level. No one was waiting for the elevator, and if anyone nearby had happened to spot our quick scuffle through the glare off the windows, they kept their peace as I left Horn Rims where he lay.

The airport train was arriving. I raced up the stairs once more and bounded onto the platform, practically strolling into the first car. In my peripheral vision, I caught a flash of gray as Hollywood dashed to join me on the train. The warning lights flashed and the doors slid shut.

Our trip to SeaTac took less than five minutes. Enough time for me to call Hollis and make sure he knew where to meet me.

Hollywood stood at the far end of the car. Alone, now. Very alert. He wasn't positive I was on to him, but he had to suspect it. He was also on his phone. Maybe trying to reach his unconscious partner. Maybe telling the silver Impala they were heading the wrong direction.

They would be too late. Unlike at other stations, a car couldn't drive right up to the airport stop. Hollywood's backup would have to leave the Impala and make their way on foot, and I'd have dealt with their square-jawed leader long before they arrived.

Most of the train passengers had roller bags or backpacks. Hollywood and I were the exceptions. The doors opened and we joined the crowd trudging along the lengthy outdoor passageway to the parking structure and the bridges leading to the terminal. He hung back, using the people for cover. It was a long walk. Exposed. If I glanced back even once, he would see it. I had to trust that Hollywood felt just as vulnerable, not knowing his surroundings and separated from his team. That he would be cautious enough to keep his distance.

As we reached the end of the passage and entered the parking structure, I broke from the pack and strode toward the first bank of elevators and the adjacent stairwell. In the glass covering an airport map display,

I caught a blurry reflection of my pursuer's tall form in his gray suit, angling to follow me like a wolf distracted from the flock.

I made plenty of noise walking up two concrete flights and banging the heavy fireproof door open to Floor 6. No one stood waiting for the elevators. Midweek and midday; if the airport was ever quiet, it was now. I hugged the wall at the side of the stairwell door and waited.

Hollywood followed my path up the stairs so quietly, I wasn't sure he was still on my trail until he cracked open the door to glance out. I stomped the door, slamming it back into him, and stepped forward to jam the dart gun hard into his jugular as he caught himself on the iron railing.

"At this range," I said, "the tranquilizer will be the least of your problems."

His handsome face hardened with anger, but he got the message. I spun him around and frisked him, finding a little Beretta Nano in a belt holster, and taking his phone. He had cash and ID and credit cards in a money clip. I walked up a few stairs, out of reach, and put the trank gun away. It was empty anyway, not that he knew that.

"Ellis Boule," I said, looking at his cards. From Los Angeles. Big surprise. "Who's your boss, Boule?"

"Call the cops if you want," Boule said. He was recovering his poise rapidly. Maybe imagining himself on a movie screen. "I'm licensed to carry that Beretta."

"You're not self-employed. Nobody who can afford to buy an office building would carry a brass money clip."

His eyes flickered. "I don't know what you're talking about."

"You don't have to. It's above your pay grade. Your boss, on the other hand, will want to talk to me."

People walked past the stairwell door toward the elevators, roller bags thumping and grinding over the cement. If Boule wanted to escape, now was his chance, while there were witnesses around.

"Talk about what?" he said.

"We can hurt each other or help each other. But we can't stay status quo. You want to call him, or shall I?"

He stared darkly at me for a moment, and then put out his hand. I handed him the phone.

"On speaker," I said. He hit two buttons and we waited as the phone rang.

"Ellis?" A woman's voice. A nice contralto.

"I'm here with the man we talked about this morning," Boule said to her. "He wants to talk."

She waited. The fact that Boule and his men had failed to capture me must have been self-evident.

"Sorry about your new building," I said. "Hope it was insured."

"Who are you?"

"Someone willing to deal, if you are. With the safe gone, I think you're low on options."

"What is it you imagine I want?"

"You tell me. Maybe I can help you get it. Or him."

There was a long pause. I figured she had already made up her mind. Now she was considering method of engagement.

"In person," she said.

"In public."

"Very well. Where?"

"I'll call you when we get there," I said, and hung up.

I put Boule's Beretta in my pocket and handed him his cards and cash.

"You pay for the taxi," I said.

EIGHTEEN

I HAD PICKED VOLUNTEER PARK as the meeting location. It was close to home, and about as open an expanse as anywhere in the city. Two roads into the park for cars, endless options for escape routes on foot. Both roads led to the park's central attraction, the broad art deco Asian Art Museum. Sitting across the road from the museum, Boule and I could see everyone who came and went. Nannies with their charges, out for a sunny afternoon, disorganized clumps of schoolchildren playing around the camel statues, and the occasional cop.

Boule hadn't said a word during the taxi ride here. Not bothering to fume about his turn of luck, I sensed. Just considering options. If those plans had included his men regrouping for another run at me, I hoped Boule had enough understanding of tactics to realize that the very public park with its security cameras was not a viable field of engagement.

I had been to the museum on field trips when I was around Cyndra O'Hasson's age. Davey Tolan and I had once frisbeed a crushed aluminum pop can back and forth through the center of the big black donut-shaped piece of art that Boule and I now sat near, until Ms. Travers had caught us. Davey and I probably earned detention for that bit of civic disrespect; I didn't recall.

A Mercedes S-Class in lunar blue eased to a stop in front of the museum. A woman opened her own door and rose smoothly out of the backseat. She would be tall, even without the heels. She would be curvaceous, even without the tailored black jacket and skirt accentuating her shape. Big black sunglasses. A lot of chestnut hair swept back from a high forehead. Elegant. Almost arrogant, as she strode across the slate flagstones toward us. Boule stood and watched her, as if hypnotized.

I didn't miss the second sedan, twenty yards behind. It wasn't another Impala, but I was pretty sure the driver had been one of the hunters in the fender-bender with Corcoran.

The woman stopped in front of us. She didn't acknowledge Boule.

"Are you a police officer?" she said to me. Her voice was even better in person.

I grinned. "You worried about entrapment?"

"I'm wondering if this will be a pointless conversation. You don't look like you can provide much help."

"At least I can hold on to my weapon."

Boule's square-jawed face reddened. "He claims to have been at the building. That night."

The woman raised an eyebrow. "The night of what? Just so we're clear."

I stood. Boule edged forward, just a little. Unarmed, but willing to defend his boss nonetheless. I pulled up my shirt to show I wasn't wearing a wire.

"The night Mickey O'Hasson and I broke into the safe in the Pacific Pearl office to take four million in gold, and he torched the place before you grabbed him," I said. "That clear enough?"

She nodded, slowly.

"So before we start really talking terms, I want to know if O'Hasson is still alive."

"He is."

"I'll take your word for that," I said. "For now. Later, I'll want proof. Did you get the gold out before the building went up?" I said.

"Which do you care about?" she said. "The gold, or your friend?"

"Both," I said.

"That's a large amount."

"You were right on top of us at the safe," I said. "You must want somebody involved with Pacific Pearl bad enough to make these guys sit and wait for weeks for that alarm to go off."

The driver of the sedan had grown impatient. He was out of the car and crossing toward us rapidly, suit jacket flapping. I looked at him pointedly.

"Marshall," the woman said. The man stopped. "Wait there." She nodded to the stone bench a few yards away. Close enough to hear the conversation without intruding.

Marshall scowled at me as he took a seat. He was bull-necked and heavy-shouldered, so that he gave more impression of width than height.

The woman took off her sunglasses to consider me. Younger than her formal bearing implied, maybe no more than thirty-five or -six. Spectacular bone structure, like a Roman statue. Her eyes were such a light blue they were nearly translucent. Cold, but beautiful.

"You could be working with them," she said. "The ones at Pacific Pearl."

"O'Hasson can confirm that I'm not. He enlisted me for the safe-cracking."

"He can also tell us your name."

I nodded. Cards-on-the-table time. "It's Shaw."

"You've learned a lot about Pacific Pearl, Shaw. Do you believe you can find who I'm looking for?"

"I found you."

"Yes, you did."

She was silent for a moment, and then took a photograph printed on cardstock from her tailored suit jacket. She handed it to me. The photograph was still warm from her body.

It was a candid shot of a man coming out of a doorway. He was very thin, dressed for winter weather in a topcoat and scarf, holding a fur hat in his hand. His face was in three-quarter view, and I could see that his aquiline nose and black goatee made almost a crescent moon shape. He looked like Lenin, or at least a scarecrow crafted to resemble Lenin.

"Tell me his first name," I said.

She understood. "Tamas."

"Fekkete."

"Yes. Have you seen him?" the woman said. Something new in her voice. Hope. Almost fervent.

"No," I said.

"Find him, bring him to me, and I'll give you O'Hasson."

"We don't need his help," Boule said.

"Find him," she said again, "by the end of this week."

"For O'Hasson, and the gold," I said.

"Half." Marshall spoke up from the bench. "Your share would have been half."

"And O'Hasson gets the other half. For pain and suffering." I looked at the woman. "Agreed?"

She nodded. Marshall stood up and started back toward the sedan, a disgusted look on his face. Boule stayed by the woman's side.

She paused in mid-turn. "You haven't asked why I want Fekkete."

"Or who you are. Or where you came from," I said. "So long as we're on the same side."

"Until Saturday," she said, her low voice nearly a whisper. "After that, I'll make other arrangements."

Arrangements that wouldn't require O'Hasson's continued health. But might include eliminating loose ends like me. The woman could threaten as well as seduce.

Beautiful, but cold.

NINETEEN

YOU TOLD THE WOMAN your *name?*" Hollis said.

We were sitting in the aft cabin of his boat, waiting for Corcoran to return from taking his wounded BMW into the body shop. Sitting, not relaxing. Since the stakeout to confront the hunters—huntress, maybe, I should call the woman in charge—none of us had felt restful.

"No choice," I said. "I had to tell her I knew about the safe, and the gold. If I didn't give her my name up front, she might have tortured it out of O'Hasson."

"And he's kept your involvement a secret so far, hasn't he? Tough little bugger."

O'Hasson was. Tough enough to last another few days, I hoped.

"You're risking a hell of a lot," Hollis said. "Four million or no. Mick O'Hasson's life or no."

"If I could see a different play, I'd make it."

Hollis frowned. We watched the Sound beyond the breakwater, where the growing wind was shoving and slicing the waves into chop. Gray clouds moved with purpose over the far horizon. We were in for another rain, unless the gale pushed the threatening front right on past us.

"Hell with it," Hollis said finally. "The deal's made. We'll see it through, if you can find this fellow she's so obsessed with."

"Obsessed is the right word. The woman didn't mention the Slatterys, and neither did I. She didn't look much like a drug lord, either, but I'm guessing that April Slattery and Fekkete double-crossed her on some deal. This vendetta against Fekkete is personal to her."

"Just to her."

"Her men might be fed up," I agreed. All except Boule. He seemed ready to follow his mistress to the gates of Hades.

"Well, I've checked what I can on Fekkete. He's a phantom. No criminal record or even a credit history. It's a fake name, no question about it. Fekkete may be the whip hand at the gym, but on paper the place is owned by a club fighter named Bernardo. He's probably the fellow you call Bomba."

I nodded. "If Fekkete were easy to find, the woman wouldn't need me. They don't know about his connection to Sledge City. That's my edge." Roddy had drunkenly declared that he expected Fekkete back in Seattle. I'd have to try to pick up his trail at the gym tonight.

Hollis got up and went into the cabin without saying more. His usual buoyant mood was tamped down by doubts he wasn't voicing. Either because he couldn't offer me any alternative plans, or because he thought I didn't share his uncertainty. He was wrong about that.

I called Calvin Lorenzo, then remembered that he preferred video. Hollis was right. To hell with it. If a murderous drug dealer knew my name, it wouldn't matter if an old reporter saw my face. I switched the call to video. Three rings and Lorenzo's shopworn face appeared on the screen, the background a blur as he sat down.

"Got your phone fixed, huh?" he said.

"Seems to be."

"I figured your ears were burning. I was gonna call you later about Gar Slattery."

"His release date?"

"It'll be next week. Maybe early, maybe late, depending on the paperwork. But the gears of correctional bureaucracy are already turning."

Next week. And the woman had given me three days to deliver Fekkete. Were the two related? Did she already know Gar was getting out?

"If he's coming to Seattle, you won't have long to wait," Lorenzo said, as if reading my thoughts.

I smiled. Maybe my first honest smile of the day. "How'd you know I was in Seattle?"

"Come on. Give me some credit."

"Don't suppose we can count on Gar honoring the terms of his parole and staying in California."

"I wouldn't suppose that either. So why'd you call?"

I held up the picture of Tamas Fekkete. "You know this guy?"

"Put it closer." He squinted at the camera, his crow's-feet reaching out to touch thin hair on either temple.

"Maybe forty-five years old," I said. "I got a name for him, but it's fake."

"Ah, yeah," Lorenzo said. "He lost his hair. If I hadn't been making withdrawals from my memory bank lately about the Slatterys and that whole mob, I wouldn't have placed him."

"Who is he?"

"Szabo or Szano or something like that. Hungarian national, I think. He was lined up as a key witness in a RICO case, about the time I was retiring. The *Times* covered the case. Karl Ekby's trial."

Ekby. The heavy hitter that Gar Slattery had mentioned to O'Hasson, when Slattery was spinning his tales of hoarded gold.

"Karl Ekby was in business with the Slatterys?" I said over the sound of Lorenzo typing.

"It would have been the other way round. Ekby was big-time. The Slatterys were tough, but if they shipped dope for Karl, there's no question who was in charge."

"And the witness, Szabo? Where did he fit?"

"He was mid-level. Importing the junk for Ekby, most likely. Everything old becomes new again, given enough time. 'Cept people. Heart disease got to Ekby before the jury could."

"So the witness never testified."

"Nope. They probably deported him, but since you're showing me a picture of the jackass, he obviously found his way back to the land of opportunity."

So Szabo had become Fekkete, running the same kind of operation in Seattle. Alongside April Slattery, who had also given herself a new name for the old game.

Then another idea came to me. Like the sun catching a solitary and invisible strand of a spider's web, revealing it to the world.

"Who would have inherited from Ekby?" I said.

"His drug biz? Or his money?"

"Both."

"Nature abhors a power vacuum. I expect the Mexican gangs tore each other apart over the territory. They've got most everything now that the Armenians don't." Lorenzo made a humming sound. "Ekby's personal dough, I'm not sure about. He was rich as Croesus. If the Feds couldn't seize his assets, they probably went to family like usual."

"Ekby's family include a daughter, or a niece? Mid-thirties now, brown over blue, body like Scarlett Johansson's taller sister?"

Lorenzo's chin rose. "You are full o' surprises, aren't you? Hang on." The next minute was filled with a torrent of typing.

"My turn for show and tell," he said.

The phone beeped and I opened up his message to find a link. It took me to a watermarked Getty Images photograph on their website. The photo was captioned *Ingrid Ekby, daughter of Karl Ekby, enters Superior Court of Los Angeles on the day of her father's indictment by federal prosecutors.* It showed the twenty-something woman in full stride, with long chestnut hair and wearing a white silk blouse and gray skirt tailored to tastefully show off a curved figure. Even at her younger age, her sunglasses couldn't hide her haughty brand of beauty.

"Thought I remembered old Karl's family showing up at court," Lorenzo said. "I'm still on the subscriber list to a few of the photo services. The freelancers made damn sure to take a lot of pictures of Ingrid. I woulda said she was built like Brigitte Bardot, but that's my generation."

"That's her," I said.

"For a week or two you saw photos of Lady Ingrid from every local outlet. I figured she would try to make something out of her minor celebrity, hit reality shows or some shit, but after Karl died she stayed out of the spotlight."

She had other goals. Personal enough that she might be willing to give up four million in found gold just for a chance to realize them.

"So you saw Ingrid? In Seattle?" Lorenzo said.

"Yeah. And that's all I can tell you. You promised me a week."

"I promised you a week before I started looking into April Slattery. Which is nearly up."

"So start the same clock on Ingrid. One week from today."

"Goddamn it."

"The full story from me. One or two names excluded," I said.

"You can't take the Fifth unless you're actually in court, wiseass." Lorenzo sighed. "Fine. A week. Then I want everything, or I'll call in every favor I've got, just to scratch this itch."

"Thanks," I said.

"Keep me in the loop." He hung up.

It had occurred to me, if not Lorenzo, that I would have to be alive at the end of the week to tell him anything.

I had a name for the huntress now, and a motive. Ingrid Ekby was after the man who'd aimed to testify against her dear daddy. And she was apparently willing to kill April Slattery just to get to him. The woman carried one monster of a grudge, considering Karl's case never made it to trial.

Ingrid's intent confirmed what I already suspected. I'd made a deal for O'Hasson's life that would require, almost certainly, leading another man to his death. Fekkete was a drug dealer and probably worse. He'd sent men to kidnap Cyndra, and he might try for her again given the chance. He would have likely killed O'Hasson, once the little burglar had retrieved the gold from the safe.

None of that made the idea sit well with me. A lesser evil was still an evil.

And evil or not, I'd see it through.

I had to get Fekkete and the gold in the same place. Ingrid Ekby wanted Fekkete. Fekkete wanted his gold back from Ingrid. Each one was bait for the other.

All I needed was a few minutes of Fekkete's time, alone. To convince him that I was the only man in the world who could make O'Hasson and his gold magically reappear.

I was sure I could do that. I had an ace in the hole.

I had Cyndra.

TWENTY

SLEDGE CITY ATTRACTED A surprisingly large crowd from nearby SODO—south of downtown—businesses after working hours. The serious fighters orbited the ring and the heavy bags lining the far wall, while the main workout area was given over to regular citizens, male and female. I blended in with the citizens.

No sign of Fekkete, but the rest of the gym's inner circle was present and accounted for. Dickson Hinch held court from the ring. He was a sight. He shadow-boxed as he talked, gliding fluidly from side to side, flicking out his hands. His torso was as pale and hairless as a snake's belly. When his shoulder and lat muscles flexed against his lean frame, they added to the image, spreading like the hood of a cobra.

I couldn't hear most of what the fighters were saying over the constant noise in the gym—the staccato thuds of gloves, metronome clicks of jump ropes—but it was clear that the topic was Hinch's last opponent. Memorializing his victory like it was the Battle of Carthage.

The doors of the back wall were open to allow a slight breeze to come through, pushing the heat around. It didn't help. I was taking it easy, paying more attention to the Sledge City goons than my own workout. A round of jumping rope. A round of ab work. Still, the sweat dripped off my nose and chin. Two women broke away from the punching bags and began removing their gloves, as a shredded trainer called that the conditioning class would be starting on the mats today.

A double-end bag close to the fighters opened up. I walked over and began tapping it with jabs, making the bag swing on its bungee cords as I listened.

"—fuckin' pussy gave up after that," Hinch was saying. "Got nothin'."

Bomba sat on the ring's edge, while the guy with the topknot hairdo I'd seen on my first visit armored up, strapping on padded chest and headgear.

"We waiting on Orville?" said Hinch.

"Hell no. You ready, Wex?" Bomba said to Topknot.

Wex nodded and stepped up onto the canvas, putting in his mouthpiece as he climbed through the ropes. He seemed less eager than usual. The fact that he outweighed Hinch by thirty pounds and had a reach advantage must not have offered much comfort. Hinch bounced on his toes.

"Dickson. Don' fuck him up," Bomba said. "He's got to fight at the quarry."

Hinch nodded impatiently, eyes already fixed on the kid.

Bomba said go. Hinch launched into a flurry of punches and kicks, all killer, no filler. Wex covered up but still took two clean shots to the head and a lot of glancing blows. Every time he dared to throw out a hand, Hinch countered it and battered him. I was quickly seeing why the light heavyweight was ranked eighth and looking to go higher. The kid tried a kick. Hinch grabbed his leg and took him to the ground with a bang that made everyone who wasn't already watching the bout turn and look.

"Time," said Bomba. It wasn't; barely ninety seconds had elapsed, but Wex wasn't going to last the round. Bomba was bright enough to call a halt before Hinch punched the kid's head through the canvas.

Hinch sprang up and swatted the turnbuckle—a high-five to himself.

I finished out the round jabbing the bag while Wex picked himself up.

Roddy came in off the street. His bruises from Bomba's fists had turned the shade of dying violets. He saw me and nodded a curt acknowledgment. He remembered meeting me last night, if not much else. I was a little surprised to see him. After the beating and the booze and the traz I'd slipped him, he must have woken late and with a headache that could floor an elk.

Orville tapped me on the shoulder with one of the punching mitts covering his hands. "You made it." When he smiled, his cauliflower ears poked out another half-inch.

"Gotta sweat somewhere."

"Well, I still got these on," he said. "Let's throw a little."

I found a set of training gloves on the communal rack and we moved out to the open area of the floor. Orville started slow, holding up the mitts for one-two and one-two-three combinations. He stuck out a paw and I slipped it and came back with a hook, and he nodded, picking up the pace, adding uppercuts and pressing me to move and escape. It felt good. I'd let regular exercise slide while building the house. We ignored the electronic clang that ended the round. Orville was strong and surprisingly quick, his pro reflexes not completely gone. He met each blow with equal force, testing. I put mustard on the punches until the mitts boomed like cannon fire.

"Nice," he said when he finally stepped back, stretching the word out to two syllables. "You got speed. Beat me to the mark a few times there."

A string of curses from Hinch interrupted. Loud enough for me to hear over my labored breathing.

"Hey," called Orville. "We got actual humans here."

Hinch and Bomba scowled but bent their heads back to the argument they had been having with Roddy.

I wiped sweat off my face with my shirt and nodded toward the fighters. "Roddy in trouble again?"

"Who knows. He's been telling anybody who'll listen that he's ready for more responsibility. Lie down with dogs, ya know?"

But before I could ask, Roddy came sidling over from the ring.

"Hey," he said to me. "Jack."

"Zack."

"You're looking for work, yeah? I remember that much."

I shrugged. "If I can't get construction, I'll take what comes."

"You want to fight? We need a sub."

On a chair against the wall, Wex had an icepack taped to his shoulder and another pressed to his neck. His topknot had come unraveled during his minute in the ring and the strands hung down the side of his face like wilted vines.

"You want me to spar Hinch?" I said.

Roddy laughed. "Fuck, no. We got matches coming up tomorrow night. Our heavyweight dropped out."

Orville cleared his throat and spat into a plastic trash can. "You ought to clear new guys with Mr. F. You know that."

"I will, I will. Fekkete will be there, he can see Zack for himself."

And vice versa. I'd finally get a glimpse of the man himself.

"These ain't the kind of fights with a ref, I'm guessing," I said.

"Naw," said Orville. Scar tissue gave weight to his eyelids, made it tough to read his thoughts.

"That a problem?" Roddy said.

"What's it pay?" I asked.

"Five hunnerd. More if you win."

"How much more?"

"A grand. Total."

I pretended to think about it. "Lemme talk to the boss. Fekkete."

Roddy scowled. "Why?"

"'Cause I want to be sure I'm gonna get paid."

"Fuck you, Jack or Zack or whatever. You don't trust me?"

"Don't know you." I shrugged, taking off my training gloves.

"Wait, wait. Look, you come on board, I'll get you the grand on top if you win. That's fifteen."

"Your boss shows me the cash first," I said.

"Now you're talkin'. Okay, I'll get you the deets." Roddy hopped back to the ring.

Orville had been diligently ignoring us, watching the women in the conditioning class. "You know who I'll be fighting?" I said.

"I stay out of the business end."

"But you think it's a bad idea."

"Depends on how much you need money. Listen," he said, "you're a tough-looking guy. That's kinda the point. They want somebody who looks the part, who can attract a few bets."

"And lose."

"That's also kinda the point. Whoever the other heavyweight is, you can be sure Mr. Fekkete expects him to break you."

"Can I trust the guy to pay me? What's his story?" I said.

"Make sure you get your five hundred bucks up front."

I nodded and Orville lumbered off toward the equipment room. An old bear returning to the comfort of his cave.

As I packed up my gear, Roddy handed me a slip of paper with *Carzell Quarry—Hwy 2—8:00* written in crude letters.

"Tomorrow night, yeah?" he said. I nodded and he slapped me on the shoulder. Best buds, now that I was ready to jump into the lion's den.

I had no intention of fighting. If I was a last-minute sub in a money bout, they might as well have tattooed SUCKER on my forehead. But all I needed was two minutes with Fekkete. Prove to him that I could make his gold reappear, and he'd suddenly have bigger dreams than some underground blood sport.

TWENTY-ONE

I FOUND CYNDRA SITTING IN the driver's seat of Addy's Subaru, parked in the little house's nub of a driveway. The engine bucked and stalled as I approached. Cyndra leapt half a foot when I rapped on the passenger window.

"Going to breakfast?" I said.

"I'm not going anywhere," she said.

"Not unless the car's in gear," I agreed. She popped the lock and I opened the door to sit next to her, one foot still on the asphalt.

"Addy said I could." Cyndra turned the key and the car bucked violently again, straining against the emergency brake. I grabbed the gearshift and whacked it into neutral before either of us chipped a tooth.

"Said you could what?"

"Practice shifting. I've almost got it." She turned the key again and the engine screamed like it was trying to be more than four cylinders.

"Ease back," I hollered over the noise. She let the gas pedal take a break from kissing the floor, and the Subaru idled with an almost human sound of relief.

"Did she say you could practice without her?" I said. The kid had borrowed some of Addy's clothes, too; a purple beanie covering her short black hair, and a KCMU t-shirt half-hidden under her overalls.

Cyndra pressed the clutch and shifted into first, then second. "I got this down on the Ford at home. I drive that one all over. This one's stupid old."

She was angry at more than the car. "Have you eaten?"

"Yeah."

"Wanna eat again?"

"Okay."

She followed me to my truck and we drove over the hill. Cyndra nodded with approval at the Dodge. "See, automatic transmission. That's better."

"Depends how many hills you climb. Who taught you to drive?"

"Farrah's sister. She's pretty cool."

"You miss home?"

"Farrah and her family."

"Nothing else?"

"Nothing. Reseda sucks. My school sucks."

"Tachelle? Your foster family?"

"Off-the-map suck. She's got like seven of us in the house, and never knows what's going on. I mostly just go to school and hang out with Farrah. I made friends with Jenna and Jerraud when I first got there, but then they moved out. Guess I will, too, soon." Cyndra didn't sound mad about it. More that her home didn't even register as something worth any emotion.

We found counter space at the Lost Lake Café and I ordered something from the chalkboard called the *leñador especial*. Cyndra ordered a side of crispy hash browns—as crunchy as potato chips, she told the server—and stole my bacon while I rolled chorizo and eggs into flapjacks to eat them like burritos.

"I have some news," I said when I was on my third cup of coffee. "I don't want you to load too much weight on it, get too excited. But I promised I would to tell you whatever I could."

Cyndra nodded, not looking away from her fingers as she slowly tore a strip of the bacon lengthwise.

"I met a woman yesterday who told me that your dad is alive. I believe her."

"Is she one of the people who took him?"

"Yeah. She'll let him go, if she gets what she wants. I'm trying to make that happen."

"What does she want?"

"Doesn't matter."

"You mean you won't tell me."

"That's right," I said.

"I can help."

"You are helping."

"By not getting in the way." She dropped the bacon and walked stiffly out of the restaurant. I tossed bills on the counter and went after her.

"Hey," I said once I'd caught up. The kid was making a beeline south. If she planned on walking home, this was the wrong direction. "Hold up."

"Go away."

"You came all the way from L.A. You want to quit now?" Cyndra took two steps to my one, and I still had to walk fast. "Or are you going to help me fight?"

"Fight?" She stopped.

"I need information. I need some leverage."

She made a face. "That's not fighting."

"The fuck it isn't. Nothing happens without intel." A passing woman frowned at my language. "These people have your dad. I need to get in their heads, and I need Mick to know he can trust me, and you can help me do that."

Cyndra looked at me closely. Maybe I was trying to trick her. "How?"

"Start by telling me some things about you two. Stuff only your dad would know."

"So you can prove you know me?"

"Something like that."

Her blue eyes were steady. "Are you helping just because of Dad? Or do you want something else, too?"

Damn, the girl was bright. I nodded my head for her to walk with me and she did. Going toward home, this time.

"Mick is what I care about," I said. "You too. I won't lie to you, there's money in this deal. If I could ask Mick, he would say that I should forget about him and get the money for you. You agree with that?"

Cyndra shook her head angrily, without slowing her walk.

"Me either," I said. "So to hell with what Mick wants. We'll save his ass. If the money tags along, great, but he comes first. Okay?"

She didn't answer. I was asking her to trust me. If Cyndra was much like me when I was twelve, trust was a long shot.

"Okay," she said finally. "I'll help fight." And a few steps later, I caught the touch of a smile in her profile. "Screw what Dad says."

That's the spirit, kid.

Kassie threw up her hands and screamed. The tower of wood blocks crashed across the kitchen table as I fell over laughing.

"Spoon!" she finally managed to spit out. We had decided that was a lot cooler than yelling the game's name like in the TV ads.

"Six to two," I said. My wins, counting yesterday and the day before, when we met. Kassie was smart, but she got nervous and her breath got shaky and her hands followed that like a dog, as Granddad would say.

"Let's play something else," she said, with a glance at the clock. I had to be gone before her dad got home. Kassie wasn't allowed to have friends in. Kassie didn't seem to *have* any friends. She was too new to the neighborhood.

Her dad's name was Trey, I had discovered. I had also learned that they had just moved in, that the house was owned by Trey's parents, who were away until Christmas, and that— big *ah-ha* here—Trey had gotten out of jail this year. Kassie told me that in a whisper, like someone might hear us, even though we were the only ones in the house. I think she was trying to impress me. It did, just not the way she thought.

Had Trey been in the same jail as Granddad? I guessed they must have been.

Whenever Kassie went to the bathroom upstairs—we had mostly played down at the kitchen table or watched TV in their living room—I had looked around the drawers and other rooms to see if I could learn more. I wanted to look in Trey's bedroom, too, and the garage, but that hadn't been possible. Not yet.

Then we heard a car turning into the driveway. Kassie always left the window open so sound could come in.

"That's Dad!" she whispered, her face in shock. She must know the sound of the Ford's engine.

"Can I go out the back?" I said. She didn't even nod yes, just ran for the door. I grabbed my coat and followed just as fast.

Their yard was tiny. Just a wide strip of grass before a really big hedge that blocked the next yard from view. I couldn't go that way, not without a chainsaw.

"There," Kassie whispered, pointing anxiously to the other side of the house, where I saw a slim gap between the house and a chain-link fence. It would take me straight to the road. That was the good part. The bad part was that the ground was all gravel. My first step crunched so loud I was afraid Trey could hear it all the way from the driveway, over the sound of him pulling open their garage door.

After that, I walked in slow motion. It took at least three minutes to make it to the front corner. I snuck away from the house and ran across the street to where my bike was hidden in the ravine.

Damn. I'd been having fun. I really wasn't learning much, hanging around with Kassie, if I was being totally real. But it was still cool.

Granddad wasn't at home. He thought I'd been spending mornings with Davey, and Davey thought I'd been spending all of my time working with Granddad and doing chores, which was partly right. I had to get my stuff done every afternoon after seeing Kassie. So Davey got the shit end of the stick.

Maybe if I got the dishes and my room clean now, I could go over there, maybe even stay for dinner. I started in. I'd just dusted the windowsills when I heard Granddad coming in the door.

"Thought you were away," he called up the stairs.

"Davey had church," I said. It was Sunday, that sounded

right. I hoped Granddad didn't know any more than I did
about when services started.

He grunted. Granddad's usual answer to any mention of
religion. He and the priest from his neighborhood in Belfast
had once had what he'd called a violent parting of the waves,
I think.

"Can I go over there tonight instead?" I called down.

"You can," he said. I almost dropped the cleaning bucket.
"In fact, ask if you can stay through tomorrow."

I came down the stairs. Granddad was in the kitchen,
stacking the cold roast from last night onto slices of bread.

"Mayo and mustard, please," I said automatically.

"I know."

"D'you have a date?" I knew what happened on *dates*.
Once or twice I came home from Davey's or another friend's
too early the next morning, and had to meet Paula or whoever Granddad was *dating*. We all couldn't wait for those conversations to be over.

"I'll be out," he said.

I knew what that meant, too. Work.

Was the job tonight? I bumped my elbow against his
jacket hanging on the hook. Felt the weight of the Colt inside.

"I'll ask Davey," I lied.

After dark, I left my bike chained up at a church a few
streets away and ran back to hide in a group of trees by the
roundabout at the bottom of our block. Wherever Granddad might be headed tonight, I wasn't going to be able to
pedal after him this time.

I wasn't really sure *what* I could do, except watch him
leave, and hope that it would give me some idea of what he
was planning and whether it might get him in serious trouble.

Granddad left the house at half past six. He didn't get
into the Chevy, which was odd. Instead he walked down

the block in my direction, and for a bad second I thought he might know where I was. The trees and the dark made me mostly invisible, but mostly didn't mean completely.

He rounded the corner and walked halfway up the lane, where a white RV with purple stripes was parked on the wide dirt shoulder. When he reached to unlock the motorhome's door, I saw that he was wearing gloves. Not the black fur-lined gloves he wore in winter, but the lighter cotton ones he wore when he didn't want to leave fingerprints.

The RV was stolen. For sure.

Granddad wasn't inside the RV for longer than a minute. He emerged and retraced his steps back to the house.

I wanted to have a look inside the motorhome for myself. It would only take a moment, and I had my picks. Once I saw Granddad go into our house, I dashed up the street.

No houses fronted the lane, and the lock was easy, so I was only exposed for a couple of minutes. I had to take my gloves off to pick the lock, but slipped them back on before opening the door. The RV looked expensive and nearly new. Dark purple stripes on a pure white background and *American Eagle* written in big swoopy letters on the side. Kind of conspicuous for a vehicle you'd steal.

With the window shades drawn, I had to squint to make out many details. The inside looked like Hollis's boat—everything a house might have, but smaller and in one long narrow space. There was a rug on the floor and a blender and other appliances resting in the sink in the galley. It all seemed super-clean and even smelled a little of plastic and leather cleaner.

Why in the world would Granddad want a big motor-home? With purple stripes?

I was turning to leave when I heard the crunch of foot-steps coming toward the RV. Familiar footsteps.

Oh, crap. Granddad was coming. Without thinking I reached out and flicked the lock closed on the door.

Hide. I stepped quickly to the back of the RV and tried a closet. It was for linens. The upper shelves were full of stacked towels and the larger compartment at the bottom held a thick patchwork quilt. I yanked the quilt out and stepped inside as a lock clunked from the front of the motorhome. Curling into a ball, there would be just enough room to hold the quilt on top of me.

A door opened just as I tugged the last of the fabric over me. Not the side door where I'd come in. The driver's door, up front. I reached out to gently pull the closet closed.

The RV's engine started. Shit shit shit. I was going for a ride.

Cold night or not, I was sweating like a pig within five minutes, trapped under the heavy quilt with my hat and coat and gloves on. I was dying to reach out and push the closet door open, just to feel the air move. But I didn't dare.

The RV stopped. The engine turned off.

Already? We couldn't have gone more than a couple of miles. I could run back home. That would be awesome. The driver's door slammed shut, and I risked cracking the closet for a look. Not that I could see much. Just the same shadowy interior of the motorhome, with a few trees and part of a street visible through the windshield.

Wait. I knew this street. Kassie's street.

I ducked back into the closet as someone rattled the side door. A moment later, I heard it open.

"Fancy shit," said a voice. I knew it, too. The vulture man.

"Nothing but the best," said Trey, Kassie's dad.

"You'll drive," Granddad said, and a moment later the engine started again. The rumble drowned out most of what they said after that, but I did catch a curse of excitement from Trey as the RV began to move.

Despite my sweat and my terror, I was a little excited, too.

We drove for half an hour, or a little more. I could tell some of the roads wound through residential streets, with a lot of sharp turns that made the motorhome list a little to the side. Then there was a long stretch at higher speed, which must have been a freeway. The RV eventually slowed, and slowed even more with each turn, and then stopped. I could hear Granddad and the men talking urgently for a minute, and then we pulled away again, one final stretch and a long curve before the motorhome stopped, reversed for a few feet, and the engine turned off.

The men got out and the doors closed. I waited. When they didn't return right away, I dared to climb out of the linen closet and stretch. My legs felt like somebody had been punching them all over. I walked shakily to move the window shade an inch and peeked out.

We were parked next to a house. A *big* house. Like, castle big. The mansion had a curved shape and seemed to stretch on for the length of the bleachers at the high school. Through the windshield I could see a courtyard, with a damn fountain right in the middle of it. Water splashing and everything.

The RV was under a long overhang or an awning. Like a rich person's version of a carport, I guessed. That made sense, because on this side of the building was an entrance. Double doors, made of carved wood and colored glass panes for decoration. Both wide open. Granddad and the men must have gone in there.

Should I stay or should I go? I knew the song—Davey was into music—and it bounced around my head while I checked the windows. If I hid in the linen closet again, there was no telling how long I'd be stuck there. They might drive the RV to Mexico, and I'd be a mummified husk by then. Assuming I was lucky enough not to be found. If I got out of the RV, they might catch me even sooner.

Then I'd be in for it. Grounded until I was eighty years old, plus hard labor. Worse, Granddad might never trust me to work with him again.

But outside sounded a lot better than going back into the hotbox. After one more peek out the windows to make sure the coast was clear, I slowly clicked the latch on the side door and crept down the steps to exit the RV.

The cold air felt great, like diving headfirst into a lake. Sweat chilled on my forehead as I edged around the rear of the motorhome.

Only to see a second motorhome, identical to the one I'd just left. It was parked a few yards around the back corner of the mansion.

What the hell? Another RV?

I looked around the grounds. A wide lawn stretched over the expanse between the mansion and water. I wasn't sure *what* water; might be Lake Washington, might be the Sound. We'd driven a long way. In the other direction, I could see the roof of another really big house in the far distance, and a stone fence with an iron gate bordering the huge courtyard, between us and the road. As I watched, a red Ferrari zipped past.

Ah. I got it.

The mansion already owned a fancy purple-striped RV. Granddad must have boosted one to match. The sight of our vehicle from the road wouldn't be at all unusual for the neighbors, or any security patrols. Not like a moving van or a bunch of unfamiliar cars. We could park here all night.

I realized I was thinking *we* and not *they*. It wasn't my score, I knew that. Still. Pretty cool. Whatever we were stealing, it must be big to need so much cargo space.

Still no sound from inside. What were they doing in there? I tiptoed to the double doors.

Man, the place was huge. The doors led into a hall—not a foyer, a frickin' two-story hall—with a staircase on one side that was wide enough to roll a piano down it. All of the lights were on. I guess they could afford it.

An intense-looking alarm panel hung open on the wall.

I didn't recognize the brand name, something German. I *did* recognize Granddad's work on the wiring inside to reroute the circuits. He sometimes made a prep run when he had a big house job, to disable the contact pads on the house's entrances and keep them from triggering an alarm. That bought him time to grease the whole system during the actual job. Maybe that's where he had been during his nights away from our house. I felt kinda good for figuring that out.

A thump echoed from way off in the mansion, past the staircase. Time for me to vamoose. I slipped into the first room off the entry hall.

It was some sort of parlor or sitting room or whatever the heck rich people called rooms that were just for show. It had that feel, even though there wasn't a speck of dust in the air. The sofa and chairs were covered in green velvet and tapestries hung on the walls in between bookshelves with rows of identically bound books. An eight-foot green plastic Christmas tree with white lights and no ornaments glowed in the corner.

Steps were coming close. I ducked behind the velvet sofa.

A two-inch opening between the sofa and an octagonal side table let me see the entry hall. I laid my head down on the perfectly clean lavender-colored carpet for a sideways view.

Trey came through first, carrying a painting in its frame. He wore a dark blue anorak and surgical gloves. Then the vulture man, with a heavy marble something-or-other held close to his chest.

Art. They were stealing art.

The men returned quickly and made another pass, this time carrying more paintings. Granddad wasn't with them. Maybe he was checking each piece in case it had its own alarm, just in case. *Always* check, that was one of his rules. I bet these people had alarms on their dinner china.

Trey and the vulture made many trips back and forth.

Downstairs, then upstairs. Sometimes they carried blankets, and I realized that was to wrap and protect the breakable pieces in the RV. No one said a word, except when Granddad directed one of them to a room that was ready for looting. I was curious why they weren't cutting the paintings out of their heavy frames. Were the frames valuable, too? Could picture frames be famous? Soon Granddad joined the loose parade, toting more small sculptures and even something that looked like an African mask. No wonder they needed a whole RV.

I was going to be left here, I realized. There was no way I was getting back inside the RV, even if it wasn't wall-to-wall with paintings and vases and other crap. I'd have to lie right here on this stupid plush lavender carpet until they left.

Don't panic, I told myself. You're still somewhere around Seattle. You've got some money in your pocket. And you've heard of buses, right? Though I doubted if Metro made many stops in a neighborhood where they drove Ferraris.

Finally Trey came down the stairs, two at a time. "That's it."

Granddad came to the entryway, carrying his toolbox, and the vulture man returned from his last trip to the RV. I slowly withdrew my head out of sight. It made me jumpy, all of them standing just twenty feet away in the quiet house. I tried to breathe extra soft.

"You got the library?" Granddad said.

"Which one? These bitches got like three." Trey laughed and the vulture echoed him. Granddad didn't. "Yeah, sure. It's done."

"Let's go."

"Quincey, you drive," said Trey. "I'm gonna close up." Quincey must be the vulture.

"Leave the alarm be," Granddad said, in the same kind of tone he used with me when he suspected I might screw up, "but lock the doors."

I heard Granddad and Quincey return to the motor-home. Trey busied himself with shutting one of the double doors. I inched my head back where I could see him. He was moving slower than he had to, I thought, throwing the bolts at the top and bottom and checking them multiple times.

Then he glanced over his shoulder, stepped back inside the entry hall, and removed something from his pocket. He placed it inside the guts of the rewired alarm panel. Then he exited and shut the door. The deadbolt clicked home. I heard the RV's engine rev, and then retreat, until I couldn't hear it anymore.

Just me, and a whole damn mansion. If it was a movie, I'd go nuts and make a roller coaster on the stairs and throw a kegger for all of my friends. But the huge place was empty and eerie, and I wanted the hell away from it.

After I raided their fridge. I was starving, among other things. I edged my way down the hallway, which had a floor so polished I could see the angels painted on the ceiling, twenty feet up. Found a bathroom and used the toilet, whistling with relief.

The kitchen—one of the kitchens, I guessed—was farther along the hall. All of the really perishable stuff was missing from the fridge, and I wondered if the owners were out of town for the holidays. Out of the whole country, probably. I bet they went to places like Switzerland and Italy. I wanted to travel outside the U.S. someday. Our trips to Canada didn't count. Too close.

Some provolone cheese and Doritos and a bottle of limonata soda fit into the pockets of my coat, and I scurried back to the double doors.

My hand froze at the doorknob. What was it that Trey had put behind the alarm panel? I swung the panel open to look.

A screwdriver. With a hard red plastic handle and a dented blunt end.

I knew that screwdriver. I'd made those dents myself,

years ago, driving a picture nail when I didn't have a hammer. Granddad and I kept it in the kitchen drawer at home.

Trey must have taken it from our house. Why?

Fingerprints. The screwdriver would have Granddad's prints all over it. Holy shit.

There was a box of Kleenex in the parlor, I grabbed a handful and fished the screwdriver out, very carefully, and wrapped it and buttoned it in my coat pocket.

I had the cell phone Granddad had given me. But he was with Trey right now. Should I call?

No. He wasn't in danger, I figured. Not if Trey was setting him up to get arrested for this burglary. I had to get home and tell him in person. Fast.

I jammed out the door and used my picks to relock the deadbolt, and then ran across the courtyard to the gate. It was made to keep out cars, not kids, and I climbed over it without even trying.

If somebody came along now, I was busted. A kid walking around in a neighborhood like this would be suspicious at any time of day. After two in the morning, the cops would probably be called before anyone bothered to ask me what I thought I was doing. I started jogging.

Half a mile down the long curved road, I came to a big brick-and-capstone sign that marked the entrance to the neighborhood. MEDINA COVE, it read in letters illuminated from behind.

Medina was on the Eastside. Hell, I was all the way across the *lake*.

At least I had all night to find my way home.

TWENTY-TWO

CARZELL ROCK QUARRY WAS about half an hour's drive northeast of Seattle, off the first winding stretch of Highway 2 that began at I-5 and extended all the way to the far side of Michigan. There was no chance of my missing the quarry. Stadium floodlights created a false sunrise on the eastern side of the access road, just as day surrendered to evening in the rest of the sky.

I'd mulled over whether Roddy's sudden invitation could be a setup. None of the Sledge City crew had reason to believe I was anything other than friendly Zack, unemployed construction worker. But it would be an easy job to bury me under a mountain of gravel at a remote mine. They could entomb me in my own truck if they wanted. I had brought Dono's Smith & Wesson nine-millimeter as insurance. One of his few possessions that hadn't burned up with the house.

As I neared the quarry, the knot of tension between my shoulder blades eased up a twist. Upwards of two hundred people, mostly men, milled around parked cars and trucks and herds of motorcycles. I could make out bright red coolers and smoke from hibachis.

A damned tailgate party.

The cars crowded into a single paved lot. That was where any adherence to order stopped. Everyone had parked at what seemed like deliberately different angles to one another, the better to sit on hoods and roofs while they mingled.

Past the parking lot, in increasing size, mounds of topsoil and sand made small hills below the looming quarry walls. The largest mounds topped thirty feet, twice that in diameter. One pile of chip rock had a Caterpillar loader halfway up its impossibly steep incline, waiting for the working week and its driver.

As I climbed out of the truck, I could smell the tang of raw earth and dust that never settled, even on a windless day. Faint shouts and cheers echoed off the piles of earth. Either the bouts had already begun, or someone had become impatient and started their own sport. It looked like that kind of crowd.

Not that I was planning to stick around and watch. I'd find Fekkete and persuade him I was his new best friend, if he wanted to see the gold again. If bracing him at the quarry proved impossible, there was another way. I'd brought one of Corcoran's little tracker disks in my bag. Slap one on Fekkete's ride, and follow him to where he and I could have a quiet chat.

A group of bikers clustered around their softail cruisers. One woman in the group looked me up and down as I passed. I returned the attention. She was little north of thirty, her brown hair still askew from the helmet, wearing black cycle boots and leathers with the top half unzipped and hanging at her waist, revealing a gold tank top with no support underneath. None required.

"Are you fighting? I think all the guys are over by the machines." She pointed vaguely toward the quarry walls.

"Thanks," I said, starting in that direction.

"Should I bet on you?" Her lazy gaze as she took a drag said she might not be talking about money.

I grinned. "Good odds."

She exhaled a long coil of sativa smoke. "Come back around if it's not exciting enough."

Motorcycle mamas weren't usually my thing, I mused while walking away. But then, it had been a while for me. Since Luce, in fact, and that meant over four months. Time flew when you were broke. And committing felonies to fill your nights. I wound through wide dirt roads left between the artificial foothills, following the shouts of excitement.

The quarry walls defined an immense ninety-degree wedge, as though a skyscraper had once rested within the huge hollow and been suddenly removed. Scars left by the digging machines formed broad horizontal stripes. Despite the man-made precision of the space, it felt primeval, as the sundered mountain dwarfed even the sky above.

At the base of a massive pile of black basalt, traffic detour barricades had been arranged into a crude square, twenty feet on each side. Two razor-thin Latino kids stood in the center, firing long jabs at each other. Hand wraps only, no gloves. The incandescent lamps overhead heightened the intensity of colors—red wraps, brown skin, yellow paint. In contrast, every hint of gray blended into a uniform deep black. It gave the fighting ring a surreal brightness, like the painter had forgotten to blend his oils into less garish shades.

Across the ring, dump trucks and other heavy equipment lined the nearest quarry wall. The closest was a yellow crushing machine, a massive snail shape with squat body and long sloped conveyor-belt neck. Men stood in close knots of conversation, ignoring the fight. Money was the real action.

I spied Bomba first, a head taller than his buddies. Then Roddy's blond locks bobbing up and down as he nodded to whatever the big man was saying.

"Hey, Zack." Roddy shifted the focus of his nods to me. "I was gettin' worried."

"Eight o'clock," I said.

"I know, I know. I just stress out. You got your gear?"

"You got my money?"

"After the fight," said Bomba, "same as for every other asshole here."

"'Cept I'm not the same. I'm a last-minute sub and I don't know you for shit."

Bomba's face crushed itself into a furious grimace. He stepped forward. I stayed put. We were nose-to-chin, with Bomba on the high side. It would have been more intimidating if his gut hadn't touched me first.

"Take it up with your boss," I said. "Where is he?"

Roddy waved his hands frantically. "Save it for the fight, man. Jesus. The money will be here."

"Right," I said.

"Fekkete is driving in with the Canadian dudes. He might be here already. Just chill." Roddy dashed off in the direction of the ring. Bomba kept up the hard stare.

"You try running out on us," he said, "and I got a dozen guys'll stomp you into a smear."

"A dozen might keep you safe." I followed Roddy.

Bomba may have been all talk, but my problem could be real. The parking lot was two hundred yards from the bowl of the quarry. No way for me to slip away unnoticed. And too far to see if my truck had become hemmed in with other vehicles in the crazy quilt of tailgaters.

One of the skinny bantamweights was being picked up off the pebbled ground to howls of encouragement and a few jeers. As I moved along the edge of the crowd, two more fighters were shepherded to the ring. One of them was Wex from the gym. Orville accompanied him, sweat towels slung over his shoulder and a battered orange tackle box of cutman supplies clutched to his chest. He noticed me and raised a hand in greeting. He looked a little disappointed to see me.

I'd lost Roddy. He could be anywhere in the growing mob, or in the labyrinth of earthen mounds around us. I retraced my steps, guessing that if Fekkete was arriving, he'd be closer to the vehicles.

Then I saw him. Or more accurately, I noticed the man whose substantial width completely blocked both Fekkete and Roddy from view. Then the beast moved aside, and I spotted Fekkete himself. Bald head, black goatee, and dressed for the event in a red tracksuit with black piping.

No mystery who the heavyweight ringer was. The two of them were like a child's picture book of comparisons, Thin and Fat. Fekkete's waist might have been the same circumference as one of the other man's thighs. His shoulder muscles looked like partly melted cannon-balls extending from out of his black tank top. He swung his huge arms, loosening up.

I walked toward them. Fekkete glanced up as I approached.

"Mr. F.?" Roddy said, as breathless as if he'd been running since he left me. "This is Zack, your sub for heavyweight."

Fekkete's pale eyes fixed on mine. He nodded curtly. He wore a gem-encrusted silver ring on almost every one of his fingers, like an especially vain caliph.

"The deal was five Cs," I said. "In advance."

He looked me over with a promoter's professional eye. Or maybe a zookeeper's, given the size of his charge. His blank stare packed far more pressure than Bomba could manage in a month of glowers.

"In advance," Fekkete said. He had a strong accent; Lorenzo had thought him Hungarian.

"Or I can offer you a better deal. If we can talk in private."

"What sort of deal?"

"A golden opportunity."

His pale eyes flashed. He slowly pulled a roll of bills from his track-suit pocket with one silver-ringed hand and held it between his finger-tips, but his mind was elsewhere.

There was a roar from the direction of the ring. We all turned to see Bomba giving us a thumbs-up. Wex had apparently redeemed himself after Hinch's thrashing earlier in the week.

Fekkete glanced at Roddy. "Are all of the first odds in?"

"Yes, sir."

"You are certain?"

Roddy shuffled. "I got the bets. No problem."

Fekkete grunted and peeled bills off the roll. "We start now."

"Not until we talk."

He gave a dismissive wave. Dammit. I wasn't going to get even ten seconds to tempt Fekkete with the gold. And it was rapidly looking like that was the least of my troubles.

"I gotta warm up," I said.

"You have so long as Roddy takes to sell you. Get in the fucking ring." He handed me the bills and walked away.

I was surrounded. Even without Bomba, who was lurking nearby, and Hinch, who was smirking at me from his vantage point on top of the excavation machine, the crowd had started pressing around the three open sides of the ring in anticipation. Short of climbing over the huge pile of basalt gravel behind the barricade square, there wasn't a direction I could go that wasn't already a dozen people thick.

"All right! We got six-to-one on our boy here. Six-to-one against Rénald. Bet American!" Roddy shouted to the crowd. "That's serious money to the winner."

Any serious money would have closed early, betting on their ringer at stronger numbers. Not many watching at ringside were willing to take a flyer on me.

Their fighter Rénald grinned and threw punches at the air. Most of the hair on his head was devoted to a Wild Bill mustache. He wore brown corduroy trousers instead of jeans. More give in the waist for that big hard-looking gut. He had more than a hundred pounds on me, and a lot less of it was blubber than I would have wanted. Rénald spun easily on his toes, all that weight flowing into each punch until it ended with a wicked snap, electric with power.

Ah, crap. I was going to die.

TWENTY-THREE

No time to wrap my hands, or to think about anything else but the few minutes ahead. I tossed my bag onto the mound of basalt behind the ring, stripped off my shirt, and started inhaling huge lungfuls. Maybe I could surprise the big fucker with speed. Or maybe I could convince him to stand in front of a dump truck while I ran him over.

"Okay, we got another hunnerd," Roddy called. "Anybody else? No? Come on, Rénald ain't that tough."

The crowd laughed. My slaughter was going to be slapstick.

The warm night would help. I was feeling about as loose as I would get. I didn't shadow-box. I just took in air and thought very hard about how I might survive.

My inaction had attracted attention. "You better fucking fight," Bomba said from his spot at ringside.

I ducked under the orange barricade. On the opposite side, spectators moved the barrier aside to let big Rénald enter. His grin was still in place, with a touch of anticipation.

"Going . . . going . . . all right, let's do this!" Roddy shouted.

Rénald wasted no time. He closed fast, looking to jam me into a corner. I sidestepped once, then again, as he pursued. I shot out a jab and narrowly ducked his answering hook. Two more jabs and a lot of backpedaling. Rénald shrugged off my punches and kept his smile. Shit. Little stings weren't going to keep him off me.

He lunged, trying to grapple. I spun to the side and he grabbed my left arm with one hand. I put everything I had into a straight right, and it gave me an instant to tear myself from his grip. The crowd jeered. I feinted a kick and it didn't fool him.

Rénald didn't seem frustrated. He just inexorably closed the distance between us, confident that I'd run out of room, or luck. I was wary of kicking, knowing he was looking to catch my leg. If he got me on the ground, his weight advantage would make the rest of my night short and extremely painful. I was so busy making sure he didn't trap me against the barricade that he nearly took my head off with a leaping left hand.

I kicked at his knee and threw a combination, not even trying for damage, just giving him distractions. He batted the punches away and lunged again. This time I was ready. I slipped to my right and stuck a knuckle-twisting jab into his throat, and stomped hard on his foot. His arm swatted me aside, almost lifting me off the ground, but he hissed with pain.

No grin anymore. Rénald came after me even faster, limping but very game. The crowd howled.

"Kill the fucker," Bomba said. Behind him, Hinch was laughing.

The mound of basalt was behind me. I feinted and ducked, desperate for any edge. Rénald threw two fast hooks. The second connected and numbed my forearm. Any more of those and I wouldn't be able to make a fist. He reached again. I slipped and turned, peppering jabs, feinting the same stomp, and when he drew his foot back in haste I spun and kicked his leg. The steel toe of my workboot speared him in the thigh muscle and he yelled.

Rénald punched me in the neck. I knew it was going to hit an instant before it did, but the knowledge did me no good. My head went as bright as the stadium lights. I was fairly sure I was moving my feet, but not certain. Where was he? The crowd howled. There. Coming straight at me, hands grasping.

I threw. Rénald barreled into me, as one of my desperate punches took him full in the nose. His rushing weight knocked me backward, toppling the barricade, and we both fell. Not as far as we should have. Rénald landed half on top of me. Something like claws tore into my back. We were on the mound of black basalt. I thrashed, almost swimming sideways in the sharp rocks. He had a grip on my arm. I punched and missed. I couldn't get my feet under me. Neither could Rénald. The gravel rolled and shifted beneath us. Rénald clutched at me, for balance as much as leverage, and I grabbed his small fingers and bent them back until they snapped. He roared and tried to tackle me, to crush me into the rocks, but his lunge had no force on the unstable mound. Every small movement brought more rocks tumbling from the steep hill above us, in a slow steady avalanche. Rénald was up to his knees in it. I stayed nearly flat. Choking clouds of slate-colored dust enveloped us. The crowd sounded like a high wind, coming in straight off the plains and picking up speed.

Rénald's meaty fist nailed my breastbone. The pain banished the last of the brain fog. I let the current of rolling basalt carry me lower, where I could roll onto solid ground. I tottered to my feet. Rénald was still struggling against the tide. I picked my way through the rocks, into his blind spot.

He knew what was coming, but couldn't free his great weight from the consuming rocks to turn and meet me. I made it quick. One punch to his neck, in just about the same spot where he'd nearly put my lights out, and a whipping hook to his jaw that shuddered from my fist all the way down to my toes. Rénald wasn't fully unconscious. He wasn't even horizontal, with the gravel up to his thighs holding him erect. But he was done.

I staggered back over the toppled barricade and into the ring. The crowd was yelling, but I was more aware of the black sweat rolling down my face. I took in huge chest-popping gulps of air and looked for Fekkete. His baleful gaze met mine.

I hope I cost you a fucking mint, asshole.

Spectators were in the ring now, slapping me on the shoulder, raising my hand, helping Rénald get free. My bag. I turned to look at the hill of gravel. The bag was gone. Buried, with my keys and Corcoran's tracker. It hadn't been far from where Rénald and I had finished our fight. I pulled away from the fans and lurched back to the mound.

It cost me four minutes of digging and two raw hands to find where the bag had come to rest. At some point during our frantic scrambling Rénald or I had stepped on it. My phone was cracked. The tracker was completely destroyed, the rubber case torn and the interior works clogged with smoky grit.

Fekkete was gone. I saw Roddy in the ring, trying to make his way toward Rénald through the knots of spectators drunkenly reenacting the fight. I shoved men aside and grabbed him.

"Where's Fekkete?" I said, lifting Roddy up onto his toes.

"Whoa, I got your money. Easy." He fumbled for the bills and pressed them into my hand. "Good fight, okay?"

"What's he drive?"

"Huh?"

I slapped him. Shook him alert. "Fekkete. What's his car?"

"Fuck, man." He flinched as my hand went up again. "It's a Boxster! You know, a Porsh. A yellow one. Don't hit me."

I dropped Roddy and ran toward the parking lot. Fekkete might still be around. Maybe I could get the tracker onto his car, somehow, in the traffic jam getting out of here. Already a field of taillights glowed, as cars negotiated their slow trickle onto the access road.

Less than one day left in my deadline to deliver Fekkete. If I missed him here, the hunters might decide they had little use for me, or O'Hasson.

There. A glimpse of yellow in the waiting line, three hundred yards farther on. Close to the road. A car near it turned, headlights sweeping across, and I caught sight of the low-slung lines of the Porsche.

Too far to run. By the time I made it to the truck and worked my way through the traffic jam, Fekkete would be miles away.

"You were a good bet." The motorcycle mama, cruising up from behind me on her Harley. "Still no shirt, too. Even better."

"I'll give you five hundred bucks to borrow your hog for ten minutes," I said.

She looked nearly as stunned as Roddy had when I'd slapped him. "You what?"

"I have to catch that car. He owes me." I held out the bills.

"Shit, cowboy." She grinned at me, half-stoned and all sultry, before swinging a leg off her bike. "I'll trust you for it."

I slung my bag over my shoulder and climbed on. The softail surprised me, leaping forward at the first touch of the throttle. I was out of practice, and even when I'd drifted around the Southeast on bikes with other soldiers, I'd been used to smaller machines. I got the Harley steady and gunned it, racing down into and along the dry ditch, passing the cars in a burst of speed. Behind me, I heard the biker chick whoop encouragement.

The Porsche was gone. He'd already made it to the access road. Which way had he turned? I pulled right and let the engine do the work as the front tire caught the earth, and the Harley carved a path up the berm that separated the quarry from the road. Dirt and rocks flew in a spray behind the rear wheel. I nearly lost control as the bike shuddered up the uneven slope. Then I was over the crest and onto the grassy earth on the other side. There. A yellow streak flashed past. Fekkete had turned right, away from the steady stream headed for the freeway. The Harley hit pavement and I flew after him.

I caught a break. A four-way stop, half a mile farther on, where Fekkete had to wait for a sixteen-wheel tractor to lumber its slow way through the intersection. I took the bag off my shoulder as I pulled up alongside, and brought out the Smith & Wesson to aim it at his front tire.

"Let's have that talk," I said.

Fekkete tried to hit the gas, and stalled the engine. Not his night.

"YOU ARE SURE THAT you can make O'Hasson do what you want?" Fekkete said, five minutes later. We had pulled over to the side, Fekkete still in his Boxster, me still on the Harley. "He will bring the gold? All of it?"

"Minus whatever he may have spent to hire muscle. That's why I need you," I said. "You protect me. I make sure he cooperates."

His eyes narrowed. "But you don't hire men yourself."

"I don't have money. That cash I made off you tonight is everything I got. And who would believe a crazy story about gold, except you?" I slapped the roof of the Porsche, friendly-like. "So I tried to steal from Pacific Pearl. My mistake. Water under the damn bridge. This way, you get half of it back, and I get my hands on O'Hasson. The little shit almost burned me alive."

I didn't need Fekkete's cold stare to tell me he was already thinking about how to dispose of both me and O'Hasson once the gold was in sight.

"How will you do it?" he said.

In answer, I showed him a picture on the cracked screen of my phone. Cyndra O'Hasson, sitting expressionless with a copy of last Sunday's *Seattle Times* in her lap. The chair she was sitting in was from Addy's dining table.

"His child," said Fekkete.

"You missed her in Reseda. I didn't."

He nodded. Almost happily. Maybe I really could make O'Hasson jump on command.

"I know a place to bring him," he said.

"So do I. I'll tell you where when it's time for you to move. Not before." I put the phone away. "No tricks."

He nodded and gave me a chilly smile. Of course I would say that. Neither of us believed it for a moment, but it was nice to observe the formalities.

TWENTY-FOUR

MY CONVERSATION WITH FEKKETE had taken longer than ten minutes, so the biker chick and I had renegotiated. With my cut lip and sore jaw, kissing and other activities proved a little challenging, but we made do.

When I woke up in the master bedroom of her surprisingly suburban house in Bothell, the rising sun had already brightened the triangular windows at the peak of the bedroom's vaulted ceiling. The woman lay on her side next to me, brunette hair touching my shoulder. Sky. That was the name she had said. I didn't know if that was her real name or a road name. Everybody I met lately was hiding an extra identity in their back pocket.

This would be a tough day. I knew these hours, the countdown before a mission. When we would plan and review and check our gear a dozen times. Some of the tasks were essential. Some of them just served to keep us calm. A lot of the time, we couldn't tell the difference.

I'd been present at a few hostage exchanges in the Rangers. Negotiating swaps between tribal leaders, mostly. They weren't the sort of assignments that earned anybody a medal. We were lucky if we went home thinking we got the slightly better part of a bad deal. The key was keeping everyone focused on what they had to lose if things went sour.

Once or twice, though, we got to bring our own people home. Captured soldiers, or men cut off from their unit and stuck hip-deep in hostile country. Those days made sense. Those days were on the side of righteousness. O'Hasson needed a day like that.

I rose and left Sky a gentlemanly note before leaving silently. Less bruised than I would have expected after my fight with Rénald. Maybe sex had beneficial properties beyond the obvious ones.

I called Hollis and Corcoran on my way into the city and arranged to meet them at Corcoran's apartment in the evening. We would all crash there tonight, to get an early start. Then I went shopping. I visited a luggage store, a costume store, a hardware store, and bought half a dozen handheld multichannel radios, spending most of the cash I'd earned the night before.

Many hours later, when I was certain I had done all that I could for now, I called Tamas Fekkete and said I would be in touch tomorrow morning at ten to tell him where to go. I told him that he could bring two men, no more. That the place I'd chosen would be very public, near downtown, and he'd have half an hour to get there before the deal was off. I hung up just as he started to ask questions.

I could count on Fekkete. He'd keep himself far removed from any danger until he thought he had the upper hand. Then he'd try to screw us over. Reliable in his unreliability.

My next conversation, with Ingrid Ekby's man Boule, was more combative. Maybe he was still pissed about my shoving a dart gun into his neck.

"You get nothing until I know Fekkete is there," Boule said.

"No bait, no trap. Fekkete won't show until he sees the gold. It's one hundred kilos of metal; no one's going to grab it and run."

"What about O'Hasson?"

"He has to be right out in front," I said. "Remember, Fekkete believes I'm forcing O'Hasson to give up the gold. He's already twitchy. Spook him, and he'll probably be gone and out of the country again before you even spit in his direction."

Boule grunted. "He'll bring soldiers."

"So maybe a frontal assault shouldn't be your first choice, for once."

"Meaning?"

"Meaning I don't trust your boys not to rush in with your asses on fire, shooting trank darts or worse at anybody who crosses your path. I'll keep Fekkete under wraps until I'm sure you're behaving."

"Go to hell," Boule said. "If you want guarantees, then tell me where the exchange will be now. Let me get my men into position ahead of time."

I ignored that. "Have O'Hasson tell you what he called his daughter when she was a baby."

"What?"

"Proof of life, Boule. Text it to this number. Do that, and I'll call you in the morning. Be ready to move."

If Boule could have sent a fist over the cellular connection, he would have done it.

"Shaw."

"I'm listening."

"You fuck with us on this, and you're done. She'll never quit coming after you."

"A woman after my own heart. Guess you feel the same, huh?"

He hung up. Sensitive lad.

If our situations were reversed, I would be just as furious as Boule. Walking into an unknown environment was tantamount to putting your head in the tiger's jaws and hoping you didn't taste good. It was a sign of his—or Ingrid's—desperation to get their hands on Fekkete that he was even willing to consider it.

But choosing the site of our exchange was my single tactical advantage. My only way to win.

Hollis met me as I hauled my shopping bags down the block to Corcoran's building. The neighborhood was mostly Cambodian. Along with a backpack, Hollis carried a paper grocery sack that smelled of vinegar sauce and ground pork and mint. Heat was already curling and darkening the brown paper in oily patches.

"Jimmy's family out?" I said.

"He's carting them off to visit an aunt. I thought I'd bring provisions. So that we don't leave them with an empty larder."

We rode up in the pink elevator—buttons labeled in English and Khmer—and Hollis unlocked the door with a key from a jangling ring the size and weight of a medieval weapon. Hollis was the sort that everyone would trust with a spare key. He set the food on the kitchen counter and motioned for me to join him at the table.

"Before Jimmy arrives," he said, unzipping the backpack. "You haven't broached the subject, but I thought I'd ask." He removed five lumps wrapped in individual chamois cloths and laid them out on the table. A mixed bag of small-caliber pistols, including an expensive-looking Walther.

"These are all clean," he said.

I considered it. Not for the first time that day.

Hollis tapped a Colt with a fingernail. "I know what Jimmy would say. He always likes a little comfort."

"No," I said finally. "If the exchange goes even halfway wrong, and the cops get involved, we might bluff our way out. That only has a chance if we're traveling light."

"I prefer the gentler path myself."

He swept the guns back into his pack just as my phone buzzed. Boule. He had sent one word: *Ounce.*

O'Hasson's nickname for Cyndra as a baby. Because she had been born premature and underweight, three pounds one ounce. She'd spent a month in the incubator, Cyndra had told me yesterday.

Her dad was still alive. Fighters, both of them.

Corcoran opened the front door and sniffed the air, his nose leading him to the kitchen.

"The fuck?" he said. "You couldn't bring something I don't eat every day?"

From the eighth floor, Corcoran's view was good enough to make out a fraction of the ghostly shape of Mount Rainier to the south. We sat on the balcony and ate while I caught them up on my conversations with Fekkete and Boule, and what I'd learned of Ingrid Ekby.

"Speaking of good-lookin' people," Corcoran said, "I don't like the idea of these assholes seeing my face. Or Hollis's," he amended. "But mine, mostly."

"We'll have masks," I said. "In fact, nearly everybody around us will have masks."

I told Hollis and Corcoran what I had in mind, and where I had gone that day to reconnoiter, and showed them what I had in the shopping bags. Their expressions were worth a tall stack of gold bars.

TWENTY-FIVE

Hollis leaned close to the windshield to peer up at the gigantic green sign as we passed underneath it.

"I said it last night, and it bears repeating," he said, his breath fogging the glass. "You're mad, boyyo."

SEATTLE EVERCON
FANTASY / COMICS / ANIME

"Thirty thousand people expected today," I said. "Nearly all of them in some kind of costume."

It was old news to Hollis. We'd waited for a dozen convention attendees in Transformer costumes to stomp robotically through the last crosswalk. Drifting through the parking garage, we followed a river of demons and heroes and sprites making their eager way toward the security line at the entrance gates.

"Cops?" said Corcoran from the backseat of the Navigator. I could almost feel him ducking his head low.

"The more the better," I said.

Hollis goggled at a girl in full Vampirella costume, wearing barely enough red fabric to make a couple of belts. "How did you know about this?"

Before I could answer, the lot attendant came to take my twenty bucks and waved us in the direction of the next available spot. Hollis slid the Navigator into place and we piled out. I grabbed my mask off the passenger seat, and gave each of them one of the laminated badges I'd acquired the day before. Corcoran stared at the badge like I'd handed him a giant cockroach.

From the back of the big SUV, I removed two hard-sided rolling suitcases, one in metallic red, the second in a shiny blue.

Hollis slipped on his hockey mask. "How do I look?" he said.

With his blood-spattered mask and soiled field coat, he made a fair Jason Voorhees, if a little short. "Unidentifiable," I said, tossing him a set of keys.

"Perfect. See you all later." As he walked off, Hollis shot a finger at Corcoran, who was trying to adjust his horribly scarred *Nightmare on Elm Street* mask.

"Fucking thing's uncomfortable as shit," Corcoran said. "And this sweater itches."

"You know where to go," I said.

"Yes, goddammit. We went through it enough times."

I joined the stream of cosplayers, carrying the empty suitcases. I was dressed in dark blue coveralls, street clothes underneath. The multi-channel radio was in my pocket. The EverCon badge went around my neck on a lanyard, just like every other attendee. Most people around us had yellow badges. Ours were green. Special access.

Before joining the crush at the entrance doors, I put in the earpiece and slipped my white mask on over it.

"Hey! *Halloween!*" said a bandoliered Wookie to my side. I gave him a thumbs-up. My spectral mask was the same as the one worn by the character in the slasher flicks. It was pale and expressionless. Unnerving. And just like the silent killer in the films, no one would expect me to speak.

The throng split itself into haphazard lines, one to each doorway. Gatekeepers wearing the red badges of conference organizers swiped each attendee's pass with a laser reader. Behind them, a table for each door, with private security personnel in blue windbreakers checking every bag.

Two pairs of uniformed cops flanked the entrances. They chatted with one another about whatever cops on easy duty talk about.

"Would you open your suitcases, please?" said the windbreaker at our door. I popped the latches to show the empty interiors.

"For all the loot," I said.

He smiled. "Have fun shopping."

The entrance doors led to a bank of escalators, leading up to the central atrium and the convention halls. At the top of the escalators was an attention deficit sufferer's nightmare. Two or three hundred people in costumes, and a few human-powered contraptions that were far beyond the usual definition and size of costumes, milled about the open floor like debutantes making their entrances. An entire cadre of Avengers pretended to do battle with a squad of X-Men. Darth Maul crossed swords with Captain Jack for a selfie. I stepped back to let a twelve-foot steampunk giraffe amble past.

Cyndra would have loved this. Maybe I could take her to a convention someday. Assuming I survived this one.

My mask from *Halloween* fit right in. Not elaborate. Easily recognizable, and less interesting for it. No one would be interrupting our business to ask for a picture, which I'd noticed yesterday happened a lot to people wearing the best costumes, or the skimpiest. One girl dressed in green hot pants as Misty from *Pokémon* had a line waiting.

I inched my way through the atrium crowd and down a lobby long enough to have served as the runway for a small plane. Booths dominated the lobby, selling everything from action figures to rare comic books to more costumes, just in case anyone felt left out.

My earpiece buzzed. Corcoran, on the radio channel reserved for him and Hollis.

"They're here," he said. "Mick O'Hasson, and two guys shadowing about ten yards off him. They're wearing sport jackets, can you believe that?"

I could. Boule hadn't known about our little costume party at Ever-Con until half an hour ago, when I'd told him.

"O'Hasson just got in line at the will-call window. One of his shadows is wheeling a big-ass footlocker on a hand truck. Is that what I think it is?"

"Let's hope so," I said.

"It's heavy enough to be gold, by the look of it. Hang on. The geek at the window gave O'Hasson a package," Corcoran said.

"Three badges," I said. "The con is sold out. And something for Mickey to help him blend in. Hold your position. Fekkete will be here before too long."

Corcoran swore. His version of acknowledging.

EverCon was a hot event. Passes had been considered impossible to get for months. I'd managed to acquire nine badges yesterday, thanks to some inside help. Three for us, three for Boule, and three for Fekkete. I wanted them here. But I also wanted insurance that neither of our guests would show up with an entire battalion.

If the atrium had been dizzying, then the enormous convention hall at the end of the lobby was a fever dream. Individual costumes were dwarfed by the displays of game companies and media showpieces. Giant inflatable anime characters lined the west wall to my left, as if waiting to play the latest *Call of Duty* on the ten-foot-wide screens on the other side of the broad aisle. The east wall was so far away it might as well have another zip code. I could watch a TV clip or a movie trailer or a video game in progress almost anywhere I looked, and I could hear all of them at once. It was like having my head stuck in a pinball machine.

No cops in sight. Maybe they didn't patrol this level often. That could be a problem. Having cops around might keep anyone from getting ideas, or getting rough.

Directly across from the entryway, a large performance stage dominated the opposite wall. Empty at the moment. It would be used in the afternoon and evening, after the larger panels downstairs concluded and thousands more people crowded the convention hall. For now, it was perfect for my needs. The closest edge of the stage offered clear sightlines to this entrance and to all aisles where someone might approach.

It was impossible for one person to cover all points of entry into the gigantic room, but the stage came close. It would be my starting position, the best vantage point.

I walked quickly across the room, weaving with the suitcases through a Rivendell contingent comparing elven headpieces and wigs. Past Vulcans and Little Ponies and a hundred other characters I didn't know. My pop culture savvy was just another casualty of ten years burned in Iraq and Afghanistan.

"Shaw." That was Boule, on the radio I had left in Mickey's package at the will-call window. The advantage of the radios was that I could hear all channels, while only speaking to one at a time, if I chose.

Fekkete would find a radio waiting with his badges, too. If he showed. The drug smuggler was slippery enough that I wasn't completely certain he would risk meeting in person, as much as he craved the gold.

"I'm here," I said to Boule. "It took you a while." Long enough that I wondered if Boule had managed to slip into the room already. I was at the stage now, looking across to the first entryway.

"The place is crowded, if you hadn't noticed," he said.

Jesus, that was nearly humor. Boule must be keyed up.

"Are you with O'Hasson?" I said.

In answer, a small figure appeared in the entryway. Mick O'Hasson. He wore a green bowler hat and green vest, easy to see even at long distance. The Irish stereotype costume had been my idea. If security saw a leprechaun, they wouldn't be surprised at seeing a box full of gold.

"I see him," I said into the radio, "but unless he ate the gold for breakfast, that's all I see."

"Where's Fekkete?" Boule answered.

"First things. O'Hasson goes to neutral ground. Agreed?"

"Agreed. But he'll do what I tell him to do. Nothing more." Boule must have O'Hasson wearing an earpiece himself, to respond to orders.

"Have O'Hasson come halfway into the room, then turn left and walk to the parade balloons over on the west wall. Under the *Sailor Moon* one."

"Which one is that?"

"Figure it out."

After a moment, O'Hasson began to walk into the room. The hunters had dressed him in dull gray sweatpants and sweatshirt, probably just stuffing Mick into the baggy clothes on the drive here. The emerald bowler hat and vest looked less jaunty than futile on his spare frame. He took each step without pause, but his progress was slow. Frail.

Stay with us, Mickey, I thought. *You're almost done.*

As he made his slow way to the west wall, I scanned the room. No Boule, or any of the other hunters I'd seen two days before. No one wearing suits or sport coats.

I had a notion of what Boule's team had been doing during their long delay before calling me on the radio. Buying costumes.

I turned to examine the crowd behind O'Hasson. Like observation training in the Rangers. Not focusing on anything, just looking at the whole field, to see if any of the grass moved how it shouldn't.

There. A man in a brown monk's robe and hood, forty yards out on my two o'clock. He kept a drifting pace with O'Hasson's progress across the floor. I watched from my distant vantage point until I was sure. Very broad shoulders on the monk. Boule's thick-necked buddy Marshall, almost certainly.

And there. Another tall hooded figure, his face hidden, hovering nearer the center of the room to my left. With one badge for O'Hasson and one for Marshall, the third man would be Boule himself. The hood twisted from side to side. Trying to locate me in the dazzling onslaught of color and sound surrounding us, no doubt.

Half of our guests had arrived. O'Hasson was about as safe as I could make him. Time to up the stakes.

I had prepared a text message for Fekkete, directing him to the convention center and the main hall. I fired the message off, adding the encouraging note that the gold was already here. That was my optimism showing. I hadn't laid eyes on the kilobars yet.

O'Hasson reached the huge red boot of the inflatable cartoon figure. Immediately, Boule piped up on the radio.

"Where's Fekkete?"

"On his way now. You better get the cheese into the trap."

"Where are you?"

"Bring it to the aisle where O'Hasson entered. When I see it, we'll meet."

I had expected the figure in the monk's hood to move, to fetch the gold. But the hunters surprised me.

A hand truck loaded with a black footlocker the size of a small ottoman wheeled into view in the entryway. Pushed by a man wearing an ivory Japanese demon mask, all grinning jaws and tusks. I recognized the tobacco-colored curls of hair around the mask's horns. Boule.

The hunters had managed to sneak extra players onto the field. Two in monk costumes that I'd spotted. But there could be more men, in different disguises. Boule was their stalking horse, easy to spot in his suit and tie. I might have fallen for it if Marshall had been more subtle in tailing O'Hasson.

"I'm directly across from you," I said to Boule, "by the stage, in coveralls and a white mask."

He spotted me and grunted. The demon mask actually went fairly well with his light gray suit. His hand truck was the heavy-duty kind, with an extra set of wheels to allow the user to push large loads without wrestling with the weight. That didn't mean Boule didn't have to put some muscle into it, to get the hundred kilos of gold rolling.

At least I hoped it was gold. If it wasn't, this could go bad long before I was prepared for that badness to happen.

The two monks held their positions, one by O'Hasson, the other where he could see all of us from the center of the room. Boule pushed the hand truck up to where I waited by the stage, with my two empty suitcases. We were near enough to the carpeted wall of the convention hall to have a relatively quiet pocket, away from the sensory overload of the main floor.

"This stays locked until Fekkete shows," Boule said through his incongruously grinning mask.

"That won't work," I said. "He'll send one of his goons to check it. The goon will give Fekkete the signal when it's safe."

"How do you know?"

"Because it's what I would do, if I were a nervous son of a bitch like Fekkete. And because I told him to stay far away until I knew O'Hasson hadn't double-crossed us with a box full of chains. Is that a box full of chains, Boule?"

"Fuck off." He lowered the hand truck to the ground, unstrapped the footlocker, and lifted one side and then the other down to the floor in two big heaves. "When Fekkete's man is here, I'll get the key to you."

I could easily pick the lock on the big box, but that was beside the point. Like I'd told Boule, no one was pulling a snatch-and-grab with that much metal.

"If Fekkete doesn't come in person, the deal's off. Permanently," Boule said.

Fekkete wouldn't trust Hinch or his other Sledge City killers with four million of anything. I was counting on his greed and suspicion to conquer his fear.

My radio buzzed. Corcoran, from his position outside.

"I got four gym rats out here, bitching at the ticket window girl," he said. "No Fekkete."

Shit. Maybe I had been wrong.

"Get gone," I said to Boule, "and send O'Hasson to me with the key."

"When they arrive," he repeated, and moved off into the vibrant forest of booths and people.

"Two of them are heading inside," Corcoran said. "I lost the others in the crowd out here. Freaks."

Where was Fekkete? Had he really decided to keep away?

I had five minutes to stew about it before Dickson Hinch and the looming figure of Bomba appeared at the entrance to the hall. They didn't have masks. That didn't matter. If Fekkete had skipped the party, my world was about to get ugly enough without any extra help.

TWENTY-SIX

WE ARE HERE." FEKKETE'S voice in my ear. He had the radio. One of his men must have passed it to him outside after picking up their badges. I exhaled a whole lungful of relief.

"Where?" I said on Fekkete's radio channel. Hinch and Bomba still lurked in the entryway, looking around for a recognizable face. Waiting for Fekkete's instructions.

"In the large room," Fekkete said in his thick accent. Maybe he'd slipped in through another entrance. Or maybe he was directing his soldiers from afar. I saw Bomba talking into a cell phone. They had spotted O'Hasson against the west wall. The little burglar was hard to miss, in his spangled green bowler and vest. He stood as ordered by the inflatable statues, looking dazed. Maybe he was in shock.

Bomba starting moving in O'Hasson's direction, bulling his way through the thickening crowd. He kept the cell phone pressed to his ear.

"I have the gold," I said to Fekkete. "O'Hasson has armed bodyguards covering him. They're dressed in brown robes, like monks."

After another moment, Bomba stopped short, still a hundred feet away from O'Hasson. He rapidly looked from side to side. Good. Keep his attention focused elsewhere. If he spied Marshall, all the better.

"Where is the gold?" Fekkete said.

"By the big stage, with me," I said. "O'Hasson will bring the key when I tell him to."

"He is doing what you say." Fekkete sounded satisfied. "The girl is here?"

"Never mind her," I said. "Send one of your men to meet me at the stage. We'll check the box and make sure."

That apparently met with Fekkete's approval. Hinch began an easy lope down the long aisle toward me. As he neared I saw that he wore a Bluetooth earpiece under his lank hair; keeping in touch with Bomba or Fekkete or both.

I used the moment to take a breath. Center myself.

This exchange would be like the kids' puzzle, getting a fox and a chicken and a sack of grain across a river in a boat that could carry only one at a time. Chicken eats grain. Fox kills chicken. Only in our case, we had enough foxes running around to slaughter an entire poultry farm.

Still no sign of Fekkete. If he wasn't here, or if I couldn't spot him, I'd have to grab O'Hasson and try to escape. Leave the gold behind, and hope it sidetracked all of the men here, every one of whom would be delighted to see Mick and me dead before the day was out.

Hinch saw me watching him, and the footlocker and red and blue suitcases at my feet. He grinned challengingly and stepped up to breathe in my face.

"Nice mask, fuckhead," he said. "But we know it's you in there, Zack."

I pressed the earpiece to switch my voice to Boule's channel. "Send the key," I said.

"The fuck are these for?" Hinch tapped the red suitcase with the toe of his cowboy boot. I caught the bulge of an ankle holster on his right leg.

"That one's yours," I said. "If there's any trouble, get those hidden under the stage."

I had examined the performance area very carefully the day before. A short black scrim hid the legs and other supports from the audience.

Curtains divided the rear of the stage from the performing area, sloping around to touch the wall.

Out of view, in the dark claustrophobic space between stage and wall, was an access door. An emergency exit, as far as I was concerned. If this all went to hell, I might need it.

Far off, at the west wall, I saw the wide robed figure of Marshall approach O'Hasson. Passing the key, I guessed. Another ten seconds, and O'Hasson began to make his slow way toward where Hinch and I waited. Bomba followed, keeping his distance. Would Marshall spot him? I hoped so. I wanted them playing man-to-man, worried about each other.

"I'm still outside," Corcoran said. "A couple of the gym rats are wandering around out here like retarded apes, but no sight of your Russian dude."

I didn't want to speak with Hinch so near. Instead I gave Corcoran a triple tap on the radio, his signal to find me inside.

Hinch was distracted. A woman sashayed past us, her black vinyl catsuit hugging every inch except for where the zipper opened in a deep V down to her navel. I wondered briefly if the word *cleavage* still applied when you could see most of a hemisphere. The feline woman returned Hinch's barefaced stare, smiling over her shoulder.

"Let's get this done," Hinch said, still watching her slink away. "I got shit to do."

Mick O'Hasson reached us. He held out a key, and Hinch snatched it away and knelt in front of the footlocker. O'Hasson teetered slightly. I bent down to murmur in his ear, under the rattle of Hinch's popping the latches on the box.

"Cyndra's safe," I said, and repeated it. I wasn't sure how well the little burglar was tracking what was going on around him. "She's okay. No matter what happens here, you stay with me. I won't let them take you again. Do you understand? Nod once."

An instant. Then his blue eyes, duller than usual but still in focus, met mine, and he nodded. I sat him down on the edge of the stage.

"Yeah boy," said Hinch. Inside the footlocker were ten small duffel bags made of thick undyed canvas. Hinch had one of the bags partway unzipped. I reached in to pull it closer. The bag was shockingly heavy.

Gold. Ten kilobars gleamed from inside the bag as if powered by a living energy.

"It's here," Hinch said, hushed with awe. Talking to Fekkete on the earpiece. "All of it."

Foxes and chickens. And four million dollars' worth of grain.

Boule spoke on the radio. "Is the gold confirmed?"

"Checking," I replied.

I'd lost Boule in the shifting waves of the crowd. And the second monk as well. Marshall and Bomba were a scant eighty feet away on my one o'clock, watching each other as much as what was happening with me and Hinch. But I'd lost the other two men.

Goddammit. Too many players. I had known going in that I couldn't watch all of them, all the time. An acceptable risk, so long as they were watching each other. That's what I had imagined while I was sitting safe and sound and making impressive plans in my head yesterday.

Dono would have snarled at me to get my ass out and be satisfied with saving Cyndra and O'Hasson.

But I could see the brass ring now. Close enough to reach out my hand and try.

I began to divide the canvas bags between the red and blue suitcases, and after an instant's hesitation Hinch joined me. Five bags apiece. Two fortunes, ready to roll.

"Stop," said Boule. "Give us Fekkete." I barely heard his demand over the cadence shouts of a platoon of Imperial stormtroopers to our left, marching in formation. Security guards walked ahead, clearing a path for them.

Fekkete wasn't coming. I'd have to play for time until O'Hasson and I could find a way out.

"Thirty seconds," I said to Boule.

Hinch spotted the security guards coming and nudged me, thinking I hadn't noticed. I slammed the roller bags closed. The guards were nearly on top of us. I shoved my blue case forcibly under the stage, hiding it behind the drapery of the supports, and Hinch hastily did the same for his red one.

As we stood up, the security guards and a double line of ivory-armored troopers passed directly in front of us. Blocking any path back to the entryways.

"Shaw," Boule said. "Don't move from that spot."

They were done waiting. I spotted the second monk, twenty yards off ten o'clock and closing. Boule's grinning demon mask, flanking us now on the right. Shit.

"I got it," Hinch said to Fekkete through his earpiece. He had edged out of reach, keeping one eye on me. "I got this asshole, too."

The stormtroopers halted right in front of Hinch and me, made a left-face to the open room, and began swinging their rifles in close-quarters drill. Everyone in the room except our little band turned to watch. The two monks and Bomba were stuck on the other side of thirty cosplayers and a hundred phone cameras already recording the show.

"We're gonna kill you, fucker," Hinch said, glancing to where O'Hasson sat unsteadily on the stage edge. "Both of you."

He was between us and the access door hidden behind the stage. I could try to coldcock him, before he did the same to me. Or I could throw O'Hasson over my shoulder and slam through the troopers like a cornerback. Crap odds of survival, either way.

"Hey." Corcoran's angry voice, suddenly loud in my ear. "I found him. Fekkete."

"Where?" I said, no longer caring if Hinch would hear.

"He's way east of you, under the hanging spaceship that looks like slug vomit. The orange one with all the neon. He's wearing a Dracula mask to hide his face, and black jogging clothes."

I couldn't see him. The spaceship Corcoran had mentioned was halfway to the other side of the huge hall, at least a hundred yards from the stage. People at that distance looked no larger than a thumbnail.

Out of time. The stormtroopers were nearly done with their show. Boule was already forcing his way through the throng of spectators, and Bomba and Marshall squared off, gladiators ready to give the crowd something else to watch.

"We've spotted him," I said to Boule. Trying to stall.

"The fuck are you talking about?" Hinch said. Starting to click that there was more going on than the gold. The mob around us cheered.

Boule wasn't falling for it. He pushed closer, near enough now that I could follow movement in the corner of my eye, as I desperately looked for Fekkete. The crowd rushed in to congratulate the platoon of troopers, momentarily blocking him.

There. Fekkete, in his vampire mask, lips so red with plastic blood I could see it even at this distance. Staring intently our way.

"Boule," I said. "Fekkete is three hundred feet off your four. Dead center in the aisle. Vampire mask." I hit the button on the radio to open up Boule's channel to Corcoran.

"Tear his mask off," I yelled. "Show them."

Jimmy got it. I saw his grotesque Freddy face and fedora suddenly appear in the crowd and close on Fekkete from behind. Boule turned away from me to look.

Hinch grabbed me. "What the fuck are you doing? We'll kill you, asshole."

But I was watching Fekkete. Hinch followed my eyes, just as Corcoran slipped up behind Fekkete and reached out to yank the rubber Dracula mask off his head. Fekkete wheeled, too late to catch Corcoran as Jimmy slid with astonishing speed into the enveloping crowd.

"It's him," I heard Boule say, just as Fekkete realized he was a target, and exposed. He tried to run for the exit. Upstream against a crushing tide. The first panels of the day had let out, and a new tsunami of humanity flooded the convention floor. Boule pursued him, and an instant later Marshall did, too. Bomba, left without a dance partner, started to tentatively go after them.

"You motherfu—" Hinch said. I caught his hand as it reached down for the ankle holster, squeezed. I have a strong grip. Inherited from Dono, like my black hair and black eyes. Hinch grabbed my shoulder, tried to yank me into an arm lock, but I was braced. We strained against each other, stalemated.

"Hey," said a girl dressed as a barbarian. Uncertain if the two nasty-looking bastards behind the dispersing mob of stormtroopers were just messing around.

"Fekkete's done," I said softly to Hinch. "You can run and try to save him. Or you can take the gold for yourself."

His eyes were crazed. Lips drawn reflexively back into a snarl. He wanted to try me. Beat me. For a moment I thought his bestial side would win out, two million dollars be damned.

He let go. I stepped back, giving him room. The girl still stared at us, along with a couple of curious stormtroopers.

"This ain't over," Hinch said, and reached under the stage to haul out the red suitcase. "Gonna fuck you up good, Zack boy." He walked away fast, loaded suitcase rolling behind him, forcing the barbarian girl and her companions to scatter.

I reached under the drapes to grab the blue case. Lifting one hundred pounds never felt so easy.

"Come on, Mick," I said to O'Hasson. "Let's go home."

He followed me down the gap behind the stage to the access door. The door wasn't locked. I spared a moment to throw the bolts, top and bottom. No one would follow.

The interior of the convention center was a well-ordered maze. We took a right, a left, and another right, moving as fast as O'Hasson's condition allowed. People swept through, rushing to their own priorities. We all nodded to one another. Our green badges assured passage. O'Hasson and I came to a stairwell, and I carried the case like a steel baby down two floors as he followed, and through wide double doors painted EXIT.

We emerged onto a narrow railed sidewalk, in the tunnel under the looming weight of the convention center. Traffic sped by, roaring motors echoing off the walls. The noise made O'Hasson flinch. We waited.

Thirty seconds later, the black Navigator came around the corner off Pike, fast enough for the wheels to squeal like a startled hog. Hollis popped the rear door before the car had come to a complete stop. I jumped the railing and helped O'Hasson step through and down to the car.

The cars behind us honked angrily. I carried the bag to the back. The cargo space was already half-full with one red suitcase.

My blue case fit neatly beside its brother. Their combined weight made the rear of the big Lincoln sag another half-inch.

Four million dollars. The curses of the furious drivers behind me didn't even smudge my exhilaration.

I tore off my mask and jumped into the passenger seat.

"No troubles?" I said to Hollis.

"None." He hauled ass toward the avenue at the far side of the center. "Though it was damn tight under that stage."

"You were as quiet as a stoned mouse," I said.

And he had been. I'd been listening, even as the stormtroopers performed their close-quarters racket. Hollis had swapped one shiny red case for another in less than two minutes. A hundred pounds of scrap metal, for a suitcase full of gold. Hinch was in for a nasty surprise.

He nodded happily. "Not bad for a hoary bugger like me, hauling such heavy things. I might just take up powerlifting."

"Invest in a whole gym."

"On that subject. Fekkete?"

"He might already be stuffed in somebody else's trunk."

That sobered Hollis. He stayed quiet as we rounded 7th Ave. and pulled up alongside the building at one of the flat emergency exit doors. He kept the engine running and his foot barely touching the brake.

"What's keeping him?" he said after a long moment.

"It's a big place," I said.

O'Hasson reached to grip my shoulder, hand quivering. The morning had bled all the energy he had, and kept right on taking. His lips were the color of bone china. "Where's Cyndra?"

"She's close, Mick. Take it easy."

He collapsed back on the seat, spent. Another minute passed. Hollis was about to speak again when the door slammed open and Corcoran came out. He opened the car door and fairly leaped into the backseat. O'Hasson gaped at him.

"Drive, for fuck's sake," said Corcoran, removing his Freddy mask. Hollis was already punching it.

"Head toward Olive," I said. I gave him directions for the next few blocks, until I saw the café on the south side of the street. Patrons sat at outside tables, soaking in the gentle sun and sipping their drinks. Two of them, one tall and one small, rose to their feet as the Navigator approached.

"Cyn," O'Hasson said as his daughter ran to the car. Hollis hadn't fully stopped before Cyndra was yanking open the door, leaping into her father's arms.

"Daddy," she said, sounding much younger than twelve.

I got out. "Take 'em to the boat. The cases, too. I'll meet you there."

Corcoran complained. Everyone ignored him. Cyndra was crying. O'Hasson looked like he would do the same, if he had anything left in him. Instead, he shook soundlessly.

"Mickey?" I said.

O'Hasson nodded. A spasm of the head, as his shaking increased. "M'okay," he said. "I'm okay."

Cyndra held on as if she'd never let go again.

TWENTY-SEVEN

Hollis took O'Hasson and Cyndra and Corcoran and four million dollars away. The tall woman waited for me by the café table.

"You zipped up," I said. The silver ring on her catsuit hung at her neck now, like a pet license on a collar.

Elana Coll smiled. "A nod to modesty when I'm off the convention floor." A very faint nod. The black vinyl was only a fraction thicker than paint. Cars passing by slowed noticeably. With three-inch heels on her boots, Elana and I were nearly eye-to-eye.

I raised an eyebrow, mock-stern. "When I asked you to help with a distraction—"

"Why be subtle?" Her smile became the proverbial Cheshire grin. "Besides, I can do more than just unlock a few exit doors and bribe people for badges."

"Were the stormtroopers your idea?" I said as we sat at her table. Talking low enough to keep the other diners out of the conversation.

"Of course. What better help than an entire army?"

"Thanks. You may have saved our asses. Especially Mick's."

"Are they going to be all right?"

I tilted my head. "He's still got cancer. She's still going to lose him."

Elana's green eyes lost a touch of their light. "There's nothing that can be done? Chemo, or something?"

"Maybe. I doubt the doctors at Lancaster explored every option. Just the ones where the state was willing to foot the bill."

"Well, he can certainly afford the best treatment now."

"Yeah." Seattle wasn't safe for the O'Hassons. But maybe they could settle in another big city, with an oncology hospital. Mick was past the idea that he might have a fighting chance, and I hadn't even thought about it. Cyndra was the one with faith.

"And I can afford a long vacation," Elana said, stretching. Her languid movement attracted a few eyes, most but not all male. "The Caribbean, I think. I've never been to the 'bean. A beach and a tall stack of trashy paperbacks."

Crime paid. I'd promised Elana ten grand, on top of what she'd had to front to get us our passes at the last minute, which had cost half again as much.

"Sorry again about the thing with Luce," she said. "I really didn't think you would be at the hangar that early."

"Forget it."

"She asked if you were in trouble of some kind. I said I wasn't sure. Which was true. You didn't share any details at the time."

"Luce already knew the answer."

"Should I tell her about it now? I mean, you were trying to save that guy's life."

"Why? So she'll think better of me?" This chat was rapidly shuffling toward a cliff.

"Yes," Elana said plainly. "Exactly that. She should know."

"I was also turning a profit. That's how this whole clusterfuck started, me breaking the law."

"I suppose. But Luce cares."

"Don't try to paint over my rough spots, Elana."

"Then don't pretend Luce's opinion doesn't matter."

Of course it mattered. That didn't change anything.

"I'll have your cut for you next week," I said, standing.

"No rush. Look after yourself." Elana gave me a sardonic wave, and I walked away.

A block later I peeled off my coveralls and stuffed them into a trash can. My t-shirt was crisp with dried sweat. I walked north, long strides, no real direction, just feeling the wind.

To hell with her. Them. I wasn't going to let anything spoil this day. We'd just scored four million bucks. I took a long breath, and let it out so slowly that my lungs ached. Knots in my shoulders that I hadn't known were there loosened with each step.

My cut would be enough money for the house, and more. Cash on hand for the foreseeable future, whatever future I wanted that to be. I'd made more profit today than my grandfather and I had in nearly a decade of stealing together. Reason to celebrate. And I would, soon.

The world was bright. Every line as sharp as a high note, every hue as rich as cream. Mine for the taking.

Granddad wasn't at home when I finally stumbled in the door at seven in the morning. It was still dark out. After leaving the empty mansion I had jogged a few miles—uphill, it felt like—until I finally found the main transit center I'd known was somewhere in downtown Bellevue. I'd waited two hours for the first bus of the day across the lake, then taken another two buses to get to the Hill, and walked down to our block. My legs hurt. My stomach hurt. I wished I'd stayed in the linen closet of the RV, even if I wound up in Tijuana.

And I'd forgotten my bike. *Dammit.*

Could I leave it where it was chained up at the church? Granddad thought I'd taken it to Davey's and I wouldn't have come home without it.

I turned around and walked back out the door.

I'd tried to reach Granddad a couple of times with my new cell phone, thinking it might be safe by now. No answer. There was a niggling worry, way at the back of my fuzzy head, that Trey and the vulture—Quincey—had something bad planned. I tried him again. No answer, again.

A block up from our home, there was a two-lot clearing where houses were scheduled to be built, sometime after the holidays. Granddad had pointed out to me how the construction crew had used heated blankets to make sure no part of the ground was frozen before laying out the forms and pouring the concrete for the first house's footings.

The crew had left the second foundation unfinished during the holidays and put up a wooden fence to keep people off the lots. I jumped it to take the shortcut. The foundation was still a big empty hole, about four feet deep. With the sky so black and overcast the hole looked like it could go down for miles, like the pit in that Poe story. I made sure not to fall in as I cut across the lot.

It was Christmas Eve today, I realized. I still hadn't wrapped the new shirt and the jars of salsa I'd bought for Granddad up at the co-op. Maybe he—

I stopped halfway through my climb over the fence on the opposite side. Trey's green Ford Taurus was parked on the street.

Was Trey here? I looked around frantically. Had he just left the Taurus to walk over to our block?

You're out in the open, Stupid.

I dropped back down, ran across, and vaulted into the next yard in one jump. The yard belonged to a family home, lots of little kid toys and a swing set. If I were lucky they wouldn't have a mean dog.

The fence was kind of sloppy and there were plenty of gaps between the boards. I peered through them, trying to spot Trey. The screwdriver he'd planted at the mansion was still in my coat pocket. I'd been very careful not to touch it.

There he came, swinging open a hinged section of the fence to enter the cleared lots. He had the hood pulled up on his blue anorak and I couldn't see his face in the dark, but I was sure that was him. I'd kind of forgotten how tall he was. He was carrying a hoe or a shovel, something with a long handle.

Trey crossed the lots and jumped down into the foundation hole. I heard him digging. He seemed to be in a rush, and I realized that the sun was coming up.

In ten minutes of fast work he was finished with whatever he was doing, and he jumped out of the hole. I could hear his heavy gasps for air. He stood there a moment—had he heard me somehow? *Sensed* me? I could take off. Jump the fence. I wasn't sure I could outrun those long legs.

Then he walked back to the hinged gate and left the

property. There was the sound of a padlock clicking shut, and a moment later his car started. I saw its headlights stutter across the fence slats and then he was gone.

It took me three seconds to jump up and over the fence and down into the foundation hole. What had Trey been doing? Digging something up?

No, I realized.

Burying something.

Daybreak had lightened the clouds overhead just enough that I could make out a fresh patch of earth, about as long as I was tall. It made a gently rounded dune, just an inch or two higher than the bottom of the foundation.

Had Trey buried some of the artwork? That was crazy. But it was still easier to think about him hiding some painting—to hang on to that hope—than the idea of what might *really* be under that mound.

I had to see.

I knelt down and started scooping dirt away with my gloved hands. It was easy. The earth was loose. The hole couldn't be too deep, right? Not if Trey had only been working for a few minutes.

But then I hadn't seen him *carry* anything to the hole. Whatever big thing Trey had been covering up, it had already been here, waiting for him.

I must have walked right past it in the dark. Scary thought. I kept digging. Dirt fell down my wrists into my gloves as I shoved big handfuls aside.

Two feet down, I hit something. Cloth. I swiped away more dirt. The sky was definitely lighter now, because it was easy to tell I was looking at blue denim jeans.

With a leg underneath.

I fell back on my butt. My hands were so cold I couldn't feel them when they thudded limply off my shoes.

Trey had buried a body.

But who? Had Granddad been wearing jeans tonight? I couldn't remember.

I jumped to the other side of the dirt patch and flung handfuls away as fast as I could. The body was lying on its side, a little curled up, so its head—its face—would be somewhere—

There. I felt it, brushing my fingertips as I grabbed that last scoop of soil.

Was it him? Slower now, I reached to brush away the earth, making myself do it before I chickened out.

Gray hair. Pale, pale skin. A sharp, beaked profile.

It was Quincey. The vulture man.

Ready for the scavengers himself now. The thought came, sounding remarkably calm, and I pushed it away just as fast.

I'd never seen a dead person before. He was so still. Not like a person lying down, but like an object. Two objects, half of a white mask and a strip of cloth, both emerging like separate pieces from the earth. Quincey's face had a rusty crooked line on it.

Blood. Pretty sure that was blood.

I was really really glad his eyes were closed.

Why did Trey bury him here? It was dumb. The body would be found as soon as anyone came to work on the house. And it wasn't like he did it in a panic. He must have dug the—the *grave*, I guess it was—before Trey and Granddad and Quincey burgled the house last night.

Brains are funny. Mine put a bunch of things in proper order just as coolly as if I'd been sitting in class and actually paying attention, instead of squatting in the cold dirt looking at a dead guy.

Trey stole our screwdriver. He dug the grave and hid the shovel nearby. He planted our screwdriver at the mansion. Then he killed Quincey and buried him. Only a block from our house.

Quincey was supposed to be found. Just like the screwdriver was supposed to be found. To point the cops toward Granddad.

I looked at the streak of blood on Quincey's face, like a worm wriggling up toward his clenched eyelid.

Real worms will be here soon.

Don't think that. No time. You know what you have to do.

I started digging. Desperate to see if Trey had planted anything else with the body. One of our kitchen knives. The hammer we kept with the screwdriver. Anything. That calm side of my brain told me how amazing it was that so many things in the house could be used to kill somebody.

Nothing was buried by Quincey's shoulders. Or on his chest. A *lot* more blood there. Had he been shot? Stabbed? More thoughts to push away as I kept digging.

It was totally morning now, and that freaked me out almost as much as touching the dead Quincey. If I was seen here—anybody walking by and taking a minute to look closely through the sloppy fence—it was real *real* trouble. Like me going to juvie hall, like Granddad going back to jail, maybe for good.

There was nothing. Nothing but Quincey, looking smaller than I'd thought he was. I guessed there might be a weapon lying under the body, but I couldn't handle that. I undeniably couldn't.

And then I started crying.

You baby, the calm part of my brain said. *Somebody will hear.*

Didn't matter. I sat there and curled up and stuck my face in my knees and elbows and just fucking bawled.

I shoved all the dirt back over Quincey—*sorry,* I told him silently—and made sure I hadn't left any footprints or anything, and then I ran back to the house.

Still no Granddad. At home, or on the phone. I swore at

it for the thousandth time. Why did he give me the stupid thing if he never answered?

Of course, there could be a reason why he wasn't answering.

Kassie's house. Trey might be there, back at home. That was where Granddad had picked him up in the RV last night. Maybe they were both there now. Go there, tell Granddad what I'd found. He had his gun. We'd be okay.

I realized I was coated in grime and snot and maybe much worse, from Quincey. Gross. I kicked off my shoes and ran upstairs to throw the mucky clothes and gloves in the bathtub and put on new ones. A quick scrub got most of the dirt off my hands and face. I took Granddad's field coat before grabbing my shoes, stuffing my feet into them as I hurried back out the door again.

Nobody had stolen my bike. That was at least one thing that wasn't world-class shitty about today. I sped through the cars driving on 23rd and up toward Interlaken.

The narrow road between Kassie's house and the brushy border of the park was busy. People leaving for work, or going out to buy last-minute presents, or outside decorating their houses. It was weird to see them doing regular things, when only a dozen blocks away there was a corpse under the ground.

The purple-striped RV wasn't here. Neither was Trey's green Taurus, at least not in the driveway. I coasted closer, to see if I might be able to tell if it was in the garage.

"Van!" It was Kassie, calling from the front door.

Dammit. Not now. If Trey wasn't here then I needed to get home and find another way to reach Granddad. Call Hollis, maybe.

"What're you doing?" she said. "Come on up."

"Is your dad here?"

"No," she scoffed. "He'd go crazy."

I bet.

"Is he at work today?" I said.

"God, you're freaky. Come on. It's cold."

I hid my bike in the brush and joined her on the front porch. She was still wearing pajamas. Green cotton with blue dots, and leather moccasins. Her face was very pink.

"Did you just get up?" I said as she led me into the kitchen.

"Kinda. Dad was out all last night, so I stayed up late. I wanted to invite you over, but you haven't given me your phone number or anything." She said it like I'd disappointed her.

"Sorry. I was out last night, too."

"S'okay. I'm making eggs 'n' cheese. D'you want some?"

I was starving, I realized. "Yeah."

"After you ran out yesterday"—Kassie giggled, remembering—"you looked hil-*arious*."

"You were the one jumping up and down." I mimed her pointing hysterically to the gap at the side of the house. "There. *There*."

She giggled again, and took some eggs out of the fridge. "After you left I had to tell Dad I was playing Jenga by myself. I think he thinks I'm going nuts. Here all alone. He says he has a big surprise for Christmas."

I hadn't thought about it before, but their house wasn't decorated at all. It was like the two of them were guests for the holidays without any hosts. I sat at the table, couldn't handle being still, and stood back up again.

"Maybe I could come visit your home? If Dad lets me?" Kassie said.

"Has your dad been here this morning?"

"I told you, he's out. You're acting funny."

When I made fists, I could feel the dirt from Quincey's grave, gritty under my nails. "Excited for tomorrow."

She gave me a strange look. "Okay."

And then Trey walked in the door.

We both stared at him. And he stared at us, slowly straightening up to his full height. He still wore the dark blue anorak he'd had on when he'd buried Quincey.

"Kassie," he said.

"Hi, Daddy!" Kassie said, like it was totally cool that she had a boy in their house.

"Who do we have here?" said Trey, still looking at me. The same words he'd used when he first saw me at home, in the foyer. Under his storm of freckles, his face turned extra pink.

"This is Van."

"Van, Kassie may not have toldja the house rules. What's the rule I'm thinking of, little gumdrop?"

He didn't sound angry. He didn't really sound like he felt much at all. And I knew that he had killed a man just last night.

"No guests," Kassie said. I could hardly hear her and I'm sure Trey couldn't from twenty feet away.

"How do you two know one another?" He was still standing in the doorway. Blocking it. I was sure he could catch me—was *ready* to catch me—if I ran for the backyard.

"From school," I said.

Bad pick. Terrible. Even Kassie winced.

Trey closed the door behind him. "Kassie goes to an all-girls school."

"Basketball," Kassie said. "I met Van when we played at Hovick Middle School."

I nodded. That was what I had meant, sure.

Trey moved into the room. He really was tall. "You kids got an early start today. Or were you here all night, Van?"

"No, sir," I said, quick as a rabbit. "My mom dropped me off."

Trey hesitated. He probably didn't know anything about

our family. It's not like Granddad would be sharing secrets over beers or anything. Maybe there was a mom, and she knew I was here.

"Van, go home," he said.

Sounded great to me. As I stood up, I saw that Trey's cowboy boots were caked with dirt from the foundation hole. He noticed me noticing.

"Whoops," he said with the same flat spookiness. "Looks like I'm tracking on the floor."

"*Daddy*," said Kassie, pleading. "Van just *got* here."

"I'll go," I said.

"Then I'm walking you out," Kassie exclaimed, and stomped past her dad to open the door. I'd have to pass him, too. My feet started moving, though the calm part of my brain that had helped me with dead Quincey seemed to have flown far away.

As I passed him, Trey put out one long finger and hooked it around my arm. I could pull away. I didn't dare.

"You say hi to Dono for me," he said. So softly I was sure Kassie couldn't hear him.

He let me go and I joined Kassie outside. We walked down the steps, and she led me around the house a little where no one could see, from inside or from the street.

"M'sorry," Kassie said.

"It's all right." It really was. I was out of that damn house.

"I wanted to—" she started. "I thought we could hang out. It's Christmas Eve."

"Yeah." Trey had said to say hello to Granddad. Did that mean he was okay? Or was it a threat, 'cause Trey had already—

"Will you see me tomorrow? It doesn't have to be here," Kassie said in a rush. "I could sneak out."

Tomorrow seemed a very long time away. "Okay."

She kissed me.

It was so shocking, I didn't do anything. Not that I had

time to, because it was already done. Kassie stepped back and tucked a lock of her orange hair behind her ear.

I was supposed to say something now. I knew that much.

"Um." More than *that*. "That was cool."

She smiled, and I exhaled.

"See you tomorrow?" she said.

I nodded and Kassie ran back up the steps and out of sight.

My face was hot. Davey would call me a pussy for blushing.

I went to get my bike out of the brush. As I wheeled it to the road, I saw Trey in the upstairs window, watching me. Seeing the proof for himself that I'd lied about my mom dropping me off. The pedals crunched under my sneaker soles as I pumped as hard as I could, standing up and just running like the devil.

At the end of the block, I stopped.

My shoes. My black Adidas were still stained and trailing dirt from Quincey's grave. The same dirt that I'd seen on Trey's boots.

He must have seen it on me, too.

He *knew*.

TWENTY-EIGHT

I T WAS BARELY NOON by the time we all regrouped on the *Francesca*, but it felt like midnight after a weekend spent scaling mountains. As wired as my mind was after the morning's action, my body clamored for a large meal and a long siesta.

Hollis had left the red and blue suitcases on the cabin floor. I unlocked both and flipped the lids open. All ten canvas sacks lay like crushed fruit within. I set one on the dining table and sat down to unzip it and remove the contents, placing them almost reverently in front of me.

"Aren't they lovely?" said Hollis.

They really were. The gold bars looked like what treasure was supposed to look like. Each one had the heft that wealth should have.

"Do you suppose Fekkete found out what we did? Before they grabbed him?" Hollis said.

I glanced over at the O'Hassons. Mickey had collapsed on the settee, more asleep than awake. Cyndra sat on the floor next to him, head by his stomach, already out. Only a kid could sleep in that position, half on and half off the couch.

"You've got a lot of room for Fekkete in your head," I said to Hollis.

He grimaced. "We set a man up to die. It sticks, somehow."

"I don't make it a habit."

"Christ. No one's saying that."

"Fekkete was a marked man before I met him." I nodded at the father and daughter across the cabin. "They got in the way. That was partly my fault. Without me helping him, Mick might never have gone near the safe."

"I'll drop the subject," Hollis said.

Corcoran interrupted by coming in from outside. He slammed the sliding door, startling Cyndra into momentary wakefulness.

"There's a guy can move some of the bars," he said. "I didn't say how many, he didn't ask. We'll get into details in person."

"The gold's probably clean, Jimmy," Hollis said. "Market value."

"Yeah, maybe. I like cash. Let the other guy worry about the damn provenance." He looked at me. "What about you?"

I hadn't reflected on much past surviving this morning's exchange. Luce would have said that I'd been thinking tactically, not strategically. The kind of thinking that made planning my future an ongoing challenge. Maybe the money would last longer if I held on to some of the kilobars for the long term.

"Let's hear what your fence offers," I said. "Then I'll decide."

Corcoran shrugged. "I'm gonna set up a meet with him. Tomorrow, or the day after. Not to trade yet, just to talk numbers."

I whistled through my teeth a little as I stood up. Every bruise from my fight with Rénald at the quarry was saluting smartly.

"If your extra berth's open, I'm going to crash until sundown," I said to Hollis.

"Be my guest. What about these?" He beamed at the suitcases like they were favored grandchildren.

I nodded at the cabin wall, where he'd recently held the smuggled bedposts. "You know where to hide stuff."

"I suppose I do at that." Hollis shook Cyndra gently by the shoulder. "Come on, love. Let's put you and your dad below."

The two of them got O'Hasson up and moving and made their careful way down the stairs.

I looked down at the small pyramid I'd made of the bars. About four hundred grand in one little pile. Despite my earlier determination to enjoy the day, my thoughts kept steering in dark directions. Was this just a hangover from the action? Dono was given to black moods after a score. Even, and maybe especially, if it had gone well. Because the fun part was over.

Fatigue, maybe. They taught us in the Army not to trust our emotions when the mission had ground us down to a nub. Use the higher intellect, and tell the reptile brain to go fuck itself with its tail.

Or maybe the fatigue was just an excuse and my mood was entirely appropriate. Sane, even. There was a whole lot of death surrounding the metal that glowed like a molten sun. The drugs that had been sold to buy it. April Slattery, murdered to find it. Fekkete, likely taking the first agonizing steps down his final path right now.

Dono would have told me to shrug those thoughts off. That all money had pain in its history somewhere, whether it came from a corporation's dividends or from the sweat of manual labor. Believing anything else was an illusion.

I didn't fully subscribe to that argument. But the gold bars seemed to hum their own tune. It wasn't joyful.

I WOKE IN THE guest stateroom of the *Francesca*. On the opposite wall, the setting sun painted a skewed copy of the porthole's oval shape. My watch alarm hadn't gone off yet. Something else had roused me.

I got up and went to check on the O'Hassons. A note in Hollis's crooked handwriting taped to my door said that he and Corcoran had gone out for provisions, and that he hoped to hell I was ready for some revelry.

Cyndra was asleep in the second stateroom. Mick sat in the main cabin, leaning sideways against the back of the settee. He still looked ready to keel over, skin hanging on his face like it threatened to slide off and fall onto the rug. A sour odor that went beyond unclean to something like decay came from him.

"Get any sleep?" I said.

He shook his head no.

"You were gone for a week."

His eyes sharpened a fraction. "Seemed longer."

"Did they keep you doped? I found a tranquilizer dart on the stairs in the building."

"Huh. So that's what it was. I was at the top of the stairs, and my arm hurt all of a sudden. Thought maybe I was having a heart attack or somethin'. Then I heard them coming and ran away."

I thought of O'Hasson's stiff jean jacket and the shirts underneath, needed to keep his thin body warm even in July. Those layers had probably spared him from taking a full dose from the dart.

"Felt like crap," he said. "Everything after that is all mashed together in my head, what I can remember."

"You torched the place. Nearly burned me down along with it."

"God."

O'Hasson was silent for a long moment. I thought maybe exhaustion had wiped his mind blank again. But when he spoke again, his voice had more strength.

"I was—I went crazy, I know," he said. "For weeks before my parole, all the meds and surgeries and shit. First it was Gar talking to me about the idea. Then it was *me* talking to *him*. If I could just hold on until I got out, and find the safe."

Slattery had set the hook deep into O'Hasson. The little thief sounded humiliated, remembering how he'd been suckered.

"I'm sorry," he said. "I am. I didn't want nothing like this. All I could think about was what Cyn might be doing, every time I woke up."

"Where did they keep you?" I said.

"Most of the time, just one room. Like a concrete shed. Outside, I think. Hot. There was a mattress and a hole in the floor like for an outhouse." He made a disgusted face. "Reeked like rhino shit, especially during the hot part of the day."

"Most of the time?"

"All of it, really. I had a scary-ass dream of being in a place with white tile and metal cabinets and shit like that. But it couldn't have been for real. I was tripping on that trank dope, thinking I was back in the prison sickhouse."

"You're safe now."

"I thought sure they were going to end me, every day. Instead of bringing me food, they'd just put a bullet in my head, or leave me without water." He stared at me. "Why did they let me go?"

I told O'Hasson a short version of the long war between Fekkete and the Slatterys, and the obsessive Ingrid Ekby.

"She let you have the gold?" O'Hasson said, stunned. "Just for finding that asshole?"

"She's nuts," I said, "and rich enough to get away with it. Whatever revenge she's after, money's no object."

O'Hasson thought about that. "Maybe not to her. Some of her boys asked me every day. What Gar had told me about the gold, how much he'd said would be in the safe, if there might be more gold somewhereselse. Those boys are in it for the profit."

I remembered the hunter Marshall, ticked off that Ingrid was willing to use the gold as bait. Dissent in the ranks. I wondered if Boule had been the one keeping them in line, or if they were scared enough of Ingrid to stay obedient.

"If I hadn't been so weak, they might have put it to me a lot harder," O'Hasson continued. "Instead they said if I helped them find all the gold, they'd leave Cyndra out of it. I didn't get it at first. Then he—*explained* it to me." O'Hasson looked ready to vomit.

"Explained that they would hurt her."

"Yeah," he said, almost inaudibly.

Everybody knew O'Hasson's weak spot was threatening his kid. The suits and ties didn't make Ingrid's men any less scummy than the Sledge City animals.

O'Hasson pointed a finger at me. "I knew you'd gotten away clean, Van. The shitheads never asked me about a partner. Never even occurred to them I might not have come alone to steal the gold. Morons."

"We stepped into a snake pit," I said. "Lucky for us that they were more interested in sinking their fangs into each other. Ingrid Ekby got what she was after. So did we. It's over. Get some rest."

"I *can't*." He waved an angry hand. "They're still out there."

Ingrid and her hunters had taken something from O'Hasson. Pride, I guessed. The belief that he could protect his daughter. And the men who did it were still walking free. Hell, they'd finally captured Fekkete. If we'd won, so had they.

"Forget them," I said. "You and Cyndra are what counts."

"Is Cyn okay?" he said. "After those sons of bitches chasing after her?"

"Your kid is tough as hell," I said, "but she needs her dad. Ask her where she wants to live, and go there. Make something good out of it."

He grinned softly. A hint of his old charm.

"Every day above ground is a good day," he said, putting mocking quotes around it. "This prison doctor would say that to me. To keep up my spirits. You believe that? I got terminal cancer, I'm in max sec getting cavity searched every time they take me for a fucking X-ray, and he wants me to stay positive. It kinda worked. He was such an idiot, I laughed every time."

He stood up to shuffle off to the lower cabins.

I foraged in Hollis's cabinets, found coffee, found booze, decided I didn't want either. Instead I went outside. The night was warm and promised to stay that way until long after darkness, even with the breeze picking up off the shore. I climbed the ladder to the flying bridge at the top of the boat. Hollis had the canvas roof folded down and the bridge was open to the sky. I sat behind the helm and watched the stars making their first hesitant gleams through the peach-colored ether.

Fine advice, Shaw, even if O'Hasson wasn't willing to listen. Take the money and build yourself a regular life. Make a few good days.

TWENTY-NINE

WHATEVER SLEEP O'HASSON MANAGED to grab that night, he was dead on his feet again by the time we reached Addy Proctor's little bungalow later that morning. Cyndra raced from the truck into Addy's arms, and the old woman clung to the girl as if a tornado was trying to tear her away. Stanley barked from the backyard, upset at not being included in the reunion.

"Big damn dog," O'Hasson mumbled. "He bite?"

"Try not to look like an apple fritter," I said.

"Good Lord," said Addy, getting her first real look at O'Hasson. "Sit down, please."

"Bed," I corrected. "Addy Proctor, Mick O'Hasson. Any other small talk can wait."

Addy bustled about, grabbing extra blankets and directing the unsteady man toward the bedroom where his daughter had been crashing during the past week. Cyndra and I were left in the front room. We mirrored each other collapsing onto the sofa and Addy's overstuffed easy chair.

"Gah," Cyndra said. "Can I watch TV?"

"Up to Addy. But far as I'm concerned, you've earned the right to do whatever the hell you want for the next year or two."

"Sweet," she said, resting her head on the arm and lying down, limp as a sock.

"You'll have to go somewhere else once your dad can travel," I said. "Not here, not Reseda."

"'Cause those guys might look for us," she mumbled into the armrest.

"You figured that already, huh?"

"Dad's still kinda freaked."

"He's gone through a lot. Think you can look after him? Not give him too much shit?"

"I guess. Can we live anywhere?"

"Let's stick to this continent," I said.

Cyndra folded herself into the corner, like she was trying to wedge her spare frame behind the floral-print cushions. "I dunno. Here?"

"Seattle's out, I told you." Off her distressed look I added, "It doesn't have to be far."

"Sure."

Maybe tiptoeing around the truth wasn't helping. I was telling the kid she had to give up her entire life. Lousy news at any age.

"Hey," I said, "you won't be alone. Addy would stick a saddle on Stanley and ride him to come and see you."

Cyndra gave a noncommittal tilt of her head. "What happens after?"

"After your dad, you mean."

Her face fell. Jesus. I was really not good at this kind of relating.

"I don't know," I said. "We'll figure something out."

"Addy said your mom died young."

Thanks, Proctor. "Yeah. I was six."

"D'you remember her?"

"Not really." Then, after a moment, "I remember the impression of her more than anything. Are you worried you'll forget your dad?"

No reply was reply enough.

"You've got time now," I said. "He's here."

She turned and stared up at the ceiling, which was a field of pristine white above the blue stenciled flowers at the top of the walls, unblemished by overhead lights or hanging plants. "I'd like to go somewhere where it snows a lot."

"So ask Mick to take you to a snowy place. Colorado, Utah. Somewhere the college students major in snowboarding."

"Ugh. College."

I laughed. "Okay. Get through middle school first."

"Bleah." She giggled. "Ugh, too. *All* the sounds." Stanley barked from the backyard, and that launched Cyndra into fits. "Woof," she said.

"You're punchy. Go play with the hound."

She headed out, and within a minute I heard the sounds of them tearing around the grass. Kids were weird. Down one second, up the next.

Give Mickey a few days of rest, get him back on his meds, and he should be strong enough to make the journey, whatever direction they chose. We'd have to establish some fake identities for them, solid enough to let O'Hasson get treatment and enroll Cyndra in school. A foundation to build their new life. I couldn't play guardian angel to the O'Hasson family forever. But letting them wander off on their own now would be like leaving an unwanted dog far out in the woods. They might survive. The odds sucked.

THIRTY

HOLLIS CALLED ME AT a quarter after two the next afternoon, while I was waiting at a stoplight on my way to Bully Betty's. I hadn't yet decided if today would be the day when I gave notice, or whether I'd stick it out and see how much I enjoyed the job when I wasn't doing it for the paycheck.

"Where are you?" he said.

"On the Hill. What's wrong?"

My phone buzzed in answer. Hollis had forwarded me a text, from Corcoran.

All good. Meet me at boat. Thanks. Sent at 2:10 P.M.

"That's it?" I said.

"'*Thanks*'? From Jimmy Blessed Corcoran? He was supposed to meet with his fence at noon. Plus, he knew I was going to be down here in Thurston County all day. Why's he asking me to come meet him?"

A hot day, and suddenly my skin went cold.

"I'm going to the *Francesca*," I said.

"Boyyo. That might not be the wisest plan."

Maybe not. But I had a sudden dreadful feeling about Hollis's boat. And Corcoran.

AT FAR END OF the big marina, Hollis's dock floated a generous quarter-mile from the offices and yacht club. I forced myself to approach slowly, checking the scattering of weekday-morning cars in the lot. Scanning every moorage slip. If there was a soul aboard any of the nearby boats, they were keeping their peace.

The *Francesca* strained gently at her lines, nudged by the current. I knocked on the hull. No answer. I grabbed the rail and climbed up and onto the foredeck. The boat groaned and rocked fractionally with my weight. I readjusted the Smith & Wesson under my jacket for a better draw and walked silently aft on the water side. No sounds or movement, other than my own.

All looked normal in the cabin through the sliding glass door. Maybe even slightly tidier than usual. I used my lockpicks to open the door and slid it wide. Listened again, and heard only the breeze through the surrounding forest of masts.

I made my way, very carefully, into the cabin and through every stateroom, checking the closets and lockers. The *Francesca* was a large boat, but even a sizable cruiser doesn't offer many places for a person to hide. I was alone.

The cabin *was* neater than normal. Most of the clothes and papers were strewn on the port side now, leaving the starboard free of clutter. The starboard, where Hollis had built his hidden compartments.

Where we had stashed the gold.

I yanked at the corner wedges and bookshelf rails, removing smaller pieces to unlock the larger ones as Hollis had demonstrated. I had to see. To make sure that the red and blue suitcases with their millions were still inside.

My hands worked as my mind raced ahead. Who had known about the secret compartments, besides Hollis and myself? Who could have opened them without tearing the interior apart by force? Corcoran, for sure. O'Hasson? Cyndra, even? They were here with Hollis and the gold, after EverCon. I had thought they were both exhausted and asleep in the forward staterooms. Had one of them managed to spy on Hollis as he stashed the cases inside?

I set about lifting the settee frame and attached flooring. The piece was long and awkward. I had to shift one side first, and then the other.

A gap below, against the spider's web pattern of strands in the raw fiberglass hull. No suitcases. No gold.

Empty.

I clutched at the wood of the wall, the larger of the two pieces that covered Hollis's big hiding place, and yanked it away in one pull.

I'd been wrong. Again.

The compartment wasn't empty.

The body of Jimmy Corcoran stared up at me.

THIRTY-ONE

CORCORAN'S FACE AND BALD pate were watery white, liver spots and freckles standing out harshly. His mouth was slightly agape. Looking even more like an eel in death. The curve of the hull held his body almost vertically, like it was propped up on display in an undertaker's window.

In the very center of his chest, a small splotch of blood stained the plaid stripes a solid rust, surrounded by darker flakes. The cotton charred by a muzzle flare from something close, something small-caliber. A teacup could have held the amount of blood that had seeped from the wound.

I touched his shoulder. Half to offer comfort that Corcoran would never feel, half to feel the encroaching rigor. He hadn't been dead long. Two or three hours in his concealed coffin, I guessed.

I let him lie, and sat down opposite him.

You shitheel, he seemed about to say. *You brought me into this.*

Yeah, Jimmy. I'm sorry.

Shove your sorry. My family ain't living off your sorry. My kids can't say shit to your sorry. You're responsible, and any apology is just you trying to skate through on chance and charm. I hate you.

I didn't have an answer. Or any argument. Jimmy was right again.

Replacing the wall would mean enclosing his body once again in the suffocating space. Instead, I took the blanket from the berth in the spare stateroom and brought it back to drape over Corcoran. The blanket had a pattern of small fleur-de-lis, white on blue. It gave his shroud an oddly ceremonial feel. Like a state funeral.

Hollis picked up before the second ring.

"Yes?" he said.

"Jimmy's dead. I'm on board your boat."

He made a sound, something like a cough that was striving to become a word.

"On my way," he managed, and hung up.

Something else occurred to me. Something I had to do while it was still possible. I looked outside to make sure there was no danger of anyone wandering past on the dock. I removed the blanket from Corcoran's body and patted down his pockets. Completely empty. Then I picked him up and laid his body on its back on the hardwood floor.

Sorry about this, Jimmy.

I put one hand under his knee and another on his ankle, and pulled hard to fold the leg up toward his torso. Corcoran hadn't been a muscular guy. His rigor wasn't too far along. Those facts combined to make the job easy, at least in the physical sense. I bent his other leg more or less to match. I folded his arms to a severe ninety degrees.

His head I left alone. Maybe it would be possible to bend it forward at the neck, to make his body into more of a ball. But I didn't want to do it. I placed the blanket over him again and sat on the captain's chair to wait.

HOLLIS LIFTED THE CORNER of the blanket to see the body. He didn't examine it, just looked down at Corcoran's face. It had been a bad year or so for Hollis. First Dono, and now Jimmy C.

"Did O'Hasson do this?" he said.

"I don't think so. They left Jimmy in the hiding space, Hollis."

He looked up from the body to me. His arm holding the blanket lowered slowly.

"Jimmy must have told them how to open it," I said.

"He would never help—"

"He would if they threatened Nakri or their kids," I said. "He'd give up the money in an instant."

Hollis's scowling face shifted rapidly to regret. "Then they made Jimmy send me that text, asking me to come to the boat. But he wouldn't allow them to lure me in. Ah, Jimmy."

The hunters. It had to be. Fekkete was out of the picture. The Sledge City fighters were vicious, but not clever. How had they found Corcoran?

O'Hasson. They had held him for a week. He'd told me himself that Marshall and the others had squeezed him for any information about the gold every day he was captive. That they had threatened Cyndra. They could have broken him. Maybe the little burglar would do whatever he was told, even after he was out of their hands, just to protect himself and his daughter. We might all be compromised.

Hollis had replaced the blanket over Corcoran. He looked dazedly at the starboard side of the cabin and the gaping compartment.

"Why would they have left him like this?" he said. "Why go to all the trouble?"

"A message, I suppose. 'Take what belongs to us, and this is what you get.'" There was a dark whimsy to the act of hiding Corcoran, like his corpse was some prank.

"I mean like this." He motioned to the lump under the blanket. "Rolled up. How could he fit?"

"That was my doing."

Hollis didn't need to voice his question.

"We have to move him," I explained. "Soon."

"Move him?"

I kicked myself for not seeing it earlier. Hollis was in shock. Mild, maybe, but still not firing on all his cylinders.

"Come on." I walked outside, and after a moment Hollis followed. I slid the door closed and we sat down across from one another.

"The quicker Jimmy is found," I said, "the sooner we can help Nakri. She'll have to know. Which means either we call 911 now and bring them here, or we move Jimmy somewhere the cops will discover him quickly. You know which choice is smarter."

"And you—you shifted him. For what? To fit into a sail bag or some horrible thing?"

I bit my tongue. Logic wasn't going to help my case here.

Hollis looked through the glass door. The wretched lump of the blanket seemed to draw his gaze as surely as his thoughts. When he turned back to me, his eyes had a sheen of tears.

"Your soul needs help, Van," he said. "I know your road hasn't been easy. I know your grandfather, for whatever love he held for you, could be a cold unbending bastard. But even he would have given our man a moment. Just one."

"Hollis—"

"You leave now. I'll look after Jimmy."

I went.

THIRTY-TWO

I REACHED ADDY ON HER phone on the third try, just as I was cresting the hill.

"What on earth—" she started.

"Where's O'Hasson?"

"I was resting. Has that been you calling?"

"Addy."

"Calm yourself. He and Cyndra went down to the arboretum. I told them to. It'll do them—"

"Driving or walking? How long have they been gone?"

"Walking, of course."

"Did O'Hasson go anywhere this morning? Did he take your car?"

"I've been asleep, Van. I was up most of the night with one or both of them. Now tell me what's happening."

I hung up.

Walking, they wouldn't have gone far. Not in the kind of condition O'Hasson was in. If the little son of a bitch hadn't been faking his weakness. Right now, I couldn't trust anything.

I entered the park off of Madison and slowed, trying to spot them on the footpaths I could see from the road. The arboretum was extensive. Gardens and shelters and small forests. There were a lot more walking trails hidden from view. If they had decided to go for a hike—

There. A flash of Cyndra's raven hair, through the trees just off to my right. I sped past and ignored the DO NOT ENTER signs to leave the truck in the nearest lot by the Japanese garden, and ran back.

"Hey," Cyndra said as I came pounding across the road. She was kneeling on the dirt path in front of a pond left by the rains, as the waterbugs skipped over the surface. I brushed past her. O'Hasson was forty feet farther along, checking out the little stone caretaker's cottage that had stood on the grounds for most of a century.

I grabbed him by his arm, my hand going almost all the way around his thin bicep.

"Move," I said, steering him around the cottage, where we would be out of view.

"Van?" Cyndra said.

"The fuck?" O'Hasson tripped, and I dragged him along without pausing.

"Jimmy Corcoran is dead," I said so the kid wouldn't hear. "Somebody murdered him this morning."

"Jesus Christ," he said.

"What's going on?" said Cyndra, running to catch up.

"It was the same men who kidnapped you, and you're the only link between them and Corcoran." I pressed O'Hasson against the gray stone wall. "So you're going to tell me what you know, or I'll put you in a sack and drop you in front of Pacific Pearl with a sign around your neck."

O'Hasson went white.

"Van, stop it," Cyndra said.

"Tell me, Mickey."

"I been here," O'Hasson said. "With the old lady, all the time."

"It's true!" Cyndra said.

"Phone calls," I said.

"Nothing." He tried to twist away.

People had always told me I reminded them of my grandfather.

Today I felt like him. I looked at O'Hasson, and he shrank back against the rough stones.

"Don't lie to me," I said.

"I swear."

"He wouldn't," Cyndra said. She pulled at my arm that was holding O'Hasson. She weighed about as much as one of the skipper bugs.

"They killed Jimmy," I said, "and they took the gold. All of it."

O'Hasson's knees buckled. His body stayed where I had pinned it to the wall.

"Did you tell them where it was?" I said.

He shook his head, as if trying to wake up.

"What did they promise you, Mickey?"

His bright eyes were wide with shock. But he didn't look away. Was he telling me the truth? Or too terrified to talk?

Cyndra pulled harder.

"Please," she said. "Please don't hurt him."

I let O'Hasson go. He crumpled to the ground, and Cyndra followed, catching him. I left them there, huddled together against the fairytale cottage.

THIRTY-THREE

I HADN'T BEEN AT MY house in a week. The wooden frame looked frailer than before, as if neglect had starved it. Some kids had been flinging rocks. Dents and splinters marked the street-side boards. I sat at the top of the stone steps, legs dangling into the space between the remnants and the yet-to-be, and thought about what the hell to do next.

Nothing could fix what had happened. The gold was gone. Jimmy Corcoran was gone. My options were down to zero.

I reached out to grab a rock myself. Maybe I could bounce it off the second-story window frame. Stuck firmly to the underside of my sleeve was a bit of curled white paper. I peeled it off.

It was round and shiny, and it took me a moment to place it. It was the back side of one of Corcoran's little GPS trackers for Cyndra, the paper you peeled away to expose the adhesive.

The bit of paper hadn't been on my sleeve before I was at the boat. It must have stuck there while I was moving—

Jimmy. I had reached under his body to lift him away from the hull. The paper had been underneath him.

But where was the tracker?

I grabbed my phone and pulled up the app Corcoran had installed for me, the one that could ask the trackers to send a signal. Turned it on. It showed one tracker currently active. I hit the key to have it give me its coordinates. A Google map appeared, with one bright orange dot blinking on it.

East. Way east, almost out of the county. A long long way from Hollis's boat.

Jimmy, you brilliant, brave son of a bitch.

You tagged the bastards.

CORCORAN MUST HAVE KNOWN they were likely to kill him. He'd done his best to warn Hollis away from the *Francesca*. And amazingly, he'd kept his head enough to palm a tracker and slap it on one of the cases.

Would they spot it? The tracker was covered in black rubber. Unobtrusive. Nobody was going to move a hundred-pound suitcase around more than they had to. I told myself all these things during the next half-hour of frantic driving, holding on to hope.

The orange dot blinked. I wouldn't ask it for another signal until I was right on top of the last coordinates. Jimmy had said the tracker had enough juice for two, maybe three signals at the most. If the hunters were in motion, driving out of town, I was fucked.

The roads grew narrower and the clusters of businesses spread farther apart. I was headed for cow country, the valley around Carnation or Fall City. My tires sang as I pressed the accelerator harder, the Dodge soaring past every citizen making their way home on Route 202.

I followed the map southeast, off the highway onto a country road. The broad expanse of the valley slowly revealed itself through the trees. On the floodplain, roads and buildings were built on man-made earthworks, four or more yards above the valley floor. The road I was driving on would become a causeway surrounded by marsh in the wet season. Now, at the height of summer, it was like an elevated track, almost as tall as the light rail running above Pacific Pearl.

A half-mile farther along, the road had deteriorated to a single lane made of cheap recycled asphalt. I passed what looked like a half-finished drainage project. A wide ditch ran parallel to the lane. A white Hino hauling truck was parked on the far side of the ditch, its flatbed loaded with a pyramid of long concrete pipes, each two feet in diameter.

I was very close to the tracker coordinates on the map. I stopped the truck. Would the tracker give me one more signal?

There. The coordinates hadn't moved. Barely a quarter-mile away, directly across a field of grasses and scrub. I pulled into the drainage site to leave the Dodge behind the big Hino truck with its cargo of pipes. The Smith & Wesson came with me.

I climbed down the embankment from the road and began to pick my way through the brush. The tips of the tallest rushes caught in my hair, every step creating a tiny avalanche of seeds. My head filled with the weighty hot smell of pollen and the tangible buzz of a hundred insects.

A farmhouse and barn came into view, a hundred yards off. I bent low. When I had closed half the distance, I began crawling.

The farmhouse, once white, was now a grayish ivory. The barn had always been brown. Elements had bleached its color and beaten it down until was a few degrees off true from any direction. The Chevy Impala parked in front of the barn was so clean by comparison that its crimson paint shined like a ruby in the middle of a cowpat. I'd seen that Impala before, when Boule and his men had come after me at the train station.

The hunters were home tonight.

There was another small square building, almost a shed, behind the farmhouse. Smooth concrete on a similar base, with a flat roof and a metal door. It might have been intended as a waterproof storage space in the event of flooding. Keep the lawnmower and the power tools safe and dry.

More recently, I would bet that the shed had held Mickey O'Hasson. A good, isolated spot for Ekby's team to hide their victim.

The sun had dipped halfway behind the far hills. Shadows stretched, tentatively at first. No lights on in the house.

Maybe I had been wrong about Ekby's team being here now. If they were away, it might mean a chance to find the suitcases in the house. But if they returned while I was tossing the place, it would be a long and dangerous run from the house to the nearest cover.

I had just decided to wait until full dark, when the front door opened and Marshall came out.

He was dressed in the hunters' usual business attire, white dress shirt and sand-colored sport coat and trousers. In his left hand he held a garment bag, and a carryall was tucked under that same arm. He pointed keys toward the crimson Impala. It beeped obediently. He opened the backseat, tossed the luggage inside, and returned to the house.

They were moving out. Now that Ekby had Fekkete and the gold, her hired guns were closing up shop.

Five minutes passed. The buzzing of the bugs increased in volume as darkness took hold. A light clicked on upstairs in the farmhouse. Someone in a blue shirt passed it. Two of them inside, then. At least.

Take them at the house? I had the advantage of surprise. They had home turf and numbers. There might be more than two of them.

You know the smart thing to do, Corcoran snarled in my mind.

Wait by the door for them to come out. If it was just Marshall alone, loaded down with more luggage, then I could choke him out, and take the other in the house before he missed his buddy. If more than one emerged—

Just shoot the fuckers.

Part of me wanted to. An unforgiving part, as ruthless in its way as Ingrid Ekby or any of her men. It wasn't like I hadn't killed before. And what was this if not another kind of war?

Then do them, and that crazy bitch.

Can't do it, Jimmy. I'll make sure your family is taken care of. I'll make their whole crew sorry they ever set foot in my city. But I can't murder them.

Idiot.

Yeah. Probably.

The porch light clicked on as the door opened again and Marshall came out carrying another two bags. Apparently that thick neck made him the bellhop of the team. He loaded them with the others into the backseat. Not the trunk.

Because the trunk was full of something else, I realized.

Gotcha, you bastards.

They had almost certainly left the cases in the car after fleeing from the marina. Why bother lugging the heavy things into the house if you were skipping town as soon as possible? Marshall went back inside, as if in a hurry to get on the road.

Now. It was dark enough. A half-mile past the farm, I could see the lights of the highway. That would be my way out of the valley.

I moved across the open ground to the Impala, grateful with every step that the farm drive was soft dirt. The car windows were down and the door unlocked. I softly pulled the trunk release and eased the lid up.

One blue metallic suitcase. I popped it open. The plain canvas duffels with their gold were still inside.

Half. A whole lot better than nothing. But what had they done with the red case in the hours since they'd left the *Francesca*? Was it inside the house?

Movement to my right, in the doorway.

I ducked behind the car. There was a shout and a bullet ripped metal from the open trunk lid. The crack of the shot echoed through the valley. I drew and returned fire through the doorway, half aiming, half giving myself cover as I dove into the driver's seat.

Another shot splintered the rear window. The angle of the Impala put the rear of the car between me and the house, but it wouldn't be long before they flanked me, or fired from the second story right through the car roof, or any number of tactics that could finish me fast. I jammed the awl point of my multi-tool into the ignition and smacked it with the heel of my hand. Pulled it out and did it again. More shouts outside. I glanced over the seat, to see Marshall running off the passenger side, headed for the cover of the shed. I let him go. The other hunter would be moving left, and that would give him a clear shot at me through the open car door.

There. He glanced around the corner of the house and ducked back. I aimed this time and blew off a jagged chunk of the wood trim at head level, just to keep him honest.

I smacked the awl one last time and pulled it out of the ignition. The lock pins would have fallen into place. Should have. Insert screwdriver. Turn. And gave thanks when the engine roared in answer.

A shot cracked off the hood, and a second went wide as I hit the gas and the Impala leapt forward, dirt flying behind it. More shots. The back window took another hole, and then I was onto the cracked and bumpy lane flying south, feeling like it was the road to heaven. Bye-bye, assholes.

The hunters still knew about the *Francesca*. I'd call Hollis, convince him to take it offshore for a while. Then we'd figure out how to set Ekby and her team up for a hard fall. Maybe find a way to plant evidence linking them to Jimmy's murder. That would be fitting.

O'Hasson and Cyndra would need protecting, too. I wasn't convinced that O'Hasson didn't have something to do with the hunters finding Corcoran so quickly. But that didn't mean I would let the vengeful—

The road was blocked.

There had been no detour or warning signs. But a giant Caterpillar bulldozer was parked across the narrow lane, its treads nearly draped over either side of the embankment. No way around it.

Oh shit. I would have to go back.

I hauled the Impala around so fast that the open trunk lid bounced and slammed itself shut.

I'd driven at least two miles from the farmhouse. The hunters must know the road was closed in this direction. That I would have to turn around and come back. Could they block the road at their end? I hadn't seen another vehicle at the farmhouse. Maybe they'd just wait and blow my tires to shreds. Followed immediately by me.

In another thirty seconds, the lights of the farmhouse in view, I got my answer.

Headlights. Big headlights, on an equally big truck with a white square face. The Hino flatbed. Two hundred and thirty horsepower and hauling six tons of concrete pipe. Far off but coming fast. Head-on.

THIRTY-FOUR

NOWHERE TO RUN. I slammed on the Impala's brakes and sent it skidding sideways. For an instant I thought it might jitter off the road into the deep ditch, but the treads held. I shifted into reverse and spun the car around, and when I hit the gas again, the Hino was only fifty yards behind me, coming down like a hammer on a nail.

The Impala's engine screamed. The Hino was thirty yards out. Ten. Its huge headlights shone directly through the shattered rear window, turning the interior of the Impala into high noon. The flatbed's bumper nearly scraped crimson paint from my trunk before the nimbler Impala won the race and started to pull away.

They didn't bother shooting at me. I would run out of road soon enough. We both flew down the straight narrow lane, rockets fired out of the same barrel.

The bulldozer blocked the road, directly ahead. A few dozen scant yards between me and the giant Hino now. Would it be enough?

I had to brake. They expected me to brake.

I kept it floored.

There was two feet of space between the bulldozer and the steep drop-off to the valley floor below. I wasn't going to make it. I didn't need to. Even if I rolled the Impala into the ditch ten feet below, it would be better than what the Hino would do to me.

I edged right. Aimed for the gap, and braced.

They must have guessed I was going to try to U-turn again. The Hino swerved left, ready to cut me off and mash me into a two-dimensional shape. Their swerve opened up an instant patch of night directly behind me, and I stomped the brakes so hard that the rear of the Impala nearly jumped into the air.

They realized their mistake, tried to veer the massive weight of the truck back to the right. It screamed past me, a hurricane inches away, and grazed my front fender, tearing it and my headlight off effortlessly. The Impala bucked like an angry horse. The Hino braked, far too late. Its tires clutched desperately at the asphalt, one long shriek of agony.

It must have only taken a second, at the speed the Hino was traveling, but I felt I had a year to watch with sick fascination. The flatbed's taillights jumped. I saw it skid, tilt, farther and farther, until it toppled, still flying forward. The rear tires, suspended in midair, nearly touched the blade of the bulldozer.

And then the Hino was gone from view, an instant before a massive kettledrum boom that reverberated for miles down the valley.

My engine had stalled. I turned off the Impala's surviving headlight and jumped from the car, gun in hand. The road was still deserted. I looked over the edge.

The Hino lay on its right side. Its thunderous path had ripped a swath of earth from the slope of the embankment and torn through an old barbed-wire fence. One of the strands of wire was still looped tight around a left rear wheel. The truck's headlights shone on, illuminating a storm of terrified insects and debris light enough to still be floating back to earth.

That wasn't the worst of it. The massive concrete pipes had snapped their restraints, scattering and embedding themselves in the ditch. And elsewhere. I climbed down the embankment.

No movement from the Hino's cab. I wasn't expecting any.

Some of the pipes had slammed forward. The metal safety barrier at the front of the truck's bed had never been designed to handle that kind of crushing impact. There was barely a square foot of the Hino's upper cab that remained undamaged.

I looked anyway. The passenger's head and torso were out of sight under one of the pipes, mashed between it and the door. I'd seen worse damage to human bodies. Not often. I'd be happy if I never saw it again.

Marshall's body was more intact, at least enough for me to identify his burly shape. I climbed up the truck, its headlights casting my giant shadow into the field beyond.

From the top, I could reach down into Marshall's sport coat. The coat and his shirt were drenched with blood and more. He had a shoulder holster with a Beretta Nano, just like Boule carried. Maybe Ingrid got a bulk deal. I set the gun and his wallet on the crushed bowl of the driver's door and used my penlight to look more closely.

The Beretta's barrel smelled of burnt powder. I checked the magazine. One bullet light. I knew who had caught it.

A royal blue magnetic keycard was tucked in with Marshall's credit cards, and a bag check tag in similarly colored plastic. Both were marked with the ornate crest of the Olympian Heights. A downtown hotel. *The* downtown hotel. Too ritzy for hired help like Marshall.

Ingrid Ekby, however. She was just the sort of clientele the Olympian cultivated.

Time for me to see how the other half lived. Or died.

THIRTY-FIVE

THE LOBBY OF THE Olympian Heights reached valiantly for the limits of tasteful ornamentation. Where a newer and hipper hotel might have gone for sleek minimalism, every wooden surface of the Olympian was carved, every surface gilded, and the Persian-inspired carpets were soft enough to absorb every click of Vuitton heels without disturbing the hushed ambiance.

Even by Seattle's indifferent dress codes, my stained jeans and torn leather jacket were going to attract attention from the hotel staff if I lingered. A group of businessmen piled out of a taxi van, airport baggage tags still on their luggage. I used the disorganized bunch for cover as they struggled with the revolving door, and crossed to the elevators.

I didn't know Ingrid Ekby's floor, or which room. But she was very rich, and always had been. Accustomed to the best. I swiped on the elevator pad the keycard I'd taken off Marshall's body, and tried the brass button for the top floor, north of the twelfth. It was marked *E*. Probably for *Executive*, or *Elite*. As much dough as Ingrid had, I doubted they had renamed the floor just for her.

The letter glowed a bright cheery red in reply. *E* for *Execution*.

I endured twenty seconds of light jazz before the elevator opened again, revealing a hallway that was the visual version of the jazz, a study in calming neutrals. Only two doors on the hall, spaced very wide. Suites, or penthouses.

I'd try the left door first, 1401. I had made it twenty steps in that direction when the door latch clunked, and I slipped sideways into the ice machine room. The steady hum of the machine covered any sound as I wedged myself behind it.

Tamas Fekkete walked past the room.

I was so stunned to see him, I doubted my eyes, and quickly moved to risk a glance down the hall at his retreating figure. It was him, no question, all the way up to his bald pate. He had changed clothes since EverCon, into another tracksuit, this one orange. He carried one of the plain canvas duffels that had held the gold bars. It looked light. That was all I had time to register before he was gone again. I heard the elevator ding and the doors open and close.

Fekkete wasn't dead. He wasn't even Ingrid's prisoner.

What the hell was happening?

I moved down the hallway and peered through the peephole of 1401. Light shone from within. Ingrid was sure to have Boule with her, and maybe a second bodyguard.

I rapped softly on the door. Waited until a shadow crossed the light at the peephole. Tapped the keycard on the lock. It beeped, and I shouldered the door open fast and stuck the S&W under Boule's nose, his hand still reaching for the latch.

"Don't," I whispered, as that same hand twitched toward his belt. He wore a suit in muted green plaid, no tie, and his hair was glossy with product. I reached under his jacket to carefully divest him of his Beretta, and checked him for a backup piece.

I spun him around and shoved him into the room. "Walk."

We could have played half-court basketball in the sitting area of the suite. Bedroom doors off to its left, and a wet bar and full dining area and kitchen to the right. Maybe the Olympian provided a personal chef.

On the fifth step Boule's weight shifted, tensing for the pivot I knew was coming. I kicked him hard at the base of his spine. He fell to land with a painful thump on his side. His head missed the glass coffee table by an inch.

Ingrid Ekby appeared in the doorway to the bedroom. She looked even better inside than she had in bright daylight. She wore a black silk tunic, belted at the waist. Her sleek hair was brushed straight back to fall below her shoulders.

She briefly glanced at Boule, before turning her freezing gaze at me.

"Scum," she said.

I tapped Boule on the sole of his leather oxford with my boot. "You. Crawl under the table and stay there."

Boule didn't move. Just stared at me, his hero's jaw tight with fury. I raised the heavy S&W, ready to bring it down on his head.

"Ellis," Ingrid said. Boule looked at her and she nodded. He gave me one last glare before starting to wedge himself between the curved gold legs of the coffee table.

"Why did you let Fekkete go?" I said to Ingrid.

"You should care more about yourself. Coming here was a mistake." She could have been speaking to a board of directors, not at all concerned that an armed man had burst into her five-star suite to threaten her.

"Murdering Corcoran was the mistake. How did you find him?"

Her brilliant blue eyes flashed to Boule, back again.

"We didn't kill him," she said.

I touched the barrel of the gun to her forehead.

"You won't shoot," she said.

"Try reaching your men at the farmhouse. Then tell me I'm bluffing," I said.

For the first time, Ingrid looked uncertain. At three inches, she couldn't miss the flecks of blood still staining my fingernail beds, left after a hasty wiping of Marshall's gore from my hands.

"It's the truth," Boule said. "She didn't order anyone's death."

Half-answers. I was fed up with those, even from myself. I walked over to where he lay under the coffee table, picked up a throw pillow from the gold chenille couch, and pinned his knee to the floor with the pillow by pressing the muzzle of the S&W into it.

"Corcoran had the gold," I said. "Fekkete just walked out of here, carrying gold. Fill in every blank, or I'll see how many limbs you're willing to live without."

"The fence," Boule said, words racing each other out of his mouth. "We found the gold through the fence. We put word out to anybody who might make a deal for the gold, weeks ago. Told them we were potential buyers. In case any more bars turned up on the market."

Smart. If April's partner Fekkete had a stash of other kilobars, apart from what the hunters had found in the safe, they might have captured Fekkete when he tried to sell them.

"The fence called Marshall last night," Boule said. "There was a meeting set for today."

"You already had Fekkete by then. What were you after?"

Ingrid spoke before Boule could. "I told Marshall to go. I wanted to make sure you were working alone."

Boule winced as I pressed down on his knee. "Marshall came back with half of the gold, one red suitcase. He said the fence had refused to tell them who the seller was, or whether the other half would be coming. That he drew on them."

"And Marshall told you they were forced to kill the fence. You bought that?"

Ingrid managed to make a shrug look elegant. "I accepted the fact that Marshall might have taken the rest of the gold for himself. If he had, it would be easy enough to confront him later. I had other concerns."

"Now I'm one of them. Marshall lied to you about more than the fence. There was no gold at the meeting. They killed the fence in cold blood, and forced my friend to take them to where we'd stashed the gold. Then they murdered him."

"Do you want an apology? You are a thief. Your friend was a thief. I honored our deal. Fekkete for the gold, and for Michael O'Hasson."

I could have gone with Jimmy to meet the fence. Would I have been able to save him if I had? Or would I have wound up sealed in Hollis's smuggling compartment right next to him?

"Where's the gold?" I said.

"Not here," said Ingrid.

In quick succession I walked through every room, keeping an eye on both of them as I searched. The red suitcase wasn't here, and neither were the canvas bags full of kilobars.

I couldn't take their lives. And apparently I couldn't steal their gold. But I could steal their revenge.

"Who are you calling?" Ingrid said.

"Sledge City Gym. Somebody there will care that Fekkete's walking around loose."

"No," she said immediately.

How about that. Actual emotion from the ice queen.

"Give me a reason," I said.

"I need him. I'll pay you." She vibrated with sudden intensity. The change was startling.

"You've sung that song before."

"The gold is in the hotel vault. I promised it to Fekkete. He has two bars to show as proof that he has more."

"Ingrid," Boule said from the floor.

"I'll get you an equal amount," she said. Making fists so tight, her nails must be cutting her palms. "But you must help us."

"Proof for who?" I said.

She didn't answer. I pressed Send and put the phone to my ear.

"Joe Slattery," she said, like the words were razors on her tongue.

I paused, and cut the call. "Joe's dead."

Ingrid made a sound closer to a raven's caw than a human laugh. "God, I wish. I've wanted nothing but his death for my entire life, it seems."

"He disappeared twenty years ago. More."

"He had to. Because my father—the great goddamn Karl Ekby—would have cut a hole in his belly and taken a week pulling out his intestines with fish hooks."

"Why?"

She looked at me as if the gun in my hand didn't exist, as if she was giving serious thought to tearing my throat out with her pearly teeth.

"Ingrid," Boule said again. His tone was tender. I remembered what Lorenzo had told me.

There were whispers about the brothers. Bad rumors. Beating the living hell out of women. Raping them.

Ingrid's veneer of calm reformed, like a thin sheet of water freezing and smoothing cracks on an icy lake. She turned and walked to the wet bar and began to rinse her hands at the sink.

"You," I said. "You and Joe. That's what this is about."

She dried her hands on the cotton bar towel, delicately, like dabbing a wound. Her makeup was still perfect. Her posture was straighter than ever.

"Me and Joe," she said. "We are tied together, aren't we? Maybe it will always be like that."

"Back in Los Angeles," I guessed, "when the Slatterys worked for Karl."

"I was barely fifteen. Joe had seen me, just once. I was late leaving my father's offices and the Slatterys came. They upset me, even then. They were frightening men."

She stepped back into the center of the room. Reclaiming her position of power.

"A month later, Joe took me right off the street near my school and into the trees. It was—it seemed like a very long time. Hours. I think he meant to kill me when he was through using me. I was an object to him. He was—*crooning*—more and more. Building up to it.

"When I realized that I was going to die, I remembered to fight, like waking from a trance. I bit him. In the neck. So hard that when he threw me off of him his first thought was to stop the blood before catching me, and I ran. I escaped."

Boule and I watched Ingrid. She might have been reading a newspaper listing, for all of the emotion her voice conveyed. But her eyes were unfocused, lost to the past.

"I cannot forget," she said. "I cannot move on. Not until."

"Did you ever believe he was dead?"

"Oh no. I could not hide what had happened. My face, my body—

both required surgery. When Karl went looking, Gar told him that Joe had run. Karl did not believe him. He asked Gar very hard with a lot of pain, but Gar insisted. One of the Slattery trucks was missing. Stayed missing. There was no sign of Joe. Karl let Gar live, to watch him. He had the Slatterys under his thumb for months. Found the banks and the deposit boxes where they hid their money. Then the truck reappeared."

"With Joe's blood," I said.

"And marks of gunfire. Karl was satisfied. I was not. Later, when Gar went to prison and April disappeared herself, I was even more certain that Joe was alive somewhere. But I had no resources. Not at that age. I hounded my father. He broke down and explained how he kept watch on the Slatterys' old deposit boxes. Trying to reassure me."

"Instead, he just gave you a focus," I said.

"April stayed hidden. After my father died, I looked. My private investigators couldn't find her. I was half-convinced that she had died herself, anonymously in some backwater town, and that my only option was to wait until Gar Slattery was released from prison and follow him to Joe."

"Let me guess. April reappeared."

"She emptied one of the old deposit boxes. The clerk called us and earned ten thousand dollars, just by getting pictures of her and her car."

"And you paid her a visit."

Ingrid didn't answer.

"She must have been pretty tough," I said, looking at Boule. "Your men got her to spill about the safe and the gold. But she wouldn't give up Joe. Just like Gar wouldn't, when Karl tortured him."

"The Slatterys are strong," Ingrid said. "They still die."

Strong, and cunning. Joe was alive. Nearby. I believed Ingrid was right about that part. Hell, I might have already seen him. Someone like Joe Slattery would want to be where he could move the pieces on the board, control his men while staying under wraps.

"April told your men about Fekkete, too?" I asked.

"Szabo, his name used to be. I remembered him from my father's trial. A distinctive man. I knew he had worked with Karl at the same time as the Slatterys. If he was April's partner, then I was certain he must have some idea where Joe is now. But he vanished before we could find him."

"So you set the trap at the safe. Hoping to catch Joe, or at least Fekkete."

Ingrid nodded minutely, acknowledging her failed gambit. "One of the last things April confessed was the alarm she had installed in her safe. It was simple enough to use it for our own purposes."

"And you sent Marshall to the fence today on the off chance it was Joe selling the gold and not me. Strikeouts, both times. You've got bad luck, lady."

"Fekkete will bring Joe to me. I will finish this."

I shook my head. "The Slatterys have the Sledge City gang. They're tougher than you." I glanced at Boule under the glass table. "And you're down to the dregs."

"Then help me," Ingrid said. "I meant what I said."

"Like our last deal."

She stepped forward. "Damn you. Don't you think I deserve to see him dead?"

I didn't answer.

"Listen." Ingrid stood directly in front of me. "Gar is being released from prison tomorrow morning. Fekkete will meet him at the airport and take him to see Joe. We'll catch them there. Everything is all prepared."

A bad thought, what sort of dark preparations Ingrid might have made for Joe Slattery. It wouldn't be a simple bullet between the eyes. Not after two decades of rot eating at the woman's soul.

"I'll win," she said.

Maybe she would, somehow. But it wasn't my fight. Let these maniacs massacre each other.

"After you're done, if you're alive," I said, "get out of Seattle. Stay out. If I find you or Boule or any of your people in my town again, it'll be war. You won't win that."

I used one of the bar towels to wipe my prints, as I ejected the magazine of Boule's Beretta and cleared the chamber before dropping the gun on the carpet.

"You were wrong," Ingrid said, just as I reached the door. "Wrong about April."

I stopped.

"You don't think I have the courage to dirty my hands," she said. "But I was the one who gave April Slattery the shot of potassium chloride. I held her under the water. I watched her die."

Ingrid raised her head, every jagged shard of willpower back where it started.

"And I felt better than I have in years," she said.

AGE TWELVE, CHRISTMAS EVE

Home, for the first time, didn't feel safe.

There had been times when it had felt a little scary, sure. I'd had nightmares like every little kid, and then Granddad would leave the lights on and a radio playing for me. He had drawn the line at my sleeping in front of the TV.

And if I'm gonna be totally honest, there were some nights since coming home from the Rolfssons' that our big house seemed a little too big, especially when dodging the creaky stairs on my way down to sneak a snack late at night.

But those are just spookhouse feelings. The kind of scare you get when you know somebody is going to jump out and go *Boo* and you'll yell and then you'll leave and go on to the next ride. Fun.

I saw a dead guy today.

I saw a *murderer* today.

And he knows where I live.

I'd tried Granddad twenty times. Hollis, too, and left him like three messages. I even tried to reach Mr. Willard, and he was scarier than any funhouse. Nobody answered. It was like the whole town had packed up and vanished.

Leaving the house might make me miss Granddad when he came home. *If* he came home. The longer he was gone, the more stressed out I got. Where was he? They had driven away from the mansion in the RV like twelve hours ago. Was he driving it out of town? Fencing the artwork they had stolen?

Or was he lying in a grave somewhere, just like Quincey?

I pictured Granddad's face in profile, half-submerged in the earth. Dead white except for the whiskers and eyebrows and black hair like mine.

No. Don't think about that. Think of something to *do*.

Something that would—I don't know—trick Trey into leading me to him, or reach somebody who could reach Granddad. Anything.

It would be dark soon.

This is a bad place to be, said that calm cold part of my brain. *After dark.*

Go to Davey's. Go to a neighbor's. Go to any business still open on Christmas Eve. Go.

Instead, I went to the pantry and moved the cans of Stagg chili and Chunky soup until I could reach Granddad's hiding place. Fight or flight. We learned about that in Science last year. If I wouldn't run away, maybe I could claw and bite. The human version.

No gun in the square hole, just ID cards and money. I'd check around the house, but I already knew every space would be empty.

I was kind of relieved. The whole shooting-Trey-in-the-leg idea that had flashed through my mind seemed like sci-fi, it was so bizarre. Still, there were other options. I had a Swiss Army pocketknife. Granddad had something better. I ran upstairs.

In his dresser drawer he kept a wooden Montecristo cigar box. It still smelled like tobacco, not the stink of cigarettes but the raw sweet aroma from a harvest. The box was full of treasures. A Zippo lighter that he filled from the bottle of butane under the stove. A silver cigar cutter. And a folding knife, with an antler handle and a razor-sharp five-inch blade. I could totally confirm the sharpness, because honing it was how Granddad had taught me how to sharpen the two little blades on my own knife.

I took it, opening up the knife for a second to look. Just holding it made me feel better.

Time for Part Two. Get the heck out. The sun was going down.

I left lights on, mostly upstairs, and in the kitchen and foyer. Then I wheeled my bike from the front porch through the house and out the back door, around to the far side. It wouldn't be visible from the street, but I could jump on it and soar down the stone steps if I had to make a run for it. Hopefully without wiping out and breaking my neck.

Then I went to hide in the backyard shed.

Trey might not show. Granddad could return at any minute. Still, being in the shed felt like having my own gopher hole. Safe from predators. I could crack the door and peer out at the house, knowing I was undetectable.

The sun was nearly down. I could see the glow of Christmas lights from the street below our house, green and white and blue and red. We didn't really decorate for the season, other than wrapping gifts and putting up stockings, which Granddad always filled with food. I think his family had gone hungry sometimes when he was a boy, and Santy— Granddad says that's what the kids had called him, or Father Christmas, which was also strange—Santy bringing them food was always the best.

Dark now. Undeniably dark.

Through the windows, I had a wide view of the foyer and most of the kitchen. Upstairs, only my room. The house looked strange at night, from this direction. Like somebody had made paintings of familiar things and pasted them to a black canvas background. Nothing moved.

Until something did.

Behind you.

Not actually in the shed, but close enough. A soft bump and the sound of scraping over wood. My hair stood up. I froze so solid I didn't even dare to reach out a finger and pull the shed door all the way shut.

To my right, something was moving along the shed wall outside. It stopped. I was sure that any second—in horror movies they always wait for a second—the shed door would be flung wide and Trey would plunge an axe—

It moved away. I heard footsteps crossing the lawn, going to the house. I leaned, just an inch, to peek through the crack.

It was Trey. Hood pulled up, tall body hunched as he skulked up to the back door of the house. I'd locked it, but I hadn't turned the alarm on. Scaring him away wasn't the idea. I just wanted him to think we were gone and see what he would do.

He opened the back door. I guess he could pick locks like me and Granddad, or maybe he had broken in really quietly. He stood there in the open doorway for a moment. Listening, I think. Then he closed the door behind him and moved so slowly into the house that he might have been pushing his way through clay.

He stopped, halfway through the kitchen, and turned toward the counter and bent a little. Was he writing something? No, opening a drawer. The same drawer where Granddad and I kept the little tools, including the screwdriver Trey had stolen from us.

I knew he couldn't be returning it. The screwdriver was still in my pocket. Was he stealing something else with Granddad's prints on it?

He finished with the drawer and continued his slow walk. A little faster than before. He must be confident he was alone in the house now. I watched him through the windows as he crossed the foyer and headed toward the stairs. Then he was out of sight.

What was Trey doing? Searching for something? He hadn't looked around downstairs at all.

Then he was in my room. He seemed very close, his tall hooded body right there at the window, and I shrank back into the safety of the shed.

My own room. It was freaky. It also pissed me off a little.

The lights went out upstairs.

I strained my eyes, trying to make out anything. But my room had vanished into the black canvas.

Trey was hiding there. Waiting. For us.

What could I do? Try to call Hollis again? Maybe we could trap Trey in the house somehow. I wished I had a button like in the crime movies, one that would slam steel plates over all of the windows and doors, sealing the exits.

I should leave, find help—even the cops if I really had to—and bring them here. If Trey was in jail, he wouldn't be a danger, at least for a while.

His messing with the tool drawer bugged me, though. Had he stolen something else? Or put something there? If cops looked in the drawer, would we be in trouble?

No matter what, I'd have to abandon the shed and cross the lawn. In easy view of the upstairs windows, if Trey was watching. Better to move fast. I slipped out onto the grass and quick-walked to the back porch, where the overhang would hide me again.

I was ten feet from the back door. It would only take me a second or two to check the drawer. I could run right back out if I heard Trey coming.

Okay. Decision made.

It was my house. I'd snuck around it enough to know just how to open the back door and step across the kitchen without making a sound. The whole time, I willed my ears to be ten times more sensitive, to catch any movement from upstairs.

The tool drawer liked to stick. I slid it open an inch at a time, careful for the squeak of rubbing wood.

Trey had put something in the drawer. A knife.

Not a regular steel knife. It was some kind of thick clear plastic, and it looked handmade, an eight-inch single piece that narrowed to a point. The handle was wrapped with athletic tape. It didn't have much of a blade, and I figured that was because the knife was intended for stabbing, not cutting.

And it was stained. Discolored at the tip and in the tiny cracks of the plastic and even a spot turning the white athletic tape a dark rusty red.

Blood. Quincey's blood.

I couldn't leave it here. It was the same trick Trey had tried at the mansion with the screwdriver, planting evidence. I reached for a paper towel and picked the plastic knife out of the drawer with two fingers, figuring I'd wrap it up and button it in my pocket with its buddy the screwdriver—

The stairs creaked.

I turned and ran for the back door, out onto the porch, as Trey thundered down the stairs. I vaulted the porch railing and ran along the edge of the house toward my bike. My hand still clutched the plastic knife wrapped in its paper towel. I jumped on the bike and pushed off, getting it moving.

I was going to win this race. I knew the yard much better than Trey did, and I would be down the stone steps before he figured out which way I had run.

Except he had gone out the front.

There he was in the corner of my left eye, rounding the opposite corner of the house. Racing to intercept me at the top of the steps. I cut right, the bike catching air on the steep slope. Trey dived and his body slammed into my rear tire. I heard his grunt as the bike flew out from under me.

I hit the ground, half on the slope, half on the stone steps. My arm banged into the steps and then into my head. Red and green from the neighbors' Christmas lights flashed and spun as I rolled all the way down to the sidewalk.

Trey. Where was he? A loud clatter as the bike crashed to the sidewalk near me. My legs scrambled. I was standing, all of a sudden. Trey was lying facedown on the steep slope, practically upside down. Moving. Getting up.

I grabbed my bike and tried to jump on it. Missed. I was dizzy. My hurt arm wouldn't grab the bars. I made it on the second try and the bike started coasting down the street. I bumped into a parked car. Kicked off again. Too woozy to run. Hard enough to stay upright and let the bike carry me.

Behind me, I heard an engine roar to life. It must be Trey. I found the pedals, somehow, and told my feet to start moving. Amazingly, they did.

The steep hill gave me wings. I flew through the second block, the third, much faster now as the street leveled out, toward the playfields leading into the arboretum park. Too late I realized I had passed all the houses and people. Past anyone who might help.

If they could. Trey was going to kill me. If I ran up to somebody and told them what was happening, maybe he would just murder them, too.

Headlights flashed as the car behind me thumped down the last block. He was coming. He was going to run me over.

The street curved sharply to the left, and I leaned into the turn, hearing the wheels hiss as I pumped harder. The headlights grew brighter. I ditched the bike and ran, straight into the trees that bordered a short hill leading down to a soccer field. My leg wobbled and I fell, tumbling at the edge of the slope. Brakes screeched on the street behind me. I glanced back to see Trey jumping out of a brown panel van. The sight got me to my feet. It felt horribly slow, working my way down the dark hill, around trees and thick bramble bushes. Wanting to run but knowing I'd brain myself on a branch if I moved faster. Trey crashed into the brush behind me.

Then the trees ended suddenly and I dashed out, almost falling onto the soccer field. Open ground. I was fast, not as fast as Davey, but I could really run, most of the time. Right now my legs shook. Trey would be able to catch up, unless I could reach the opposite slope and the arboretum on the other side. Plenty of hiding places there.

A branch snapped and I heard him curse as he broke

through the brush to the field. I was halfway across, the yellow boundary line glowing up ahead. Legs still moving. I'd hit the wall soon, that moment when my body would stop doing what my calm cold brain told it to.

Go. Go.

Ten yards to the trees. Five. None. I dashed into a narrow split between two trunks as Trey's huff of effort sounded near enough to chill the back of my neck. I kept going, slipping and sliding on wet leaves as I pushed through the brambles, up the slope, ignoring the pain in my hands. Too dark to run now. Thorns and spindly winter branches grabbed at my sleeves and jeans. Slowing me down even more. Trey was a freight train, smashing his way through everything. He was catching up.

I ducked behind a thick tree stump, fell to my knees. Tried to quiet my gasping. Would he run right on past?

No. He'd stopped, almost. Twigs crunched under his feet, as he searched for me in the dark.

If he missed me, I could double back. Get help. If he didn't . . .

I reached into my jeans pocket, found Granddad's folding knife. Opened it. Fight or flight.

It was so hard to see. Even in winter the trees let no light in from the city or the sky. I focused on the last place I'd heard Trey, listened for the squeak of his soles on the sodden ground.

There. Right next to where I crouched. Leaves shifted underfoot as he turned, seeking.

I plunged forward with the knife held in two hands, almost diving. The blade met something, and Trey yelped. I bumped my head off his knee and the knife fell away as he yelled and cursed. I scramble-crawled away in a panic. Up on my feet, moving, I didn't care which way.

Lights now, through the trees ahead. Streetlamps. The road through the arboretum. Get there. Hide.

I hurtled out of the woods. Trey was so close. I could hear every one of his staggering steps over the bang of my heartbeat. The road. I was on the pavement.

Headlights boomed, closer even than Trey. I turned, knowing I was about to be flattened, but the headlights veered away and there was a scream and a terrible thudding sound.

I fell down, right on the yellow dashed line in the middle of the road. The pavement was cold against my face.

Granddad was there, bending down, lifting me up.

"*Daideo,*" I said. Grandfather.

"Van," he said. "What happened?"

"I lost your knife," I said. And started crying, for the second time that day.

Big baby.

THIRTY-SIX

Just after the witching hour, Seattle was as quiet as it ever got, resting until the eruption of the next working day. I had the sidewalks outside the Olympian hotel and into downtown all to myself.

Ingrid Ekby was insane. She had murdered three people that I knew about, to devise a slim chance of avenging her own horrific rape. She'd kill more before she was done. Without hesitation.

I agreed that she deserved to see Joe Slattery dead. If someone had ripped my life apart the way that Joe had done to her, I'd sign that same contract with the devil.

But Ingrid would pay any price, overlook any collateral damage, to see her vendetta through. She hadn't spared a thought for Marshall or her other man, dead at the farmhouse. Corcoran, and the fence. All the same. She would undoubtedly have sacrificed Boule or me or O'Hasson with as little hesitation.

I passed a tree-lined courtyard at the back of Benaroya Hall. A pair of skateboarders clattered through tricks on the steps and wheelchair ramps. The boards reminded me of Cyndra, who I had frightened so badly just that afternoon. I wasn't sure how to make up for that, if it could be fixed at all. Even Hollis had me on his shit list. One winner of a day.

At least I knew where my feet were taking me.

Luce lived in a one-bedroom apartment above the bar that she owned, near Pike Place. My grandfather had owned the bar, called the Morgen, originally, in partnership with Luce's uncle. Most of the time, Luce used the adjoining staircase in the back room of the bar that led to her hallway. There was also an exterior entrance to the building. I pressed the intercom button, not knowing if it actually worked. I'd never heard it buzz while Luce and I had been dating.

Midnight. Luce might still be in the bar. Or out. Or with someone. I pressed it again.

"'lo?" came her electronically garbled voice over the speaker.

"It's Van."

There was a pause. "What's wrong?"

Trust Luce to know this wasn't my attempt at a late-night hookup.

"Five minutes," I said, amending it with, "If you can."

Another few seconds ticked by before the lock answered with a harsh drone. I pulled the door open and walked up the long flight to the first story of apartments. Luce waited in her doorway at the far end. I hadn't woken her. She wore jeans and her faded Karen O t-shirt with the sleeves cut off, instead of the oversized cotton tees she favored on warm nights. Her blonde hair was pulled back and held in place with a large black claw clip. Her feet were bare.

"Sorry to surprise you," I said.

"You often do." Luce walked back into her apartment. It was a feminine space, lots of snapshots and soft textures, and it managed to be cluttered and spotless and homey and precise through a method I hadn't quite figured out. Like the woman herself. I waited as she retrieved her mug of tea from the bedside—hardback book open on the blanket, no sign of any other recent company—and followed her into the tiny kitchen where I declined a cup for myself and we sat in the only two chairs at the table.

"Jimmy Corcoran is dead," I said.

Her face hardly changed at all, but sadness was suddenly there, in her eyes and in the set of her mouth.

"Today?" she said.

I nodded.

"How?"

"He was killed. Shot."

Luce took in my soiled appearance. I was sure she had spotted the gun in my jacket pocket before I'd even crossed the threshold.

"Has Jimmy's wife heard yet?" she said.

"I expect so."

Luce leaned back. She'd known Corcoran as a friend of her uncle's, and of Dono's. A presence for her whole life. Even if she and Jimmy weren't close, it was still a loss, another permanent absence in a generation with whom we had few surviving connections.

"Was it a job?" she said. "Something that you were part of?"

"Yes."

She tilted her head in a question. "But that's not all of it."

"Jimmy got involved because he wanted to make money. I'm not making him out to be better than he was. He also helped some people along the way. He figured that made the hazards worth it."

"Regular people?"

"At least one kid you could rightfully call innocent."

"And you wanted me to know that," Luce said, catching on, "because you can't tell Jimmy's family."

My long exhalation sounded more like a sigh than I'd intended. "I just wanted to say it to somebody who knew him," I replied.

"I understand." And after a moment, "Elana had told me it was some sort of rescue effort."

Dammit. "Elana talks too much."

"I sort of forced her to tell me."

"Dangling something shiny in front of her, I bet. Freaking magpie."

Luce laughed softly. I hadn't had the pleasure of hearing her laugh in many months, and it gave me a feeling like a drink of hot cider on a frozen day.

"I should go," I said.

"If you want." She stood up when I did. "Thank you for telling me about Jimmy. What he did. You were always good at protecting people."

"From some things."

"You know how to protect yourself, too." There was sadness again, in a different key now.

True enough. I wasn't looking to turn back the clock. Luce and I were better off as we were. If we tried to right all of our wrongs, we'd be as crazy as Ingrid Ekby.

THIRTY-SEVEN

A NIGHT WITHOUT DREAMS, EVERY second of it, until my calendar app beeped to remind me I had half an hour before my appointment with Dr. Mattu. I showered and dressed and skipped the usual coffee to get out the door on time.

The smell of Mattu's lapsang steeping in its pot permeated the outer office. He popped his head out.

"Here? Great. Let's start early." He disappeared before I could reply.

"You look tired," he said, pen already scratching as I sat down. "Dreams?"

"I want to talk about purpose," I said.

The scratching stopped. "Beg pardon?"

"You cautioned me about using the house as a crutch. I haven't been doing that the past two weeks. I've pursued that other work."

"The work you didn't want to do," Mattu said.

"Yeah. And it made money, and it still wasn't satisfying. Not completely, anyway. But on the way, I helped some people."

He straightened in his chair. "Which was fulfilling?"

"For me."

"Helped them in what way?"

"Out of danger. Into a safer place, at least."

"That's good," he said with some hesitancy, "if you weren't the one who put them in danger in the first place. And if you didn't deliberately put yourself in harm's way for the thrill of it."

I shot a finger-gun at Mattu. The irony of that gesture probably wasn't lost on him, either.

"You recall our first sessions," he said, "when we talked about the attraction of war for you."

"Not violence," I said.

"Not killing, certainly. You are not a psychopath. But the acceptance of your fellow soldiers, the rush of combat." Mattu spread his hands wide. "Those are hard to surrender. War is terrible, and it can also make you happy."

"Purpose."

"Correct. So if you're diving into trouble, ask yourself why."

"Because it feels right," I said.

"Are you looking for praise? Tangible rewards?"

I liked the money fine. It just hadn't been enough for me.

"Is it some form of penance?" Mattu said.

"I don't think my sins are so heavy that I have to get myself dead."

"Look at the kind of situation. You could help people at a soup kitchen. Instead, you put yourself in physical jeopardy."

"I'm accustomed to that."

"Perhaps. Also, you might be gambling."

I frowned. "Meaning what? I live for the risk? Sounds like we're back to me being a war junkie."

"High risk, high reward. Your sense of satisfaction might come from winning."

I knew enough about gambling to know it was less about winning than surviving. For as long as you could. The crash was inevitable.

"I do like winning," I said. "Achieving objectives, the Army would call it."

"But?"

"If I just wanted to bust heads, I could stick with bouncing. Or MMA."

Mattu's picture window looked out onto a pinched atrium with a Zen garden. Its rocks had been raked into wave patterns, by an unsteady hand. I sometimes wondered if it was a test. Did patients with OCD fight the urge to go out and make the waves even?

"Making a change," I said.

"Yes?"

"The situations are dangerous because I can handle danger. If I can't handle it, I want to stay out entirely. It's about using what I've got. If I could make soup, I'd be in that soup kitchen."

"Then maybe the answer is to find something that helps people and matches your skills. Firefighting, or police work."

I looked at him.

He cleared his throat. "Perhaps not police. We can delve into your complicated feelings about the law another time. You might also volunteer with veterans' services. Either the VA, or something local for soldiers in need."

I had thought of that. And there was a germ of an idea there, lying dormant.

"Thanks. This helped," I said.

"Do you realize this is the most open you've been with me in the months we've been meeting?"

"Enjoy it while it lasts, Doc."

And, for once, my joke got a laugh.

I HAD TO SQUARE things with O'Hasson. A lot of things. Accusing him of selling us out, threatening him in front of his kid, who I'd terrified in the process. I had to try to make things right with Cyndra, too. That might be impossible. Mickey could be my warm-up. At least I could tell him I'd recovered half of the gold. His share should pour some oil on the waters.

No answer at Addy's door, except for Stanley barking from the backyard. Maybe they were all out at the movies or something to take their minds off the last week.

I was debating whether to go up the block to my house, or to walk the other direction to the arboretum and revisit the site of my fiasco with O'Hasson, when Addy's Subaru coasted down the block. Cyndra glowered at me from the passenger seat as Addy pulled in. Great.

"Perfect timing. Help me unload these," Addy said, popping the trunk. Cyndra jumped out of the car and skirted the house toward the backyard before I could say anything to her.

I slung the handles of Addy's grocery sacks over my arms, loading myself like a pack mule to carry the trunkful of food in one trip. "Where's Mickey?"

"He's not here?"

"I knocked."

"Sleeping again, I expect," Addy said.

We went inside. Addy let Stanley in and started putting the food away. Cyndra stalked inside and into the bedroom, and came out again, fast.

"Where's Dad?" she said.

"Not there?"

"No." The girl went past me, all gangly elbows and knees, and into the front room. "Dad?"

"He might be out for a walk, sweetheart," said Addy.

Cyndra shook her head emphatically. "He's not. He's gone to find them."

I set the bag I was holding down. "Them? The men who kidnapped him?"

Addy frowned at me, maybe disagreeing with my mentioning O'Hasson's ordeal in front of the kid.

"What makes you think Mickey did that?" I said to Cyndra.

"He's been talking."

"Talking about wanting to get back at them?"

"Van," said Addy. Cyndra caught her warning tone, too, and glanced at her uncertainly.

"Go ahead," I said.

"He kinda sleeps," she said, "and kinda doesn't. I dunno. But he talks. Like he's still there. He says *please* and *don't* and *water*. Sometimes he just says *fuckers* over and over and . . ."

"All right, enough," said Addy. "Van, I need to speak with you."

"It's true," Cyndra said, waving her birdlike hands in frustration. "He wants to hurt them back. I know he does." Stanley whined, upset at the mood.

"I believe you," I said, "but even if he were strong enough, even if he decided to go, he wouldn't know where to find them, Cyn."

"But what if he *remembered* where?"

"Enough," Addy said again, with more heat. "Let's all calm down. Your father will be back soon."

Cyndra stomped and wheeled around to race off to the bedroom. The door slammed.

"That was just marvelous," Addy said.

"What if she's not wrong?"

"Good God, Van. That poor man is so worn down he can barely stay alert for more than an hour at a time."

Or that was what he wanted us to think. I'd stopped believing I could anticipate Mickey O'Hasson.

"Did he leave a note?" I said.

She sighed and walked around in a fair imitation of Cyndra's stomp to check the kitchen counters and her desk. Stanley nosed at her each time she passed.

"Nothing," Addy said, gesturing to the desk.

"Does he have any money?"

"I left him forty dollars in case he needed to order food. Hardly enough to finance an airstrike. Or even much of a taxi ride." She glanced at the cubby where she kept her checkbook and other papers, and paused.

"What?"

"My ORCA card is gone." Mass transit. Buses and local trains.

"So he's not out for a walk," I said.

"Don't start." She reached out to hold Stanley's snout and keep him from pushing at her. "He couldn't possibly have gone after them. You said."

But Cyndra could be right. What if O'Hasson had figured out where they'd been holding him? What if, in his addled state, revenge was worth everything?

"Lend me your car," I said.

"Why?"

"I'm going to drive around and visit some places where my truck might be recognized."

She reached into the pocket of her cardigan and handed me her Subaru keys. "Could he really do it?" she said before I was out the door.

"I would," I said.

AFTERNOON TRAFFIC WAS ALREADY heavy, and getting heavier by the hour. It took me until early evening to check all of the places O'Hasson might know or have gone in Seattle. I asked about him at the twenty-four-hour pharmacy, saying he was an uncle stricken with dementia. I tried Hollis's marina. The hulk of the burned-out office building. The rental car company at SeaTac. Even Lloyd's Own, the bar where he'd first spun me the story about hidden treasure. No one had seen the frail ex-con with the surgical scar.

Eventually I was out of options, and my headache reminded me that I hadn't eaten today. I stopped at Mama's in Belltown, which had been one of my favorite haunts when hanging around Dono's old bar. Time had forced Mama's to adapt from the dive covered in kitsch art I'd grown up with, but I could still order an Elvis burrito with extra corn tortillas without looking at a menu. Comfort food, when the rest of the world was chewing on me.

What the hell was O'Hasson up to? If Addy was correct, he could barely handle the walk up the hill to the bus stop. Cyndra thought her dad was out for blood. After seeing how deeply Ingrid Ekby's men had wounded him, I leaned toward the kid's way of thinking. But could little Mick O'Hasson, dying burglar, really shoulder that kind of weight?

The plate arrived. My phone rang. Maybe that was the man himself. I stuffed a bite into my mouth and answered.

"She's gone," Addy said. "Cyndra."

I made an interrogative sound.

"She—I think she stole your truck."

I slapped a twenty down on the table and ran out the door, an instant ahead of my chair toppling to the floor with a bang.

"SHE FOUND THE SPARE key you left me," Addy explained as I dashed into the house past her. "Did you know she could drive?"

I was already tearing apart the bedroom, looking for some clue. "She didn't take her backpack this time. I can't track her again." Where the hell would Cyndra go? She knew even fewer places in Seattle than her father.

"We should call the police," said Addy.

"What has Cyndra been doing since I went looking for Mickey?" I said.

"She stayed in her room for a time. Then I convinced her to have some food, and she played that mining game on the computer, like she's done every day. She can't have gone far, can she? She's only twelve."

"She made it a thousand miles on the train." Being tricky must be in the O'Hasson blood. Cyndra was a renaissance delinquent. Between low-level hacking and driving, I wouldn't be surprised if—Wait.

"Was Cyndra on her old laptop? Or this one?" I thumped the flat screen with my fist.

"Mine. She likes the screen size."

"Were you using this to talk to Enid and the others about the shell companies?"

Addy's face blanched. "Why?"

"Because I'll bet the kid found a way to trace everything you've looked at."

I turned on the monitor and was greeted by an imitation 8-bit rendering of a castle. Cyndra's supposed play on *Minecraft* while she was otherwise occupied. I shut down the game and checked the browser history. Cyndra had deleted the entire day.

"She doesn't want us following her," I said, grabbing my phone.

"Tell the police that she's been gone about an hour."

I wasn't calling the police.

Juniper Adair answered.

"Send me the camera feed," I said immediately. "I want to see what's at Pacific Pearl."

"What? The man called two days ago. Told me they don't need the photos anymore."

"The camera's still running."

"Well, yes, but—"

"Then send me the goddamn feed."

"What camera?" Addy asked me. "Who is that on the phone?"

"Someone with a lot to lose," I said so Juniper would hear.

Juniper sent the latest photo. It showed the same picture I'd seen in a hundred of her raw images, half of the squat bulk of the Pacific Pearl freight office, captured by the hidden camera across the road.

"It's just the building," she said.

"Back it up. Look for anything in the last hour. A car passing on the road, or someone walking by."

Juniper was smart enough not to argue. Maybe realizing that if she didn't cooperate, my next step would be to come to her house and look through the images my own damn self.

"Here," she said after two minutes. "I'm sending you every picture that's got something in it besides the building."

The sun was below the hill now, but during the past hour it had been high enough that the colors in the images were suffused with a gilded glow. I swiped through the series Juniper had sent, spotting the mottled paint of my Dodge's roof immediately, like blue alligator scales at the bottom of the picture as the truck passed the camera.

"She's been there," I said to Addy. A few more images of cars passing, the light already fading. Then, in a picture gray from dusk, a small thin figure in the distance, crossing the railroad tracks to the left side and behind the building. Just clear enough to make out a white shirt and very short, very dark hair.

Half an hour ago. Cyndra might still be nearby, poking around. I could—

Then I realized I had seen something else, and flipped back to make sure.

The door. The man-sized exit, at the side of the two rolling doors of the loading bays. In most of the images the door showed as a flat rectangle in the same ugly brown as the rest of the freight building.

Then, in just one picture of a passing car, the door was open. Not much. Such a small amount that Juniper probably hadn't noticed the difference. But the door was definitely cracked, as if someone inside had eased it open a couple of narrow inches to look out.

Cyndra wasn't alone there.

"What?" said Addy, catching my tension.

"Call the cops," I said. "I'll meet them there."

THIRTY-EIGHT

I LEFT ADDY'S CAR ON the far side of the elevated light rail tracks and ran at a low crouch along the support columns toward Pacific Pearl. Already I could see my Dodge truck, parked sideways a few dozen yards from the freight company's lot. The lot's exterior lights were switched off, leaving the squat cinderblock building completely dark.

Cyndra wasn't in the Dodge. But through the window I could see her laptop computer lying on the passenger-side floor. The driver's door was unlocked. I searched the cab. The Smith & Wesson was gone. Did Cyndra have it? Was she skulking somewhere around the building right now, looking for her dad?

There was no sign of the cops. Perhaps they'd done a drive-by already and left. I couldn't wait.

The razor-wired gate was wide open. I ran across the street and the lot, straight into the deepest shadows by the loading docks. With its brown solidity and barred windows, the freight building might have been a prison from two centuries ago. Bleak and unforgiving.

I circled the building, looking for Cyndra, watching for signs of anyone within. A single car passed by the lot at high speed, hurrying on its way to less desolate parts of the city. That was the only sound.

No kid. No nothing. If it weren't for my Dodge abandoned outside, I'd have been convinced everything was squared away and looked for Cyndra elsewhere.

Instead, I picked the Medeco lock on the rear door. I had to make sure.

I knew the layout now, and moved quickly through the rooms without needing my penlight. The office space with its roller chairs, and the file cabinets just beyond. Moonbeams through the window grilles divided the interior into smears of bile yellow and black.

When I reached the loading bays, I paused. The broad cool room was as quiet as the rest. But there was a smell here, fresher than the undertones of diesel and coolant. An organic stink. Blood, or shit, or both.

I followed the smell into the ratty communal room off the loading bays, with its big wooden cable-drum table and spindly chairs. One chair had been knocked over. At the far end of the long space, past the table and the emergency exit, a shabby black curtain stretched across a doorway. The animal smell must be coming from behind it.

Crossing the room, I saw blood splashes and spatters on the cement floor, outside the black curtain. Smears on the walls as well. I touched one. Still sticky. I stood to one side and peered through the inch between the curtain and wall.

Beyond the tattered velveteen cloth was a space about the size of the main room in my studio apartment. It was a slaughterhouse. Fekkete was lying on his back, still wearing his orange tracksuit, in the middle of the bare floor. Another man's body lay beside him, facedown. The body wore a navy suit, and a crushed pair of horn-rimmed glasses lay near his foot.

Boule was a fraction more upright, his shoulders awkwardly propped against built-in shelves along the wall. His head lolled, joining the collection of dirty junk on the shelves. His wrists were bound behind his back.

More blood here, much more. On Fekkete's face and chest, and on the floor, in thick drops and tiny pools. The confines reeked of recent death.

Boule exhaled, and coughed wetly. I checked for signs of life on the other hunter and found none. There was no point in my checking Fekkete. The front half of his head had been beaten almost concave.

I knelt by Boule and grabbed his hand. "Can you hear me? Squeeze."

His fingers gripped mine. His face wasn't the unrecognizable paste that Fekkete's was, but it wasn't good. One eye was puffed shut, and if he lived he would need a set of new teeth. Under his tan skin he had the undead sallowness of internal bleeding.

"Seh me ub," he rasped, surprising me. The *B* sound made flecks of pink mist.

"Where's Cyndra?" I said. "The girl. Was she here?"

Boule nodded. "Girl. 'ngri."

"She and Ingrid. Where are they?"

"Zho. Helb me." Blood dribbled from his jaw.

"Joe," I said, "and Gar. The Slatterys have them. Do you know where?"

He nodded a clear affirmative, and twisted, trying to show me his bound wrists. "Clinig," he said through the pain.

"I'll get you to a doctor. After you tell me. Where are they?"

His head tilted. Trying to shake no. "Clin—"

Then he was out. I felt for his pulse. The tap against my fingertips was strong enough, but very fast.

As I stood, I saw a familiar piece of white strap. A handle, on the plain canvas bag that Fekkete had carried away from Ingrid Ekby's hotel room. It was buried in the junk on the shelves above the unresponsive Boule's head. I opened it. The two gold bars she had given Fekkete were still inside. His down payment on betraying Joe Slattery. He must have concealed the bag here on the shelves, before the violence started.

I could guess how it had gone down. Fekkete had tried luring Gar or Joe or both to Pacific Pearl, a place they would deem safe ground. Ingrid and her men had been waiting. But the Slatterys had been too shrewd, or maybe Fekkete had tried to play both sides against the middle.

It didn't matter now. The Sledge City crew had come out on top. Fekkete had been judged a traitor and beaten to death. It wasn't hard to imagine Dickson Hinch and the others having their fun. They had left Boule alive. He would know where Ingrid had the red suitcase with their two million in gold.

Ingrid and Cyndra had been taken elsewhere. For other purposes. Where could they have gone? And why?

Ingrid had told me she had made preparations for Joe's death. A place, presumably. Not the farmhouse; Marshall had been moving out. Somewhere else where she could take her time torturing and killing Joe. Then the Slatterys had turned the tables. Had they forced Ingrid to take them to her intended murder room? My gut turned over at the thought.

Hydraulic brakes squeaked on the other side of the loading bay doors, over the weighty rumble of a diesel engine. One of the refrigerated trucks.

Hinch and the others, returning to move the bodies. Time to leave.

The emergency exit in the communal room was our way out. I could carry Boule to the Dodge, get him conscious and talking. Once I had Cyndra I'd dump him outside the nearest ER. I went to disconnect the fire alarm.

The door had been nailed into the frame. Dead solid. It would take a crowbar and half an hour to open.

I could run for it. Dash through the far side of the building, and count on foot speed to give me enough distance before anyone started shooting. If I were willing to abandon Boule to his fate.

Boule knew where Cyndra was. It wasn't a choice.

A loud steely clatter from the bays, the sound of someone unlocking one of the rolling doors. Another minute and they would be inside.

The lights were still off. I needed them to stay that way. Dirt and paint chips scattered as I wrenched open the fuse box, flipping the master breaker down and snapping off the plastic switch for good measure.

Back into the curtained room, stepping over Fekkete's body. I needed a weapon, too. The beam of the penlight confirmed that the contents of the shelves were useless. Crumbling magazines and twisted nails and rolls of old strapping tape. The only objects with any weight at all were the two gold bars in their plastic wrap, dense but small.

They were coming. And I had nothing but my two hands.

An idea struck. I tore at the dusty tape with my teeth and nails, peeling long strips away from the roll.

From the loading bay, the door rattled as Hinch or one of the others wrestled it up the first foot. I clicked off the penlight and worked by feel alone. Peeling more tape, winding it around the first gold kilobar. Then around my knuckles.

The rolling door made a sustained thunder and final boom as it opened to its full height. At the edges of the curtain, the yellowish moonlight grew brighter. Boule's labored breathing made a liquid rhythm.

Someone swore as they tried the light switch. Then footsteps. One step at a time, feeling their way in the dark.

"Get a flashlight." Hinch, his usual lazy drawl trimmed by anger.

"Where? The truck?" That was Wex, the kid with the topknot.

"Look the fuck around, dickhead."

I finished with the last strip of tape, pressing it hard into my palm as I counted the sets of footsteps. Hinch plus two men. At least two. I moved to one side of the curtain that separated us. My eyes had adjusted and the fabric showed as a black maw in the gray wall.

One man coming toward me now, edging through the dark along the wall with the useless exit door. Another crossed the center of the room by the round table. Slow steps, and heavy.

"Bomba," said Hinch. From closer than I'd thought, somewhere near the fuse box. "Drag those pussies out here," he said.

I pressed my back against the sheet metal wall next to the black curtain, the steel cold through my shirt. I was already sweating.

Hinch by the fuses, five yards away. Wex somewhere off in the loading bays. Bomba coming right toward me.

Cyndra, God knew where. I curled my hands into fists, slowly, feeling the weight.

One more deep inhale. Knees bent, coiling.

All right, you sons of bitches.

Bomba's steps reached the curtain, and moonlight flooded in.

Let's get mean.

A kilo of gold, with as much of my two hundred pounds behind it as

I could throw, smashed Bomba full in the face. His nose and cheekbone collapsed in the split second before his head snapped back. He toppled, and I came right behind his falling body. Rushing through the half-open curtain toward Hinch.

Hinch was fast. Hinch was expert. He could barely see me in the half-light from the loading bay, but he knew an attack was coming, and he dipped and sidestepped and slapped a palm out like a striking adder in one fluid motion, measuring, ready to throw the big counterpunch. I wasn't obliging. In the last rushing instant I fell to one knee, swinging my fist in a vicious haymaker. Hinch belted me on the meat of my shoulder, just as the world's most expensive brass knuckles fractured his shinbone. He screamed. I swung again and missed as he fell with another cry of agony.

A shadow blocked the moonlight. Wex. I rolled on the cement, not caring about direction, as the muscular kid almost fell over me in his haste. My roll brought me up against Bomba's writhing form. He grabbed me reflexively with his big hands, trapping me on the ground. I heard him gag through his ruined face. Wex found my leg, held it. I kicked at him in the dark, thrashed against Bomba. The huge man's grip tightened.

"Kill him," Hinch yelled from somewhere in the black. I couldn't get a clean kick at Wex. He grabbed my other ankle, pinned it. They had me. Bomba rolled onto his side, blindly straining to crush me from behind in a bearhug.

His face was near mine. I headbutted him in the spot where I'd crushed his nose. Twice, three times. Blood sprayed the side of my neck, and Bomba's hands fell away. Wex sacrificed his grip on my leg to punch me in the gut. I slammed both fists, both gold bars, down onto his skull. He went instantly limp.

The gunshot from the dark was like a bomb going off, dazzling and deafening. Hinch. Unable to stand but not done fighting. I shoved Wex off of me and rolled as Hinch fired again and again, the muzzle flaring like a strobe. He may have hit Wex, or Bomba, or both. I went for the cover of the table. A bullet shredded a plank of the wood, so close to my face I saw it in the split second of illumination.

"Fuck you," Hinch said, and fired again. When that flash faded there was neither darkness nor light, only the phantom spots left behind in my vision.

Was he out of rounds? I had no idea what he was holding. A heavy enough caliber to make any wound a permanent problem. I wedged my bound fingertips under the big round table's base and lifted, straining with everything I had.

"You motherfu—" The cable drum crashing onto its round edges cut off his words. A shot sliced the air above my head with a sharp *whap*. I bent low and shoved, rolling the man-sized drum in front of me, toward where the muzzle flare was still glowing. It bowled over Hinch just as a final shot went into the ceiling. He screamed, and flailed at the crushing weight, for the spare second before my armored fist connected with his head.

I left him alive. Half by choice, and half by chance.

THIRTY-NINE

BOULE HAD REGAINED CONSCIOUSNESS during the chaos. Once I got him outside the loading bay, he pushed away from me and shambled to lean against the Pacific Pearl truck. Its idling engine radiated heat I could feel, even though I felt powered by a blast furnace myself.

I yanked open the passenger door and dragged Boule toward it, sweeping an orange tackle box off the seat to make room.

"Zhow you," Boule mumbled. The blood on his face had dried and it cracked and flaked with every move of his torn lips. I watched to make sure he didn't collapse during his tortoise climb into the passenger seat. He used his right arm exclusively, his left cradled protectively to his body.

He pointed south. And I realized what he had been trying to say earlier. He had been trying to tell me where Cyndra was. Where Ingrid had prepared a place for Joe.

WE MADE IT THERE in fifteen minutes, staying off the freeway. I stopped the refrigerated truck one block away and one over, where there would be little chance of it being spotted. Boule had zoned out again during the drive, his head lolling against the doorframe and broken arm in his lap. I left him there.

An alley cutting through the middle of the block was the quickest path. I tucked Hinch's Luger pistol, wrapped in a rag, into the back pocket of my pants and vaulted the chain-link gate. The Luger had two rounds left in it, after all of Hinch's wild shots at me.

I emerged from the alley. There it was. Right where all the terror had started.

The steel frame of the six-story building had survived O'Hasson's blaze, but most of the windows were missing or charred completely black. On the ground floor, a new fence made from sap-wet sheets of plywood looked incongruously clean.

Above the fence, its plastic splintered by heat and high-pressure water, was the empty socket where the sign for the urgent care clinic had once been, on the ground floor of the now-destroyed building.

Clinic, Boule had said through his mouthful of splintered teeth. He hadn't been asking for a doctor. He had meant here.

I was an idiot for not realizing it before. Boule and his hunters had set the trap at the safe. They would have had to lay in wait close by, in shifts. And they would need somewhere to take Joe Slattery after capturing him. What better place than in the same building? Ingrid owned the whole fucking thing. The old clinic was ready and waiting.

O'Hasson had told me his vague recollection of a frightening place with tile and steel tables. A nightmare, he had believed. The hunters had hit O'Hasson with the tranquilizer that night, at least partially. Mick hadn't taken enough dope to put him all the way out, and he'd managed to fight back with his firesticks before they finally grabbed him. He'd still had a fingernail grip on consciousness when they brought him inside the clinic. Maybe Boule and his men had been rushing to grab their gear before the whole building went up. They had been lucky to make it out alive, just as I was fleeing the building on the opposite side.

O'Hasson had thought the scary place had been his drug-induced hallucination. But it was very real, I knew now.

Ingrid's murder room. And Cyndra was somewhere in there.

I slipped across the street and behind a Chevy Malibu with deflated tires. A sliver of darkness showed in the plywood fence, where one sheet tilted outward on hinges.

No sound from within. I put a finger against the plywood and pushed. It swung wide, silently, and I glided inside.

As if in answer to my movement, I heard a cry from deep within. A woman's cry.

The glass of the lower panes on the wall had been shattered by fire or by firefighters, making a path for the torrents of spent water. I knelt and crawled under the knee-high window frame.

Beyond it was a hallway, half-filled with burnt debris and covered in sludgy muck that had never completely dried after the fire. Most of the ceiling was intact. The cry of pain had come from the other side of the hallway wall. If there was a door leading in that direction, it must be around the far corner.

I didn't like the hall. It was too confined, too obstructed. With some of the walls half-collapsed, any escape route was uncertain.

Another sound. A man's laughter, high and hearty. It echoed off the blackened metal air vents and bubbled glass.

I inched my way through the wreckage. If a board or a piece of charred drywall blocked my way, I moved it aside, as slowly as if I were doing a curious form of tai chi. Making a path I could follow in the dark at a dead run, carrying the kid.

At the corner, I stopped. A low murmur of talking from the second door down on the right. A light behind that door switched on, and the hallway was suddenly cast into green-tinted funhouse shapes. Warped walls and twisted angles.

I heard a heavy door close, and a shadow blocked the mossy light. I drew back, around the corner. A flashlight shone past me and footsteps—casual, relaxed—came toward me.

The moment he stepped into view, I stuck the muzzle of the Luger behind his cauliflower ear. He froze.

"Hello, Joe," I said.

The man I'd known as Orville turned his head. His scarred eyelids widened at the sight of me.

"Drop the flashlight," I said.

"Zack," he said in his high hoarse voice. "Or whatever your name is."

"Down."

He let go of the flash. I moved behind him.

"Nobody's called me Joe in fuckin' years and years," he said, as I began to pat him down. "I wouldn't even let my sister say it. She might make a mistake where somebody could hear. Then suddenly today, I'm Joe to everybody."

"Pick whichever you want for your gravestone," I said.

"How'd you know?" He sounded amused.

"I thought you'd be somewhere close. Then I found your cut kit in the truck tonight." The same orange tackle box he'd been carrying at the quarry.

"Had a feeling about you," he said. "That you'd be money, or trouble, or something. Would have known it was you in the mask at the geek convention, just by how you moved. Quick."

I hadn't spotted him. But then Joe was very good at hiding.

"Never forget it, once I see a guy fight," he continued. "You ain't small-time like O'Hasson. What are you?"

"Last of the independents. Go." I motioned back to the doorway from where he'd emerged.

He turned his head to me and grinned. In the sickly light of the hallway his face was something out of an old-time Universal movie, green and white and monstrous.

"Ain't got shit," he said.

I kicked the back of his knee and he went down on it. Chuckling in his high voice all the way.

"Where's the girl? O'Hasson's kid?" I said.

"Ah, she's right back there," he said. "The little gash came looking for Daddy. Sweet, yeah?"

I whipped him across the temple with the barrel of the Luger. "Call your brother out here," I said.

Joe was a big man and he'd been hit plenty in his life. The cut on his head from the blow bothered him about as much as an ant's bite.

"Leave now," he said. "Live until tomorrow."

I pressed the Luger under his eye.

"Won't matter," he said in that same bemused manner. "You can't get to them in time. The Ekby bitch made her little playroom too tough. Gar will slice them up. You'll fry anyway."

He meant it. Joe Slattery was the rarest of breeds, an animal unafraid of pain or death.

I shoved him to the ground with a kick, and faded back to look through the doorway.

Beyond a scorched reception area stood an intact wall with a closed steel door in the center of it. Wire mesh glass covered the span on either side of the door from waist height to ceiling. The clinic had weathered the blaze well. The wired glass was only partly cracked and melted, and the door looked solid enough to withstand a hydraulic battering ram.

That was the murder room. Where was Cyndra?

Joe had climbed halfway to his feet. I grabbed him.

"Move or I put one through your spine," I said. I hauled him stumbling into the reception area and slammed his face up against the green-tinted glass as I tried the handle on the steel door. Locked.

Through the mesh window, I saw Gar Slattery jump behind a line of wide silver lockers, now greasy and seared. His hand whipped up to the top of the metal row to yank down a pistol-grip shotgun. Shit. I retreated back behind the metal door, pulling Joe in front of me. If Gar's shells could pierce the door, his brother would be first in line.

Two rounds in the Luger, against Gar's twelve-gauge. Double shit.

The chamber beyond the door had been some sort of lab once. Exposed pipe jutted out from the tiled walls, and the table was stainless steel, like O'Hasson had described. Ingrid Ekby lay partly over the table, shirtless, her bare legs off one side. Handcuffs held her wrist against one table leg. She seemed only half-conscious. I couldn't see Cyndra anywhere.

"Joe?" Gar yelled from his hiding place. It was the first time I'd had a glimpse of Gar. Prison had bleached his skin and thinned his mop of hair to strands, but he was still as tall as his brother, and fitter.

"I've got Joe," I called to Gar. "Let them go."

"Cut off her fuckin' face," Joe yelled. He was pushing against the door, fighting me. I rabbit-punched him on the back of his bull neck. His forehead smacked the metal, trailing a bloody smear as his knees buckled and he sank to the floor. I stuffed the Luger rag from my pocket into his slack mouth.

"Gar," I called. "You hurt them, I give it right back to Joe. Cops are coming. Time to make a deal."

"I'll blow this whore's head off," Gar said.

"Then Joe's dead and you don't get your money. You want to live under a rock like Joe? So shit-poor that nobody will find you?"

Silence from inside. I didn't like it. I risked a look through the glass.

Gar had opened the locker nearest him. At my angle, I could make out Cyndra's raven hair, where she lay propped up inside. Jesus, was she dead?

The ex-con watched me as he hauled Cyndra to her feet. She stood, wavering, his broad hand gripping the back of her neck. She was dressed in the same clothes I'd last seen her in. She looked unharmed, at least physically. Her elfin face drooped in the uncomprehending daze of shock or drugs. On a shelf above her in the big locker, her father's burglar kit from our break-in rested alongside bottles of antiseptic and stacks of gauze. Part of Ingrid's preparations, maybe intended to keep Joe alive for as long as possible. I ducked back as Gar leveled the shotgun at me.

"Joe, say somethin'," Gar shouted.

"Unlock the cuffs," I said, "and I'll step away from Joe."

He didn't reply. Thinking it over, I hoped. If Gar could catch me even a few feet away from his brother, I'd be sunk. Even firing through the wired glass, he'd have a fine chance of rearranging my guts with buckshot. I fished in my pocket for my lockpicks.

Gar must have decided it was a good gamble. I heard rattling as he grabbed Ingrid's cuffs.

And I began to pick the lock on the steel door with my free hand. Very quietly.

"You put the women up to the glass," I yelled to cover the slight ticking of the pins. "I'll put Joe on this side."

I heard the cuffs fall to the floor with a clack. Then a hard slap, and Ingrid's muffled cry. The simple spring lock was giving me trouble, one-handed. Joe was coming to. I gave up on the lock for a moment to kick him facedown on the floor and plant one foot on his back.

"The girls come out, Joe goes in," I said.

"You fucker. Lemme see him," said Gar. He had moved. Looking for an angle to shoot through the glass, maybe.

Joe fumbled dazedly to take the rag out of his mouth. My narrow advantage was getting slimmer every second. I felt the last pin in the lock surrender as Joe tried to shove himself up to his hands and knees. I dropped the lockpicks and stepped back, wheeling Joe around for a shield as he rose to his feet. A shove from me put him in front of the window to my left.

"The girls," I said again.

Gar was moving inside the chamber. If he stepped where I could see him through the window, or if he turned away to collect Ingrid or Cyndra again, that was my chance. Pull the unlocked door open and put the two rounds from the Luger through his heart and head before he could blink.

Then it all went to hell.

A loud thump sounded behind us. Joe and I both swung around.

It was Boule, staggering like a walking corpse against the open doorway. He weakly tried to raise an automatic pistol. Joe rushed him. I knelt and fired, trying not to hit Boule, and the bullet tore a finger-width chunk out of Joe's trapezius muscle as he slammed into the stricken Boule and the two of them disappeared into the shadows of the hallway.

A blast from Gar's shotgun exploded the glass above my head. Flying shards tore at my scalp. I fell behind the shelter of the closed door. Gar was at the window, trying to point the shotgun downward at me along the wall. I fired at him and more glass cracked as Gar shrieked and disappeared back into the chamber.

Gunfire from the hallway. I pointed the Luger in that direction, knowing it was empty, just as Joe's arm came around the edge and aimed Boule's automatic right between my eyes.

FORTY

JOE SAW THE LOCKED slide on the Luger and his big dentured grin split his face in half.

"Get up," he said.

I rose. He came into the room. Blood dribbled down his shirtfront from the light wound to his shoulder. He ignored it. The back of my neck became warmly wet as the cuts on my head dripped.

"Kept some'a these hidden in the Pearl trucks." He chuckled, showing me the automatic. "Guess April told these assholes 'bout the guns before they dunked her. I got the last laugh on that, right?"

Gar appeared warily at the broken mesh window.

"Open the door," Joe said. "We got this boy now."

The door opened. Gar pointed the shotgun at me. Behind him, Ingrid stood half-naked in the back corner, shielding Cyndra, who was sitting down on the floor, a small slack bundle against the tiled wall. Ingrid's face and breasts were scratched. Sweat and fouler elements left from the fire matted her fine hair.

"Go right on in," Joe said. He and Gar both covered me as I entered the chamber.

"Who is he?" Gar said to his brother.

Joe chuckled. "A clever one. Coulda used him back in L.A. He's the guy took our gold away."

"So kill him," Gar said. His hands tightened on the shotgun. I felt a hollow spot, right at my beltline, where the first shell would rip me in half.

Joe shook his head. Not saying no. Just mocking exasperation.

"He's fucking dangerous," Gar insisted. "Don't play around."

"Let the child go," Ingrid said to Joe, her voice stretched taut. "She can't hurt you."

Joe's grin didn't change, but his eyes became something less human.

"Say please," he said. "Make it nice."

Ingrid shuddered, almost imperceptibly.

"Get over there," said Gar, waving the barrel of the shotgun. I put the steel table between us. If he pulled the trigger, maybe it would buy me an extra tenth of a second.

"You don't need the kid," I said.

"I do," Joe said. "I deserve it. Do you know how long I've been waiting? A fuckin' lifetime." He stepped toward Ingrid and she shrank back against the open locker. "Now I unnerstand why."

"No time," I said. "Ingrid's man gave you up to the cops. You can't go back to being Orville."

"Orville's a loser," he said lazily, his eyes roaming over Ingrid's body. "The old busted pug. I live real good most of the time. Sun and fun. Orville just lets me visit the West Coast. Get close to where it all started."

"The cops know Gar is with you."

Joe shook his head again, disdainful. He reached out with the pistol and traced Ingrid's jawline. She met his gaze. Her eyes leaked tears, but she wouldn't look away.

"Had you so young," he said to her. "Wonder if you're just as honey-dripping now?"

Gar banged the open door with the grip of the shotgun. "For fuck's sake. Let's get out of here."

"If you want your gold, you need us alive," I said. Joe didn't react. Gar paid more attention. "I stuck fifty of those kilobars into deposit boxes yesterday. I know where Ingrid has more."

"Where?" said Gar.

"He's shitting you," said Joe, close enough to Ingrid for his fetid breath to ruffle the hairs hanging in front of her face. "Shoot him if you want. Just keep the mess off my table."

From behind Ingrid, Cyndra made a small cry, like someone emerging from a dream.

"I'll trade the money," Ingrid said, "for the girl's life."

"Now we're talking," said Gar.

Ingrid looked at me. I understood, somehow, what she wanted me to do.

"Come here, kid," I said, and rounded the table to lift Cyndra from the floor. She weighed nothing. I carried her back across the chamber to Gar's side.

Joe nodded. "That's right. Give us a little privacy. Plenty of time for the fresh little thing later."

I put Cyndra down. Under the steel table.

"Joe," I said. Gar looked back and forth between us, uncertain. Joe finally tore his eyes from Ingrid and turned to me.

"It ought to be you," I said. "You earned it."

He chuckled again. "Yeah."

The gun he'd taken from Boule lifted to point at my heart.

I will never know if Ingrid Ekby fully understood what she was doing. Perhaps she was just grabbing frantically at the nearest thing within reach. She snatched O'Hasson's open burglary kit from the locker shelf and spun full around to swing it at her tormentor's head with a scream of rage. Joe raised a contemptuous arm to block the bag. Shattering O'Hasson's collection of homemade firesticks.

The bag exploded, dousing both of them in liquid flames. Joe shrieked and shot Ingrid in the chest before the terror sent him into flailing, infernal spasms.

Gar fired a blast at the falling Ingrid, too late to make a difference, too late to recover as I sprang at him. I caught the shotgun in two hands and slammed it into his face like a man heaving a barbell. Gar crashed into the table. I wrenched the gun from him and reached to yank Cyndra from the floor.

Joe Slattery's entire body was ablaze. He lurched toward us. Seeking a final hellish embrace.

I ran out the door with Cyndra limp in my arms. Slammed it shut behind us and put my back against it. The left side of the chamber was engulfed. Fire lapped greedily out the broken window. Gar banged the handle and threw himself at the door on the other side, every desperate blow vibrating through my entire body. I pressed back, harder. The steel grew hot so fast, it was like the element on a stove. Gar had enough breath left to scream. Joe had already stopped.

FORTY-ONE

THE MOMENT WE WERE out of sight of the devastation, I pulled the truck over to check Cyndra. Her pupils were slightly dilated, and her pulse on the slow side of acceptable. When I dropped her wrist, it settled back into her lap, not fully limp, not conscious of motion. It wasn't shock keeping her numb, or at least not only that. She'd been doped.

I guessed that Boule and the hunters had stuck to their weapon of choice and brought tranquilizers with them to subdue Joe. Slattery had seized the opportunity and dosed Cyndra with some brand of opiate. To keep her compliant, while the madman had his sick fun with Ingrid.

Cyndra stirred. Her eyes closed completely and her breathing deepened. She looked very much like she must have years ago, before her father went to prison.

Maybe Cyndra had been so drugged she wouldn't remember the night's horrors. I'd never prayed. But if I had, sparing the girl those memories would have been worth every word.

ADDY WAS AWAKE, SITTING in the front room. I carried Cyndra inside and ignored Addy's exclamations and questions until we had the girl tucked under the red-and-white checkerboard quilt in the spare bed. I checked her pulse and eyes one more time. Stanley vacillated in the hall, toenails tapping nervously on the hardwood. He chose to stay with Cyndra as we retreated.

I went to the kitchen and took down the rum left from last winter. Addy had placed the bottle out of her way on the cereal shelf after I'd moved out. I took a glass from the dish rack and filled it. Drank a mouthful. It poured pepper-hot down my raw throat to settle into my belly. The second drink was less of a gulp.

Addy was talking. I tried to focus.

"—she hurt?"

I shook my head.

"Thank the Lord. Her father's in Virginia Mason. He collapsed while he was downtown, without any ID. The hospital called me after he regained consciousness."

"Will he make it?"

"Yes. He's very weak. They're keeping him for a day or two, while he gets back on medication. What happened to you and Cyndra?"

Addy followed me out to the backyard. It was so far into the night that even the insects were quiet. I stood and inhaled rotting bark and far-off car exhaust and the rose bush that had somehow survived Stanley's rampages.

"Can you talk about it?" Addy said.

Once I started, I could do nothing but. I told her about the gold. About EverCon. The rabid dogs from Sledge City. The dead men in the back room of Pacific Pearl. I spared nothing. If Addy had any positive opinions left about my character, I tore them right down to the ground. Theft, coercion, assault, or murder. Everything was copy.

My throat dried and it never occurred to me to drink. Gar Slattery. Ingrid Ekby. Cyndra, in the hands of monsters. And Joe, whose scarred and grinning face seemed to beam horribly from my last blinding, blazing sight of him. Consumed.

Addy listened to it all, until the stars had faded in the eastern sky. When my words ran out she quietly asked about Corcoran and his family. More about Cyndra, and what she may have endured.

I answered her questions. Then Addy got up to walk to the kitchen and brought back a ceramic mixing bowl filled with rags and water. Instead of setting the bowl down, she cradled it with both arms.

"You've done a lot of wrong. It's inexcusable." Addy took a deep breath and shivered. "But without you, Cyndra might still have followed her father here to Seattle. Without you, she would certainly have died tonight. And right now I don't have enough in me to give a good goddamn about anything or anyone else but that little girl. So clean yourself up, and then leave her to me."

She went inside.

I washed the crusted filth from my arms and face and neck. My body felt like I'd spent the night in a threshing machine. The next time I sat down I would not be getting up for a long while. I wrung the last rag out over my head, over and over, letting the drips sluice through my hair and sting the lacerations on my scalp.

The sun cut its first flaxen slice out of the horizon. Every room in Addy's home had gone dark and quiet. I walked around the side yard to the street, and on up the block.

High above, the empty framework of Dono's house stretched toward a cloudless heaven. Dew hung expectantly from the beams. Sunlight finally touched the upper rafters and seeped rapidly down to the lower floors, stilling the nascent drops as it touched them.

Before ten minutes had passed, the wooden skeleton of the house was blanched dry and rigid. The day would be a hot one.

AGE TWELVE, CHRISTMAS DAY

Hours later, after Granddad had sent Hollis home, we sat together in the front room. Granddad in his usual wingback leather chair, and me on the short sofa. I'd fallen asleep there, not meaning to, while Granddad had been out. Setting things right, as he called it.

He'd said that, like whatever was wrong wasn't my fault, and that it would be simple to fix. I knew at least one of those was a lie. His car—well, the car he had been driving—had killed Trey dead. Granddad had dragged the body off into the trees almost immediately, right after he had bundled me into the backseat. We were out of the arboretum before another car passed.

That wasn't going to be easy to clean up. Was it?

Riding in the car, I had told him—between wiping my eyes, so embarrassing—about Trey and Kassie and Quincey, and that I had been at the mansion when they had burgled it. He had turned from the winding road to look at me.

"Fucking hell," he'd said. And he hardly ever talked like that.

I had a lot of questions, but Granddad had told me there would be time later. Hollis was at the house minutes after we arrived, which I didn't understand, but I was too groggy to ask how.

Now I was rested and sitting on the hearth in front of the fire Granddad had built, and eating leftover fried chicken from the fridge. Life was weird.

Granddad took the bloodstained plastic knife out of his pocket. The sight of it made me stop chewing.

"You know what this is?" he said.

I nodded. "Trey used it to kill Quincey."

"I expect so. I found it on the hill in front of the house, right there."

"I must've dropped it. I'm sorry."

The corner of his mouth twisted up. "Now that's the last time you'll apologize tonight, Van. Yeah?"

I nodded.

"You're not in trouble. If anything, I'm more to blame. For one, I stupidly left my burner phone in my car back here in Seattle. That's why you haven't been able to reach me. And then there's this." He tapped the knife. "You know that in prison, men have to defend themselves. I made this—started making it—in jail."

"A shank," I said.

"Where'd you hear that? Television, of course. A little old, that word, but yes. It's a blade. I started making it in the shop from a piece of plastic I'd traded cigarettes for." He turned the knife over, considering it. "Making something like this can be a slow process. A few passes on the belt sander each day, while the guards and other cons are distracted. I would hide it in the shop in between." He tossed the knife onto the coffee table. "And then hardly before I'd started, the damn thing went missing."

"Somebody stole it?"

"I wasn't sure. But it worried me, because my fingerprints would be on the plastic. It would be simple for someone to finish the job, make it into a weapon and use it in jail, and I'd be sunk. Then somebody popped to me that our friend Trey was the one who had it. That was bad news."

"He didn't like you?"

"Liking didn't enter into it. Trey is mad. Crazy, not angry. You understand?"

"Yeah."

"If Trey had the blade, then he would find a way to use it. To manipulate the situation. Some men are like that. They see a weakness and they can't help themselves. They have to sink their teeth into it."

I was definitely done with the chicken now.

"Trey was released before I could do anything about the problem," Granddad said, in a tone that made me think it was very lucky for Trey that he hadn't stayed in jail. "After I got out—the night of, in fact—he and Quincey got hold of me and said they wanted to meet to discuss a job. They needed my contacts to sell the artwork from the mansion. That's when I had a small idea of what Trey intended."

"To frame you for the mansion. And Quincey."

Granddad chuckled. "I wasn't that clever. I thought he was going to use the blade to force me to give up my share. Buy the damn thing back from him." He shook his dark head. "The man was a thief, and sometimes violent. I knew that much. But he was much worse besides. A psychopath. You know that word from TV, too?"

"Uh-huh."

"Well, it's often used wrong. Not every psychopath kills people. Trey figured he could tie me to the burglary with our screwdriver, and frame me for Quincey with the blade. You see the tape he wrapped around the handle? I will wager you that under that tape are my prints, clean as ever. If the case ever got that far, the forensics lot could find them. No one would ever connect Trey with either crime."

"But if you were arrested, you could tell—" The look on Granddad's face stopped me. I knew what he was going to say before he said it.

"There would be no arrest," Granddad said. "I would just disappear. That's why Trey was here tonight. He knew I was due back from Portland with the money, after fencing the artwork."

"He was going to kill both of us," I said. Wow, my voice sounded calm for something like that.

Granddad nodded. "That's why I was upset when Trey saw you, here at the house. You were something I cared about."

A weakness he could sink his teeth into. I shivered.

"He's dead, right?" I said.

"You don't have to worry."

"I'm not. Not about him coming back, I mean. What about his . . ."

"I've moved him. And Quincey."

"Where?"

"That doesn't matter," he said, standing up, and I could tell sharing time was about over. "I want you to get some sleep."

There was one more thing, and I asked it, knowing it might tick Granddad off. "Why were you casing Trey's house?"

That twist of a smile again. "Saw me there, did you? I was waiting for a time when he and the girl wouldn't be home. I went in and searched the place carefully. No blade. So"—he stretched and yawned, his arms nearly reaching the ceiling— "Plan B. Carry out the burglary—Trey wasn't a fool, it was a good score—and then Hollis and Willard and I had planned to have a long talk with the man when I got back from Portland."

Which explained how Hollis had been here so fast. After Trey had been—Ugh. I was pretty sure the sound of Granddad's car hitting Trey would be bouncing around my head for a long time. Worst earworm ever.

"Enough of that," Granddad said. "Go to bed. Happy Christmas."

It *was* Christmas now. Past midnight.

Kassie.

"Go," Granddad said.

I went upstairs and stripped down to my shorts. Halfway

through brushing my teeth, I heard Granddad go out the front door and down the porch to the steps. Toothbrush still in my mouth, I walked into his bedroom to look out his window to the street. Almost all of our neighbors had unplugged their Christmas lights for the night, and our block was back to its usual weak yellow color under the streetlamps.

Granddad stood on the sidewalk. A dull brown panel van was parked in front of our driveway. Its door opened and Mr. Willard got out. Easy to recognize him; he looked almost as large as the van itself.

The bodies are in the van, I thought, and shivered again. And then I realized: That was the van Trey had chased me in. He would have had to put me and Granddad somewhere, after—

Nope. Definitely not thinking about that anymore tonight.

In the morning, after breakfast, I told Granddad I was going to Davey's. He had rescued my bike from the bushes sometime during the night; I found it leaning on the front porch, with a few new scrapes. I jumped on and pedaled up to Kassie's house.

There was another car in their driveway, a Cadillac. Not an old convertible one like Hollis drove, but new and wine-colored with a white leather roof.

I went up and knocked on the door, hoping Kassie would answer. When it swung open an older lady in red glasses and a red polo shirt with green Christmas trees on it blinked her eyes at me.

"Um," I said. "Is Kassie home?"

She looked a little puzzled, but called for Kassie and kept looking at me while we waited.

"Are you a friend of hers?" the lady said.

I nodded, and then remembered manners. "I'm Van."

"How do you do," she said, like we were at tea or something.

Kassie came running up. "Van!" she said. Her face looked happy, right then, but her eyes were a little red. "Come in."

"Merry Christmas," the lady prompted.

"Right. Merry Christmas." Kassie grabbed my arm and tugged me inside. The house smelled of bacon and muffins, and even though I'd eaten, my mouth watered. The lady shut the door and followed us, almost hovering.

A tall old man with white hair and freckles stood cutting celery at the kitchen counter. I got creeped out. The man looked a lot like Trey, same height and everything. Plus the carving knife.

"Van, this is my grandpa and grandma, Earl and Liesl," Kassie said, very formally. I guess she got that from the grandma. I said hi.

"Merry Christmas, Van," said Earl. "How do you two know each other?"

Even his questions sounded like Trey's. Coming here was a bad idea.

"Our schools meet," Kassie said smoothly, "for sports."

"What do you play?" Liesl said.

I remembered what we'd told Trey about Balewood playing Hovick. "I write about the basketball games. Girls' and boys'. For the paper."

"We've been trying to get to one of those games," said Liesl.

"Since Trey can't. Or won't," Earl said, muttering.

Kassie tugged again at my arm. "Let's go out back."

It was freezing outside but I didn't mind at all. At least I wasn't in that kitchen.

"Did you and your grandfather already open presents?" Kassie said. "What'd you get?"

"Money, mostly. Granddad never knows what to buy."

Then, in case that sounded ungrateful, "I got a couple of Game Boy games I asked for. And a multi-tool."

"What's that?"

I pulled it out of my pocket and showed off the pliers and files and screwdriver and other things. Kassie loved how it all folded up. She said it was like a boy's version of Polly Pocket, and then she had to explain what the heck that was.

"What did you get?" I said.

Kassie's face crumpled. "We haven't opened yet. We're waiting for Dad."

Right. I felt stupid.

"He's coming," Kassie said. "He said he'd be late, last night. But he's coming."

Trey wouldn't be, of course. I knew so many things that Kassie and her grandparents didn't, I wasn't even sure what I could talk about. If I should talk about anything at all.

I hadn't told Granddad I was going to see Kassie. He would have ordered me to stay away for good. Too risky, he would have said. No connections.

So why had I come?

"Let's play something," I said. "You pick which."

She smiled, and tucked her hair behind her ear, like when after she'd kissed me. "I'd like that."

It felt cruel somehow, keeping my mouth shut. This Christmas would just get tougher for her, the longer her father didn't show. And the really bad news about him would arrive soon enough, I guessed. I knew what was coming, couldn't help it, couldn't ever tell.

But I could be here. Try and make right now a little better.

"Six to two," I reminded her. "I'll let you win today. My gift."

Kassie laughed. "You are so mean."

Sometimes I was. Not today.

FORTY-TWO

Mick O'Hasson had drifted off. The second time he'd zoned out since we'd started talking. Not fully asleep, just coasting on whatever cocktail of drugs the doctors had prescribed for him, while he lay in his hospital bed regaining strength.

I was riding a little high myself, on a fistful of painkillers. Even with pharma blunting the worst of it, my neck wouldn't turn all the way to the left, and I limped as I made my way down the hall to splash cold water on my face at the drinking fountain. One nurse looked at me sideways, maybe suspecting that I had wandered away from my own sickbed. Ten minutes left in visiting hours. I'd intended to come earlier, but after leaving Cyndra with Addy, exhaustion had knocked me down and kept me there most of the day. When I finally rose, I moved like I was underwater.

O'Hasson was awake again when I stepped back into the room. He looked at me and sniffed.

"What were we talking about? Cyndra," he said, answering his own question. "The old gal told you she's sleeping a lot, right? Must be why I nodded off. Power of suggestion." His mouth twitched, just a hint of his habitual grin returning.

"Addy's worked in hospitals. She says a lot of rest is what Cyndra needs most right now."

"And she doesn't remember what happened to her?" he said. I'd told him Cyndra's story already, but I couldn't blame him for wanting some reassurance.

"She remembers driving to Pacific Pearl and sneaking up to the building and moving some pallets to look through a window. Then somebody stuck a bag over her head. After that, she has just vague impressions of being in a truck. They must have doped her almost immediately."

Mick bowed his head, and it took me a moment to realize he was giving thanks.

"That's what Cyndra can remember right now," I cautioned, "and she's handling it like a champion. But Addy told me she's woken up a few times, crying out. She's going to need help, Mick."

"I wanna see her."

"One of us will bring her by in the morning. Hey."

"I'm here," he said, jolting back to full consciousness.

"I'm sorry for threatening you. Especially in front of Cyndra. It was stupid of me."

O'Hasson shook his head, making the vinyl underneath the cotton pillowcase squeak. "Screw that. Your buddy died."

"Doesn't justify it."

"You got Cyndra back for me. That's it, far as I care." He stuck out a hand. I shook it.

He looked around the austere room, with its flat white walls and curtains the color of a parched desert, and every piece of furniture on casters. "Am I sick of these places. In the morning, I'm gone."

"Not yet. The doc's got a specialist coming to talk to you tomorrow." And before O'Hasson could get more than half a word of protest out of his mouth, I added, "Let the cancer clinic here take a look at you. You can afford better than the state minimum now."

"I know my own fuckin' prognosis."

"Then you're guaranteed not to get any bad news. How many patients can say that?"

"Nowhere to go but up? That's your sales pitch?"

"Your daughter will kick your ass if you don't. That's all the pitch I need."

He laughed, not quite able to turn it sour. "Look who's the sympathetic type after all."

THE FOLLOWING MORNING, HOLLIS and I agreed to meet at Bully Betty's, before the bar opened for the day. He came straight from the funeral home where he'd been helping Nakri make arrangements for Corcoran. Lifting the metallic blue suitcase over the sill of the bar's service door made my bones creak. My body was stiffer than ever, but my mind was finally letting me rest. I was coming off of the first real sleep I'd managed in two days.

"Damnation," Hollis said. "You got it back."

I gave him the short version of events as I unlocked the door and put on a pot of coffee. By the end of it, Hollis was seated in a booth, looking like I'd slapped him with a dead squid.

"Jesus, boyyo," he said at last. "Jesus."

"Yeah, he probably helped me out, there at the end."

"The woman killed herself. And took both those sinful fucks with her."

"I don't know if Ingrid intended to die. But I'm sure if she knew it meant taking the Slatterys with her, she'd have made the same choice a thousand times over."

"Laughing as she falls into the abyss. God, the madness of it," Hollis said.

Ingrid Ekby had given her life—and maybe her humanity—to find and kill Joe Slattery. He'd damaged her so deeply that the wounds had never healed. Because she wouldn't let them? Or because she had tried and found it impossible?

"And that's half of the gold there? The suitcase you took off the bastards who killed Jimmy?"

"Less O'Hasson's share, yeah."

"What about yours?"

"We'll get to that. How's Nakri?"

"Forged of steel, that lady. She'd have to be, married to Jimmy." Hollis allowed himself a small smile. "Maybe all Cambodian women are that way. Or she's holding herself together for the children."

I had seen the news story. Seattle man found shot and robbed in Magnuson Park. Corcoran's kids would go on thinking their stepdad had been the victim of an unsolved mugging, though I'm sure Nakri would believe there was more to the story than that. We couldn't tell them any part of the truth, even if it meant knowing that the men who'd killed Jimmy C. had come to bad ends themselves. That knowledge might not be any solace anyway.

Hollis cleared his throat. "Listen, about what I said. You moving Jimmy like that—"

"It was unacceptable."

"I couldn't have done it. And it had to be done."

"Jimmy would have treated me better, if the situation were reversed. No matter what he thought of me personally."

Hollis hesitated, and then got up and found mugs and poured the coffee for us. He nearly spilled the hot brew while shying away from a thatch of dreadlocks dangling from the ceiling.

"This is a very strange place, did I mention?" he said.

"Weird enough to suit me."

"D'you know why Jimmy needled you so much? He was scared of Dono—hell, nothing to that, sometimes even I was frightened of your man. And you're so much like him. But." Hollis waved a finger at me. "You've compunctions your grandfather didn't. Ideals. Jimmy was a little scared of those, too."

"Here's to him," I said.

We drank. The coffee helped my aches as much as the codeine.

Hollis looked at the blue suitcase, leaning against the stool at the end of the bar. "It should feel like more of a victory, shouldn't it? We've got the money. We lost Jimmy, but damn near every one of those shit-eaters paid with their lives, too."

Ten dead. Maybe eleven. I'd lost count.

"War doesn't work like that," I said.

"No. I suppose not."

"Having the gold didn't make me happy," I said. "Too much blood on those bars. Stealing it was fun. Getting O'Hasson away from Ingrid's men was even better."

"And the girl? You saved her."

"That was best," I said.

"A good day."

"Good is the correct word."

"So you're not keeping your share? It's for Jimmy's family?"

"I kept some. Add the rest to Nakri's cut. I trust you can come up with some tale."

"What about rebuilding your house?" Hollis said.

"I'm giving up on the house. Selling the land."

Hollis had trouble swallowing his mouthful of coffee. "Wasn't the whole point of this—" He left the obvious ending hang.

"Money to rebuild the house was one reason. The bigger motive was giving me something to do that I could do well."

"Safecracking."

I smiled. "At the start, yeah. But mostly the planning, and the execution. The job we pulled at EverCon was the most focused I've felt since leaving the Rangers. And I want a little more of it."

Hollis scratched his cheek, contemplating. "Just what are you getting at, lad?"

I leaned back, feeling the leaden burn of pain, the price of the fight. Enjoying it, just a little.

"How would you feel about some pro bono work?" I said.

FORTY-THREE

I FOUND ADDY AT HER kitchen sink, washing the breakfast dishes. She would no more let plates sit dirty than I would have left my service rifle caked in mud. I picked up a towel decorated with sunflowers and started drying the plates in the rack.

"Cyndra asleep?" I asked. She nodded. Addy and I had been edging around one another for two days. Sea urchins under the same rock. She hadn't said a word about everything I'd confessed to her, not that I wanted or needed absolution. Our brief conversations had stuck to the neutral topic of Cyndra.

"I've been talking to Tachelle Tyner," she said. "Cyndra's foster mother. I told her that Cyndra followed her father up here without his knowledge, which at least keeps me on the side of honesty."

"They must be ready to chew live scorpions," I said.

"Between summer vacation and the natural defense network of Cyndra's fellow teenagers, Tachelle only realized she was gone a couple of days ago. I was informed that Cyndra has been a challenge."

"As the kid would say: Duh."

"Miz Tyner and I made the informal agreement that Cyndra would stay here until her father is well enough to travel south. Sparing them the trouble of fetching her."

"I'm sure she jumped at that."

"In a flat second. I don't care for that woman at all."

I leaned against the counter next to the sink so I could see more of Addy's shining, wrinkled face. "You don't want Cyndra to leave."

"It's best for her to be at home. Her friends are there. School."

"What if she stayed?"

"She can't."

"What if she wanted to stay near you? Would you want that?"

"Van, please stop."

"No." I took a wet serving dish out of her hands and put it aside. "Goddamn it, Addy. You were right when you called me out for being deceitful. So let's lay it out. Mickey will need a lot of professional help. Cyndra might need even more, when her memories start flooding back. And they will. You think the Tyners can handle that? Or that they even give a shit?"

"They wouldn't let us—"

"I won't give them a choice. I don't care if it takes bribing Tachelle or false records to prove you're Cyndra's great-fucking-aunt or what. I'll make it happen. *We* can make it happen. If you want."

Addy burst into sobs. It startled the hell out of me. I'd hardly seen the tough old woman so much as get misty before. I jumped forward to hug her for a long moment and then guided her into the front room to sit in her overstuffed peach chair.

She cried for a little while, fishing Kleenex out of the knitted cozy on the lamp table next to her. I sat on the floor and held her hand. After dabbing the last of her tears and a hearty blow of her nose, she tossed the final tissue aside.

"I keep harping on you for your secrets," she said.

"Doesn't mean you can't have your own. Mine tend to involve felonies."

She laughed a little. "You're right. We all have bits of our past we've kept quiet. Or set aside. That's easier, sometimes."

I waited.

"I had two babies," Addy said. "With my first husband. One was still-born. We never legally named her, but I always called her Lanie. My boy Dwight died of pneumonia when he was four."

"Addy."

"It was many, many years ago, Van. It startles me sometimes how much time passes when I don't think of them." She shook her head. "I've been thinking about them a lot this past week."

"Cyndra likes it here. She likes you."

"It might not be possible for long," Addy said, maybe to herself. "I'm not young. If her father dies, Cyndra could want something else for herself. Someplace better."

"So we'll just have to make it so good here that the kid never wants to leave."

Addy sighed and turned bloodshot green eyes on me. Her armor back up, with a chink or two. "Are you serious about bribing the State of California and all that rubbish?"

"Damn right."

She huffed again, less emphatically. "Then I guess I'm serious about finally cleaning out the project room."

"I'll help."

"Damn right indeed. I can't lift those boxes."

"With everything, I meant."

"I know," Addy said. "I know."

FORTY-FOUR

THE CLERK AT THE front desk of the Olympian Heights gave me a smile that was eighty percent solicitous, and the rest uncertain. Even sporting a good suit and tie, along with my new hair and glasses, I guess I gave the impression of being out of my natural element.

"Checking out," I said. "Room 1401. Ms. Ekby."

I tilted my head a tiny fraction to indicate the lobby behind me. The slim clerk looked over my shoulder to see the statuesque woman in a silver-gray Prada jacket and skirt and large Persol sunglasses. She stood halfway across the long hall, next to a neatly stacked line of embossed leather luggage. Her brown hair shone like silk.

"Ah," he said, brightening, "and I hope everything went well on her side trip?"

"Vancouver was very successful, thank you. As was her stay. Thank you for retaining the room while we were called away."

"Of course, of course. The Olympian is always delighted to help with unexpected needs. Leave it on the same card?"

"Please. And we have one bag in your care." I handed him the claim card that I had removed from Marshall's body. I had scrubbed the blue plastic very clean, of prints and of blood. "A red metallic suitcase, quite heavy."

"Certainly. Shall I call a bellman?"

He should. Two young Ethiopian men raced forward and assisted me in trundling the luggage to a minivan cab. I rolled the hundred-pound suitcase myself, and duked them each twenty dollars for their trouble. They returned to the lobby with excellent impressions of Ingrid Ekby.

The cab took us the handful of blocks to King Street Station. If the driver thought it unusual that a woman with five thousand dollars' worth of luggage was taking the train, he kept it to himself. A fast trip and a solid tip.

On the pavement in front of the train station, taxi gone and suitcases back in their neat row, we waited.

"My," said Elana Coll, "that was positively graceful."

"You looked the part."

"Me, and a lot of padding." She rolled her shoulders. "Don't stare. They're not real, you know."

"You don't need the help anyway."

"I may keep this wig. I'd love to hold on to the luggage, too. But I suppose monogrammed initials make that a bad idea."

"Very." We had moved fast to pack Ingrid's room and secure the suitcase. The police hadn't yet identified the bodies found in the incinerated clinic, so complete was the destruction. As soon as the investigators and the press learned that the dead included Ingrid Ekby and the Slattery brothers, every law enforcement agency west of the Rockies would be swarming the city.

Elana's green eyes flashed. "You should keep your new look, though. Van Shaw as a blond. Kinky."

Hollis's Cadillac turned into the loading zone, sparing me further grief. He gaped through the window at the two of us, almost sputtering while I loaded the luggage in the trunk—barely enough room, even with the wide beam of the Caddy—and opened the door for Elana.

"Such a gentleman." She smirked.

The Caddy pulled a fast U-turn and proceeded without pause onto 2nd Ave. Hollis shook his head as if he'd walked into a cobweb. "Take those things off before I crash, please."

I removed the wig and glasses, gratefully. The makeup Elana had painted on my cheek to diminish my scars could wait. Overkill, maybe, since I'd kept my face angled away from the hotel cameras. But better safe than sentenced.

Over two million dollars in the suitcase. Hollis had arranged with one of his many contacts, this one engaged in some sort of Balkan financial market, to take the kilobars off our hands for a small percentage of the take. The bulk of it would be converted to untraceable cash. I'd already picked the recipients. A foster aid charity, a children's defense fund. Leo Pak had told me about a hunger program for vets that had put food in his belly when he'd been too far gone to handle such trivial things himself. No end of need out there.

"Everything good?" Hollis said.

Two million, funneled anonymously and tax-free. Addy had assured me that her friend Enid had the know-how to set up a shell corporation, just as capably as she could trace one. Enough money to make an impact. Let the damned gold change a few lives for the better.

"More than good," I said.

FORTY-FIVE

CYNDRA AND I SAT on a bench at the edge of the skate park by Seattle Center. Cyndra wrestled with her skateboard. I wrestled with Stanley, keeping him from racing into the midst of the skaters zooming up and down the terra-cotta-colored ramps. I'd offered to switch, but Cyndra knew she had the easier job.

She held the skateboard between her knees and a socket wrench in her hand. A gallon Ziploc bag holding bolts and bearings and four new skateboard wheels in electric green waited to the side. Stanley had his jaws around one of the old black wheels she had already removed. He gnawed at his prize.

"How long do we got?" she said.

"Have," I said automatically. "At least an hour." Her dad was at Mason again for an MRI. His second this week. The doctors were gearing up for something, O'Hasson thought, and while they never said yes or no, he figured they were going to take a crack at scraping his skull. Those were the words he had used, and his grin when Addy had winced could have lit up her whole house.

"Ouch." Cyndra stuck her knuckle in her mouth. She'd lost some skin to the board's rough grip tape.

"You've been to skate parks in L.A.?" I asked.

"Sure. Lotsa times."

"And done that?" I nodded to the teenagers catching air on the quarter-pipe.

"Have *you*?" she said.

"Nope. Too chicken."

She smirked and finished putting the bearings and wheels on, giving each axle nut an extra-hard yank with the wrench. I thought she was about to reach for her backpack, which was full of the helmet and other gear that Addy had insisted Mick buy for her. Or else she was going to skate off without it, just to try and prove something to me. But instead she sat and gazed out of the park, toward where the Needle pointed up at a pure azure sky.

"Addy said she wants me to stay here," she said. "If."

Mick had talked to Cyndra, leveling with her about his condition and promising to fight it. She was old enough to think ahead for herself, to what she might have to do if that fight didn't go their way.

"Do you want to stay?" I said.

"I think so."

I nodded.

"But I don't know," she said.

"Okay."

Both of us turned as a hoot went up from a group of skaters in the park. One of them had bitten the dust and was making comedy out of it by faking injury.

"It's okay not to know," I repeated. "Addy just wants you to understand you've got options. You get me?"

"Uh-huh."

"We can all figure it out together."

"When the day comes," she said, as if she were finishing a sentence I'd started. "Dad used to say that, when I was little. Worry about it when the day comes. Trying to, like, calm me down when I would get crazy about stuff that hadn't happened yet."

"Did it work?"

"Doubt it." She reached for her helmet.

I watched as she kicked off into the swirling riptide of skaters. Stanley barked encouragement. Before two minutes had passed, Cyndra was yelling and whooping right along with the rest of them. Flying across the hardscape, her wild grin back in place.

Mattu had told me—after I'd convinced him to devote our session to something other than my own sleep habits—that kids Cyndra's age could compartmentalize tough emotions just like adults. Distraction was a positive thing. If we were honest with her about her father's chances, and her own trauma, that would let her engage with the ordeal—Mattu's phrase—in her own way.

I knew something about keeping parts of yourself in separate boxes. Even walled off completely, when the truth was too painful. I also knew, without Mattu having to say it, that cracks would form in those walls. Nightmares. Bursts of rage or fear. Cyndra was a survivor, and survivors carried wounds.

We'd help her heal those, Addy and Mick and me. When that day came.

Today, we were all alive, and flying.

ACKNOWLEDGMENTS

Thanks to the following people for helping me through every day of EVERY DAY:

To my agent, Lisa Erbach Vance, of the Aaron Priest Literary Agency. An appropriate start, as Lisa was the first person outside the family to champion my work, and remains the first stop for both encouragement and reality checks on manuscripts, a balance she strikes with elegance.

To my editor, Lyssa Keusch, at William Morrow, a wonderful collaborator and friend, without whose enthusiasm and insights both the novel and I would suffer. Liate Stehlik, Danielle Bartlett, Kaitlin Harri, Richard Aquan, Miranda Ottewell, and Priyanka Krishnan are the amazing people who whip the books into shape and help them find an audience.

To editor Angus Cargill at Faber & Faber, with gratitude for his guidance, and to the wonderful Faber team of Daisy Radevsky, Sophie Portas, and Luke Bird. And to Caspian Dennis of the Abner Stein Agency, for representing us splendidly on the far shore.

To Áine Kelly of Galway, for her valuable help in Irish Gaelic and invaluable friendship. To John Pullman, Martin Naborowski, and the gang at Pullman's for their expertise and showing by example every week what a gym should be. To buddy TL Frasqueri-Molina and the one and only Jason Marsden, for their experiences and tips in navigating pop-culture conventions from large to independent-nation-sized.

To the terrific teacher and author Jerrilyn Farmer, and the rest of our Saturday morning writing group—Beverly Graf, Eachan Holloway, Alexandra Jamison, John McMahon, and Kathy Norris—for their quick pencils and quicker minds.

My usual disclaimer: This novel is fiction, and I reserve the right to mess with jurisdictions, geography, methods, or anything else that will keep the story moving, keep the lawyers bored, and keep potentially dangerous information where and with whom it belongs. Beyond those guidelines, I aim for accuracy. I am deeply indebted to the professionals, named and anonymous, who have lent their hard-won knowledge to the work. From the veterans of the United States Army, those include Christian Hockman, Bco 1/75 Ranger Regiment, and Matt Holmes, 82nd Airborne, 1st Brigade combat team. As always, the really cool stuff is theirs, and any mistakes are mine.

Thank You, Dear Reader, for picking up this book and giving it a shot. In this world of constant distraction, a little attention is a sincere compliment.

And finally to Amy, Mia, and Madeline, for making every one of my days a celebration.

Also by Glen Erik Hamilton

ff

Past Crimes

COME HOME IF YOU CAN . . .

Answering voices from his past, Van Shaw – soldier and former thief – returns to Seattle after a decade's exile, only to find a whole heap of trouble, and himself the prime suspect in a brutal attack on his grandfather, Dono.

Plunged back into the dangerous underworld he had vowed never return to, Van finds that the secrets held by those closest to him may be the deadliest of all.

'This guy has got what it takes.' Lee Child

'Lee Child's hero, Jack Reacher, may just have a fresh rival . . . The flashbacks to his past, and the dark characters he encounters along the way to this personal epiphany, make Hamilton's first Van Shaw novel and his formidable protagonist hard to resist. There will be more; Shaw is too taut and smart a hero for there not to be.' *Daily Mail*

'A zipline ride of a thriller . . . Hamilton has crafted a compelling new hero in Van Shaw.' Gregg Hurwitz, *New York Times* bestseller

ff

Hard Cold Winter

Former Army Ranger and thief Van Shaw is thrust into a maelstrom of danger as lethal and unpredictable as the war he left behind in this emotionally powerful and gritty follow-up to Glen Erik Hamilton's acclaimed debut, *Past Crimes*.

When an old crony of Van Shaw's late grandfather calls in a favour, the recently discharged Ranger embarks on a dangerous journey to the Olympic Mountains, in search of a missing girl tied to his own criminal past. What he finds instead is a brutal murder scene, and a situation in which everything may not be as it seems . . .

'A very good thriller indeed . . . Make no mistake, Van Shaw is a remarkable fictional creation.' *Thriller Books Journal*

'A real page-turner.' *Trip Fiction*

'Brimming with action, conflict, and realistic and compelling characters . . . Aficionados of the genre will eat this one up.' *Library Journal* (starred review)